ISABELLA'S
HEART

ISABELLA'S HEART

Diane Merrill Wigginton

JEWELED DAGGER
PUBLISHING

JEWELED DAGGER PUBLISHING COMPANY
www.jeweleddaggerpublishing.com

Designed by Fine Design

First edition February 26, 2016

Second Edition April 4, 2017

978-1-946146-05-2—Isabella's Heart eBook
978-1-982936-20-4—Isabella's Heart Paperback
978-1-946146-03-8—Isabella's Heart Hardback

This series is about family and so it is to my family that
I wish to dedicate this book,
for without family I would have no inspiration or
desire to follow my dreams.
You truly do bless and inspire me every day, warts and all.

Prologue

JANUARY 29, 1783

LONDON, ENGLAND

A Pub on the Wharf

T HE NIGHT WAS RIPE FOR celebration as Charlie and his two companions set out for what they all hoped would be a pleasant adventure. It was Charles Philippe Deveraux's nineteenth birthday and he was going to show his buddies how the son of a duke celebrated in style.

The White Boars Pub, a somewhat unseemly establishment, sat in the middle of the busy London Wharf District, with a reputation for attracting a most unsavory clientele.

Stepping through the well-worn doors of the dimly lit pub, Charlie and his two companions were nearly overwhelmed by the initial stench of sweat and piss emanating from the unclean rabble assembled within.

It was almost too much for the three young noblemen, but they were determined to find what they came this far to find: excitement!

Charlie Deveraux, Thomas Swift, and Ashton Longmire had left the university earlier that day, determined to break free of all conventional constraints and find some trouble, come hell or high water. And if trouble was not to be found, it would not be for lack of trying.

Oxford was a prestigious university, but Charlie found the constant constraints and protocols suffocating. He missed his home, and the freedoms he had enjoyed growing up. But most of all he missed me, his twin sister.

His mind wandered momentarily back to a simpler time, when we climbed the large, old trees that surrounded our chateau in France. Hiding in the large branches, we lay in wait to bombard our two younger siblings, Honore and Nicolette with our ammunition of rotting fruit.

What mischief we always seemed to find ourselves in, Charlie recalled. He allowed the memories to flood his mind only briefly, because they were just too painful otherwise.

He and I had always been close. In fact, he couldn't remember a moment in his life when I hadn't been by his side, until the day we had been loaded into carriages and sent to separate schools, several hours apart, three years ago.

He had taken a lot of ribbing from the other boys in his dorm when he first arrived at his boarding school. He would sit at his writing desk and pen lengthy letters to me every other day, then wait with anticipation for my reply.

Before he knew what had happened, one of the young men he roomed with ripped a letter from his hands and began reading it aloud to everyone that would listen.

Charlie had been humiliated and shamed by all the young men in the dorm. After that, he just stopped writing all together and concentrated on his studies.

But that was then and this is now. Charlie was out with his two best friends. They were there for one reason, to have some fun and just maybe, if they were lucky, find a little trouble to get into.

I

 GREW UP IN A LOVING home, overlooking the Bay of Biscay, in France.

Our lavish home and lands were awarded to Father for services rendered to the crown during the Seven Years War, a battle fought throughout Europe for political domination. My brother Charlie and I were blessed to grow up in this loving home, with plenty of sunshine, sand, and room to run free. Of course, we had the normal teachers, siblings, and parents who occasionally tried to come between us, but Charlie and I always managed to thwart their best efforts.

Charlie was named after my mother's brother, who died at the age of five, when Mother was just an infant.

I was named after a beloved grandmother of my father's.

As twins born of one womb, I often felt as if we were of one mind. I would think of something and Charlie would know exactly what I was thinking and vice versa. We had a strange connection that gave us an advantage over other children. I always knew where to find Charlie, even when he didn't want to be found. In turn, Charlie always knew how I was feeling, even when I insisted that I was fine, when I truly wasn't. We each shared an intuition about the other that some felt was abnormal or not of this earth, and yet I never gave the matter much thought because this was just the way our minds worked. I guess I always knew we were different from other children, and I was all right with that because I considered it a gift we were given, not a curse.

Charlie was very handsome, with dark auburn hair like Mother's and striking blue eyes like Father's. He was blessed with a natural athletic ability and physical appeal that drove all the young ladies around him to distraction.

I, on the other hand, had dark hair like Father's, with streaks of red running through it that showed up when I spent too much time in the sun. My eyes were the same jade green as Mother's, but from time to time, tiny flecks of blue would appear when I was distraught or scared. I was also blessed with my mother's curves, which I found vexing when I wanted to keep up with Charlie, or run free through the countryside, masquerading as a boy.

Eventually, I learned to use my God given gifts to my advantage when it came to my male counterparts. I found that it was infinitely easy to sway them to my way of thinking, when it suited me, by simply pouting or giving them a well practiced look. Charlie said it was the devil in me that made me so good at it. But I say it was the need to survive in a male dominated world that made it necessary for me to resort to such tactics.

Our parents had a strong loving bond that often manifested itself in ways that embarrassed Charlie and me. We especially despised their public displays of affection when they were anywhere near us. We made funny faces and acted as if the life was being sucked from our very souls. This was done in hopes of distracting them, but it never seemed to work. Mother and Father ignored our antics, choosing instead to stare longingly into each other's eyes and laugh like children sharing a private joke.

Mother referred to us as her little angels when we were born. Yet it didn't take long for us to earn reputations as petits diables, titles we earned because of our devious or creative minds. It really was a matter of perspective. We had a way of coming up with new and innovative ways of tormenting our younger siblings, Honore and Nicolette.

Honore was named after Father's best friend and confidant who was a permanent fixture in our home. We affectionately referred to our little brother as Honore the Younger, a nickname he despised for some reason, so we never missed the opportunity to take our digs. Honore was three years our junior, while Nicolette was two years younger than Honore.

Nicolette was a pleasant child but a bit quiet in comparison to the rest of us, and it often felt wrong to torment her as we did. But Charlie and I dealt out our brand of torture to our two siblings equally. Unfortunately for Honore and Nicolette, Charlie and I had a little sibling rivalry of our own going on, and it knew no bounds. When I say sibling rivalry, I mean we both tried to out do the other, especially when it came to annoying our younger siblings.

That was, until that dreadful day when our parents came to a decision that changed everything. They decided that our education was better served abroad, at separate boarding schools in London.

We were told it was in our best interests, and that we needed to develop healthy relationships with other young men and women outside of our small, but intimate circle of two.

To say that my life was turned upside down would be an understatement.

I broke down and clung to Charlie as if my world had just fallen apart. This did nothing to sway our parents' decision. I felt off kilter and my life took on a new direction altogether, one fueled by anger and general mistrust of all people who weren't my brother, Charlie. I will say that the unfortunate experience did teach me a few things that came in handy later on. I learned to think and to do everything for myself. I became strong, self sufficient and independent minded.

There were some harsh critics among my peers who called it something else altogether. They said I was tough, inflexible, and far too stubborn for my own good. There were even those who claimed I possessed a few severe character flaws that would prove to be of detriment to me later in life. Yet, I was deaf to their criticisms, as it didn't serve my purpose at the time.

My challenges and problems stemmed more from a broken heart than anything else. I felt incomplete, as if a part of my vital organ had been ripped from my chest, while it was still beating.

Most children our age might have pleaded with their parents to reconsider, but not Charlie. He resigned himself to his fate, obediently stepping into the waiting carriage and graciously waving farewell as it pulled away.

It was safe to say that I was not like most children.

As I looked into my parents' eyes that day, I vowed I would never forgive them for their betrayal. Then I took it one step further, like the proverbial knife to the heart, some would claim and I swore to them both that I would never again darken their door step.

I was fearless. But I think we are all fearless, until the unthinkable happens. Straightening my spine and drying my tears, I climbed into my waiting carriage, alone, with nothing but my sheer determination to keep me warm. I steeled myself against the urge to glance back at my appalled parents, standing in the drive, clinging to one another.

I'm sure the consensus between them was that I would come to my senses soon enough, that I was merely being a dramatic sixteen year old girl, and that the entire matter would blow over quickly enough and all would be forgiven with time. Instead, my resolve was only strengthened with each passing mile, and determination became the air I breathed.

To say that I was shaped into the person I've become today and that it can all be traced back to that one defining moment in time is a valid, but far too simple explanation.

So now I tell you my story, as I recall it.

2

The Sisters of Our Lady's Finishing School
For Young Ladies Located in the English Countryside

HEARD THE CLOCK IN THE hallway chiming 4:00 a.m. as I tossed and turned restlessly. Unusual visions clouded my normally peaceful dreams.

I saw three young men sitting in a tavern drinking ale, as the foul stench of urine and unwashed bodies assaulted my senses. An overwhelming feeling of dread and fear coursed through my veins as I twisted in my sheets. I tried to study the young men enjoying themselves while they celebrated their special occasion, but I couldn't see their faces clearly. They were seated next to others, and people were mingling around them.

I asked myself, *'why do I feel so ill at ease if the young men are having a good time? But more importantly, why am I having this dream at all?'*

I had never stepped foot into such an establishment. So why was this happening? I felt sick to my stomach and I didn't like the crude behavior I was forced to witness, but I couldn't turn away. A bead of sweat trickled down my forehead, and an image of a white pig kept running through the tavern, between my feet, when I looked down. It was as if I was there with the men who were laughing and having a good time. That was strange that a pig was allowed to run free in a place where people were gathered and food was being served. Nothing in this dream made any sense to me.

Suddenly, one young man excused himself and staggered to the back of the tavern. He began to heave up the contents of his stomach and I felt a sharp pain in my own stomach at the same time. Wrapping my arms about my middle, I tried to comfort myself.

Making his way back to his companions, the young man placed his hand on the shoulder of one of his friends, "Hey, Tommy, I think I've had enough celebration for one day. I'm going to find our room and sleep off this pounding in my head," he said, throwing a few coins onto the table, before he headed for the door.

"Hey, Charlie, wait up, I'll go with you," Tommy shouted after him. "Ashton, the party is over, let's go," he called to the third man seated across the table from them.

Slowly looking up from the woman's neck he was nuzzling, the young man acknowledged his companions.

Why had that man called out my brother's name? Again, nothing made sense to me. My brain seemed to be in a fog. I felt nauseous and dizzy.

Downing the contents of his mug, Ashton kissed the cheek of the young woman seated on his lap. "Well, sweetheart, you heard the man, party's over and I'm going to need my leg back," Ashton retorted, immediately standing up and unceremonious dumping the scantily clad woman onto her ample backside before she could get her footing. Staggering toward the door behind his friends, Ashton trotted to catch up, while slipping his coat on.

The three men came together half way down the block, laughing about the crazy night they had just had. Propping Charlie up between them, they stumbled their way down the street, as they looked for the sign of the Royal Crown Inn, where they had secured lodgings for the night.

Realization struck me like a bolt of lightning. The man they kept calling Charlie was my Charlie, my twin brother, whom I hadn't seen in three years. He was celebrating his nineteenth birthday with his school chums and I was a witness to their garish self indulgence.

The clarity of colors in which I was now seeing everything seemed to pop out at me, as if I were standing right next to them. The fog had lifted from my befuddled mind, and now I felt as clear as day. It was as if I was the fourth person standing alongside the noisy, rambunctious trio. I had always been aware of Charlie and his whereabouts in the past, but in an intuitive way. This was definitely very different than that.

As I was digesting this new information, I again felt a shroud of darkness as thick as London fog descend upon me. My insides began to twist into a knot, and it felt like a fist to the gut.

Five, very rough looking men had been watching the antics of Charlie and his companions, and suddenly appeared, seeming to come out of nowhere, surrounding the three of them.

"You boys need some help finding lodgings for the night?" The larger man asked with a thick Irish accent.

"We know our way around just fine," Ashton answered curtly, his blond good looks contorting into a grimace, as he tried to focus his eyes on the man speaking to them.

"You heard my friend, *Monsieur. Casse-toi!*" Charlie asserted, as his natural French accent came out stronger than his English.

"Now, now, my young friends, there is no call for you to be so unfriendly. We just thought that maybe you gentlemen needed some assistance finding some accommodations." The large man spoke again, trying to sound friendly and genuine, as he took two more steps toward the three men in the center.

But there was nothing genuine or friendly about him. There was something in his stance and overall demeanor that spoke volumes to me.

"My friend just told you. We are fine, and truly don't require your assistance, so bug off," Tommy chimed in, as an uneasy feeling began to crawl up his spine.

Suddenly, Charlie sobered up, looking directly at me, as if I was standing next to him. I felt his fear and uneasiness, as his heart and mind raced. He was trying to send me a message. Had he felt me beside him all along?

Charlie stood a little taller and turned to look at the large man. I could tell he was simply posturing, in hopes that his full height of six feet three inches would be of some deterrence to the intruders. "If you are looking for money, we spent it in the pub tonight," he responded, while reaching into his trouser pocket. He fished around for a moment, hoping that he had remembered to place his dagger in it before he left his dorm room earlier that day. I felt the same sickening feeling he got when he realized the dagger wasn't there. My heart sank, and his fear now became my fear.

Trying to think fast, Charlie decided to take another approach, "What do you know? I seem to have a few coins left over. This should be sufficient for your needs, boys. Why don't you have another round of drinks on me?" Charlie suggested, pulling three silver coins from his pocket and flipping them at the large man, who let the coins land at his feet and roll into the gutter.

"Now is that any way to treat a Good Samaritan, who just wants to help you find a comfortable place to lay your pretty little heads down for the night?" Someone else said, standing directly behind Charlie, causing him to jump in surprise.

"Now look what you've gone and done. You've insulted my friend and hurt his feelings by throwing money at him," another man chimed in, as he took two steps closer, tightening the circle around the boys. Two large rats scurried from the gutter where the coins landed. I noticed that the salty sea air was especially pungent and thick at that moment, and it assaulted my senses. I felt myself physically shiver as if someone had just walked over my grave.

I cried out to Charlie and his hapless companions, but the sound froze in my throat, and my blood felt like ice as it tried to move through my veins. I wanted to warn them, or scream that they should run!

But it was already too late. The men were closing in on Charlie, Ashton and Tommy, and I could feel my stomach churn, as tears bathed my cheeks.

Charlie once again turned and looked directly at me. I could hear his words even though his lips didn't move. "*I feel you there. I know you can see me. If we survive this fight, you have to find me. I know you can find me, Bella.*"

Turning away from me now, Charlie got into a defensive position and the three of them placed their backs together in a triangle formation. This was the classic stance of the Musketeers. Charlie and I had learned it when we took fencing lessons from a man we called Uncle. He had taught many a Musketeer how to fight at the academy.

I was suddenly struck by Charlie's loyalty to his two friends. He had obviously cared enough about them to teach Ashton and Tommy what to do in a situation such as this.

I didn't want to witness what came next, but like a carriage mishap on the side of the road, it was impossible not to stare and wonder if anyone lay dead next to the overturned wreckage.

Punches began to fly as fists connected with solid bone. The sickening sound of a grown man's fist connecting with another man's jaw made me clench my stomach as the taste of bile lingered in my mouth. The smell of desperation hung heavily in the air, and I cried out for my brother as he fought for his life.

3

Just Between Friends

Y VISION STOPPED THERE AND I was left to wonder how it all turned out. A scream that had been stuck in my throat the entire time suddenly erupted from my mouth, as I bolted upright in bed. Fear and pain gripped my chest as tears streamed down my face. "Charlie! Oh God please, not my Charlie."

My sweat drenched sheets clung to my body and convulsive shivers shook me to my core. I couldn't think, nor could I stop shaking. Fear gripped me by the throat, zapping every ounce of strength I had. My limbs felt weak, like noodles that sit too long in a pot of boiling water. My face felt swollen and my ribs hurt like I had just been through a terrible accident. I couldn't explain why I was no longer connected to Charlie, or why my vision started, then abruptly ended.

It was as if Charlie shut me out of his mind, shielding me from the horror that was about to befall him.

I sat on my bed for the longest time, consumed with grief and fear, trying desperately to form a coherent thought. Finally, I leaned over, fumbling in the dark, to light the candle that sat on my bedside table. Climbing from the bed, I stumbled before opening the doors to my armoire, then began to rummage about until I found what I was searching for. Pulling out a pair of boy's trousers, a shirt and a cap, along with the bandages I used to bind myself up, I quickly dressed. Fumbling about, I found the old jacket and boots I kept in the back corner of my dressing closet. I always kept them safely tucked away for those times I wanted to ride without being recognized or bothered by social convention.

If Charlie had been killed, surely I would have felt something by now, like the splitting of a mighty oak tree by a bolt of lightning, I would have felt the confirmation of such an act. But I didn't feel myself split in two. I simply felt consumed with grief for the horrific act perpetrated against my brother. Slowly the feeling of rage began to stir inside of me, becoming all consuming as it mixed with desperation and the need to be whole again. My emotions propelled me forward, placing one foot in front of the other.

Slipping everything but my boots on, I extinguished the candle and piled my hair under the cap. My disguise was now complete. Ducking quietly out the door and down the hall to the back staircase, I listened for a moment, making sure that no one was wandering about this part of the hall.

The only noise I heard was coming from the kitchen as the cooks prepared the bread for baking. I exhaled, realizing that I had been holding my breath, and my heart felt like it was going to pound its way through my chest. Tiptoeing down the stairs and past the cooks was no easy task, but I waited for the right moment and made my way to the side door. Silently lifting the latch, I opened the door just wide enough to slip through, then closed the door behind me. I froze when the top hinge squeaked slightly, quickly closed my eyes, I said a little prayer. Then easing the latch back into place, I said another prayer that my absence wouldn't be discovered for hours. By then it would be too late for anyone to do anything about it.

Stopping long enough to slip my boots on, I stayed in the shadows, just in case anyone was up rummaging through the garden for fresh herbs. Finally, making my way to the barn, I eased the heavy wooden door open, and listened for any noise of men moving about.

When I was satisfied that the only noises were those of the horses shuffling about in their stalls, I pushed the door open wider. Growing up with horses, I knew how to saddle one for myself, and didn't require the help of a stable hand. The only thing left to do now was to pick the right horse for the long ride to Oxford. I needed a horse with lots of heart, and not one that had gone barn sour, or become fat and lazy. No, I needed a horse that was willing to run and not stop until I had reached my destination, and I had just the right horse in mind.

Making my way along the wall of closed doors, I peeked into a darkened stall, trying to make out the horse standing in the shadows. "Third stall on the right…oh sorry, Rosy, wrong stall, sorry girl," I whispered shutting and latching the top of the door. "Must be the forth stall on the right." I whispered to myself as I gingerly unlatched and opened the next stall door to check. "Yes. Good morning, Dodger, my handsome lad. I have an important mission for you today," I whispered, greeting him with a gentle pat on the nose and a cube of sugar, before slipping a feedbag over his head so I could saddle him quietly.

"Hey, what do you think you are doing, young man?" the farrier, Tucker Parker, growled as he grabbed me by my coat, spinning me around. If it had not been for his strong grip on my collar, I would have hit the ground hard.

"Shhh!" I said, almost jumping out of my skin. "Tucker Parker, you scared ten years off my life," I scolded pushing him off of me, as I leaned down and picked my hat up off the ground. "Keep it down before you awaken the entire place," I groused, while dusting the hat off and placing it back upon my head. Then narrowing my eyes at him, I began tucking my hair back under the hat.

"Sorry, Isabella, I didn't realize it was you. I thought someone was stealing a horse," he replied, in a hushed tone. "Which begs the question, where exactly do you think you are going at this hour of the morning?" he asked, standing in front of me with his hands on his hips.

"I have to take care of something and I don't need the entire Order of Saints coming down upon my head, if you must know. So you can help me, Tucker, or get out of my way," I said in a loud, angry whisper.

"Why didn't you come and get me to help you?" he asked. Then taking a second look at me, as if he was truly seeing me for the first time. "And why are you dressed like a boy, if you don't mind me asking?"

"I have a long ride ahead of me and I don't want to attract any unwarranted attention, if you get my drift," I added as quietly as I could, while throwing the blanket and saddle over Dodger's back. "And why I didn't seek you out at this wee hour of the morning is a silly question. You have known me for three years now and you know my history and general mistrust of men," I replied, struggling to secure the saddle properly.

Taking hold of my arm, Tucker pulled me around to face him. He had a strange look in his eyes, before he stepped in even closer, as if he intended to kiss me.

Panic set in and I suddenly experienced a strange ringing between my ears. Bringing Tucker up short, I placed my hands against his chest, and gave him a hard shove, to stop any further advancement. "Have you lost your mind, Tucker Parker?" I cried, sounding a little harsher than I intended.

"You use to like it when I kissed you, Isabella Deveraux."

"That was a long time ago." I said, brushing him off as I turned back around to finish saddling Dodger. "I'm not that scared little girl any longer, trying to figure out which way is up."

Taking a hold of my arm gently, he forced me to stop and look at him, "Then I will go with you, to make sure nothing happens to you."

"No, you can't," I answered rather sternly.

"Why Izzy?" he asked, with that hurt look he always gets when I said or did something he didn't quite understand.

The sound of pain in his tone almost made me feel bad for being so harsh. But dealing with Tucker's delicate ego is not something I could handle, so I did what I always do in a situation like this, I pushed him even further away. "Tucker, I don't have time for this," I replied, irritated he was distracting me from my task.

"Oh now, look here," he said, pointing at the strap, as if I had never saddled a horse in my life. "You're doing it all wrong," he said, shoving my hands out of the way.

"Keep it down, before you wake the entire stable up," I scolded with just a hint of derision in my voice.

Tucker proceeded to undo the leather strap, and then cinch it back up exactly as I had done it in the first place, only tighter. "If you don't do it tight enough from the beginning, the saddle will slip and you will end up on the ground a mile down the road. You know Dodger is a prankster," Tucker continued to pull on the strap until Dodger voiced his distain, by stomping his hoof and swatting Tucker with his tail. "Dodger always inflates his belly when you slip the saddle on his back."

"Thank you for your unwarranted assistance, but I really must be on my way," I stated flatly, changing out the feedbag for a bridle.

"I can't let you go off on your own, willy nilly through the countryside. What if something happens to you? I would be responsible," Tucker countered, stepping in front of me, trying to impede my progress. Then reaching up, he took a hold of Dodger's bridle, and refused to let go.

"As if you have anything to say about the matter," I stated under my breath. Gingerly stepping around him, I placed my booted foot in the stirrup and swung myself up onto the saddle. Leaning over, I secured my other foot in the other stirrup, while avoiding eye contact with him.

Grabbing a hold of my leg, Tucker squeezed it tightly, until I finally turned giving him my full attention. Only when I looked down at him and smiled, I patted the jeweled encrusted dagger in my pocket and said with a dangerous glint in my eye, "I am fairly confident that anyone who is stupid enough to get in my way will be dealt with, in a swift and deadly manner, if you get my meaning."

To emphasize this bold statement, I leaned over even closer to his face, "If you and I were ever truly friends, this would be where you turned loose of my horse and wish me a safe journey."

Shock, surprise, and then finally hurt showed on his handsome face once again. "You're not coming back are you, Izzy?" he quietly stated. Taking a deep breath, I let it out slowly, and then shook my head no. "What do I tell them, when they find you missing?" he asked, still hanging onto the bridle.

"Just lead Dodger out of the barn quietly and go back to bed. You don't have to tell them anything. Just feign ignorance. That's what I would do," I said, deciding to change tactics. "Please, Tucker, I truly have to go now, before they discover me missing," I quietly pleaded for his cooperation.

"Just be safe and don't take any unnecessary chances," he said gently. Tucker's brown eyes clouded over, before he turned away to hide the feeling he was experiencing. Quietly, he led Dodger from the stall and out into the courtyard before regaining control of his tangled emotions, I could see a physical change come over him as he closed himself off to me behind a wall of civility. Slowly looking up from the ground, but not directly at me, he asked, "before I turn loose of this horse, Isabella Deveraux, just tell me the general direction you will be traveling should I be called upon to point the search party in the right direction. Of course, only if something should happen to you and you are never heard from again," Tucker concluded morbidly, as he turned his soft brown eyes toward me again. "Should there be a need to go in search of your cold, lifeless body along the roadside somewhere," he concluded dryly.

"Oh, now you're just being obtuse and trying to get under my skin, Tucker Parker," I replied, slightly put off by his coldness. "I am heading for Oxford."

"That is almost two and a half hours away," he cried as his face registered shock and alarm all at once. He couldn't decide whether to turn loose of Dodger's rains after all, so I made the choice for him. I could read Tucker like a book, and regardless of my desire to spare his feelings, I had neither the time nor the inclination to coddle him.

"I will only ride Dodger an hour and a half, tops. Please, Tucker, stop worrying. I will be fine, but I really have to leave now," I said, kicking Dodger in the side as I yanked the reins loose from his grasp. "Sorry, Tucker, see you when I see you," I called out quietly.

"Not if I see you first," he answered back, under his breath.

4

A Bold Move Indeed

NCE I WAS ON THE MAIN road, I kicked Dodger hard and rode him like the Devil himself was nipping at my heels. I tried to pace myself and save Dodger's strength as much as possible, but I kept seeing Charlie's scared face in my mind and urged Dodger to go even faster.

My gut told me that Charlie and his two friends were in a bad situation, and I felt sick. At the same time, I hoped to arrive at the school and discover that it had all been a bad dream, the wild imaginings of my crazed mind. I said a little prayer that Charlie would be in his dorm room, cracking jokes with his friends. But something in the pit of my stomach kept telling me that it was all true.

I had learned years ago to listen to those strong promptings and not brush them aside. That loud voice that screamed out its warnings in my head had saved Charlie and me more than a few times.

As I rode, my mind took me back to the summer of '78', when Charlie and I were visiting the Smith family.

Every summer our family would join the Smiths' at their lake-side chateau in the countryside. They had geese, dogs, horses, and large trees to climb. But the best draws were the two Smith boys, John and Niles. Our families were so close back then that I can scarcely believe how it all came to an end that summer.

The four of us were close in age and had developed a bond that allowed us to slip back into a comfortable friendship each summer. We ran about the countryside freely for two weeks, without a care in the world.

1778 was the year Charlie and I had turned fourteen, and I was particularly anxious that summer because I had developed a crush on Johnny. He was two years older than me and I got these butterflies in my stomach every time he looked at me.

The summer before his body had begun to change and now his manly form had become very desirable. His shoulders had broadened and his voice changed, but the most impressive change in Johnny was the loss of his baby fat. When he took his shirt off to jump into the water that summer, I gasped out loud.

Charlie looking at me and suddenly his eyes got big and he had a strange look on his face. It was the same look he had when he wanted to tell me a secret, but this time it was as if he had read my mind and already knew my secret.

It was strange that I could have those feelings for a boy and yet it felt so right. I even let Johnny kiss me behind the tree fort.

We were all enjoying a carefree summer, when the tragedy struck.

Our families had gathered by the lake. The four of us were headed for the docks when I had a premonition. I had never experienced anything that strongly before and decided to listen to the voice in my head. I tried to redirect the activity away from the lake, but Johnny and Niles wouldn't hear of it, their hearts were set on play-ing pirates and nothing was going to stand in their way. Luckily, I managed to convince Charlie to play a game of hide and seek with me instead.

An hour later, the boys over turned the small boat in the middle of the lake. Johnny was a strong swimmer so he swam to shore to get help, but was forced to leave Niles behind, clinging to the capsized boat. He had never learned to swim very well, and by the time help arrived, Niles was nowhere to be found. His body floated to the top of the water and was retrieved from the north shore three days later.

The Smiths' were devastated and something inside of Johnny snapped that day. Neither Johnny nor our friendship was ever the same after that. We heard rumors and whispers that Johnny had to be institution-alized a year later.

Our family never went back to the Smith's chateau, and Charlie and I lost touch with our friend. The recollection still makes me tremble with fear when I think of how close Charlie and I came to death that day.

I pulled my cap further down over my hair and gave Dodger his head. I leaned over his neck and spurred him onward, as his powerful legs ate up the miles between The Sisters of Our Lady girls' school and Oxford. I pushed Dodger to his limits, stopping only once half way there to water him. I was never one to abuse an animal but dread continued, like a never ending circle in my head. Urgency continued to pound in my head and all I could see was Charlie's face before he closed his mind to me.

I finally reached the stables at Oxford, when I came to a skidding halt inches from a young stable hand who nearly jumped out of his skin. Dodger was wet and lathered, his nostrils flaring from endless miles of running.

I flipped the rains to the young man as his face registered shock. "Walk him for no less than twenty minutes, and whatever you do, don't feed or water him until you have completely cooled him down," I said in a tone that left no room for argument. I turned and started to walk away when I realized I didn't know where I was going.

Turning back around, I called out to the young man, "Excuse me, but could I bother you for directions to the Head Master's office?"

"Who?" The boy asked as if confused by the simple question.

"The man in charge, the gentleman who runs this fine establishment for higher learning," I impatiently persisted.

Then waving my free hand around in a circular motion, to suggest he hurry up, yet the young man continued to stare at me, clearly confused by my female presence, on an all male campus.

"Grrrr…" I growled deep in my throat, as I grew increasingly impatient with the delay. "If you are still confused young man, I am a girl dressed as a boy and that was the sound of my soul dying slowly,"

I grumbled. "Please point me in the direction of the Head Master's. I will take it from there." My nerves were shot and so was my backside from so many miles in a saddle.

"Oh, you must mean Dean Sinclair," the gawky young man finally answered.

"Yes, the Dean," I replied, with a forced smile, while rubbing my sore posterior and lower back. "Where might I find the gentleman?"

"Follow that path between the two buildings then stay to your left and you will arrive at the main building. His office is at the top of the stairs when you go in the double doors," he answered, staring at my outfit then looking back at my face.

"Thank you," I called back to him as I waved good bye, over my shoulder.

Being in such a rush, I nearly ran headlong into another young man as I came around a corner. "Oh, I am terribly sorry," I apologized, as he grabbed hold of my arm, dropping the books he had been carrying.

"No, the blunder was entirely mine. I wasn't watching where I was going," he apologized, pushing his glasses back into place with his finger.

I quickly leaned over, retrieving his books and handing them back to him. "You dropped these, and again I am terribly sorry for running into you." I didn't wait for his reply because I was a girl on a mission and I was in a hurry.

"Can I help you find somebody? You look a little out of place here."

"That is because I have never been here before and I am looking for Dean Sinclair's office," I replied, while continuing on my way.

"I can show you where to find the Dean if you like," he said with a hopeful tone as he ran to catch up to me. "Let me introduce myself," he said stretching out his hand as I continued to walk, "My name is Timothy. Timothy Jones. And you are?"

I stopped and looked at his outstretched hand, somewhat frustrated by the delay. "Isabella Deveraux," I replied, taking a deep breath.

Stretching out my own hand, giving him a half heartedly hand shake. "I don't wish to be rude, but I am in a bit of a hurry and the young man in the stables already gave me directions. I am sure that I will be fine, and thank you for your concern. Good day to you," I said briskly, before walking away.

"We really don't get many young ladies on the campus. I just want to make sure that you don't get lost," Timothy continued as he tagged along beside me.

"I really don't think that I will get lost, since this path leads straight to the main building, where I will go through the large doors and straight up the stairs. I was told the Dean's office wouldn't be hard to find. Was I misinformed or does that about sum it up?" I conceded, slightly irritated that he was still following me.

"Well... yes... I mean no... but..." Timothy stammered.

"But what, Timothy?" I asked impatiently, looking him in the eye. "I have an important matter to discuss with the Dean, so if there is nothing more, I must be on my way. It was a pleasure to meet you, Timothy Jones," I retorted, before turning on my heels and continuing down the path.

"Well, I will be around in case you find that you are in need of my help. In this area, just in case you need anything," he continued to speak, even though he was unsure that I was still listening, as he indicated the bench he would be occupying while emphasizing the word 'anything' again before I was halfway out of ear shot.

"Thank you, Timothy Jones. You have no idea how much comfort that brings me, just knowing that you will be waiting right there, for my return," I stated dryly under my breath.

I finally arrived at the large building at the end of the path. Self conscious of the fact that I looked out of place, I ducked my head down and hurried up three steps and through the doors.

Once inside, I took a deep breath to steady my nerves. Orienting myself with the building, first I looked left and then right, and decided that my best bet was to go straight ahead. Spotting the staircase at the end of the hallway, I subconsciously checked my cap again, before heading up the stairs.

Prominently posted on the door it read, College Dean, Emerson Sinclair. "This must be the place," I muttered to myself. With my hand on the door I took another deep breath to quell the nerves bubbling up from my empty stomach. Plastering a pleasant smile on my face, I turned the knob and went inside.

Positioned in front of the Dean's office door was a rather stern, plain looking woman, with her hair pulled back and pinned in a tight bun, causing her already severe features to stand out. Her pinched up face was too small for her prominent nose and weak chin. While the stern woman continued to peer at me over the top of her thick rimmed spectacles, one question plagued me. Had the Dean hired a relative out of pity, or necessity?

"May I help you, young man?" she asked, while looking me up and then down suspiciously.

The way she acted, you would think she was guarding some precious commodity behind those heavy wooden doors. "Yes, Miss Sinclair..." I said reading the name plate on her desk. "Is the Dean in? I need to speak with him." I stated drolly, and then removed my cap allowing the full extent of my unruly hair to tumble down my back.

"Oh, umm, I'm afraid that won't be possible, Miss, the dean is very busy and can't be disturbed. Would you like to make an appointment?" Her tone let me know that I was not getting through that door anytime soon.

"Would the dean be available to speak with a member of the Deveraux family, Miss. Sinclair?" I stated in my best upper crust tone that assured her that I would not be put off. "And yes, just in case you were wondering, I am related to the very same Deveraux who is responsible for funding the construction of your new library and research department."

"Please give me one moment, Miss Deveraux and I will see …" she said, almost cringing as she jumped up from her desk.

"Lady Isabella Deveraux," I corrected, letting her know that I had not missed the slight.

"Of course, Lady Deveraux, I will only be a moment." She nearly tripped over her chair as she bowed and curtsied at the same time.

Moments later I heard Dean Sinclair's jovial tone, which sounded forced, as he emerged from his office. "Lady Deveraux, how may I be of service to you this fine day?" he crooned, taking me by the arm, to maneuver me around Miss Sinclair's desk and through his office doors. "Please, come in, come in."

Before closing the double doors, Dean Sinclair turned to Miss Sinclair, "Please prepare us a pot of tea. I am sure Lady Deveraux has traveled a great distance and would love some refreshments."

"Please, Dean Sinclair, I don't wish to be a bother," I protested even though my stomach was growling.

"No bother at all, my dear… no bother at all." Taking his seat behind his grand mahogany desk, Dean Sinclair folded his hands and smiled pleasantly, "Now what can I do for you, Lady Deveraux?"

"I'm looking for my brother Charlie. If you could tell me where I might find him, my business with you will be concluded," I cheerfully informed him.

"I'm sorry, Lady Deveraux, but your brother is not here."

"What do you mean he isn't here? Where is he?" I asked as dread welled up from my stomach.

"I really can't tell you, Lady Deveraux. Your brother just said he had some matters to attend to and that he would be back in a few days."

I quickly stood up, unable to decide what to do next. Suddenly I couldn't breathe or catch my breath, and I brought my hands to my chest.

Seeing my distress, Dean Sinclair came around his desk, pouring me a glass of water at the same time, handing it to me in one fluid motion.

"How can you be dean of this school and just allow people to come and go as they please? Aren't there classes he should be attending?" I questioned, while hyperventilating.

"I assure you, Lady Deveraux, this is a university of the best quality and not a prison. Young men are free to come and go as they please," he informed defensively.

"Ha," I scoffed, nearly chocking on the water I'd just swallowed. I was struck by the injustice of society and the double standards that forced me to dress like a boy and sneak about just to check on my brother. But here at the university for wealthy young men, they were allowed to leave whenever the mood stuck them.

"Please forgive me, but I came a long way to see my brother, and you are telling me that you have no idea where he went? How do you think my father is going to react to the news that his eldest son is missing?"

"He is not missing, Lady Deveraux, of that I can assure you," Sinclair said. "I already told you, that your brother informed me that he —" Sinclair was suddenly distracted by a commotion coming from the other side of his office door, when without warning the door flew open, and a man barged in.

"Sinclair, old man, I have a matter of some urgency to discuss with —" the man's words freezing in his throat mid sentence.

"Grand Poppy, what are you doing here?" I cried, while tears of frustration and pent up anxiety rolled down my cheeks, the moment I saw my grandfather's face.

"Darling Isabella, I did not expect to see you here!" my grandfather, Lord Jonathan Stewart exclaimed, throwing his arms around my shoulders and giving me a great big squeeze.

"Charlie is missing. All three of the boys have been taken," I blurted out.

"I told you, Lady Deveraux, your brother is fine. But I don't recall mentioning his companions, who accompany him." Sinclair nervously laughed, while trying to make light of the entire matter. "Besides, your brother left yesterday morning, with the promise that he would return in a couple of day."

Looking up into my grandfather's face as tears rolled down my pale cheeks. "I saw it, Poppy. I saw everything and it was awful."

Patting my hand, grandfather looked over to the dean nervously. "Your grandmother woke me early this morning and insisted that I come down here and check on Charlie. I think she had a terrible dream as well," he whispered, trying to hide his own fears he had attempted to push aside on his long ride to the university.

Collapsing in his arms, I was comforted by his strength and allowed myself a moment of weakness.

"Could someone clarify what is going on? Because clearly, I am in the dark and I don't understand what the two of you are talking about," Sinclair demanded, clearing his throat, while looking at the two of us as if we should be committed to the nearest asylum.

"There is no time, Dean Sinclair. Time is of the utmost urgency. I do apologize, but Isabella and I really must be going," Grandfather announced before clearing his throat. He had some misgivings about discussing such intimate family matters in front of his longtime friend, Emerson Sinclair.

Miss Sinclair picked that moment to walk through the doors, bearing a tray of tea, crumb cakes and cookies, with the announcement of, "Tea is served."

"Terribly sorry to put you through all the trouble, Miss Sinclair, but we are just leaving," grandfather apologized, stepped to the side, allowing her to carry the tray into the room.

I sheepishly grinned at her, then taking a napkin from the tray, I wrapped two cakes and a cookie up, running to keep up. Grandfather managed to get half way down the stairs before I caught up to him.

We began our long trek back to the stables in silence, which was just fine with me, because it gave me time to eat one of the crumb cakes.

"You might want to slow down before you choke on those cakes seeing how you don't have any tea to wash them down with," he called over his shoulder, giving me a side long glance.

"What? Oh," I uttered, looking at the crumbs left in my napkin. "I didn't have time to eat earlier and I am starving. I think my stomach just took a bite out of itself," I said sardonically. "I would have grabbed a cup of tea on my way out, but felt it might be frowned upon and considered very poor form."

"Really?" he quipped, emphasizing the single word.

Grandfather's carriage was waiting in front of the stables and I frantically looked around for the young man who was seeing to my horse, Dodger.

"Just a minute Poppy while I take care of something," I called out to him, before running to the stables.

"Just be quick about it," he called back impatiently.

I found the young man in one of the stalls brushing Dodger's coat. Dodger was enjoying life with his nose buried in a feedbag, devouring a portion of well deserved oats.

"Listen, I want to thank you for your help earlier, and if it wouldn't be too much to ask, I need to request another favor," I began, then reached into my pocket and pulled out three coins, the amount easily three month wages for the lad.

Placing the coins in his hand, I folded his fingers over them, and looked directly into his eyes. "I need you to take Dodger back to The Sisters of Our Lady School, and find a young man by the name of Tucker Parker. He will take Dodger off your hands. You can find him in the stables."

"But what do I tell this Tucker Parker fellow when I see him?" he asked with some hesitation, mixed with surprise, as a smile began to form on his lips, when he realized just how much money I had given him.

"Tell him there won't be a need to send out a search party for me after all," I smirked.

"What?" he asked, shocked at such a strange message.

"Just tell him that Lady Isabella reached her destination safely and that she is with her family in London," I said. "Oh, and one more thing — tell him I said that I will see him when I see him. He'll know what it means. Can you do that for me?" I asked, making him repeat the instructions back to me word for word.

I thanked him for everything again, then turned and ran all the way back to the carriage, only to find Grandfather waiting impatiently, checking his pocket watch.

5

The Search Begins

I T ONLY TOOK GRANDFATHER A moment to begin his inquisition as I closed the carriage door behind me. Grandfather rapped on the roof with his walking cane, giving the driver the signal to head back home.

"I was curious about the statement you made earlier in the dean's office," Grandfather said, pausing a moment to carefully phrase his question. "When you said that you saw everything in your dream, what exactly did you mean?"

Squirming slightly under his intense stare, I cleared my throat before answering. "Well, in my dream I saw three young men entering a pub," I answered, wrinkling up my nose slightly, as the memory of the pub's fettered stench assaulted my senses again. "And there was a white pig with tusks running about, which, when you think about it, doesn't make any sense at all, because who would allow a pig to run about their establishment?" I mused out loud, as I rambled on.

"Yes, yes then what happened?" his hand impatiently waving in the air, wanting me to get on with the story.

"Yes, of course. Sorry," I apologized, feeling slightly embarrassed for rambling on.

Closing my eyes so I could once again focus on my dream, I continued to explain. "I saw Charlie get up from the table, and walk to the back of the room to throw up." Opening my eyes, I stared intently at my grandfather, to gauge his reaction to my next statement.

"Now this is the part where it gets very strange, because when Charlie got sick, I felt sick as well, and nearly threw up."

Grandfather sat quietly while I continued to describe the scene to him, and I could tell that the wheels were turning in his head because he placed a finger over his mouth the entire time.

He always did this when he was deep in thought. Grandmother told me once that he did that to keep from thinking out loud and disturbing the person speaking.

"Charlie walked back to the table to inform his friends that he was going back to the hotel, because he was tired and not feeling well. He called one of them, Tommy, and the other one…. Ah… Ashton, that's it, the other one's name was Ashton. Then Charlie walked out of the pub. It really is a disgusting place," I informed him as an aside. "Then Tommy yelled at Ashton, to come along. They all met up outside and were staggering down the street together, minding their own business, when they were accosted by a group of five very rough looking men."

I shuddered as the entire scene played out all over again in my head. Suddenly, I opened my eyes, to stop from seeing the rest of the dream.

"So, what happened next? Why did you stop?"

"Because the rest of the dream is just too brutal to relive in my head, that's why," I stated emphatically.

"All right, point taken. I'm sorry, Bella. So where do we begin searching for them?" Grandfather asked.

Peering out the window I forced my mind back, trying to remember every smell or impression that might help us know where to start looking. "Oh! I remember," I said suddenly. "It was near the water, because I could smell the sea air, and I had a salty taste in my mouth when I first awoke, and I could hear the bells chiming from the buoys."

"That's good! Now we are getting somewhere," his eyes sparkled with relief as he looked up to the carriage roof in gratitude, as if thanking the Heavens above.

"Poppy, I need to tell you the rest of the dream," I quietly said, almost hesitantly.

"Only if you are feeling up to it," he said gently.

"But I am afraid it gets worse, much worse," I added gravely.

Part of me wanted to spare him the gruesome details and part of me needed to share them with someone else before I exploded. I could hardly bear reliving it all over again, as my voice caught and I stifled a sob.

"Well, go on then, out with it," Grandfather insisted. I could hear the fear in his voice as he prodded for more.

With quivering lips, I continued. "Charlie tried to buy the men off. He even offered to pay for their drinks, but they weren't interested in the money, Poppy. Why didn't those men want the money?" I asked. My chest felt tight and I struggled to breathe, as my mind recalled every gruesome, agonizing feeling, when the man's fist hit Charlie's jaw, and how I felt chilled to the bone as Charlie fought back. Tears ran freely down my cheeks now and I squeezed Grandfather's hand.

"It's alright, Isabella, you can tell me," Grandfather added, choking back his own emotions.

"They started beating Charlie… and the sound of men hitting each other still rings in my ears. Oh Poppy, I can still smell their desperation and feel how scared…" My words faded away as the memories flooded my mind. The emotions overtook me and I just wanted the images to stop. I buried my face in Grandfather's coat and cried.

Handing me his handkerchief, Grandfather placed a hand on my back, comforting me until I had no tears left.

"Now when you say this all came to you in a dream, how can you be sure that it is real?" he asked cautiously.

"Do you doubt me?" I sniffed, sitting up to look at him.

"No. Of course not, but how can you be sure that you interpreted everything in this dream of yours correctly?" Grandfather pointed out.

Wiping my tears, then blowing my nose, I took a moment to compose myself. "This one was different from anything I have experience before, Poppy. It was as if I was standing there next to him. I could smell and feel every one of Charlie's emotions. When he got sick, I felt sick and when he was scared, I felt that fear. His pain was my pain, I don't know how else to describe it. We were completely connected. Charlie knew I was there too. He looked directly at me as if he was trying to tell me something."

Then suddenly, I remembered. "Poppy! The men's faces, I know what they look like! I don't think I will ever forget their faces," I cried, grabbing his lapels and pulling him close to me. Suddenly, I let loose of his coat and sat back, exhausted, against the seat.

"Extraordinary," he added, and then scratched his head. "Your grandmother has never been able to do that. The only person to have come close to that would be your mother." Grandfather mused, looking at me as if he was seeing me for the first time in his life.

Opening the back panel of the carriage, Grandfather instructed the footman to head for the London Wharf, promising him extra pay if he got us there quickly.

6

Getting To The Heart of the Matter—The London Warf

RRIVING AT OUR DESTINATION TWO hours later, Grandfather insisted that we get out and walk.

"When you mentioned in your dream that there was a white pig running around the pub, that got me to thinking," he announced, taking my arm and wrapping it around his as he pulled me down the street with him.

"I have never actually seen a live pig running free in any establishment, mind you, but I have seen a place called The White Boar." Leading me to a spot directly in front of a pub, Grandfather pointed to a sign hanging above the door.

"That's it! That's the pig I saw running around in my dream." Recognition hit me like a bucket of cold water.

I turned loose of Grandfather's arm and ran to the door. Shoving it open, I stepped inside the darkened room. The overwhelming stench of piss and fermenting beer nearly knocked me off my feet, assaulting my senses all over again. Memories began to flood my mind all at once, as if it was yesterday.

Even though the pub was nearly empty, the room suddenly filled with people, and the entire scene from the night before began to played out before my eyes. I recognized the five men sitting at the back of the pub, before they attacked my Charlie.

Retrieving a handkerchief from my pocket, I placed it over my nose to keep from gagging as I wandered over to the table where Charlie and his two friends had been sitting. Touching the table with my hand, tears sprung to my eyes, as each person's emotions lingered still, palpable and strong. Heading for the back of the room, to the table in the back, I touched it with my hand and saw the despicable men who sat there the night before. I began to shake uncontrollably. There was pure evil in their intent and I quickly lifted my hand to break the link with them.

Looking up, I found Grandfather studying me, watching my every reaction. "This is where they sat," I said, looking down at the table again. "The evil men, who took Charlie."

Then feeling the need to distance myself from the evil I felt, I rushed back around, to the first table and touched it. "Charlie was here, Tommy was next to him here, and Ashton sat on the other side across from them both, with a girl on his lap."

Suddenly turning on my heels, I ran to the door, and then down the street in the direction my brother had walked, as Grandfather followed silently behind.

Stopping in front of the cobbler's shop at the end of the block I recognized the sign hanging there, squeaking as it blew in the wind. "This is where they were surrounded, Poppy. This is where everything went wrong," I shivered, standing there in the middle of the street.

People walking by gave me strange looks, but I didn't care; my brother was gone, and I felt an emptiness that couldn't be filled by anyone but him.

Dark spots on the cobblestone street where blood had dried I knew was Charlie's and his friends' and, just maybe, some of it was from the five mysterious men as well. Charlie was a professionally trained fighter, after all.

Silent, bitter tears ran down my cheeks, I wiped them away with my sleeve. Taking several deep breaths to gain control of my emotions, I needed a minute to think. Looking around in the gutter, I moved some debris with the toe of my boot, until I found the three coins Charlie had tossed in the air.

Bending over to retrieve them, I wiped the dirt off on my pants. "These are the coins Charlie tried to give the men to make them go away," my voice faltering as I placed the coins in my pocket.

"It looks as if someone threw up over here a few hours ago," Grandfather said, as he stood a few feet from me, examining the gutter. "Most likely your brother or one of his companions. If they were as drunk as you said, a fist fight would have done the trick," he added absently, almost to himself as he pondered something in his mind. "Do you think the five men could have been sailors, Isabella?" He asked as an afterthought. "I know the harbormaster, and he knows everything that happens on these docks. Perhaps if you could describe these men to him, he might be able to tell us something about them," he smiled, as hope sparked life back into his eyes.

"Come along, it's a long shot, but maybe it will pay off." Grandfather grabbed hold of my hand, pulling me behind him, unwilling to slow down until we reached the harbormaster's office.

"Harry Kerr, as I live and breathe, how are you doing today?" Grandfather called out his greeting as we entered the small office, sounding jovial as if nothing was amiss in the world.

"Can't complain, business is good and the Missus is happy, so I am too. What can I do for you, Lord Stewart?" Harry replied.

"I would like to introduce you to my granddaughter, Lady Isabella Deveraux. She was just telling me about a group of men that she saw hanging around the docks yesterday, causing some trouble. Do you think you might be able to tell me anything about them if she describes them to you?"

"Well, I can certainly give it a try," Harry said, eyeing my strange attire. "Are you sure you grabbed the right grandchild, Lord Stewart? This one looks more like a boy than a girl," he teased.

Taking off my cap, my hair spilling down and I curtsied for the man. "It's a pleasure to meet you, Mr. Kerr. As my grandfather mentioned, there were five men hanging about the wharf yesterday. There was one man in particular, who seemed to be the ring leader. He was a rather large man, well over six feet tall, with very broad shoulders. He had the most stunning black hair and beard that came to about so," I indicated, using my hand to show how far his beard hung down. "He had a distinctive accent, I think Irish, or maybe Scottish, I can never tell the difference... oh and he had a large scar over his left eye, like this," I added, using my finger to trace a line over my own brow, trying to be as specific as possible. "The scar had to be at least three inches in length."

"Do you have any recollection of this man, Harry?" Grandfather casualy asked.

"It sounds like the man from The Three Sisters ship. I think his name was Shames something... Oh, I can't remember his last name off hand. Just a minute, and I will look him up in my ledger," Harry said as he stepped behind the counter and flipped open a book. "He was just in here last week now I know he is in here somewhere," Mr. Kerr muttered absently to himself, thumbing through the pages.

"Yes, here it is," he said, pointing to a line in his book, "Shames O'Malley, a great beast of a man. I wouldn't want to meet him in a dark alley," Mr. Kerr admitted with a shudder. "I get a case of the willies every time he comes in here. A nasty piece of work, if you ask me. He and his whole crew can go to the Devil, for all I care."

"Can you tell us where his ship is from, and if it is still in port?" I asked with hope that Charlie and I would soon be reunited.

"I haven't lost my mental capacity just yet," Harry replied, touching his finger to his forehead with a wink. "The Three Sisters ship is out of Dublin, and they are a discontented lot, every last one of them. They come over here every three or four months with a load of whiskey, ale and beer to sell to the local merchants. They may be a surly lot, but those Irish know how to make spirits," he conceded with a smile, as he came out from behind the counter. "I understand that O'Malley's group trades with most of the pubs and restaurants along the wharf, as well as a few of the finer pubs in London," Mr. Kerr said, standing next my Grandfather. I could tell he was maneuvering himself for a long winded conversation, and as a general rule, grandfather is willing to shoot the breeze with just about anyone. But today was different, and we didn't have time for idle chitchat. "You know, Sam was telling me just the other day... why, you remember Sam Reburn —"

Grandfather interrupted Harry mid sentence, "I am terribly sorry to cut you off, Harry, but we have to find Shames O'Malley and his ship. We need to speak with him regarding a matter of some urgency," Grandfather asserted cordially.

"Oh, you won't find Shames O'Malley or his crew around here. You will have to set sail for Dublin. They let out of here before the sun rose this morning," Harry said with a puzzled look. "I opened up just after eight this morning and they were already gone. Funny thing about that, they were scheduled to be docked for another three days. I guess they must have sold all of their goods and decided to head for home early."

Grandfather and Harry Kerr turned to look at me when I gasped out loud and clutched my stomach. Another audible groan escaped my mouth before I could stop it. Turning on my heels, I ran out the door. Suddenly, I couldn't breathe and needed air, and I needed it now. Gulping air like a fish on shore I was sure I was going to be sick.

I couldn't think, my mind suddenly felt foggy. I didn't know which way to turn, but what I did know was I couldn't stay here.

Turning left, I started walking.

"Isabella! Isabella! Where are you going?" "Wait!" Grandfather called out to me. I could hear the concern in his voice as he closed the gap between us, but I didn't care. I continued to walk quickly, wiping tears from my face with my sleeve as I went.

"Isabella! Stop please!" Grandfather clamped a surprisingly strong hand on my shoulder, bringing me to an immediate and abrupt stop. "Where are you headed?" he asked, in a tone that was both laced with frustration and concern.

"I have to find him, Poppy. I don't know exactly what that means yet, but I will figure it out. He's counting on me. I can't let him down." Hysteria began to take hold of me. "I am going to find him! I have to find him!" I screamed, pounding my fists against his chest.

Wrapping his arms tightly around me, Grandfather pulled me close as I crumpled to the ground, taking him with me, as my wobbly legs refused to support me any longer.

Devastation overwhelmed me and I sobbed uncontrollably, clinging to my grandfather's coat for dear life.

I desperately tried to make sense of what had happened and yet my mind just couldn't reconcile the events that had transpired.

Charlie and his companions were gone. The culmination of fatigue, hunger, and distress causing the air around me to feel heavy and electrified. My tongue had a metallic taste to it, and the hairs on my arms stood on end, just like they did on those rare occasions when I had been foolish enough to stand outside in a thunderstorm.

It was as if the world around me was completely normal one moment, and then flipped upside down the next, conspiring against me with the universe to force a change.

Limp in Grandfather's arms, I marveled at the peacefulness of unconsciousness, as my mind seemed to slow before it shut completely down. For a few moments, before letting go, I could still hear Grandfather calling my name over and over again, then there was nothing except peace and quiet. A space between conscious and unconscious, where everything around me continued as normal, but I deemed them of little consequence as they ceased to matter any longer, and I allowed myself to float away.

7

My Mind is Made Up

USHED WHISPERS, AND AN OVERALL feeling of being cold assaulted my senses. Water constantly dripping down my back and the sounds of moans, born of pain and fear, surrounded me on both sides.

"I'm coming, Charlie. I will find you!" I shouted in my mind, "I swear it."

Suddenly, waking from my fitful dream, I sat straight up in bed. "Charlie!" I screamed, shaking uncontrollably. It took a full minute before the fog cleared from my eyes and mind as I thrashed about, fighting against the hands that tried to hold and comfort me.

"Isabella, stop fighting me. You're safe now. I'm here," Grandmother insisted, letting go of my shoulders; she grabbed for my hand in an attempt to reassure me.

"How did I get here?" I cried, looking around the room that I recognized as my mother's, in my grandparent's home, in London.

"Grandfather brought you here yesterday. He was beside himself with worry. You collapsed in the middle of the street and he couldn't rouse you," she continued talking as she walked over to the servant's call rope and gave it a pull. "You were unconscious when he arrived with you." Coming back to the bed, she sat down on the edge and gently laid her hand across mine. "This happened to your mother once. Oh, you should have seen your grandfather and me. Your mother scared me half to death."

"But why did it happen?" I asked, still trying to piece everything together, as recollection flooded back and my heart began to ache all over again.

"I don't know, but when it happened to your mother, it was after a terrible trauma. The trauma was too much for her to bear, and she collapsed and slept for three days. I think maybe it is a protective mechanism that flips in the mind when you cannot immediately reconcile what is happening."

The door opened and a maid carried in a tray, setting it down on the table. She proceeded to pour two cups of tea, leaving them on the tray for us.

Grandmother picked up a robe at the end of the bed and helped me into it.

"Here you go, Miss, a nice warm pair of slippers will do the trick," the maid cheerfully quipped, as she placed them on the ground at my feet. "I have soft boiled eggs and a bit of toast, guaranteed to make you right as rain before you know it."

"Isabella, this is Maria. She is an excellent lady's maid, and will be with you as long as you decide to stay with us," Grandmother announced while walking over to the tray of food. "Everything looks excellent, Maria."

"Thank you, my lady," Maria replied. "Now, Lady Isabella, if you will have a seat right here," Maria said, leading me by the arm to the settee, as if I were an invalid. I was about to say something snide, when I heard a knock on the door.

Grandfather cleared his throat and pushed the door opened farther. "I heard you were awake and thought I would stop in to see for myself. Well, you don't appear to be any worse for wear," his booming voice reverberated through the room.

"Sorry that I gave you such a scare, Poppy. I'm fine, really," I smiled up at him. "I just feel so silly making everyone fuss over me like this."

"Nonsense, we just want to make sure that you are alright," he chided, taking the seat next to me on the settee. "And when you are feeling better, I will see to it that we get you back home to your parents."

Choking on my tea, I sputtered and coughed as Grandmother took the cup and saucer from my hands to prevent them from ending up on the floor. Grandfather gave me two swift claps to the back, nearly toppling knocking me on to the floor.

"I left there three years ago, vowing never to go back, and I meant it," I said vehemently.

"Don't you think three years is long enough to punish your parents? They were only doing what they thought —"

"Let me stop you right there, Poppy!" I demanded, holding my hand up. "My brother and I were literally ripped apart. I didn't know how to be without him and then suddenly, I am kept from him for three years."

"That was your choice. The family has been together since then, and you have refused to have anything to do with your mother or father," Grandmother gently admonished, trying to play the peacemaker. "Can't you put your anger aside and let bygones be bygones, Isabella?"

"Your parents miss you so very much, and it pains us all that you have refused to see them," Poppy continued, where Grandmother had left off.

"I am not going home and that is final," I said, stomping my foot to show that the matter was settled.

I stood and walked over to the fireplace in silence and stared into the flames. The sound of the fire crackling and popping was somehow soothing to my raw nerves.

Neither one of them said a word, but I could feel them communicating silently behind my back. They had developed their own code, born from so many years together.

I closed my eyes to the pain I felt every time I allowed myself to think about my family and how much I missed them. I had tried hard to put the last three years behind me, but memories of that day never failed to invoke strong emotions. I prided myself on being tough these days. I had honed the skill of putting up walls, tall, strong, impenetrable walls. They encircled parts of me that were frail, and vulnerable to the outside world. These were the parts of me I kept hidden from all those who attempted to get close to me. It was like a knife to the heart and all I wanted to do was throw myself down on the ground, and curl up into a tight little ball, and cry like a baby. But crying never solved anything, and it certainly wouldn't bring Charlie back to me now.

I took a deep breath. Quickly shoring up my crumbling walls, that were too raw and sore to the touch, like an open, festering wound.

Besides, there were other things more important at the moment. Like Charlie, who was out there, taken by some crazed madman for reasons I could not even fathom, and for a purpose I didn't dare try to guess.

Grandfather finally broke the silence, "You and your mother are just alike. The most obstinate, stubborn people I know," he concluded in frustration, getting up from his seat to pace the floor.

I turned my back to the fire, bolstered by its heat licking at my heels. I began again, slowly stoking the flames that had been burning inside of me for three long years. "Well isn't that rich" I scoffed. "I told you yesterday that I was going after Charlie. Did you think that I ramble on just to hear the sound of my own voice? I am going to find him, mark my words. So you can help me or you can act surprised when you awaken tomorrow morning and find me gone. Either way, I will not be stopped," I proclaimed boldly, allowing my words to sink in. "But know this, if you choose not to help me, there is a question you will be asking yourself for years to come," I announced defiantly.

Grandfather stopped mid stride, turning to face my determined gaze. "Oh, and just what question might that be, my obstinate, bull-headed granddaughter?"

"You will be asking yourself, if you did everything humanly possible to save your grandson. So with or without your help, I am going to

Dublin to find Charlie, by any means necessary. And God help this Shames O'Malley bloke, because when I get my hands on him, rest assured he is a dead man," I declared, with a murderous glint. "And I promise you both, that I am going to find Charlie or die trying!"

"That is crazy, Isabella. Do you hear yourself?" Grandfather cautioned, taking my hands in his.

I gazed into his aging eyes, and a part of me wished that I could let go of the anger that festered deep inside of me. I even wished that I could be different. But I wasn't. So letting go or giving up was not part of my character makeup, and my firmness of purpose was born from desperation.

Taking Grandfather's face in my hands, I kissed his cheeks and hugged him tightly, before turning and doing the same to my Grandmother.

"You can help me Poppy, or I will go around you. And even if I have to stow away on one of those ships in port, to get there," I added softly, with a steely resolve, refusing to give even an inch, "I will do so."

Seconds, then a minute passed by as he stared back at me. "Alright, I believe you," he said in defeat. "I will take care of the arrangements today," he continued, as his demeanor and countenance seemed to shrink a couple of inched.

"Jonathan!" Grandmother shouted, sounding exasperated by the two of us. "I don't believe what I am hearing. You aren't seriously considering letting her go off like this."

"You heard the girl. She is going one way or another. It would benefit all concerned, if I were to see that she arrived there safely and in one piece," he said, sounding irritated by being called into question. "Besides, she will be safe with me by her side."

"Jonathan!" Grandmother shrieked.

"What?"

"This is ludicrous. I will have no more of this crazy talk from either one of you," Grandmother protested.

"But Clarisse–" Grandfather sputtered, before Grandmother interrupted him again.

"No, Jonathan. Don't you, Clarisse me. You and I both know what the doctor said about your heart. I will not lose you this way. You will not be going, and that is final!" She announced.

Grandfather looked at me with derision and mockery in his tone, "Now I remember where you and your mother get your stubborn streaks."

"Jonathan Stewart, you stop it this instant."

"Well, it's the truth. The women of this family have all been cursed with the same affliction — you are all obstinate. Why, even Isabella's father claims that she has been stubborn as a mule from birth."

"I'm right here. I can hear what you're saying," I complained, stepping between the two of them. "And might I add that your statement could be viewed as highly inflammatory and offensive."

"No offense, Bella, my dear. I love you dearly, but you are one of the most bull-headed people I know, besides your mother and grandmother, of course," he said flatly, giving Grandmother a stern look over my head, daring her to disagree with him.

Letting out a deep sigh, along with the rest of my pent up anger, I knew my grandfather spoke the truth. "No offense taken, Poppy. To tell you the truth, you wouldn't be the first person to say as much to my face."

"I don't know about this Jon. Angelina is going to be furious. And I don't even want to imagine what Jude will do when he finds out," she continued, as she pushed her way past us both, to take a seat on the settee. "He will take us apart with his bare hands. I'm serious, Jonathan, our son in law is going to kill us."

"No he won't," Grandfather assured, with a wry smile. "Because I'm going to send Isabella to Dublin with an army of mercenaries at her disposal. They won't let anything happen to her, I guarantee it," he said over his shoulder, reassuring Grandmother as he walked toward the door. "Just get her packed and be ready to leave when I get back," he said, stopping at the door with his hand on the handle. "This may take some time, so don't hold breakfast or lunch for me."

"I hope you don't think I will be sending you unchaperoned, with an army of mercenaries, my dear," Grandmother said pointedly.

"Of course not, Grandmother, that would be absurd, even ludicrous." I retorted.

8

An Army of My Own

RESSED IN A MODEST BLUE gown, with my hair combed and piled upon my head, I was pronounced adequately prepared for a sea voyage. That was after Grandmother grilled me in the proper conduct of a young lady of my status. I was further informed that, "Proper young ladies did not run about the countryside disguised as a boy." Grandmother's words, not my own.

At that point, I was willing to agree to anything, just to get out of the house and on my way, while stuffing the additional boy's attire and boots I had obtained from a stable hand into my trunk when no one was looking. After all, one never can tell when being mistaken for a young lad might come in handy.

One hour later, I was standing on the wharf, with a trunk full of dresses that I didn't need and Maria, my new handmaiden, at my side.

Grandfather seemed anxious as we walked along the docks, so being the grateful granddaughter that I was, I decided to lag behind and supervise the unloading of trunks, giving him time to conclude his business with the mercenaries. I found great irony in a ship named The Sanctuary, manned entirely by a crew of mercenaries. Stepping onto the deck thirty minutes behind grandfather, my senses were on high alert as I began assessing the men that I would be placing my trust and life in. They were a rag tag group of men, to be sure. One only needed to look at them to tell that. But I was willing to keep an open mind, if it meant getting Charlie back alive.

A man high up in the rigging gave a high pitched whistle, causing another man to call out something that belonged on the seedier side of London's night life. This ruckus was cut short mid sentence, when the Captain fixed his men with a steely stare and shouted in a deep, booming, Irish voice, "Enough!"

The captain's slow menacing glare caused each man, one by one to turn back to what they had been doing, casting their eyes and heads downward.

The captain was formidable looking, standing over six feet tall. Fit and muscular, he commanded attention, the kind of man, one would envision as the leader of a group of mercenaries, and yet the one characteristic that struck me the most was his glaring stare. It caused the hairs on the back of my neck to stand on end and a shiver to crawl up my spine.

His piercing blue eyes seemed to look straight through me, and disassemble me piece by piece, while measuring my worth all at the same time. And by the look he was giving me, I was found lacking, a burden he suddenly realized he had been saddled with.

He wore his sun streaked blond hair tied back, which only added to his menacing good looks. My immediate impression was that of a dark and brooding man, haunted by some unresolved tragedy in his life. I can't really say why that image popped into my head, however images often flashed through my mind like a moment in time, giving me insight or a feeling about a person. This is how it was with my grandmother, as well as my mother.

"Captain Aiden Townsend, allow me to introduce you to my granddaughter, Lady Isabella Deveraux," Grandfather said, with just a little too much pride.

I rolled my eyes because of the fuss he was making. "Please forgive my Grandfather, Captain Townsend, Isabella will be adequate for the duration of our journey. Lady Deveraux is my mother," I said, offering my hand to the good captain, while I fixed him with a bold stare of my own.

Ignoring my outstretched hand, as if it wasn't even there, the captain redirected my attention to his left. "Allow me to introduce you to my first mate, Caleb Daughtery," the captain said, stiffly.

First mate Daughtery was also an attractive man, just a hair shorter than his captain. He had brown hair that was pulled back as well, and his hazel eyes merely danced with humor. Intuitively, I knew that the two of them had been childhood friends.

"Mr. Daughtery, it's a pleasure to meet you," I said inclining my head.

"Oh no, Lady Isabella, the pleasure is all mine, I assure you," he said, in an accent that matched the captain's before giving me a genuine smile that caused a spark of mischief to dance in his eye.

"If you gentlemen will forgive me, I would like to get settled in. So I will say my good-byes here, Grand Po — I mean Grandfather," I coughed to cover up the correction, before completely slipping up and using the childhood name Charlie and I called our grandfather.

"Give your old grandfather a hug child, if you're not too old for such things," he pensively said, pulling me into his embrace. "I have it on good authority that you will be safe, my dear."

"I am not afraid, Grandfather, and I promise to return with Charlie by my side," I assured him, emboldened by the gravity of the adventure I was about to embark upon.

"Then perhaps when you return with Charlie, we could have a candid discussion about you forgiving your parents and reuniting with your family once and for all."

"One mountain at a time, Poppy, one mountain at a time," I whispered in his ear, as I pulled away from him.

"You are so much like your mother," Grandfather sighed.

"I am nothing like my mother," I bristled.

"Oh, but you are more like her than you will ever realize," he said with a last hug and a kiss on my cheek, before turning loose of me.

I turned, giving the captain my full attention now. "How soon till we set sail for Dublin, Captain Townsend?" I asked, suddenly anxious to be underway.

"As soon as your grandfather is safely on shore, my Lady," he stiffly replied, with a nod of the head. Then turning to his right, he signaled to a young man standing a few feet away. "Please allow me to introduce you to Jamie, our cabin boy. He will be happy to show you to your quarters. I hope the accommodations will be suitable, since we aren't accustomed to taking on passengers," he added as a dig.

"Let me assure you, Captain Townsend, if I had to sleep in a row boat all the way to Dublin, I would make do. There really is no need to make a fuss on my account. I promise not to be a bother. In fact, you will hardly notice me on board. If you will excuse me now, I am anxious to settle in."

"When you see the size of your accommodations, my Lady, you might prefer that rowboat," first mate, Daughtery teased, causing me to smile.

Grandfather gave me one last wave good bye as he descended the gangplank.

I heard the captain start calling out orders, as Maria and I followed the cabin boy to my quarters.

9

The Prodigal Son Returns Home

"OIST THE ANCHOR, FURL THE sails. Get a move on men, we have urgent business in Dublin," Captain Townsend called to his crew.

"And eventually the prodigal son does return home," Caleb somberly said in Townsend's ear, as he took a moment to study his friend.

"I can hardly imagine my father throwing his arms around my neck to welcome me home," Aiden replied dryly, scowling at some unknown tormenter.

"Shall I change the subject?" Caleb asked somberly.

"I would be grateful if you did," Aiden answered, wishing to discuss anything other than his father or his homeland.

"What do you think about our new charge?" Caleb inquired, following Aiden as he headed to his cabin.

"Can't say that I gave her much thought," Aiden replied gruffly, trying to sound convincing.

"Tell me you didn't notice the way she smelled like lavender and the first blush of spring," Caleb insisted, taking a hold of Aiden's arm, turning him around, forcing him to look at him.

"I didn't notice," he said emphatically, avoiding eye contact.

"Liar!" Caleb insisted, pointing his finger at his friend. "I have always been able to tell when you are lying to me, and I just want you to know I am not fooled."

"What do you want to hear, Caleb?" Aiden's calm demeanor began to slip. "Do you want me to tell you that Lady Deveraux's scent lingered in my nose even after she left the deck? That I could get lost in the depths of her eyes and never come back?"

"At least it would be honest. Shauna and your son have been gone three years now. You're not a bloody monk," Caleb said, sounding almost desperate.

"Tend to your own needs, dear friend, and leave me out of it," the captain answered.

"You are allowed to have feelings for another, Aiden. Any woman will do as long as she has a heartbeat," Caleb said, letting out a frustrated breath. "It is possible to enjoy the company of a woman, without disgracing the memory of those who came before her."

Captain Townsend ignored Caleb as he reached his cabin. Opening the door, he tried to fling it shut in Caleb's face, but was impeded by a boot blocking the door.

Caleb, only momentarily put off, was not deterred, and followed Aiden into the room. "I do not understand this emotional exile of yours!" Caleb said, slamming the door shut behind him.

"And if I were to spend time with a young woman just to ease myself, it certainly wouldn't be with her," Aiden proclaimed with fervor.

"And what is wrong with this one, if you don't mind my asking?" Caleb asked, slightly surprised by his friend's reaction.

"Agh," the captain's expression of exasperation and Irish distain came from deep in his throat. Aiden turned to glare at his mate who had the bad form of persisting in this particular line of inquiry. "Have you lost your bloody mind man? I truly don't need that kind of trouble."

"What makes you think she is trouble?" Caleb queried.

"Did you see her eyes?" Aiden scoffed.

"I can't say that I was actually looking at her eyes, old friend," Caleb laughed.

"Enough, Caleb! Lady Isabella is our charge. I'll not be mucking up the waters where I make my living," Aiden proclaimed emphatically, pointing his finger towards the door. "Besides, that one is not only a lady, but a highborn. Don't you think she has better things to do than hang out with the likes of you or me?" He interjected, indignation etched his words.

"Have you forgotten where you came from yourself, old boy?"

"Hardly," Aiden answered, as his eyes snapped at Caleb like a whip.

"Then I have only one thing left to say to you," Caleb announced with a smug smile on his lips.

"Oh and what might that one thing be?" Aiden asked, quickly tiring of their so-called friendly banter.

"Tis a fool that loses out because he did not recognize the prize that was set before his very eyes," Caleb quipped as he walked to the door.

"And what brilliant philosopher might you be quoting from now?" Aiden asked, with derision dripping from his lips.

"That would be me," Caleb said glibly, standing at the door with his hand on the latch.

"Just make the arrangements for supper if you're not opposed to performing your duties as first mate, Daughtery," Aiden yelled at Caleb's retreating back, "or I will show you who the real fool is, my friend," Aiden murmured under his breath. "We will see in the end who is the real fool indeed," he concluded, turning back to the paperwork sprawled across his desk.

10

Dinner is Served, Anyone Order a Side of Crow

"**I** WANT TO THANK YOU FOR the generous invitation to dinner, Captain Townsend," I said, entering his private quarters with Maria close behind.

"I assure you that it is my pleasure, Lady Isabella," Aiden replied stiffly.

"What lovely quarters you have," I added, looking around at the spaciousness of it.

"Please make yourself comfortable," the captain insisted, sweeping his hand toward the sitting area.

"Nothing like the little clothes closet you currently occupy, is it?" Caleb teased, causing Aiden to send a severe glare his direction.

"Well, you have to admit, the berths are rather small," Caleb said sheepishly, while shrugging his shoulders.

I had to stop myself from laughing outright, because the two of them reminded me of an old married couple, bickering over trivial matters. "Please don't concern yourself over my accommodations. I can assure you that I am not here to sightsee, gentlemen," I admitted, turning my head to the side, pretending to study something that had caught my eye, effectively covering my laugh, when I cleared my throat.

"And exactly why are you here?" Aiden asked bluntly.

"What?" I questioned, coming back to reality.

"I said, why are you here?" the captain questioned again, sounding impatient because I made him repeat the question.

"Didn't my grandfather fill you in on all the details of why we are heading to Dublin? Do you truly not know the reason your services are needed?"

"Yes, of course I do. He told me why he was retaining my services and what it is he wished me to do. The only thing I don't understand, is why you are tagging along?" Captain Townsend asked, narrowing his sardonic blue eyes at me, in a clear attempt to intimidate me.

"Tagging along!" I cried in outrage. Turning on the captain, a small growl of frustration escaped my lips. Closing my eyes, I took several deep breaths to calm myself, while I clenched and unclenched my hands. "Before you dismiss me as some simple maiden off on a jolly jaunt through Dublin, I need you to stop and consider something."

"Oh, and what is that?" Townsend asked, with such an air of smugness about him that it grated on my last nerve.

"I am more than a simple maiden here to rescue her brother and his rich school chums," I answered boldly, while coolly glaring back at the captain.

"Oh, really?" Townsend's replied, with a cynical tone. "Please explain how you intend to help me retrieve your brother and his two friends from a band of Irish thugs?" Aiden said, finessing the question when I didn't back down.

I would rather have burned my own eyes out than have been the first one to look away. "If I felt I would be a hindrance to you or your men, I can assure you that I would be the first one to step aside, but I am perfectly capable of taking care of myself," I admonished, digging my fingernails into the palms of my hands to keep from screaming at his arrogant face.

"Oh, really?" Aiden retorted once again, with an air of superiority mixed with sarcasm.

Precisely at that moment the cabin boy knocked on the captain's door, but neither one of us looked away or blinked. We were too busy sizing each other up.

"Oh look, supper is served," Caleb announced, in an attempt to defuse the tense situation quickly developing between the captain and myself.

"I have certain talents that can be useful in this particular situation. Perhaps my grandfather forgot to mention it to you; or perhaps, my grandfather figured you to be a more evolved individual, considering your line of work," I said with a derisive scoff. "Apparently he was wrong, and I can only assume that he didn't realize that your hubris was overshadowed by your inability to comprehend matters better." I finished by raising an eyebrow to signal my challenge.

Then stepping even closer to the captain, I slowly looked him over from head to toe, and with a tone of smugness of my own that clearly called into question his manhood, I made a derisive sound that said to anyone in the room with eyes that I found him lacking.

Now I will be the first to admit that I received immense pleasure by calling the captain out. He was smug and too self assured for his own good. His handsome features registered surprise at my boldness, and his cool demeanor of control suddenly faded for the second time that day.

"Did you just call me dense?" Captain Townsend said with sudden dawning, as he turned to Caleb. "She just called me stupid," he repeated with indignation.

"Don't be ridiculous, Aiden. Lady Isabella would never say such a thing," Caleb protested, as he turned to me with a pleading look of mercy upon his face. "You didn't just call the captain stupid, did you, Lady Isabella?" warning me off from this line of rhetoric with his eyes.

"Please forgive me, Captain Townsend. It seems I made a mistake. You don't lack the capacity to comprehend my meaning after all," I sweetly said, with a wicked smile.

Caleb immediately turned to face his friend and place a strong hand against his chest. "Can you even defend yourself with a sword?" Aiden fired back, with an arrogant glare that was like a harsh slap to my face.

Captain Townsend stood before me with his arms folded across his chest, as if he already knew the answer to this question. Taking another step toward me, he pushed Caleb aside when I did not immediately answer. Now, standing toe to toe with me, he was so close that I could feel the heat of his body through my gown. "Well?"

A smug smile began to form on his lips now, confident that he had me on this account.

Now it was my turn to slowly smile up at him. Not the pleasant smile of someone greeting a friend or even trying to be cordial — the self-satisfied, wicked smile of a person who just discovered that they suddenly had the upper hand. I honestly think at that moment I would have been willing to fight Satan himself, if it meant wiping that arrogant smug smirk from the captain's face.

"Yes, my dear, Captain Townsend. As a matter of fact, I can fight," I replied with confidence and a smug smirk of my own.

Confusion registered almost immediately across his countenance, as crystal blue shards shot from his eyes. "And where did you acquire such skills, might I ask?" His skepticism was clearly stated in his tone as he pinned me to the wall with his stare.

My jade green eyes shot back with self assuredness, refusing to back down. "I trained with some of the best swordsmen in France." I knew it was childish to gloat, but I didn't care. "Would you care for a sampling of my abilities?" I taunted, with the confidence of a well trained student.

"Aye," the captain simply answered, seeming unsure that he had heard me correctly.

Turning my attention to Caleb, I fixed him with a cordial smile. "Mr. Daughtery, would you be up for a little physical activity with me in the morning?" I sweetly purred, seductively.

I knew that I was being spiteful and that my words could be misinterpreted as inappropriate, but I had to smile to myself. I had finally wiped that smug expression from the good captain's face.

Looking confused for just a moment, Caleb didn't miss a beat. "It would be my pleasure, Lady Isabella," he said with a most ungentlemanly smile. Then, as if he remembered where he was, Caleb suddenly looked up at Aiden, and cleared his throat, "If that is agreeable with the captain, of course," he corrected, casting his gaze sheepishly to Aiden, who scowled and nodded his head in the affirmative.

I was counting on Caleb's eagerness to assuage the tension in the room.

"Then, I believe, good sir, we have ourselves an exhibition in the morning," I retorted, with a very large smile on my face, when I cast my confident gaze back up to Captain Townsend.

"Then perhaps a little light fair to sustain you until then," Aiden suggested, while narrowing his eyes at me. Then glancing over my head to glare at his friend, Aiden swept his hand toward the table.

"I do believe I am suddenly ravenous," I countered, with a devilish grin.

I I

A Duel of Wits, by a Pair of Fools

"RULY YOU WERE JESTING WHEN you said you would dual with the captain's man," Maria scoffed as she pulled a sensible gown from the trunk, holding it up for my inspection.

"No, Maria, I was not jesting. This is no joke, I assure you. I will prove myself worthy to be part of my brother's search party, if it is the last thing I do," I retorted, turning around to face her. "Maria, put that dress away. I need the trousers that I hid at the bottom of the trunk. Oh, and the boots as well," I added impatiently, while I wrapped bandages around my chest to bind my breasts.

"You cannot be serious," Maria stood with her mouth hanging open, the dress draped over her arms.

"I am very serious, Maria, and if you won't help me, I will do it myself," I finished tying the bandages, and then slipped a white linen shirt over my head. When I had tied the shirt closed I turned, giving Maria a stern look, assuring her that I would not back down.

She gave a sound of exasperation, and then folded the dress up and placed it back in the trunk. "Alright fine, I will get them for you," she grumbled, rifling through the trunk in search of the items.

"I want the short pair of trousers that tuck into the boots," I absently instructed, as I sat down to pull on my socks.

"Now I know why your grandmother insisted I come along with you. I think she was afraid you would run amuck, and she wanted someone with enough common sense, to pull you back from the edge when you leaned too far over the cliff."

"Oh Maria, I hope you don't intend to run on like this every time I make a decision that you don't agree with. Otherwise this is going to be a very long trip and you will grow hoarse from talking to yourself," I teased, "because I'm not really listening."

"Aye, go on now, you cheeky girl," she muttered under her breath, digging into the trunk with earnest this time, looking for the pair of men's trousers I had asked for.

"Admit it, Maria, you are actually having fun, and we are only one day into our journey," I joked, tweaking her cheek.

"You are a handful, that is for sure. Why, one only need look into your eyes to tell that about you," Maria retorted with a scowl.

"Did you put my jeweled dagger someplace?" I asked, looking about in a panic, when it wasn't where I had left it the night before.

"I put it with your sundries, Miss," Maria absently gestured with her hand towards the smaller trunk in the corner while she continued digging through the trunk, still looking for the trousers. "I didn't want it to get lost."

"Maria, this room is the size of a bread box. How could anything get lost in here?" I added in exasperation. "I always sleep with it on the night stand, but I can see I'm going to have to put it under my pillow from now on."

"Pish, posh," Maria mumbled. "Here they are!" she announced, triumphantly pulling the trousers from the trunk. "

"Thank goodness. I thought I was going to have to go out there in my present state of undress."

"Not if I have anything to say about it, Missy," Maria scolded, rolling her eyes at me. "Now let's get you dressed properly for this duel you have involved yourself in."

"You truly worry too much, Maria, this will be a piece of cake," I said with confidence while slipping the trousers on over my stockings.

Tucking my shirt into the pants, I tightened the drawstring, and tied it securely.

Slipping on the knee length, black leather boots, I tucked the pant legs inside. Finally pulling on the coat, I turned around in a circle, giving Maria a good look at me. "Well, how do I look?"

"You look right fetching, my Lady. Like a scrawny boy who needs to eat more. Now, what do you want to do with this hair?" Maria asked, reaching across me to retrieve the hairbrush.

"A plaited braid, if you please," I asked nicely, pulling out a leather tie instead of a ribbon.

"We won't mention this event to your grandmother when we return," Maria warned, waving the hairbrush at me as if she would hit me with it if I crossed her.

"Not a word," I quickly agreed.

It was ten o'clock and the air felt brisk when I stepped out onto the deck; my dagger safely tucked into the pocket of my pants. Several whistles went out as I made my way to the upper deck, but I barely noticed because my heart was pounding loudly in my ears.

I had been brash and arrogant the night before, but it was worth it to see that smug smile leave the captain's lips when I told him I could duel.

The entire circumstance of last night was made all the more enjoyable when I turned to the first mate and invited him to be my partner. Clearly Captain Townsend saw it as a snub, and for some reason this brought me even more pleasure.

I didn't miss the small twitch of the captain's lips either, or the sudden disbelief that momentarily registered on his face and in his eyes, before he quickly covered it up.

I must say the entire event had been very satisfying, to be sure. Right up until this point. Coming face to face with the stone faced, brooding Captain Townsend, and his disapproving glare was now causing me some anxiety. I felt a sudden shudder make its way up my back. I straightened my spine just a little more, and allowed my eyes to wander the deck.

My stomach had been churning since I left my cabin, and I was very aware that it was unseemly, as well as unladylike to dress like a man, but I had a point to make. A point that would be impossible to make dressed in a cumbersome dress and several layers of petticoats. I took a deep breath and placed a confident smile on my face before I made my assent to the upper deck.

"Lady Isabella, I trust you slumbered soundly," Caleb greeted me pleasantly, as he ushered me over to where the captain stood.

I was somewhat leery of the captain's stern looks and it did little to breach the chasm of tension that now lay between us.

"I did, Mr. Daughtery, and thank you for asking. The ocean rocked me soundly to sleep last night." Then sweetly smiling up into his face I added, "I really can't remember when I have slumbered more soundly."

I could feel the captain's piercing eyes boring a hole into my head. His intense glowering stare sent another shiver up my back.

"Good morning to you, Captain Townsend," I sweetly crowed, turning to make direct eye contact with him, refusing to show him any outward signs of the inner turmoil I was feeling.

"I trust you are well rested then, and ready to fight?" Aiden inquired, dispensing with pleasantries. "Do you prefer sabers, swords or a rapier? Because I am afraid we don't have proper fencing foils lying about."

"We will go with the lighter weight rapiers," Caleb said, quickly stepping in between us and giving his friend a strange look over his shoulder. Taking hold of my arm, Caleb led me to the stairs and quickly down to the lower deck.

Before descending the steps, I turned to look at the captain, and found him staring at me, with a scowl marring his handsome features. Immediately glancing away, the captain walked with purpose to the upper deck railing for a front row view of our exhibition.

Suddenly feeling self-conscious, I turned away as well, and took the hand of Caleb Daughtery when he offered it to me. Squaring my shoulders, I allowed him to lead me to the lower deck, where a pair of fencing rapiers and sabers had been laid out.

Picking up the rapier, I weighed the piece in my hand as I took several practice swings, mentally preparing myself for the fight ahead. I would prove my worth and value on this mission, if it was the last thing I did. I could not fail, but more importantly, I would not falter, because my brother's life depended on it.

Standing mere feet apart, we both took the classic stance in preparation for our friendly fencing exhibition.

Giving Caleb permission to attack first, I gestured with a wave of my hand. Daughtery attacked and I easily parried, then countered back, with an attack of my own, forcing him to retreat several steps. Jabbing Caleb in the chest area with the dulled end of my rapier, I hit my mark. The crew standing around on deck, jeered, calling into question the first mate's manhood. He took it all in good fun, but attacked with more zeal and vigor the next round.

Resetting, we began again trading attacks and parries back and forth for about twenty minutes. We began to perspire with all the physical activity, so Mr. Daughtery decided to call for a small break. Slipping his coat off, Caleb deposited the garment with a crew member.

I removed my coat as well and wiped my forehead with the sleeve, before depositing the coat on a pile of ropes. Noticing that the rowdy crowd of men had suddenly gone silent, I looked up to see what had caused it.

That's when I came face to face with the unsmiling, yet ever handsome, brooding Captain Townsend.

"How about we engage in a real dual, my dear?" the captain challenged, his voice seductively deceiving as he broke the tension between us by giving me a half smile. His blue eyes seemed to spark like the sky during a thunderstorm, causing my breath to catch.

Dumbfounded for a moment, as my mind scurried to assimilate and assess the situation, I asked for the only thing that came to mind,

"May I please have a drink of water first?" I queried, locking eyes with him.

"Since you asked so nicely," Captain Townsend said, with a sardonic smile. "Rogers, fetch Lady Isabella some water," he bellowed in my face while maintaining direct eye contact.

Mr. Rogers ran to do the captain's bidding, bringing me a ladle full of fresh water. He handed it to me, and I gratefully sipped it slowly trying to buy time.

Realizing what his friend had in mind, Caleb stepped forward. "Aiden, I must protest. What you are proposing is wrong," he said sternly, as the casual exhibition turned serious and the crew of rugged mercenaries looked on in disbelief.

"Anyone can have a leisurely game of back and forth exchanges for fun or even show, but your enemy is not going to follow the rules, nor will they give you a chance to catch your breath between bouts," the captain said, putting his hand up to stem the flow of any further protests from Caleb.

Turning his back on Caleb so he could focus his full attention back to me, Townsend continued to speak, but this time he was playing to the crowd, who had gathered for the show.

"Although you and my first mate here seem to know your way around a rapier, we are going in with swords, Lady Isabella. Of course, if you would prefer not to continue because you are too tired. . ." Townsend began, leaving the question open ended as he gave me a patronizing smile. Then turning his back to me, Townsend faced his crowd, as they began to jeer and yell loudly.

Paralyzed by indecision, and the dangerous glint I witnessed in Townsend's eyes, I chewed on my bottom lip, still trying to think clearly.

Turning about in a circle, while shrugging his shoulders, the captain truly was a showman, as he expertly worked the crowd of men up into a frenzy. As if to say the show was over, the captain looked at me and smirked, then shrugged his shoulders as he turned his back to me again.

"Well, lads, I do not think the lady is truly up to the challenge. I would suggest you all return to work." Some light laughter erupted as the men slapped the captain and first mate on the shoulder and turned to resume their duties.

I picked up the two sabers and weighed them both in my hands, then choosing the one in my left hand, I threw the other at the captain's feet. The blade landed with a loud clank and skidded to a halt against his shiny leather boots.

Turning around, Captain Townsend's jovial smile quickly faded as he noticed the sword in my hand. Then slowly looking down, he scoffed, and bent down to retrieve the sword at his feet.

"It seems I was wrong, lads," Townsend announced loudly between clenched teeth. "It would seem the Lady has a backbone after all."

The thought flashed through my mind that these blades had very sharp edges and were void of guarded tips for safety purposes. I quickly pushed the thought from my mind and remembered that I truly had a reason for being here — my brother — and I would never turn tail and run from anyone, especially someone as smug and self righteous as Captain Aiden Townsend.

We walked in a circle like two wild beasts at the ready, each taking the measure of the other. The tension was thick as everyone on deck fell silent again. Caleb again tried to protest, but Captain Townsend gave him a look that silenced him at once. I felt like I vibrated with the silent tension that existed on deck as I prepared my strategy.

I made the first move while Townsend still looked at Caleb. Thrusting my sword, I caught the captain off guard by cutting the button from his woolen coat.

Lifting his eyebrows in a manner that could have suggested either a question or a challenge, Townsend licked his lips and gave me a smile. It was not a pleasant smile, in fact it wasn't a smile at all, but a grimace meant to warn me of the impending danger ahead.

The crew suddenly went crazy. They shouted and jeered again as I heard money called out and odds exchanged. The captain lunged forward, and I deflected the attack with my sword, easily stepping to the side and swinging. We exchanged thrusts and parried back and forth, moving around in our tight little circle for several minutes. I refused to back down or give an inch as he pressed his advantage of height and strength, pushing me back against the masthead.

I sidestepped him as he swung his sword, and then pulled up short at the same time as I ducked. I figured it was his way of giving me a warning. But I didn't need a warning because I was playing for all the marbles in my brother Charlie's bag.

Knocking Townsend in the stomach with the hilt of my sword, I stepped to his right and repositioned myself to the ready. The sardonic smirk was back as he lunged at me, taking several heavy swings with his sword, and nearly knocking me over. We locked swords, and he came in close, growling under his breath. "Do you concede?" he asked, holding tightly to my free hand, keeping me momentarily still.

"No!" I said, as that one word dripped with derision from my lips.

Not giving him a chance to reset, I pushed off from him and swung hard, forcing him back. The surprise I saw in his eyes was gratifying, if only for a split second, before regaining his composure and retaliating in kind.

He forced me back as he went on the attack, and I caused several crew members to scramble for safety, as I beat a hasty retreat.

A low animalistic growl escaped my lips as I attacked in frustration. My muscles were beginning to burn in my right arm, and I let my guard down for just a second. That was all it took. The captain's sword inflicted a nasty gash on my left arm, several inches below the shoulder.

A small cry escaped my mouth. Captain Townsend froze in mid swing, and then lowered his weapon. The smugness instantly drained from his face, replaced with concern.

Maria made her way to the deck, drawn by all the commotion and noise. I heard her gasp and I looked at her for a split second, but I didn't really see her. My mind was already going through the evasive moves I had been taught. Maria closed her eyes and began to pray, as the entire crew on deck fell silent.

Then I remembered the reason I was there, on that deck, in the first place. Looking down at my arm, I could see the cut was deep and the blood had begun to flow from the gash. This was no time to wallow in my pain. Moving my arm to make sure it was still of use to me, I blocked out the pain, and concentrated instead on the moves I intended to make.

I turned my full attention back to the captain and gave him a murderous stare. I felt something snap inside of me. Like the floodgates being opened, all I could see was Townsend. Everything and everyone else faded away.

The captain wore the strangest look on his face as I raised my sword above my head and set myself to the ready.

Narrowing my eyes at Townsend, I prepared myself to fight, as if it were a matter of life or death.

I was fighting for my brother's life!

"I think it is time for you to concede," Captain Townsend stammered as he lowered his guard. "Look, your arm is hurt and —" the captain said, pointing at my arm with his free hand.

Cutting him off, I lunged at him, and he deflected my blade, but stumbled backward several steps, while still attempting to reason with me. I refused to hear him out. I was now focused on the task at hand.

"I thought you said you knew how to fight," I taunted, causing the crew to go crazy again. "Or perhaps you would like to concede?" I jeered.

Aiden lunged and half heartedly swung his sword, which I easily blocked. Lunging back in turn, I managed to put the captain on the defensive. Seeing a moment of hesitation from him, I delivered a kick to his lower left leg, throwing him off balance. He grunted and fell to the deck onto one knee.

I circled around behind him as my breath seemed to come in harsh, angry gasps. Giving an extra push with my booted foot in the middle of his back, I managed to knock him down on all fours.

The captain snorted in frustration and pounded a fist into the deck in a show of anger of his own. Then slowly rising to his feet, he looked over his shoulder at me, and I saw something in his eyes besides surprise at my underhanded tactics it was determination.

Growling somewhere deep in his throat, Captain Aiden Townsend looked like an angry bull preparing to charge. Turning towards me he lunged, slashing with his sword, a move I had anticipated and easily sidestepped, deflecting his emotionally fueled advances.

This caused another loud outburst of laughter from the crew.

We circled each other again, both of us taut and on edge as we lunged at one another, simultaneously locking blades. Aiden's left arm snaked out and grabbed a hold of my waist.

Pinning me tightly against his larger frame, our swords rested between us. "You need to concede, and I will allow you to save face," Townsend said between clenched teeth. His rage was clearly manifested by his ragged breathing as he leaned in even closer to my face, to emphasize his displeasure.

"Your hubris is astounding, sir, or is it that you are worried that you might be bested by a woman!" I sweetly asked, just before stomping on the instep of his foot with the heel of my boot.

"Ouch!" he yelled. "Why you little —" he began to say, before letting out another growl of displeasure.

I pushed off from him when he was momentarily surprised by my move, and my blade caught the back of his hand, when we came out of the clench. Looking down, he couldn't believe what he saw. The back of his right hand was bleeding from a two inch gash.

I didn't give him time to ponder whether I had done it on purpose. I immediately lunged at him, and our swords clashed back and forth as we took turns attacking one another.

I was physically tired and backed up, trying to step out of his reach, but he was relentless. Stepping back several more feet, I soon realized my mistake when I came up against the masthead once again.

Quickly dropping his blade to block me, I found myself trapped as I quickly shifted, attempting to turn to my left.

Raising my arm high above my head to strike back at the captain's trap, he gave my blade a mighty blow, knocking it easily from my tired hand. Moving quickly, he pinned my right arm above my head, with his left hand, trapping my body between himself and the masthead.

I found it difficult to breathe as he pressed his hips against mine in a show of superiority. The crude shouts of encouragement from his crew made my cheeks turn crimson. He leaned his face down close to mine as if we were merely lovers exchanging lurid thoughts of what we might do to one another later.

He smiled seductively and I could see he felt self assured of his manly prowess. "Do you concede now?" he purred in my ear. His mouth was now so close to mine, I thought he meant to kiss me.

"Are you truly so sure that you have the upper hand?" I said, tilting my face up just a touch more toward his, just to show that I was not intimidated by him.

"If this had been a real fight, my lady, you would be walking through those pearly gates to greet Saint Peter, by now," he retorted with a smirk and a small chuckle to top it off.

"Oh," I said, feigning surprise and shock. "Then this must be when I shout out loud and clear so everyone can hear me say that I concede," I continued, attempting to play coy, as I cast my eyes downward.

"That would be the customary thing to do," he retorted, as his continued smugness radiated from every pore.

Looking down to where his hips connected with mine, I made a slow but assessing trail back up to the captain's eyes. Giving him a shy smile I sweetly asked, "I was wondering if you could point that thing in a different direction. I hear they can be dangerous."

"Only when placed in the hands of amateurs," the captain purred seductively again.

"And what if I said I had a little surprise of my own, just for you?" I sweetly responded, pressing my chest into his as I seductively smiled up at him.

He chuckled again, and moved his face to my ear as he inhaled deeply of my scent. "Mmm... What a delicious and unexpected occurrence. Perhaps we could discuss the matter over dinner tonight in my private quarters," Aiden purred again. Locking eyes with the rakishly handsome captain, I raised my eyebrows. Then giving the captain a seductive smile, I chuckled in response. "Oh Captain Townsend, I find men as a whole an easy lot to manipulate," I replied. "And if this had been a real fight, you too would be walking through those pearly gates to greet Saint Peter himself, having been unmanned by a woman," I said, pressing the tip of my dagger into the delicate fleshy parts of his crotch, for emphasis.

"Ouch!" he growled, squeezing my pinned wrist tighter, as he backed his hips up a couple of inches to avoid another nasty poke from my dagger. "You don't fight fair," his angry tone told me he was not pleased by my unorthodox tactics.

"And neither will the enemy. I believe those were your words, were they not, Captain?" I said smugly. "So I have only one question for you, Aiden, are you ready to concede?" I asked, giving him a wicked smile.

Bringing his sword blade close to my throat he growled in response.

"Ah, you men are all the same. Stubborn as mules till the end, and certain in your convictions that you belong on top," I quipped, lifting my chin higher to avoid the sharp edge of his blade.

"Not necessarily, I have been known to concede the top position from time to time," he added with a devilish smile, and a lift of his eyebrows.

"You don't say," I volleyed back. "But more to the point," I added with a swift poke to his groin again, "We seem to have a bit of a standoff."

"Aye," he responded, with a sound that came from someplace deep in his throat. "And how do you suggest we end this said standoff, short of you unmanning me or me slitting your pretty little throat?" Aiden asked, trying to maintain a pleasant tone.

"Ah, you think my throat pretty," I sarcastically taunted. "Might I suggest a draw? I will be allowed to accompany you in the search for my brother and you can keep your precious manhood," I said happily, knowing that I was about to get my way.

"Where did you learn to fight like that?" he inquired, sounding grudgingly impressed.

"My honorary uncle is a Musketeer for the French Government," I bragged, feeling just a bit prideful. "By the way, would you mind lowering your sword just a smidge? I don't believe I will be able to continue standing on my tiptoes much longer?" growing tired of his sword under my chin.

Looking down at my feet, then smiling back at me, he replied, "I was wondering how you happened to grow an inch taller all of a sudden," he teased while relaxing his arm and lowering his sword slightly.

"Could I trouble you to turn loose of my wrist as well? I think I've lost all the feeling in my fingers," I pleaded, felling self consciously as our bodies continued to press intimately together.

Raising that damnable eyebrow again, he realized where my actual discomfort lay. "As you wish," he gallantly responded.

"Might I suggest, you put your little sticky thing away, and then I will lower my sword," he suggested, almost comically.

My eyes shot up looking at him suspiciously. I was trying to gauge his sincerity.

I studied him for a long moment before speaking, "You drop the sword first then I will put my little sticky thing away," I countered, mocking him somewhat sarcastically.

"Why?" he questioned innocently.

"Why do you think?" I countered facetiously.

"Oh, you don't trust me," Aiden said, feigning shock and hurt on his face.

"Perhaps it would be advantageous to both parties involved if we had an impartial third party intervene," I stated dispassionately, causing him to throw his head back and laugh.

"Did they teach you proper negotiation skills in finishing school?" he mocked looking back down at me, but instead of looking into my eyes he was staring at my lips.

The lack of food, my inability to breathe, the extremely tight quarters, added with the gaping gash in my arm, caused me to feel light headed. Suddenly my knees buckled.

The captain caught me under my arm and propped me back up. "Perhaps my giving you space wasn't such a good idea," he teased.

"As much as I am enjoying our duel of words, I would appreciate it if you would get on with it," I suggested somberly, praying that I could stay on my feet long enough to reach my cabin.

Turning his head to the side Aiden hollered, "Mr. Daughtery, your assistance, if you please."

Daughtery cleared his throat first then leaned over and spoke in a hushed tone. "Please, don't mind me."

"Would you mind being of some assistance to the young lady and myself. We seem to be at an impasse," Aiden said holding my gaze with his piercing stare. "It seems neither one of us is willing to put down our weapon first, due to a lack of trust. Therefore, Lady Isabella suggested that we have an impartial third party intervene on our behalf. That is the way you put it, is it not?" he finished, cognizant that I had been staring at his mouth the entire time.

I had picked a point of reference to stare at while he droned on, to keep myself from falling over. The fog in my head grew thicker, just before I began to see stars. I tried one last time to clear my head by taking another deep breath.

"Did you hear what I just said?" Aiden repeated. Absently, I bobbed my head in agreement.

"Is she alright, Aiden?" Caleb asked, sounding concerned when he looked at my pale face.

Dropping his sword to the deck with a loud clank, Aiden removed the dagger from my hand. Impatiently, he shoved it into Caleb's hand. "Here, just take the damn dagger," he uttered.

"Ouch, that hurts!" I screamed, while trying to push against the captain's solid chest. "I never conceded to you," my words slurred together, just before I fainted.

Instantly, Aiden's desire for playful banter was all but gone.

"Isabella," Aiden shouted, shaking me like a rag doll.

"What the hell did you do to her, Aiden?" Caleb growled, in a tone not only accusatory but angry. "Aiden, her arm!" He shouted, pointing to the pool of blood on the deck, where I had been standing.

"Stupid girl," Aiden cursed. "Why didn't she tell me she was hurt?" Cradling me in his arms, Aiden shoved his way through the crowd of men gathered around trying to get a better look.

"Out of the way, you bunch of lazy vagrants," Aiden shouted, irritation edged his tone as he impatiently pushed his way past them.

"Move back, there's nothing to see here! Somebody fix those sails before they are shredded by a sudden up kick of wind. You all know what to do, run the damn ship and clean up that mess on my deck," he yelled over his shoulder at no one in particular.

"I'll get the doctor," Caleb called out to Aiden, before he ran off.

"Her grandmother is going to kill me for letting something happen to her," Maria exclaimed, following right on the captain's heels.

12

Let the Operation begin

ICKING THE DOOR OPEN, AIDEN entered his room, making his way to the bed. "Would you mind throwing those covers back?" he asked impatiently, waiting for Maria to comply. Then laying me gently on the bed, he began to tear my shirtsleeve, to expose my arm. "Damn it woman, why didn't you tell me you were hurt!" he muttered at my unconscious form.

"Captain Townsend, please!" Maria gasped in shock.

"I brought the doctor, how is she?" Caleb blurted out as he came through the doorway with the doctor close behind.

"Still unconscious," Townsend answered.

"Hey, what are you doing? Get your hands off me you, you big ah… ah, *espe'ce de con*!" I whispered, slowly regaining my bearings.

But still feeling groggy and slightly violated, I grabbed at my shirt, that laid torn open. The captain had exposed more bear skin than I was comfortable with.

I attempted to cover myself. "Ahh…" I gasped, making a guttural sound deep in my throat. "What have you done to me? There's so much blood," I yelled in surprise.

"What did she just call me?" Aiden asked, confused by me suddenly switching to French.

"Sorry, my head was a bit fuzzy and I couldn't remember the English words for, "you big, *stupid idiot*," I said with indignation dripping from every word.

I found myself suddenly fending off hands that dared to reach for my shredded, blood soaked shirt. "Stop it. Leave me alone," I demanded while shoving and slapping at their hands. "Take your hands off of me. Have you gentlemen never been taught decorum?"

"You keep that fire burning inside of you. You're going to need it, judging by the look of that wound," Doc said as he peered at my arm and adjusted his glasses. "We are going to need plenty of boiling water, Caleb. Hand me my bag, if you wouldn't mind, Captain?"

I looked between the three men with ever growing doubt that any of them knew what they were doing. Searching about the room for Maria's friendly face, I pushed past the captain with my good hand, trying to move him out of my way. "Maria, oh where did she toddle off to?" I called out.

I spotted Maria, standing in the far corner quietly crying. Once again I tried to get off the bed and past the two men who were prodding at my arm.

"Maria, stop that caterwauling this instant and do something," I scolded with an air of authority, as Captain Townsend shoved me back against the pillow.

"And just where do you think you are going?" he asked, with a tone that was beginning to grate on my nerves. "The Doc here needs a look at that arm," he stated flatly, while grasping my sore appendage tightly, holding it steady for the doctor to examine.

"Ouch!" I screamed louder than before. "*Merde!*" I cursed in French and punched Townsend in the arm with my good hand. "I don't bloody think so," I boldly proclaimed. Without another word, he took hold of my wounded arm and ripped the sleeve completely off, then pinned me against the bed with a large hand against my good shoulder.

I was so shocked by his sudden and decisive action that words escaped me and I laid there with my mouth agape.

"I am afraid this is bad," Doc said, pushing around on the arm.

"That truly hurts, you know," I said, finding my voice once again.

"I am sure it does, my Lady," Doc replied, half heartedly, still poking at my sore arm.

He was a middle aged gentleman with shabby features. Not dirty, but just not crisp. His shirt and trousers looked as if he had been sleeping in them for a week, while his hair was disheveled and uncombed. That confused me, because when I sniffed him, he smelled sterile.

"Ouch! Bloody hell! Get your filthy hands off me," I yelled, pulling my arm from the Doc's vice like grasp, as I fixed him with a dirty stare.

"Hand me a clean towel from the cabinet above your head, Maria," the captain ordered; "You need to lay still, Lady Deveraux. I will not have any more of your nonsense."

"Like hell you say," I bristled and narrowed my eyes at the captain. I fixed him with a nasty glare that would have withered most men in an instant, turning them to nothing but a pile of ash where they stood.

"Don't think you scare me, young lady. I have just battled one of hell's own minions up on my deck and I have to be honest with you, that was truly frightening," Aiden teased, trying to lighten the mood, as he took the towel from Maria.

"That minion you speak of will be the least of your troubles if you don't get your bloody hands off me this instant! That I can promise you!" I said tersely, giving him a wicked glare again as he tightly wrapped the towel around my arm and squeezed.

Unfazed by my angry outburst, Aiden ignored me and continued to call out orders. "Caleb, get the Lady a glass of our best whisky," he said, pointing at a carafe sitting on the counter.

"I don't drink, sir," I stated emphatically.

"Well, you do today," Townsend said, motioning for Caleb to hurry with a silent gesture he sent over my head.

"That wound needs to be closed soon before we have some real problems," Doc said, continuing to speak with Aiden as if I wasn't there.

"Define problem," I questioned, trying to get the doctor's attention. But he was too busy having an entire conversation with the captain without using any words.

"Hey Doctor, I'm right here, talk to me. What do you mean by a real problem?" I asked, starting to feel panic rise up in my chest.

"The shirt has to go, it's covered in blood and will contaminate the area," the doctor informed Aiden.

"Caleb, run down to the galley and tell Cook I need him to boil me up two pots of water. Then stick these instruments in one pot and continue to boil them for ten minutes, but don't take them out," Doc instructed, handing Caleb some surgical instruments, wrapped in a towel. "Instead, I want you to bring the entire pot back here to me, and have someone bring me the other pot of boiled water, plus some fresh water when it is ready," he instructed, continuing to bark out orders to Caleb as he ran out the door.

"Got it Doc," Caleb called over his shoulder from half way down the hall.

Maria handed Aiden the glass of whisky Caleb had given her just before he left the room.

"I need a fire going in that stove over there to heat the tool," Doc said, looking at Aiden who nodded his head.

"What tool?" I asked, anxiously.

"Maria, make sure she drinks this," Aiden instructed as he handed the glass back to her, "And make sure you keep pressure on that wound."

"Wait! What tool are you intending to place in the fire? More importantly what are you intending to do with it after you have placed it in the fire?" I called out, trying to make eye contact with anyone who would answer my question. Instead, everyone continued to move about the room, avoiding direct eye contact with me, as if I were invisible.

"You know what? I think we can just wrap my arm up. It's truly nothing more than a scratch after all. I will be good as new in a couple of days," I reasoned out loud, while scooting to the edge of the bed.

"Oh, no you don't, missy, you will stay put," Doc insisted, forcing me back on the bed with a wave of his hand. Picking up my wrist in one hand, while glancing at his pocket watch, he checked my pulse again.

"You better drink up now. We don't have much time," Doc said, taking the glass from Maria and pressing it into my hand.

"I told you, I don't drink," I replied, with less veracity in my tone this time.

"Drink!" Doc said sternly, pushing the cup up to my lips and tipping it so the amber liquid spilled into my mouth. Taking a sip, I began to cough and sputter as the liquid burned my throat.

"Keep going, I assure you, it gets smoother with every sip," the captain said reassuringly as he strolled back into the room. The cabin boy followed close behind, his arms loaded down with firewood.

Coming up behind Maria, Townsend tapped her on the shoulder and took her place when she stood up. Taking hold of the towel, he continued to squeeze tightly, despite my protests. "We will know you have drunk enough whisky when you stop complaining," he said flatly, raising an eyebrow and inclining his head toward my glass of liquor.

After fifteen minutes, I managed to get two thirds of the glass down and was feeling no pain at all. I began to laugh uncontrollably every time I hiccupped.

"What is so funny, missy?" Doc asked, standing over me to check my pulse again.

I giggled, then blew air between my lips, "I can't feel my lips."

"She's ready," Aiden proclaimed, taking the glass from my hand. "It would be such a shame to waste a perfectly good glass of whisky," he reasoned and then downed the remaining contents of the glass to steady his own nerves. He set the empty glass down on the table with a satisfied sigh.

"I also think we are ready to lose the shirt." Taking hold of the blood stained shirt by the tails, Aiden pulled it over my head and off in one fluid motion.

The only thing protecting my modesty now was the bandaging I used to bind my chest that morning.

"Jesus, Mary and Joseph!" Maria exclaimed out loud.

"It's alright, Maria," I slurred, "The shirt was old anyway." I suddenly looked about as if I had just discovered something odd. "Did it suddenly get cold in here?" I asked, as a shiver shook my entire body.

Caleb returned from the galley with the pot of boiled water that contained the Doc's tools. "Wow," the first mate exclaimed, as he walked through the doorway and saw me scantily clad.

"Put your eyes back in your head, Daughtery," Aiden said drolly, placing a blanket over me. "You act as if you have never seen a half naked woman before."

"Who says I have?" Caleb quipped.

"Everyone who will be assisting in this room is to wash their hands in the bowl, making sure you dump the water out between each person," the doctor instructed making certain everyone was listening.

"Oh, hi ya, Mr. Dottery…no, no, no, that's not your name," I giggled, "What's your name again?"

"It doesn't matter, love, I'm sure you will have a whole bunch of new names for each one of us in a few minutes," Captain Townsend said, blandly making sure he kept his voice smooth and even. "Time to move you over to the table, that's a girl," he said, pulling my good arm around his neck, so he could lift me up and carry me to the large wooden table draped with a clean sheet. "Maria, fetch me that pillow for your mistress's head, if you please," the captain instructed, while sitting on the edge of the table making sure I didn't roll off.

"You're cute!" I drunkenly said, turning onto my side, trying to prop my head upon my hand unsuccessfully, and bobbing my head as I reached up to tweak the captain's nose. "You really have pretty eyes. You know, if you weren't so stern and stiff all the time, you would be pleasant to be around," I slurred.

"I will keep that in mind. You are much more fun when you are sloppy drunk. You should think about taking up drinking as a hobby," the captain suggested while pushing me back over onto my back. "You are going to want to lie still for this part."

"But what fun would that be?" I pouted. "Then I couldn't talk to you anymore. Has anyone told you that your lips look like two soft pillows?" I asked, reaching my hand up to touch the captain's lips before he slapped it away.

"Hush child, before you go and embarrass yourself," Maria chided me as if I was ten years old.

Turning my head to the other side, I looked up at her. "Oh, hi Maria, I wondered where you ran off to. Is my bed ready yet? I'm really feeling sleepy now."

"Yes child, I changed those dirty sheets for you and the pillow is all fluffed," Maria replied, holding my hand, plying me with placating words meant to comfort me.

"Let's get started," Doc said when he finished laying his tools out on the table, several inches from my head. "Caleb, you will be at the head putting pressure on both of her shoulders, here and here," he indicated, pointing with his finger. "Aiden, you will hold the rest of her still using any means necessary, but keep her still. We don't want this scar to be worse than it needs to be. Maria, I need you to hand me what I ask for. Everything is arranged in order, just the way we discussed earlier."

"Aye," Maria said as her voice shook.

"What is he talking about?" I asked as panic began to seep into my inebriated consciousness. "I'm not going to like this, am I?" I questioned, looking up at the captain.

"No," he admitted, shaking his head somberly.

I looked around frantically, no longer feeling so jolly, as my heart started to race. Unable to breathe, I was suddenly overwhelmed with the desire for self preservation and began to struggle, and thrash about.

"Shh, Shh, now, why don't you just look at me?" Townsend suggested, distracting me from what the doctor was doing. Aiden was acting as if I were merely a spooked colt preparing to bolt. "What color are your eyes?" he continued in a hushed tone from the side of the table, "You know, I don't think that I truly took a good look at them before."

I turned my head to look at him, suddenly grateful to have a place to focus my anger instead of lying there helpless.

"Now?" I scoffed, "You want to discuss the color of my eyes right now?" I said with scorn, letting out an incredulous laugh. I saw him incline his head as his eyes looked past me, and then the real panic set in.

"Wait! Wait, I'm not ready," I cried, licking my lips, searching my mind for a plausible excuse to stall.

"It's probably better if you don't think about it," he soothed, his tone like soft, gooey caramel as he continued to speak quietly to me. He redirected my attention back to him by climbing upon the table next to me.

Following the captain's slow intentional movements with only my eyes, I found it hard to lift my head, because Caleb was applying pressure to my shoulders.

"What do you think you are doing, Mr. Townsend?" I asked in my best highborn tone of distain.

"Please, call me Aiden. I feel we have become so close in such a short amount of time, Isabella. May I call you Isabella? It really is a beautiful name, the way it rolls off one's tongue," the captain continued to talk as he inched himself even closer.

"No!" I stated emphatically.

"Now why do you have to be like that, when we have come thus far in our burgeoning relationship?" he said, smiling pleasantly the entire time.

"What do you mean?" I asked as alarm bells went off in my head.

"Oh, Holy Mother!" I heard Maria exclaim, causing me to turn my head in her direction as I heard her gasp.

Maria was ringing her hands together, with her head bowed and eyes closed, as if she were praying.

I quickly twisted back around to find Townsend's face looming only inches from mine as he made his move. Aiden hovered above me before covering my smaller frame with the majority of his own solid form. "I didn't realize your eyes were so green, and what's this? You have little specks of blue in the back ground. What a surprise!" he added, drawing my attention back to his face with a hand gently placed on my cheek, as I tried to look around, "Just keep looking at me."

"You realize I can't breathe because you are crushing my lungs," I admonished with a degree of scorn, fueled by self-indignation.

"But can you move?" Aiden asked, raising his eyebrows at me.

Those blasted eyebrows of his. "No, of course not," I answered, with trepidation.

"Good," he smiled. "Do it now, Doc." Aiden called, nodding of his head.

At first the pain was bearable when the Doc doused my wound with something. My whole body felt somewhat numb from the liquor I had consumed, but soon I began to gulp for air as tears ran down my face and pooled in my ears.

The doctor cauterized the wound, after the cleansing process, and seconds felt like an hour as the searing pain became unbearable.

I screamed as I had never screamed before in my life. Catching my breath became impossible, as Aiden's full weight bore down on me to prevent me from thrashing about. Stars shone in my peripheral vision, gradually crowding in on me as my head began to spin, getting lighter and lighter, until unconsciousness engulfed me. Every thought simply melted away as my body sought the blissful release into my mind's unconscious recesses while my body attempted to come to terms with the trauma that had befallen it.

For most people, this would be a peaceful space of sweet nothingness; an empty slate that is void of fears and worries, but for me, the peace was short lived as my mind and body fought against each other. I found myself stuck in a state of abyss, in a dark space where I was tormented by the very gift of sight, granted to me by my ancestors. I was trapped in the far recesses of my own mind, unable to look away and helpless to intervene in any way.

My own unconsciousness, forced me to bear witness to the atrocities perpetrated upon my brother Charlie and his two friends, at the hands of a man with a heart and soul as black and shriveled as Satan's himself.

13

Throw Down the Gauntlet and Pass the Bread

 LAGUED BY HELLISH NIGHTMARES OF inhuman treatment and despicable living conditions, I tossed and turned with fever, unable to escape my own unconscious thoughts. Filthy pigsty, and deplorable living conditions swirled together inside my mind.

But above all this, I couldn't seem to break free from the pounding pain in my own head. The need to stop the unbearable sensation was nearly too much for me to bear. I could hear my cries for release, and began to question whether they were even my cries at all.

Anxiously, I waited for help to come and stop my suffering, but no one came to my aid. I felt lost, trapped in a thick fog and feared I would suffocate or be swallowed whole by it.

What was the meaning of this madness?

Locked up for hours on end, unable to break free of the shackles, rusting cuffs and manacles that chaffed and rubbed at my skin as hunger tore at my belly, like a wild animal. I could feel my soul weighted down and sinking further into a mire of despair, afraid that I would never be able to claw my way out of it.

"Charlie, I'm coming for you, just hold on a little longer," my mind screamed out in desperation, "You have to hold on, Charlie."

I could see his face, contorted in pain as his freed hand reached out to mine. "I will find you, Charlie, I swear it. I swear on my life, I'm coming for you. Don't give up. Keep fighting." Just before our fingers touched, I felt an invisible force pulling at me, separating us, as if we were being ripped apart all over again.

Fury seethed deep inside me like a wild beast. Angry tears spilled from my eyes, ran down my face and pooled in my ears. I could hear distant voices calling out my name, cutting through the thick fog that had been choking me. I felt my fevered brow being bathed in blissful coolness and I begin to relax, as a deep sigh escaped my lips. The morbid feeling of dread and despair still hung over me like the smoke of a funeral pyre, yet I no longer desired to strike down the first person I laid my eyes on. A sense of lingering madness continued to plague me and I had to fight my way past it.

What did it all mean? An eternity seemed to pass before I felt the fog completely lift.

A voice spoke soothing words in my ear, someone was attempting to coax me from those darkened places that had imprisoned me for so long. Hands touched my brow, smoothing matted hair from my face. Then someone lifted my arm, moving it about, testing the mobility.

"Ouch," I cried out weakly as my eyes fluttered open, then closed again. The blinding light that streaked through an opened portion of the crimson red and gold curtains helped lend visibility for the examination.

"It is so nice of you to finally grace us with your presence, Lady Deveraux," said the man sitting on the edge of my bed, moving my arm up and down.

Opening my eyes just a crack again, I could make out the form of a thin man in his forties, with salt and pepper hair. The man's hair was neatly combed forward and his glasses rested on his nose. He had a pleasant enough face and a comforting mannerism, but I had already decided that I did not care for him, because he caused me pain. "And you, good sir, would be the perpetrator of this pain in my arm," I stated, accusingly.

"No, my dear, that would have been inflicted upon you by the black-hearted, fiend who attacked you. I am simply the local physician, retained by the gentleman of the house, Lord Townsend," he said with a somber face.

"Who the Devil is Lord Townsend, and what do you mean by finally gracing you with my presence?" I asked, posing the question to the good doctor, while sitting up a little straighter in bed.

My eyes scanned the room and found nothing that looked familiar. "And where exactly am I? What the bloody hell is going on here?" I demanded, pulling away from the unfamiliar man. "Stop touching my arm, that really hurts." I added with a degree of petulant distain. "People who take such egregious liberties of unconscious victims should be persecuted," I grumbled under my breath as I cradled my wounded arm.

I was feeling out of sorts and slightly off kilter, as I scooted away from the man who was now looking at me suspiciously.

"Well, I can't say they didn't warn me about you, Lady Deveraux," the man said, pushing his gold rimmed glasses further up his nose, with one finger.

"My name is Doctor Goodman, George Goodman. Lord Townsend retained me to oversee your recovery," he continued, trying to reassure me of his excellent qualifications. Reaching across the bed again, he captured my arm once again so he could rebandage it.

"Where is Maria, and who is this Lord Townsend you speak of?" I questioned, looking about and wondering to myself if somehow I had awakened in a different moment in time.

"Lord Aiden Townsend is your… a hum… solicitor," Doctor Goodman stammered, and then looked away, seeming to be embarrassed by the situation.

Clearly the doctor had been misinformed regarding my relationship with this Townsend person, and I for one intended to set him straight.

I had no more than opened my mouth, when there came a loud knocking at the door. Startled from my intended tirade on the matter, the doctor and I both turned our attention to the door that was suddenly thrown open.

"Oh good, you are awake. We were starting to worry that you might never wake up, my love," Aiden said, using a particularly sweet tone I had never heard from him before.

Why is he using that tone with me, and why did he just call me his love? He was being unusually attentive towards me, considering we didn't know each other well at all.

Maria followed closely behind Aiden with a tray of tea and biscuits.

"Why does everyone keep saying that? And can you explain to me why the doctor here thinks that you are my... a hum...?" I began to loudly protest, using the same speculative tone the good doctor had just used.

The teapot Maria was carrying clanked loudly against the cups and saucers. "Please forgive me, Lady Deveraux, the tray slipped in my hands."

Momentarily startled, I blinked my eyes against the bright light, and sat up a bit straighter in bed. Focusing my attention on Maria, I glared at her and then folded my arms over my chest. Then remembering my original focus of inquiry, I turned back to Aiden Townsend with a questioning glare.

Clearing his throat, Aiden gave me a sheepish look, and then ignored my question all together, as he turned to speak directly to the doctor, "How is she doing today, Doctor Goodman?"

"She is doing well and should be as good as new in a few weeks," he answered, giving me a curious look over Aiden's shoulder. "However, I am concerned that she doesn't seem to know who you are. Perhaps she also hit her head when she was attacked and I should —"

"Very good, Doctor Goodman, but I truly don't think that will be necessary," Aiden said, cutting the doctor off.

"I would be negligent in my duties if I didn't at least examine her head for contusion. If she does have a head injury, this could be a serious sign," Doctor Goodman continued, turning back to me, with a curious glance as he narrowed his eyes.

"Why does he think that you —" I began to say, when Townsend closed the doctor's black bag with a resounding snap and, looping his arm through the doctor's arm, escorted him to the door.

"I have left your wages downstairs with my butler. Please stop into the kitchen on your way out, Maggie will have some fresh tea and hot scones ready for you before you leave. I have been told they are the best scones in the county." Aiden's jovial tone was deceiving as he seemingly rushed the doctor on his way, promptly shutting the door with a resounding bang the moment Doctor Goodman crossed the threshold.

"Would you please tell me what is going on around here? I am getting the distinct feeling that something very underhanded has occurred, so you better start talking," I protested, attempting to stay calm, even though I could feel the blood pounding in my head. I took a slow, steadying breath to calm my nerves and quiet the hysterical voices in my head.

"Shhh! Keep it down!" Townsend said, motioning with his hands. "The walls have ears," he continued in a hushed voice as he slowly walked back to my bedside. "You have been unconscious for three days."

"I've what?" I gasped in disbelief, a little louder than I realized.

"Shh…shh…" Townsend cautioned again, the tone of his shushes sounded almost harsh. Aiden took another cautious look back at the door over his shoulder. "As I was saying, you have been asleep for three days. I didn't know what else to do, so I brought you here to my home in Dublin. When you didn't immediately wake up I became concerned and called on Doctor Goodman to get a second opinion. I've known the man most of my life, and I pray he knows how to be discrete. But since I never trust anyone completely, I had to come up with a plausible reason for your presence in my home. So I told him that I was your solicitor," he concluded, looking around the room for a chair.

"You what?" I scoffed, in disbelief, not sure I had heard him correctly.

"Oh, Lady Isabella, I have been so worried," Maria cried out, interrupting my tirade. With tears in her eyes, she placed a napkin on my lap and a cup of tea in my hand. I could see her hands shaking before she placed them into her apron pockets. "You looked so pale and kept crying out for your brother Charlie."

Aiden pulled the chair up to the side of the bed next to me and sat down. I could see the concern in his eyes as he looked at me and studied my reaction. "That wouldn't be judgment I hear in your tone now, would it?"

"What do you think, Lord Townsend?" I quipped, sarcastically. Then lowering my eyes, I stared at the cup of tea in my hands for a full minute, trying to digest this new information.

"Has there been any progress in your search for my brother?" I quietly asked, looking up slowly. I gazed boldly into Aiden's eyes, refusing to look away even though his intense stare unnerved me.

"I have men out scouting the towns and countryside, discretely asking for information about three young, well bred, English men, that have recently arrived in Dublin. But so far nothing has come of it." Aiden's eyes shifted slightly as he cleared his throat. "Are you certain that they are here?" he asked gently, while holding my gaze.

"Is there a ship in the harbor by the name of *The Three Sisters?*" I asked intently, already sure of the answer before I asked it.

"Aye," Aiden answered.

"And is that ship captained by a man named Shames O'Malley?" I again asked a question that I knew the answer to.

"Yes, but Captain O'Malley and his crew weren't aboard. They left a skeleton crew of four men behind to guard the ship. The rest of the crew left for parts unknown," he said still trying to read my reaction.

"Honestly, how hard is it to find a man who is as distinctive looking as Captain O'Malley?" I questioned, accusingly. "Tell your men to start looking around pig farms," I suggested.

"Why?" he questioned.

"Just do it," I added dryly.

"You are talking about half of Ireland," he answered, looking at me closely before asking suspiciously, "Where would you have gotten such information, when you have been unconscious for three days?"

"Call it a feeling and leave it at that," I responded, averting my eyes. "You never answered my question earlier," I said, changing the subject.

"Oh, and which question would that be?" Aiden asked with a half smile.

"Why does the doctor think that you and I are involved?" Now it was my turn to scrutinize him.

"It's the perfect cover story," Aiden announced, nonchalantly.

"A perfect cover story for whom, Captain Townsend, or should I address you as Lord Townsend?" I said petulantly, punctuating his name for emphasis.

"It really would be more appropriate for you to call me Aiden, if this is going to work," he countered, leaning forward in his chair to give me one of his steely glares.

"If what is going to work? You really haven't told me why you feel the need to put me in such a compromising position and impugn my good name."

"My men and I are not known as mercenaries in this part of the world and that is by design. I am from here, and it would put my family in a difficult position," he said, giving me an intense look.

"So you intend to destroy *my* good name and reputation, to save your family some embarrassment? How terribly gallant of you, *Lord* Townsend," I replied with a disapproving tone.

"Which could actually workout in our favor, if you would allow me to finish?" he argued, sitting back in his chair, slightly irritated that he had to explain himself to me. "Shames and his men will never see us coming if we play our cards right."

Running his hand through his hair, Aiden crossed one leg over the other. "I apologize for the damage to your reputation, but we can sort everything out later." He continued impatiently, as he raked his fingers through his hair again. "Meanwhile we will be free to move about the countryside, unimpeded and without drawing too much attention to ourselves."

"Except, of course for the part where everyone believes me to be a woman of loose morals," I said snidely, trying to pick a fight with him.

"I would appreciate it if you would let me finish," Aiden blurted out in a frustrated tone. "The kinds of places this Shames O'Malley and his crew travel, will barely notice if a Lord is showing his benefactor about, from inn to inn."

"I'm not sure," I hesitanted.

"Of course, if you think you're not up to it, we can simply leave you here to recoup from your injuries," Captain Townsend taunted.

"I didn't say that I wasn't up to the challenge, Captain Townsend, I'm just not certain about the benefit of such an arrangement nor am I sold on the necessity of it," I challenged.

"Aiden," he corrected, with a seductive smile.

"And there is no other way that we can search for Charlie and his school mates, unless we pretend to be…?" I asked with a hint of suspicion, unable to finish the sentence. Everything about this situation galled me to no end.

Aiden chuckled sarcastically. "Yes of course, there is another way, there is always another way to do anything, but you have to ask yourself, at what cost?" he concluded, and then started to pace the floor in front of my bed like a caged animal.

"We could reveal ourselves as mercenaries, looking for three English lads and hope that we get to Shames and his men before they slit the throats of your brother and his companions, who, I might add, would most likely end up dumped from the nearest cliff or bluff, never to be seen or heard from again," Townsend stated bluntly, stopping in front of the bed, to glare at me with his hands on his hips. "Or we could go with my plan, which has the best chance for success."

I didn't know if Townsend was just arrogant or cocky, but his bedside manner left something to be desired.

"You have made your point, Townsend. I will, of course, leave the details entirely up to you, since you are the so called expert," I said, taking a deep breath to quiet the sudden flames of anger that began to build again. The man was an insufferable, arrogance bore. "I will do my best to play the part of your adoring whore," I added with a disdainful smile. I felt frustrated by the entire situation.

"Good." Aiden bobbed his head, satisfied that he had made his point. "You rest now, and I will check in on you before I go out this evening," Aiden asserted stoically, clasping his hands behind his back.

"And where would you be off to this evening, Captain... I mean Aiden?" I asked, while trying to act mildly disinterested. I cast my eyes downward and adjusted the napkin in my lap then, lifting the cup of tea to my lips, I gave a more convincing smile this time.

"One must pay homage to the Right Honorable Lord Lieutenant of Ireland, if one wishes to move about and conduct business in Ireland," Aiden replied, nonchalantly, trying to act as if it was no big deal.

"That sounds intriguing," I added, placing my cup back down on the saucer before giving him a passive glance.

"Not really. The entire evening will be very stuffy and boring, if you ask me," he replied, refusing to make direct eye contact with me. He was almost trying too hard to convince me that his entire evening would be dull, tedious and monotonous. He gave a last, half hearted, yet polite smile before heading for the door.

"If you say so, but what would I know? I've been asleep for three days. At this point anything sounds exciting, compared to that." I smiled sweetly. A plan had formed even before Aiden closed the door.

"Maria, order me a bath and find out as casually as possible about the dinner Lord Townsend is planning to attend tonight. I want details. Who will be there, what the dress is and what time he is leaving," I demanded between sips of tea and bites of the biscuits she had slipped me while Townsend was telling me about his very dull evening plans.

"Lady Isabella, you've only just awoke from a three day sleep. You have not yet recovered," Maria argued. "I don't think it would be wise for you to go out this evening."

"Yes, Maria, I have been asleep for three days," I stated mildly, taking another sip of tea. "But look at it from my point of view. If I didn't sleep for another two days, I would still come out ahead." Placing the cup of tea on the nightstand, I hung my feet over the edge of the bed. "Please, Maria, give me your hand. I would like to get up from this bed."

Coming to stand beside the bed, Maria just shook her head wanting to scold me. "I'm not sure about this, Lady Isabella."

"You're not going to make me get out of this bed on my own, are you?" I queried, cognizant that she was feeling guilty over the entire matter.

Maria, blew air out from between her teeth. I had learned this meant she was conceding, and I had won. "You are a conniving sort, Lady Isabella. Brave, but definitely conniving. I will see to that bath immediately," she announced, heading for the door with the tray of dishes in her hands.

"Oh, and Maria, could you have the cook send up some soup, if she has any. I'm starving. I swear I could eat a horse."

"Of course, my lady, I will return shortly." Maria turned and curtsied like I was the Queen of England.

"Be off with you, or I will banish you to the Towers," I teased, giving my best upper crust rebuff.

"Then who would be left to scrub your back and do your dirty work?" she replied over her shoulder as she stopped to pick up another cup on her way out the door.

"Good point," I said under my breath. I scooted to the edge of the bed, and stretched my back where it was stiff. "Oh Maria, one more thing,"

"Yes, my lady?" Maria answered, in an exasperated tone, as she turned back around.

"Bring me something for the pain. My arm is starting to hurt."

"I will return shortly," Maria replied, with concern now etching her words.

14

A War of Wills

HE CLOCK STRUCK SIX THIRTY.

Maria covertly obtained the information I had requested. The formal dinner would be served promptly at seven thirty on the dot. Which meant Lord Townsend would needed to leave the house no later than six forty five and would be dropping by to check on me any minute now.

My hair was swept up on my head with cascading curls down the back. Crystal adornments were fastened in place, catching the light just right, every time I moved.

The dress I chose to wear was a green velvet gown with a floral design down the front split of the skirt, allowing a slight glimpse of delicate petticoats when I moved. The collar of the gown skimmed my shoulders in an elegant, but seductive way as it crested my shoulders, before dropping off to a three-quarter length sleeve which served to cover my bandaged arm.

I wore a pair of delicate emerald drop earrings and nothing more. I could scarcely recognize myself when I looked in to the mirror.

"Maria, you are a treasure. You have turned me from pitiful sow's ear into a silk purse."

"I am only too happy to further the cause, my Lady," Maria replied, feigning humility.

"Oh Maria, your humbleness is most refreshing," I laughed as much from Maria's antics as I did from my own delight of her handy work.

A loud knock on the door interrupted our levity. Swallowing the last bit of elixir Maria had given me, to dull the ache in my arm, I handed the glass back to her.

"Good luck, my dear," Maria said, squeezing my good arm, before running off to the changing room.

"Come in." I called across the room, turning around on the stool I sat upon.

Aiden stepped into the room and immediately looked towards the bed. A curious look crossed his face. Scanning the room, he found me seated on the stool in front of the mirror. Surprise creased his brow.

"What are you about, madam?" he cautiously asked.

"I felt the need to get out of bed. And since I went that far I thought I might accompany you to dinner," I answered, innocently smiling at him.

I didn't miss the way he took a step back when I stood and turned in a circle, giving him a complete view of Maria's work.

"But it will truly be a very dull evening, with a bunch of stuffed shirts," he stammered, trying to discourage me as he took a few steps towards me.

"I've been asleep for three days," I stated flatly. "I'm sure I will find the clinking of silverware and crystal stemware entertainment enough. Besides how will it look if my... a hum... guardian leaves the house without me?" I innocently reasoned. "One never truly knows who is watching."

Aiden cleared his throat as he stepped closer. "Well, about that —" he began.

"Surly this Honorable Lord Lieutenant of Ireland fellow would be a good place to practice, if I am to play your paramour," I stated, cutting him off.

I had smoothly argued my point, and at the same time pinned Lord Townsend to the wall, like a bug, with my stare. Like a proverbial fly, stuck to a pin board, Aiden had no way out and no other choice but to except defeat.

"About that," Aiden said, shifting uncomfortably before taking another step in my direction.

"Yes," I said coyly, tilting my head to the side and arching my eyebrows innocently, giving my best effort to look guiltless of any act of perceived scheming.

"I must reiterate the facts to you. People don't know what I really do and to maintain that ruse I needed a plausible explanation for your presence," he reasoned, arching an eyebrow in response. "You were unconscious, so I figured what's the harm." He smiled unapologetically.

"So what did you think would happen when I awoke from my long sleep? That there would be no harm, no foul and no consequence to your actions?" I asked pointedly.

"Well, no," he said with a devil may care smile.

Oh, he was a shameless rogue, in his navy blue evening coat, crisp white shirt that framed his tanned features, and sandy blond hair perfectly combed. Not to mention the way his teeth glinted at me every time he smiled with that infuriating smirk. It was simply galling. How I wanted to slap that look of arrogance from his face.

"And then there is the permanent damage you have done to my reputation," I added with a hint of castigation in my tone. "So the deed is done. I will play along, but you will need to give me time to get into character. I have never been anyone's lover before."

"How can I make this up to you?" He replied, letting his charming smile do most of his talking. Taking my hand in his, Aiden looked into my eyes and I was momentarily trapped, in the liquid blueness of them. "You realize that no one can know the truth, for your brother's sake," he reiterated.

"Yes, yes, I realize that," I began, breaking the momentary spell between us. I felt a pang of irritation as my heart was racing. Disentangling myself from his grasp, I retrieve my wrap from the stand. Handing it to him, I turned around, presenting my back to him. "We might as well finish slogging through the mire," I stated, "I've come this far."

"That's the spirit," he encouraged, and then looked at the wrap in his hand. "But I am afraid that this little wrap won't do at all. If you are going to slog through the mire with me, you are going to need something a little thicker," Aiden mused, almost to himself.

"This should do nicely," Marie exclaimed, coming out of her hiding spot in the changing room, to hand Aiden a full length, black wool cape with a hood. "It simply wouldn't do, if my Lady were to become ill her first night out," she added, avoiding eye contact with Aiden.

"Thank you, Maria. How fortuitous that you just happen to have the Lady's wrap ready," Aiden said, draping the cape over my shoulders.

"Perhaps, Lord Townsend, you will give me the particulars of all my many duties as your... a hum... ward," I said, while walking toward the door.

15

Into The Lion's Den We Go

HE CARRIAGE RIDE WAS SHORT and relatively comfortable, except when it came to discussing the particulars of our so called relationship. He reminded me again of the need to keep up appearances, no matter what. Just listening to the smooth deep timber of his voice in the dark, was pure decadence, like letting rich confection melt in your mouth. I was again infinitely grateful for the dim lighting of the carriage's interior and the distance between us as he sat opposite me. I finally breathed a decent breath of cool air as we stepped out of the carriage.

The residence of the Lord Lieutenant of Ireland was a virtual palace, with thirty seven palatial rooms and more than one hundred staff. To say the place was beautiful would be an understatement.

Aiden had informed me that it would be a small intimate gathering this evening with the Lord Lieutenant and his family. But he had neglected to inform me exactly who the Lord Lieutenant of Ireland was in relation to himself.

Aiden wrapped my arm around his as we approached the large wooden door, to complete our ruse.

"Good evening, Lord Townsend. How good to see you again," the butler greeted.

"Good evening, Godfrey, nice to see that you are still alive and kicking," Aiden answered pleasantly as if the two of them had been long time friends. "Allow me to introduce you to Lady Isabella Deveraux of Bayonne, Isabella, Godfrey."

"It's a pleasure to meet you, Godfrey." I smiled.

"I assure you the pleasure is all mine, Lady Deveraux," the butler smoothly replied, graciously inclining his head to me. "Please come in," he offered in a well rehearsed monotone voice, as he swung his arm in a wide ark, bidding us to enter.

"May I take your coats?" he asked as soon as he had shut the massive wooden door behind us. Aiden shrugged out of his overcoat and then reached out to remove my cape, handing everything to Godfrey who then handed the garments to a maid waiting patiently in the corner.

"This way, please. They have been expecting you." Godfrey directed us in his droll, monotone voice, making me smile as we made our way through the foyer and down a long hallway to a set of double doors.

Opening both doors, Godfrey swung them wide. "May I present his Lordship, the Viscount of Buckinghamshire and Lady Isabella Deveraux of Bayonne," Godfrey formally announced us, as Aiden and I entered the room with our arms interlocked.

I nearly missed a step, forcing Aiden to pull me into the room, as I turned my head to look at him. "His Lordship the Viscount of Buckinghamshire," I whispered in disbelief, under my breath.

"Shh..." was the only response Aiden gave as he smiled broadly, fastening his social mask firmly in place. Inclining his head, Godfrey smiled while backing out of the room. I could have sworn he winked at Aiden before closing the doors.

The room was huge and very grand, with bold red and gold carpet throughout the entire room meant to warm up the ostentatiously large space. A blazing fire burned in the oversized fireplace, removing the chill from the enormous space. Candelabras and chandeliers glowed brightly, giving off a feeling of intimacy and warmth, despite the rooms size.

"Aiden, you are home! Oh how I have missed you so." A beautiful blond girl cried, just before throwing herself into Aiden's arm. "You really shouldn't stay away so long."

"Who is this beautiful, grown woman throwing herself at me?" Aiden teased, holding the young lady at arm's length, pretending to give her a stern look.

"Oh Aiden, you are such a tease." She laughed, hugging him tightly again.

"Why, this couldn't be my little sister, Evelyn, could it? The last time I saw you, I swear you were only this tall," Aiden said, indicating with his hand, his mid-waist level. "You must be sixteen by now."

"Eighteen," Evelyn quickly corrected him.

"Evelyn, allow me to introduce you to Lady Isabella Deveraux. But I better warn you, if you're not nice to Lady Deveraux, she just might give you that spanking, I'm sure is well deserved," Aiden said with a wink and a kiss to Evelyn's cheek.

"She better not." Evelyn laughed, then gave me a disapproving look.

Aiden took a hold of my arm, pulling me along with him as we walked over to a lovely, middle aged woman with blond hair fashioned neatly upon her head.

"Mother," he said, with warmth and joy in his tone. "I trust you have been busy trying to keep these two scoundrels in check."

"I am afraid, dear son, the two of them are lost causes. So I have given up trying," she replied eyeing the two men in question standing three feet away from her. "Why didn't you tell us you were coming? We would have arranged a party for you," she scolded as she came to her feet so she could put her arms around her son, and squeeze him tightly.

"Mother, this is Lady Isabella Deveraux," Aiden said turning to me, and giving me a push, toward his mother. "Isabella, meet my mother, Lady Townsend."

I curtsied, bowing my head. "It is a pleasure to meet you, Lady Townsend," I said, smiling sincerely.

"Oh please, it is just the six of us, you must call me Judith. You are lovely, my dear," she stated, very matter of fact.

"Thank you, Judith, you are far too kind," I replied graciously.

Lady Judith, had elegant features. She wore a rust colored, satin gown with crystal beading adorning the top.

Aiden inclined his head toward the two gentlemen who came to stand by Judith.

"Isabella, allow me to introduce you to my father, the third Earl of Buckinghamshire, the Right Honorable Lord Lieutenant of Ireland, John Townsend," Aiden said politely, without much warmth.

"Oh my dear, that is just a bunch of pomp and circumstance. Please, you may address me as Lord Townsend," John benevolently said, blowing a puff of cigar smoke above my head. "And this is Aiden's' younger brother, Ian," he gestured to his right.

I smiled and inclined my head toward them both.

Lord Townsend's wife just rolled her eyes and took me by the arm. She led me to the table elegantly laid out with crystal goblets, delicate china and freshly polished silverware.

"Please, my dear, sit here next to me." Lady Judith tapped the chair with her hand, as Aiden rushed over to pull the seat out for me. "He has always been such an attentive dear," she gushed, looking up at her son adoringly. Standing by her own chair, Lady Judith waited for her husband to come and assist her with her chair, but after several awkward moments, Aiden pulled out his mother's chair.

Ian slipped into the chair next to me, while Aiden was occupied with their mother. Aiden reached for his chair next to me, and then gave a slight growl under his breath, while Ian grinned up at him like a fool. In the end, Aiden conceded the loss and took the seat across from me.

Ian leaned over and smiled at me. "Aiden has always been a bit slow on the up take, you know. I attribute it to his constant need to please Mother," he said chuckling to himself, as if he had just told me a funny joke.

Inwardly I groaned, thinking to myself that this could turn out to be more tedious than sleeping for another three days. I snuck a quick glance at Aiden, who was busy entertaining his younger sister, Evelyn.

"So, tell me son, what have you been up to these days?" the Earl inquired.

"I'm still shipping goods back and forth between the islands," Aiden answered with a polite smile that didn't quite make it all the way to his eyes.

"When are you going to give all that up, and take your rightful place in the family business?" the Earl chided.

"We have already had this conversation, Father. I told you before that I no longer have the stomach for it. I would appreciate it if you would oblige me by changing the subject. I really didn't come to fight with you this evening," Aiden retorted flatly, giving his father a measured look of tedium. "Besides, I know Ian is eager to fill the vacant position I left behind. And let's face it, this works out well for everyone involved."

"What do you mean by that?" the Earl questioned.

"This way, Ian doesn't have to come up with a clever way of doing away with me to get the position he has wanted all along," Aiden stated glibly, while giving his brother, Ian a bored stare.

"Doesn't that red herring ever get old with you?" Ian quipped while rolling his eyes at Aiden. "After all, it has been years since you turned your back on your family, for this shipping venture you call a career. Is it my fault Father hasn't given up hope of enticing you back? Personally, I send out small prayers of thanks every day for your prolonged absence." Ian finished with a biting jeer directed at Aiden.

"On second thought, Father, perhaps it is time for us to revisit the topic of the family business. Now that I see with my own eyes what little you've had to work with," Aiden shot back, unable to hide the vicious yet cutting tone in his words, while looking directly at Ian.

"Boot licker," Ian mumbled under his breath.

"What did you just say?" Aiden hissed between his teeth.

"Boys, boys, mind your manners!" Lady Judith intervened, with a distinct tone that meant business. "We have a guest present, and I will not have you two shaming this family with your public displays of distain and animosity for one another."

Ian's face turned a bright shade of red from suppressed anger, as he picked up his glass of wine and drained the cup in one swallow. He then motioned to the footman to refill his cup, which he drained once again while glaring menacingly at Aiden.

Aiden simply smirked in Ian's direction and turned to say something witty to his sister Evelyn, causing her to burst into laughter.

"My dear, what is it you do?" the Earl asked me, clearly trying to give his two sons time to cool off.

"Do, your Lordship?" I asked, in surprise.

This fumbling for words caught Aiden's sudden interest, as he waited for my answer.

"Yes, yes, my dear, I mean for fun," the Earl quickly clarified.

"I have only just finished my schooling, so I haven't truly had much time for doing anything fun, but I do like reading and horseback riding," I answered, grasping for something to say, while feeling slightly caught off guard. I gave Aiden a quick look, as I was unsure what Lord Townsend expected of me.

"What is it you enjoy reading?" Lady Judith asked, trying to soften the briskness of her husband.

"I just finished reading a book by Adam Smith, entitled: Wealth of Nations. I must say that I found his analogies fascinating," I said, turning my attention to Judith.

"You don't say? And what does this Adam Smith say about the wealth of our nations?" the Earl questioned, sounding a bit skeptical that I would have read such a book, let alone understood it.

"Basically, he suggests that it is not the silver or gold that one possesses, which makes them wealthy, but the commodities that rise and fall with supply and demand. For example, the products that people use on a daily basis, like milk, wheat, fabrics, you know, that sort of thing," I said, feeling pleased that I could discuss something of intelligence, rather than the usual mundane societal affairs or the weather. "He talks about the commerce of our wealth and the taxations of it all. But if the poor are taxed at the same rate as the wealthy, how can that be fair to all?"

"You don't say," Aiden's father countered with a smile, as he winked at Aiden. "So, what do you think, Lady Deveraux? Do you agree with him?" he asked, sitting back in his chair with his glass of wine, still skeptical that I understood what I was talking about.

"I do to a point. I feel that if people are taxed to the point that they can't make a living on their properties, then they will abandon them for other pursuits," I replied.

"What other pursuits would that be, my dear?" he questioned.

"Well, for instance, your Lordship, if a farmer can't feed his family because his taxes continue to increase every time he comes out slightly ahead, he might think that stealing from his neighbor would be a worth while pursuit. This farmer goes to the adjacent county and robs or steels from his neighbors and is content with this arrangement, as long as it puts food on the table and takes care of his problem. Do you see? I think that Mr. Smith isn't taking into account the poorer members of our society that must scratch out a living with their bare hands. I think that he is talking about the upper five or ten percent of society that are involved in the trade industry and deal in commodities. Those people in our society who don't really get their hands dirty in the traditional sense of the word. So I ask you, what happens to the other ninety percent of the people in our society?" I questioned, looking around the table.

"I have never looked at it in those terms, my dear," the Earl said, looking at me funny. "Who told you to think in that way?"

"Forgive me, Sir, but I am afraid I don't understand your question," I said, with a slight tilt of my head.

"What my father is asking you, my dear, is who told you to think such a thing?" Aiden stated dryly, attempting to clarify his father's statement.

I turned to the Earl, trying to remember that I was a guest in his home.

"I can assure you that the thoughts and opinions I have expressed are entirely my own. Nobody has ever told me how to think, nor would I allow it. I have been forming my own opinions ever since I can remember, and in my family, such free thinking has always been encouraged, regardless of how radical it may seem to others," I bristled with indignation.

"Bravo, my dear," Lady Judith gave a small cheer.

"Here, here," Lady Evelyn echoed.

"Perhaps, my dear, this is not the appropriate moment to unleash the full fury of your temper upon my father's insensitive nature. I'm afraid he does not truly understand the working mind of a modern day woman, and therefore I will have to proclaim ignorance for him," Aiden explained while eyeing his father disapprovingly.

"Well, perhaps this would be the perfect moment to signal for the next course of our meal to be served, Father, before we have a woman's rally break out before the desert," Ian said drolly, rolling his eyes and dabbing his lips with the cloth napkin in his lap.

"That is a very good idea, my boy," the Earl agreed, looking to his head footman and signaling for the next course to be served.

"I think you mean splendid idea, darling, before you stick your other foot in it," Lady Judith said sarcastically. Aiden smiled, then wiped his mouth with his napkin, before his father saw him smirk with approval.

The rest of the evening went by quickly, and I even managed to earn Lord Townsend's begrudging acceptance before the night was through.

As we prepared to leave, Aiden slipped a proprietary arm around my waist as his younger brother Ian joined us in the foyer as Godfrey retrieved our garments.

"I hear there was a bit of a dust up during dinner, Lord Aiden, and for once it wasn't between you and Master Ian," Godfrey casually commented in Aiden's ear as he slipped Aiden's coat on him.

"Oh, there was a dust up between Master Ian and myself, but it was the one between Lady Isabella and my father that caught the most attention this evening," Aiden replied, putting the emphasis on the word Master to get under Ian's skin.

"Very good, Sir," Godfrey quipped, cheerfully.

Godfrey then turned to Master Ian with a somber, disinterested stare upon his face, and slipped his coat on him without any niceties at all. It was very apparent that Godfrey disliked Ian for some reason.

Aiden smiled, then slowly looked me up then down with a critical eye. "It would seem to me that Lady Deveraux has the misfortune of being a nonconformist, with a brilliant mind. Because she is not only eloquent, she is exquisitely brilliant and opinionated all at once," he said while slipping my cape over my shoulders. "Which in Father's opinion, is a sin." Aiden chuckled, lifting my hand to his lips to place a kiss on the back of it, as he gazed lovingly into my eyes.

The affect of his complete attention left me momentarily mesmerized. And then, as if out of nowhere, I was suddenly afflicted with a case of butterflies in my stomach. Which caught me completely by surprise.

"Darling, are you all right?" Aiden asked with concern. "You look pale to me."

"I'm fine. Just a little tired, that is all," I declared, with a shy smile.

I remember thinking to myself, *wow he's very good at this role playing. I could almost believe his act. He honestly knows how to lay it on thick for the butler and his brother Ian.*

Godfrey cleared his throat. "Very good, Sir. I took the liberty of calling your carriage around for you. It should be waiting out front."

"Thank you, Godfrey. If you ever get tired of working for my father, you know where to turn," Aiden teased.

"Good to know, Sir," Godfrey inclined his head, then smiled at me drolly. "I trust you had a pleasant evening, my lady. I do hope you enjoyed your visit."

"It was a most interesting, if not stimulating evening, Mr. Godfrey," I stated.

"You would make a very fine diplomat, my lady." Godfrey smiled, inclining his head again.

Ian rolled his eyes and walked out the door with an exasperated sigh.

"What do you suppose could be wrong with Ian?" Aiden chuckled to himself.

"Your mother claimed he was dropped on his head one too many times, as an infant, Sir," Godfrey offered up, as an explanation.

"That would explain a lot." Aiden stated under his breath, before walking through the door and stepping into the waiting carriage.

I found myself staring out the window for the majority of the ride home. I tried to get comfortable, but my arm was paining me, so I closed my eyes and rested my head in the corner. Even with my eyes closed I could feel Aiden's eyes on me.

"Why are you staring at me?" I asked with my eyes still closed.

"How do you know that I am staring at you? Maybe I am staring out the window," Aiden replied.

"But you are not staring out the window," I contradicted, "I can feel your eyes boring into my brain."

"Perhaps I am intrigued by you," he finally answered.

"Intrigued by me? Don't be ridiculous," I scoffed.

"Yes, Lady Isabella Deveraux. I am intrigued by you. I also know that you are hiding something from me, and I intend to find out what it is," Aiden said, with a wicked smile.

Opening my eyes to casually gaze at him, "I assure you, Lord Townsend, I am merely a woman in search of her twin brother. That is all. You may keep your suspicious mind off of me and on more pressing matters, like finding my brother and his two companions. That is what my grandfather paid you for, if you will recall."

"How could I forget?"

By the time we returned Aiden's residence, it was well past midnight, and I was exhausted. Beads of perspiration had broken out on my forehead, the truth was, my arm felt like it was on fire.

Maria fixed me up before I crawled between the soft sheets of the bed, grateful to be able to lay my head down.

Apparently, being asleep for three days, did not equate to being able to stay awake for three nights.

16

And The Truth Shall Set You Free

LUMBERING SOUNDLY, I DREAMT OF hay carts moving down rutted dirt roads driven by nervous men with darting eyes. Scanning their surroundings suspiciously, they appeared ready for action at the least bit of provocation.

I knew I was having one of my special dreams by the clarity and vividness of my surroundings. I could feel myself being drawn into the scene, as if I were there, experiencing it all first hand.

The fact was, I couldn't remember the last time I had had a normal dream of walking through fields of wild flowers with bunnies hopping about. No, my dreams were of strange men doing unspeakable things to other men. Not the sort of thing I would wish upon anyone, not even my worst enemy.

The dirt roads they traveled were more like well worn paths, the kind a sheepherder might use rather than people traveling in carriages. The path led up a hill and into a small town.

Why can't I see Charlie or his two friends in the cart? I prayed for a sign, anything that would indicate where they could be located and in what direction they were headed.

As a vendor's sign came into view the first cart rounded a corner. It was hanging above the establishment and it read The Copper Kettle Inn. I wanted to cry out for joy, but I knew that one sign wouldn't be enough to identify this particular inn. The Copper Kettle Inn had to be about as generic as one could get. There were probably twenty of them throughout Ireland, alone. No, I would need something more to go on.

A heard of sheep passed in front of the carts, causing them to come to a complete stop. One of the men sitting in a cart seemed agitated, as he waited for the old sheepherder to move his flock from one side of the road to the other.

Then it happened — I got the distinct impression of the word meat, but it was spelled funny. The word had an "h" at the end. I didn't quite understand it yet, but knew in my mind that it had to mean something.

My eyes flew open, and I sat straight up in bed. "Maria!" I screamed. Throwing the blankets off, I jumped out of bed, ran to the heavy curtains and threw them open. The sun was up.

"What time is it?" I muttered to myself.

"What's wrong?" Maria asked, rushing into the room, with a startled look on her face.

"I had a dream," I shouted, taking her by the shoulders and giving her a sturdy shake.

"Like your grandmother?" Maria asked.

"Yes! I need clothes, Maria," I blurted out franticly. "Now Maria, I need clothes now!"

"What kind of clothes?" she asked, throwing her hands in the air, looking perplexed.

Stopping a minute to think, I now threw my hands in the air. "I don't know," I stated with a shrug of my shoulders.

That moment, a loud knock on the door startled us both, and simultaneously we yelled, "Come in."

Aiden opened the door and poked his head into the room, "Excuse me, but did you say, come in?" he cautiously asked, before stepping through the door.

"Yes!" We both answered again, then looked at one another. With a shake of my head to clear my thoughts, I turned back to Aiden.

"I just wanted to be sure," he said stepping into the room, before shutting the door. "You're not dressed," he stated.

"I was unsure of what to wear," I said plainly.

"Caleb is back and he has intel. We have to leave soon," Aiden remarked, somewhat impatiently, as if I was holding things up.

"Leave for where and for how long?" I asked, feeling confused.

"We are leaving for the mid east region of —"

"Meath," I blurted out before he could say anything more.

"How could you know that? Caleb just told me." Aiden stood perplexed, his mouth gaping open as he stared at me.

"How long will we be gone? Will I be riding horseback, or in a carriage?" I questioned, hoping to distract him from further inquiry on the matter.

"I don't know how long we will be gone, but you need to pack quickly," he added, still looking at me funny. "We will be taking the carriages. If anyone is watching us, we will appear to be a normal couple traveling through the countryside. Maria, you will be accompanying us as well, but you both need to hurry," Aiden ordered as he turned to leave. "Oh, and Isabella, wear something pretty and be quick about it, we don't have all day!" With that Aiden rushed from the room, banging the door closed behind him.

Forty-five minutes later, Maria and I were in the foyer as the foot-men carried our trunks out to the waiting carriages. I had chosen to wear a green wool traveling dress because the weather threatened to be unpleasant.

Maria had had the forethought to stop by the kitchen to gather a basket of food for the road. I was certain the men had eaten, but Maria and I on the other hand, had not had time for a proper meal before our departure.

Aiden and Caleb came down the stairs together. Both were handsomely outfitted in day coats, crisp white linen shirts and black breaches tucked into their leather boots. Caleb wore a gray coat with a green silk cravat, while Aiden had opted for a navy coat, camel vest and black on black silk cravat. They both looked very dashing in their finery, which seemed a far cry from their previous attire as mercenaries. I scarcely could pick which one of them I found more appealing.

"May I say, Lady Isabella, you are the picture of radiance," Caleb gushed, taking my hand in his and placing a chaste kiss on the back of it.

Aiden simply took the basket from my hand, and offered me his arm, which I felt obliged to take.

"Well, do I get any details?"

"Come my dear, perhaps you will allow me to surprise you with our destination," he said, speaking unusually loud, while giving me a look that said, *'Don't speak.'*

Leading me to the first carriage he helped me up the steps then handed me the basket. Turning around, Aiden prevented Maria from climbing into the carriage behind me. Instead, he took her by the hand and led her to the second carriage.

"If you would be so kind as to keep Mr. Daughtery company on our long journey, Maria, I would be eternally grateful. Lady Deveraux and I have a few things we need to discuss in private," Aiden said, helping Maria up the steps. He promptly shut the door behind her before she could protest.

Aiden then walked over to the first carriage and climbed in, shutting the door behind him. Taking a seat close to me, he rapped on the ceiling of the carriage with his silver handled walking stick.

The two carriages pulled out, with twenty well armed men on horseback and another three horses in tow.

"So, do you care to tell me what that was all about back at the house?" I asked, while staring out the window. Then turning to look at Aiden, I noticed he was sitting very erect.

Placing his hat and walking stick on the bench across from him, Aiden turned in his seat to face me. Placing his leg upon the bench, he adopted a very relaxed, almost casual stance, as his leg brushed up against the side of mine.

"I think we will play a little game," Aiden suggested, "one that will allow us to become better acquainted. Maybe we will even come to an understanding and trust one another," Aiden said crossing his arms over his chest. "And since this will be a long trip, I would suggest you make yourself comfortable"

"And this little sordid proposition… I mean game of yours, it will go both ways?" I inquired, suspiciously.

"Yes, and the rules are simple, but not negotiable," Aiden stated, fixing me with a serious stare.

"Alright, I will bite. What exactly are your rules, Lord Townsend?"

"Any question asked has to be answered honestly and completely," Aiden said, narrowing his eyes slightly.

"And what will be gained by this little game of yours?" I asked, turning around on the bench to face him as I placed my back against the carriage wall opposite him.

"As I said, knowledge and trust will be necessary on this mission, so we will both come out winners," Aiden concluded somberly.

Aiden clasped both hands around his bent knee and interlocked his fingers, trying to appear completely at ease, but there was something in his eyes that made me suddenly leery.

"This sounds like it might be a very taxing and possibly arduous game filled with pitfalls and traps. Perhaps you wouldn't mind if I take in a little nourishment, since I had to forgo breakfast this morning," I replied, reaching into the basket to retrieve some hard cheese and bread. "Would you like some?" I offered, holding out some cheese.

"No, thank you. I had breakfast, but please, by all means be my guest," Aiden asserted, impatiently waving off my offer.

Biting into a piece of cheese that tasted like heaven itself, I couldn't help but express my joy with a small sigh. "I'm sorry but this is just so delicious. Please get on with your little game of trust."

"Certainly," Aiden said, angling his head to one side, as he studied my face. "How did you know that we would be heading for the little township of Meath?" he asked suspiciously. His harsh gaze told me that this would be no simple little game of trust, but an all out inquisition. I choked on the piece of cheese I had just bitten into.

Aiden pulled a flask from his front coat pocket, removed the cap, and shoved it into my hand, once my convulsive coughing had eased.

"I told you before that I don't drink," I hoarsely replied, lifting my chin just a bit.

"Maybe you will make an exception just this once," he asserted, sarcasm dripping from his lips. "Seems to me, you might need something to wash the crumbs down with, seeing how your mouth just went dry," Aiden replied, as his narrowed eyes followed every twitch and uncomfortable breath I took.

Taking the offered flask from his hand, my fingers brushed his, and a spark jumped between us, shocking me as I looked into his eyes intently staring back at me. I took a small sip, to appease him and tried to hand the flask back to him.

"You can do better than that. Take a real drink, like this," Aiden prodded as he took the flask back and showed me how it was done. Handing it back to me, he watched to see if I was brave enough to take his challenge.

Rolling my eyes in exasperation, I threw my head back, letting the liquid flow down my throat. I tried to swallow quickly, but it burned a trail and left me gasping for air.

"There now, isn't that better?" Aiden said, slapping my back a couple of times, until I began to breathe again. "I knew you had it in you," he laughed, then settled back into his spot on the other side of the bench. He slipped the flask back into his jacket pocket.

I eyed him, unsure of his motives or where he was going with this line of questioning. After all, did he truly expect me to answer him honestly? I barely knew the man. Cautiously, I settled back against the carriage wall, and tossed the cheese and bread back into the basket, deciding I was no longer hungry.

"I apologize if my question made you uncomfortable, but I must insist you answer," Aiden casually stated, as he folded his hands around his leg again and waited.

I hesitated for a moment, to give myself time to come up with a plausible explanation that would not cause Lord Townsend to turn our carriage around and head for the nearest insane asylum.

"Tell me something, Captain Townsend. Just how open-minded are you?" I asked cautiously.

"Come, come now, I thought we had gotten beyond all that formality. I really must insist that you address me as Aiden, even when we are alone. If you get accustomed to the use of my given name, you will be less likely to slip up when we are in public," He said, impatiently. "And as to your question, I have been described by many people as being open minded. I'm a bloody mercenary, for crying out loud."

"That doesn't answer the question, Captain... I mean Aiden," I corrected myself.

Reaching over to open the window, I let the cool air in before continuing. "What I am about to tell you sounds crazy, but I assure you that I am not." I took a deep breath to build up my courage. Turning to face Aiden once again, I stared into his piercing blue eyes, determined to make him understand everything I was about to reveal. "The only reason I hesitate to answer you is because most people tend to get uncomfortable with things that are unexplainable or unknown to them," I said, shifting uncomfortably in my seat, suddenly feeling self-conscious. Explaining a family phenomenon is difficult enough to those who love and accept you, but to explain these things to people who don't, well, let's just say, you're asking for trouble.

"Well, out with it then," he growled, growing impatient.

"I have these dreams, well, not just me, you see my mother and grandmother also have these dreams as well, and they are difficult to explain." I chanced a quick glance in his direction to see if he was grasping what I was trying to say to him. I searched his posture for any sign that he intended to change course for the nearest asylum, or stop the carriage on the side of the road and burn me at the stake. "These dreams aren't normal dreams. They are about real events that are occurring or have occurred. In my dreams, I can see things as if I am there, next to the person I am dreaming about. Do you understand?" I asked, taking a deep breath and holding it, as I turned to look out the window again and wait for his reaction.

Minutes passed and still he didn't say anything. Finally I turned to look at him and found him pondering my words with his chin on his hand, staring at me.

He had the strangest look in his eyes and I couldn't determine what he was thinking. I found his silence disturbing. Unable to take it any longer I blurted out, "Do you or do you not understand what I am telling you?"

"Are you trying to tell me that you can see things that are happening to someone else when you are asleep?" Aiden questioned, narrowing his eyes in disbelief.

"I don't necessarily have to be asleep, but yes. I can hear, smell, sense, and feel what they are experiencing," I shyly replied looking away, suddenly feeling unsure that I had done the right thing by trusting him with the truth. "My dreams tend to be about Charlie, my twin brother. I guess it has always been that way with the two of us." Bringing my eyes up to meet his gaze directly, "I know that this all sounds a bit crazy, and sometimes I think I might be losing my mind, but I can assure you that I'm not crazy. I am telling you the truth."

"But how does it work?" he asked, trying to understand.

"It runs in my family and I was taught that it is a gift, not a curse. We just accept it as normal." Pulling my jeweled handled dagger from my pocket, I handed it to Aiden to examine. "My mother told me when I was younger that I was to carry this dagger with me at all times because someday it would save my life. It would never occur to me that she could be wrong. So I carry that dagger faithfully, wherever I go. Maria makes sure of it. And I know that someday my life will be saved because of it."

"So do you know where your brother is right now?" Aiden asked, as he handed back the dagger.

"It doesn't work like that. I can't just make it happen. It is completely involuntary, and sometimes it isn't a dream at all, but a feeling about something or an impression of some kind. It's usually about someone I am connected to, but not always," I said, feeling a bit flustered because I had never really had to explain my gift to anyone.

"You mean you can connect to someone like your brother because you are related?" Aiden asked, trying to clarify.

"Exactly like my brother, because we are twins. We always had a very intense bond and we were inseparable since the day we were born. He knew what I was feeling and I could always find him when no one else could," I explained excitedly because Aiden didn't look at me like I had three heads.

"So you are telling me that you have a special connection because you and your brother… I'm sorry what was his name again?" Aiden asked, trying to remember.

"Charlie. His name is Charlie," I added. "I awoke this morning from a dream, and that is how I knew about Meath. Charlie and his mates are being transported in a hay cart."

"Yes, yes, you and Charlie are close, so you dreamed about him this morning, and that is how you knew where we were headed." Aiden mused absently, trying to make everything clear in his own mind. "This is extraordinary."

"I'm not crazy. I'm still the same person I was yesterday, I just have a different skill set than most people. I'll prove it to you. There will be a very deep rut in the middle of the road, just before we get to the top of the steep hill going into the township of Meath," I said defensively, feeling the need to prove myself to him.

"Well, that is a given. Most of these towns have heavily used dirt roads leading into the townships," Aiden replied skeptically.

"Yes, but this one was caused by heavy rains two months ago and the town has not gotten around to fixing it yet. More than a few people have lost a wagon wheel there. Just after the deep rut and steep climb, the road will bend around to the left and there will be a sheepherder's trail. There is a sheepherder who crosses the road, two times every day at the same time. And if that isn't enough to convince you, the first sign you will see as we enter the township of Meath will be The Copper Kettle Inn," I said triumphantly.

"Extraordinary," Aiden absently commented, rubbing his chin with his index finger and thumb.

"You already said that," I informed him narrowing my gaze, trying to determine if he felt I was a fraud.

"I am just trying to wrap my mind around such a thing."

"The proof is in the pudding, so we shall see when we get there if I am right or if I am wrong. After all, I have never stepped foot in Meath before," I announced as I turned in my seat so that I faced forward. Then I straightened my back a smidge and placed my hands in my lap.

The minutes passed in awkward silence until I could stand it no longer. His eyes were boring a hole into the side of my head, and it was beginning to make me feel uneasy. So I decided to turn the tables. "I feel I have been extremely honest with you, so I was wondering if you would do me the same courtesy?" I began, slowly shifting in my seat, so I could study his reaction to my question.

"All right, my dear, fair is fair," he responded with such self confidence it was somewhat galling.

"If you hate your brother so much, why do you give up your position and title to him so easily?" I asked pointedly.

"Uh, uh, uh," Aiden stammered a moment. "You realize that you have asked two questions," Aiden said, wagging his finger at me, and sounding superior while attempting to sidestep my question all together.

"Stop deflecting and just answer the question," I quipped, growing perturbed by the one sidedness of his inquest.

"My brother and I have a complicated relationship," Aiden replied, no longer smiling. Instead his mood shifted, becoming suddenly somber.

"That is not an answer," I replied while reaching into the food basket to retrieve some dried fruit, which I offered him.

Waving me off, he shifted in his seat. "When we were younger we were very close. One might even say we were good friends. We shared everything with each other. We ran about playing our boyish games of make believe and tormenting the staff as young boys will do. Then one day something changed. Or more accurately, Ian changed, almost overnight. It was about the time I turned eighteen and Ian was sixteen. I can only guess at the reason of course, since Ian never came out with it straight away. But I believe that must have been when Ian realized that only one of us would inherit the family title and lands," Aiden spoke with a somber, faraway look in his eyes. "Nothing was the same after that."

"But you still haven't answered my question," I chided, suddenly feeling sorry for his childhood loss. I touched his arm, trying to lend some comfort. I couldn't imagine how I would have felt if Charlie suddenly turned on me.

"My brother is a dangerous man, and that is all you really need to know." I saw the pain reflecting in Aiden's eyes, before the walls he kept between us went back up. "So save your pity for someone who deserves it. I have enough money to live comfortably. I refuse to choose title over family. Besides, I've already lost everything that ever truly mattered to me once. A title is just society's way of making sure that one person feels superior over another. I simply choose to remove myself from that game," he concluded, with eyes that seemed to look right through me.

I was stunned by his ever changing moods as I sat pondering his words.

After a few minutes of silence, Aiden came back from the dark place where he had escaped. "It would seem that it is back to me then," Aiden interjected as he rubbed his hands together.

"Please proceed. It appears that my life is an open book compared to yours," I said, tilting my head back and dropping a piece of dried apricot into my mouth.

"What did your grandfather mean when he said you should forgive your family?"

Slowly chewing, and then swallowing the apricot with a gulp, I found my mouth suddenly dry again. "Well then, why don't you ask me something easy?" I scoffed sardonically as the apricot got stuck half way down my throat, leaving a bad taste in my mouth. I threw the other apricot I was holding out the window and took a moment to compose my emotions.

I turned back around, confident that I had my emotions in check. "I don't see how your question is the least bit relevant? And how is the answer to such an impertinent question going to help rescue three young men?" I queried.

"Again, it goes back to trust," Aiden stated, in a frank matter. "Are you going to answer my question or are you going to continue to... what was the word you used... oh yes... deflect?" A smug smile had formed on Aiden's lips, as if he had just bested me.

"First of all, I am not deflecting," I stated defensively. "And secondly, if you are expecting me to share something that personal with you, after your feeble answer," I stammered. "Well ... then, you... you... have a lot of nerve." Our eyes clashed and I huffed, folding my arms across my chest. "So let me just be perfectly clear when I say, you first!"

Brushing a stray hair from my face, I sat glaring at him and waiting for him to make the next move.

Several more minutes passed between us in silence before Aiden raised one eyebrow at me, and I thought to myself, 'that damnable eyebrow again.' He reached into his pocket to pull out his flask. Removing the cap, he placed it into his pocket. "Cheers," he said, raising the flask to his lips.

"Ahh," came the deep, satisfied sigh, from his throat, as he turned and offered me the flask.

Waving him off, I replied, "No, thank you. I really don't want any just now."

"Might I suggest you have some, because this portion of the game is much like ripping a bandage off, when it is stuck to the scab. It's going to hurt like hell," Aiden added with a strange look in his eye.

Studying his face a moment longer, I took a deep breath then blew it out slowly. Without a word, I reached out, taking the flask from him. Tipping my head back, I drank deeply just as he had done a moment before. But instead of a satisfied sigh when I was done, I began to choke on the horrible stuff.

"I promise I will fill my flask with the good stuff next time," Aiden chuckled to himself, and retrieved the flask from my hand, before continuing to speak. His tone suddenly turned serious. "Listen up, because I won't be repeating anything I am about to divulge to you. And when I have finished, we will never speak of the matter again." There was a touch of sadness in his eyes as he looked out the window gathering his thoughts, before he continued. "Do we have a deal?"

"Deal," I quietly replied.

Taking another swallow of the liquid from his flask, Aiden placed the cap on the container, and shoved it back into his pocket.

"I was married once. Her name was Shauna." Aiden paused a few seconds, taking a deep breath before continuing. "My wife and I had a son named John, but we called him Johnny. We were very happy, the three of us, in our little home together," he added somberly.

Aiden seemed to have been transported to a faraway place, as he continued his story. "I was working for my father at the time. He was grooming me to take over the family business for him when he stepped down as Lord Lieutenant of Ireland." A muscle convulsed in Aiden's jaw as he clenched and unclenched his teeth. "Shauna and Johnny died three years ago during the influenza outbreak. I was away, conducting business for my father when word came that they had fallen ill. I did everything in my power to return as quickly as possible, but by the time

I reached our home, they had been dead two days. I was told that they had passed within hours of each other. They both died without me by their side, and I blame myself," Aiden concluded somberly. As he lifted his eyes to look at me, they shone with deep emotion and unshed tears.

I swallowed hard, so filled with emotion that I could not speak at first. Finally gaining control, I placed a comforting hand on his knee, "How can you be to blame for an illness that took so many lives?" I softly asked.

"I wasn't there when they needed me the most," Aiden replied. "I put business and money before my family."

"But you can't continue to blame and torture yourself for something that was out of your hands," I insisted.

"I guess that is the difference between you and me. I take responsibility for my actions," Aiden said, striking out at me.

I refused to take offence. In fact, my heart went out to him, as I forced back tears I desperately wanted to cry for his loss.

"A few years ago my parents decided that Charlie and I needed to finish our education. They also decided that it would be best if we did that at separate schools. Charlie and I were opposed to this arrangement, but it was of little consequence to our parents. Charlie and I had never spent a single day apart since our birth, so the mere thought of being separated for years was abhorrent to us both," I mused, as my voice caught in my throat.

I was feeling the pain of his loss and mine all at once, and it was nearly too much for me to bear. Blowing my nose in a hanky I kept in my pocket, I looked away, embarrassed by my show of emotions.

Finally taking several deep breaths, I shook my head and turned toward Aiden to finish my story. "In the end, Charlie was placed in one carriage and I was forced to watch it pull away from our childhood home, without me. I was bitterly angry, so angry in fact, I told my parents that I would never forgive them for their hand in such a betrayal. To this day I have not seen, nor spoken to either one of them."

"So I guess you know how to hold a grudge," Aiden coolly stated, while gazing into my eyes. "Sometimes fate has a way of taking the ones we love far from our hearts, leaving us filled with much regret," he finished, before averting his gaze out the window.

"Yes, this may be true, but it is never more keenly felt than by the one who is left behind," I replied with a sniff, chancing a glance in Aiden's direction.

He sat silently for several more minutes that felt like forever, before bringing his gaze back around to me. "You are decidedly one of the most determined individuals I have ever met," Aiden said when he finally spoke.

"Is that a compliment, or a nice way of saying that I am as stubborn as a mule?" I questioned. Suddenly feeling uncomfortable, I gave a nervous laugh as he continued to scrutinize me with those probing eyes of his.

"I think, Lady Isabella, that it is simply a statement of fact," Aiden quietly said, with a good humored chuckle.

"I still don't know whether to take it as a compliment or an affront?" I bantered. Shifting in my seat, I glanced away, desiring to be anywhere but where I currently sat. I was bombarded by his scent that filled the carriage and reminded me of his proximity. He smelled fresh and clean like a spring breeze mixed with saddle oil. The combination was intoxicating.

Flashes ran through my mind, of the day Doc cauterized my arm. Aiden had restrained me by laying on top of me, staring into my eyes. At the time, I realized he was attempting to distract me from the pain, but it was still a disconcerting feeling to have his hardened muscular frame covering mine, as it all came rushing back to me. Suddenly, I felt bombarded by inappropriate thoughts that assaulted my mind, and, without meaning to, I gasped out loud.

"Are you alright?" His concern was touching.

"Yes, yes," I answered, grateful that he couldn't read my thoughts, like Charlie could. Worried that he would see a look of guilt reflected in my eyes, I refused to look at him, "could we stop for a few minutes? I just need to stretch my legs."

Aiden rapped on the roof with his walking stick and one of the footmen opened the slot in the back of the carriage to communicate with him. "Yes, Sir, did you need something?" the young man inquired.

"Lady Isabella needs to stop and stretch her legs," Aiden replied.

"Of course, right away, Sir," the man answered, closing the slot with a brisk flick of his wrist.

"Are you sure that you are feeling well enough to travel? Maybe this was a mistake, bringing you along. It hasn't been very long since your injury, and the doctor did say that you would take several weeks to heal," Aiden commented, with an edge of real concern in his tone. This caused me even more discomfort because of the direction my thoughts had led me.

"I can assure you that my arm has not bothered me once this entire trip." I lied of course, because I didn't want to give him a reason to send me back. "I just have a cramp in my leg," I stated, this time looking him in the eyes. "I will be fine with a quick walk and a bit of fresh air. *And a small nip of painkiller, Maria packed for me, I thought to myself.* "I will be right as rain."

Our caravan of two carriages, two drivers, four footmen and twenty heavily armed men on horseback continued twenty minutes later, with Maria and Mr. Daughtery joining us in our carriage. I couldn't tell if this new arrangement displeased Aiden or not, but he wore a disagreeable scowl for the next hour of our journey.

We stopped several hours later to stretch our legs again, eat, and rest the horses for an hour before returning to the road. I found the light drizzle of rain rejuvenating and the smell invigorating. The rain was never enough to halt our trip, but it was enough to leave little mud puddles in the rutted roads, causing the carriage to rock back and forth a little more.

To pass the time we talked on many different subjects and occasionally I would chance a look in Aiden's direction, only to find his eyes had been watching me.

Aiden sent three men ahead of us to secure lodgings, and an hour later we rounded the bend in the rutted dirt road that lead into the township of Meath. Now it was my turn to study Aiden's face as he suddenly became interested in the scenery outside the carriage window.

As we came around the sharp bend in the very rutted road of the township of Meath, we sat behind two carts waiting patiently for the herd of sheep to finish crossing. My eyes remained locked on Aiden's face, as I studied the reaction so plainly written upon it. At first, his eyes reflected his sheer disbelief, then his astonishment, and finally an expression of acceptance for what he could not explain.

The carriage driver pulled up to the front of the inn, where Aiden's men stood waiting for us. Stepping through the open door, Aiden quickly turned when a man whistled loudly, calling to his sheepdog. The dog, a border collie, worked feverishly gathering any straggling sheep that had fallen behind as they crossed the road.

Caleb, then Maria, stepped out of the carriage ahead of me. Taking a hold of the hand Aiden offered me, our eyes locked as I stepped down from the carriage. Following the direction of Aiden's head as he nodded toward the shepherd, I turned to witness with my own eyes the scene unfolding just as it had in my dream only hours before.

A man with a herd of fluffy white sheep and black faces was crossing the road, heading down the hill on the other side. A black and white dog nipped at the heels of those sheep foolish enough to fall behind. The man was dressed just as I had seen him in my dream, in brown trousers, thick black boots, and a heavy, brown, wool coat to protect him from the elements of the cold Irish winter.

I felt Aiden's eyes on me, but I didn't care, I had made my point. Turning around I walked directly past the hanging sign, without so much as a glance up. I knew that it read, The Copper Kettle Inn, without having to look at it.

I could feel Aiden watching me walk away, so I straightened my spine and took a hold of Caleb's offered arm. I allowed him to escort me through the hotel doors.

I had been confident that the shepherd would be there with his sheep. But now Aiden knew as well, that everything I had told him was the truth and not simply the mad rantings of a delusional, crazy woman.

17

The Proof Is In The Pudding

IDEN'S MEN HAD SECURED AN entire floor of rooms. Two of those rooms were connected and opened to the other, making it more like a suite instead of three separate rooms. Maria was already in our room unpacking one of my trunks, laying out clothes for the next day, while I stood at the window watching the retreating figures of the sheepherder and his flock.

Aiden knocked on the door and after a few seconds opened it without being invited in. He stepped into the room and closed the door behind him in a most proprietary way.

"Caleb has ordered dinner for us. If you don't mind, I have asked that it be sent to our room, and by our room, I mean my room," Aiden said so frankly, as if it were an everyday occurrence that I have dinner in a room with a man, alone.

"Maria, would you give Lord Townsend and me a moment alone please," I softly said, without turning around.

"Yes, my lady. I will be in the next room, if you need anything."

A few seconds passed before I turned to find Aiden standing next to me, with a strange look in his eyes. "I'm sorry that I doubted you," he said, reaching a hand out to tip my chin up with his finger, forcing my eyes upward to meet his.

I realized that I had been holding my breath, as I lifted my chin just a touch higher. "I accept your apology, Lord Townsend," I whispered quietly. I watched his head slowly lower until our lips touched, kissing me so tenderly at first it took my breath away.

When he finally pulled away, he could see the unspoken question in my eyes. "Just keeping up with appearances. After all, we wouldn't want anyone to question our commitment to one another, would we?" he stated glibly, looking past me to the street below, before clearing his throat and leading me into the other room.

"Why, of course not, that would be preposterous," I agreed with a degree of sarcasm in my tone. And yet I didn't fail to notice that my heart seemed to still be pounding in my chest.

Stepping back over to the window, I opened it, allowing the cold blast of air to cool my cheeks. The distraction of the cold air also helped me to put the reality of my situation back into perspective.

Aiden walked up behind me, causing my heart to skip another beat. "May I take your coat?" he asked, close to my ear. "If you feel uncomfortable being alone with me you may leave at any time. Look, I have even left the door open to the next room where Maria is busy unpacking as we speak."

"Don't be ridiculous, I am fine," I replied, unfastening my coat and slipping it off to give to him.

"Good, I was looking forward to dining with you this evening," Aiden admitted, taking the coat from me. He laid it across the back of the settee, as a knock sounded at the door. "Please, sit," he indicated the settee with his hand.

Aiden went to the door and opened it for a young man, carrying a large tray. He entered, walked over to the table by the window, and set the tray down.

Aiden waited by the door for the young man to leave, handed him a few coins and thanked him for his trouble.

Rubbing his hands together, Aiden headed straight for the tray and removed the cover. Inhaling deeply, he sighed in delight. "I don't know about you, but I am famished," Aiden said with enthusiasm, placing the cover back over the food. My lips still tingled from his kiss only moments before.

Pulling out a chair from the table, Aiden stood behind it, and waited for me to catch on. "Why you are most gallant, Lord Townsend," I gushed. "How lovely that I am witness to this side of you again, so soon after our dinner with your family," I commented, taking the seat he offered me. Then cautiously, I watched him through my eyelashes, as he walked around the table and took the seat across from me. Aiden moved with a certain poise and sophistication I had not noticed before.

"I have to confess that I am somewhat naive when it comes to men and women. So perhaps you might fill me in, as to how far you intend to take this… um… ruse of ours?" I broached the subject, attempting to clear the air.

"I feel we are being watched, and I would hate for the mission to go wrong because we didn't play our parts," Aiden said, trying to convey just how important it was. "My men reported to me yesterday that there have been two men hanging around my house ever since we arrived in Dublin. And just before I came upstairs, I was informed that we have had two riders following us since leaving the house this morning. So you see, it is imperative that we don't let our guards down, for any reason. Your brother's life may depend on it."

"I am not questioning you or your men's ability to do their job, Aiden, I was only questioning how far you and I will be required to play our parts?" I pointed out. "Maybe I am going about this all wrong," I said, fumbling for words and feeling very awkward.

"Have you never had a boyfriend?" Aiden inquired, sounding astounded by my naiveté.

"No! I mean no." I blushed again. "I have been busy with my studies," I said defensively. "Besides, I didn't realize that would be a requirement for this mission, or I might have left the all girls school sooner so I could be better prepared, of course," I stated glibly.

"That's not what I meant at all," he quickly corrected while searching for the right words.

"Please explain, exactly what you did mean, Lord Townsend? Because I'm not entirely sure I understand what it is you want from me."

"What I want?" Aiden cried, as if he didn't understand the question.

"So keeping up with appearances is the only motivation behind this dinner of yours?" I questioned suspiciously. I was famished and needed nourishment to think straight. I took a couple of bites of food, and studied his reaction.

"Nothing!" Aiden blurted out.

"Nothing!" I said sharply. "Really?" Throwing my napkin on the table, I stood, and walked to the window, suddenly feeling the need for some air.

"I thought we had moved beyond this point earlier. I thought we had made progress," Aiden complained, as he threw his napkin on the table as well and walked over to join me at the window. "I thought we could at least be friends," he said, roughly spinning me around to face him.

I put my hands up, to keep him from coming too close, but it didn't deter him. His heart was pounding, and his muscles flexed into tight cords in his chest. I watched the war raging in the depths of his indigo eyes.

"I have learned that friendships with men come with strings and entanglements. So, I ask you again, Lord Townsend, what exactly is it that you want from me?" Fury now crackled through me like lightning. I stiffened in his arms as my eyes sparked defiantly.

"Touché, my dear," Aiden replied, staring at me intently for a full minute, trying to decide what he would do next. "Tell me, Isabella, how did one so young become so disenchanted with the world?" Before I knew what had happened, Aiden pulled me to him, kissing me despite my struggle. His rough embrace caught me off guard as I continued to push hard against his chest.

My breath caught in my throat and I felt my lips being parted as his embrace turned less rough. I closed my eyes as the velvety texture of his tongue gently explored mine, and without thinking, I found myself melting into him. I could feel his thumb against the side of my jaw and it sent a thrilling sensation down my spine that reached clear to the pit of my stomach. I heard myself sigh and the sound echoed in my ears.

I suddenly realized that I no longer felt tense or ready to scratch Aiden's eyes from their sockets. I decided instead, that I rather enjoyed the soothing blue color of his eyes exactly where they sat.

Slowly, Aiden pulled away, and I realized that I had not taken a breath. Opening my eyes slowly, I brought my hand up to my lips that felt swollen, and I was confused by the puzzled expression on his face.

"What makes you tick, Isabella Deveraux, and why do you feel the need to be so tough?" Aiden whispered. Not exactly the question I would have gone with.

Pushing away from him, I backed up to the window, and turned so the air could hit me squarely in the face. "You can't lose what you never had," I wispered, almost wistfully to myself.

I took several deep breaths, filling my lungs and slowly letting it out again, until my heart resumed a normal beat. Then turning to Aiden, once again composed and confident, "I do believe I've had quite enough of this game of yours for one day, Lord Townsend, so if you will excuse me, I am terribly exhausted, and wish to turn in."

I turned to leave when Aiden reached out a hand, and gently grasped my arm. "Please, Isabella, don't go." Aiden's eyes pleaded with me.

I nearly changed my mind when I looked at him and the plea written in every angle of his beautiful face. "Thank you for the lovely invitation, Aiden, but I am too worn out to spar with you anymore tonight." Emotion caused my voice to crack, and I could feel tears forming at the back of my eyes. I wanted to trust someone, but I was not yet ready to fully trust him.

I looked down at his hand still resting on my arm, and then slowly brought my gaze back up to meet his. Our eyes clashed and I wished in that moment that I could read his thoughts. Aiden's hand fell away as I focused my eyes on the door at the far side of the room, connecting the two rooms.

Straightening my spine, I willed my legs to propel me forward, towards that door, and to the safety that lay on the other side of it. I did not fear for my safety in the normal sense of the word. I was not afraid that he would physically harm me. I had already proven I could hold my own when it came to Aiden Townsend.

On the contrary, I trembled at the mere thought of a much deeper pain, that I imagined Lord Townsend capable of inflicting — the emotional kind of pain that comes with no outward appearances or scars, but hurts just as much as a blade to the heart. He could leave the kind of scars that produce gaping holes, that can't be seen with the naked eye. The emotional kind of torment that would be left behind in the wake of one, Lord Aiden Townsend, who, like a hurricane could cut a wide path of damage that could cripple a person for life. And I, for one, did not intend to get caught up in the path of hurricane Townsend, when this mission came to an end.

18

What Dreams This Way Come?

HE FITFUL NIGHT'S SLEEP WAS not entirely of Aiden's doing. I tossed and turned as visions filled my mind, with secret handshakes, dark meeting places, and angry men. An image of a large, old, oak tree inside a heart kept dancing through my head. I couldn't make any sense of it, and as the night wore on, this pattern repeated itself three more times, before the dream changed.

A farm house on the outskirts of a town came into focus. It was secluded from other dwellings, and I could see men lingering about on the porch and around the sides of the house as they watched and waited. I recognized the two carts sitting outside the barn door, as a large dark form immerged from the main house. The dark figure seemed to be giving orders to one of the men on the porch who ran to do his bidding. He gathered men as he made his way to the darkened barn.

A lantern was lit before the three men stepped through the doors. A few minutes later, six men immerged from the barn. Two of them shuffled their feet as they walked because of the shackles around their ankles and the gunnysacks over their heads. The sound of the chains clinking together twisted my insides until I wanted to scream. Unable to lift a finger to help them, I felt useless. I could only watch helplessly as they were roughly pushed and shoved into the back of the waiting cart.

My heart began to race, and then suddenly it was in my throat. I recognized the first man led from the barn in shackles as Charlie.

I said a little prayer of thanks with one breath and cursed the Devils who had him with the next. Charlie was still alive and that was what really mattered in that moment. *"I'm coming for you Charlie. Just hang on a little longer,"* my mind screamed out to him over and over again.

Breathing a momentary sigh of relief, my heart sunk once again when I realized that there were only two men being loaded into the cart. What had happened to the third man? Was he still alive?

Sacks of grain were piled up around Charlie and his friend to camouflage their presence in the cart. One man sat in the front of the cart the entire time, waiting for it to be loaded with its human cargo. His face was slowly coming into focus, and I held my breath. I could feel my heart begin to beat wildly in my chest. Shames O'Malley, that blackhearted pernicious creature himself, sat in the front of that cart, holding the leather straps in his beefy hands.

I felt physically ill, and I couldn't breathe. Tears dampened my face. *Please, dear Father, don't let them come to harm,* I prayed. *Think, think, think… damn you…damn you to hell.* Anger seethed from my pores, as the two carts pulled away from the farmhouse.

Looking toward the farmhouse now, I saw the outline of a man left behind, then I noticed another man who stood beside the barn. Speaking to someone else inside the barn door. Moments later he shut the door and blew out the lantern he was holding.

I awoke with a sudden understanding. *The third man was still in the barn. He was alive. Why else would they leave people behind, to guard the farm?*

I jumped from my bed, not caring that I startled Maria in the process, and ran to the door separating my room from Aiden's. Quietly tapping on the door, I called out to him, but there was no answer. Turning the knob slowly in my hand, I cautiously opened the door and stepped inside the darkened room. "Aiden," I loudly whispered, taking two more steps forward and calling to him again. "Aiden, wake up," I said walking in even farther.

"You choose now to change your mind?" Aiden asked in a groggy voice.

"What?" I said, tip toeing toward Aiden's voice in the dark. "No!" I said, aghast at his forwardness.

I heard Maria striking a match in the other room to light a candle. Suddenly remembering the reason I'd come through the door, I whispered in the dark. "I know what's going on."

"What are you talking about, Isabella?" Aiden yawned and rubbed his eyes.

"They have left —" I said.

"Who has left?" he asked, cutting me off.

"Shames O'Malley has moved on, taking Charlie and one other prisoner with him. I really don't know which one they took, but I am certain I can locate the farmhouse where they have left the third man." I blurted out, talking without taking a breath between sentences. "Please, you have to get up and get dressed this instant. We have to stop them," I said, speaking excitedly. "Shames left the farmhouse, and has taken Charlie with him. We don't have any time to waste."

"Slow down now," Aiden said, sitting up in bed, and reaching for my hand in the dark to pull me toward him as Maria walked into the room with the lit candle, bathing the us in an eerie light.

"I need more to go on than that," Aiden insisted, still half asleep, rubbing the sleep from his eyes. Aiden squinted when Maria shoved the candle near his face.

"Maria, go lay out my heavy black cloak and the gray dress for riding. I will be right there to change," I ordered in frustration because nobody was moving as fast as I needed them to. In my mind I could see the cart getting farther and farther away with every passing second.

"Please Aiden," I pleaded, as I turned my attentions back to him. "You have to wake everyone up and we have to leave right away or we may be too late —"

"Too late for what, Isabella?" he asked in confusion. "I really need specifics, woman."

"It's a secluded farmhouse, on the edge of town, just east of here —" I replied.

"I need more than the general direction to head in," Aiden demanded, cutting me off again.

"If you would shut up a minute instead of interrupting me every time I open my mouth, I would have told you that the place has three buildings. The main house, a barn and a work shop. Shames left two men behind to guard the prisoner. They are keeping him in the barn," I stated defiantly, feeling a bit smug because I was able to give so many details.

"But that still isn't enough to go on. How am I supposed to find this farmhouse?" Aiden questioned, with a skeptical tone.

"There you go doubting me?" I quipped defensively. "I thought we had gotten past this," I jumped to my feet.

Aiden's hand reached out, grabbing me by the wrist, before I could turn and leave. "It's just that I … well —"

"It's just what, Lord Townsend?" I said, glaring down at him in the dark.

Pulling me back down to the edge of his bed, I heard a sound of exasperation expelled through Aiden's lips.

"Fine, tell it to me again. My men and I will try to find this farmhouse you speak of."

"Nice try, Townsend, but I'm coming with you and I will give you the rest of the details once we are on the road," I defiantly said, yanking my wrist free from Aiden's grasp, nearly knocking the candle over that Maria had left for me on the night table. "That way you won't leave me behind," I cried, glaring at him in the candlelight. "That is what you were planning to do once I gave you all the details, isn't it?" I accused.

"How the bloody hell did you …" Aiden began to say, then swore under his breath.

"It won't take me but a minute to get dressed. I would suggest you do the same or *I* will leave without *you*," I warned.

"The hell you say!" Aiden spat, jumping out of bed and spouting a string of expletives under his breath as I walked away.

I could hear him yanking on his trousers, none too gently, I might add.

Turning around once I'd reached the door, I took a deep breath to steady my nerves. Holding the candle tightly, I willed my hands to stop shaking, as I addressed Aiden. "I feel it only fair to give you warning, Townsend, I intend to retrieve my brother myself, and I won't allow anything, or anyone, to get in my way. Not even you."

Turning my back to Aiden, I walked from the room with purpose and closing the door. I could feel his eyes boring a hole through the wall, as a fresh string of expletives fell from his lips, basically his calling into question my parentage, as I retreated to my own room, shutting the door behind me.

I could hear Aiden stomping about in his room through the walls, but I didn't care. I was determined to find out for myself why Shames O'Malley left the third man behind. But more importantly, I was going to find out exactly where he was headed with my brother.

And when I located the shiftless, good for nothing, conniving bastard, I would see him dead, by my own hand.

19

And Then There Were Two

WENTY MINUTES LATER, I WALKED out of my hotel room, headed for the stairs, my disheveled hair still in the same braid I had worn to bed the night before. Maria followed me down the stairs as I quietly gave instructions to pack everything up and have it loaded into the carriage and ready to go upon my return. I was confident that we would be moving on as soon as our business concluded at the farmhouse. I walked out the front door of the inn just as Aiden, Caleb, and five of his men came around the corner, with a horse saddled up and ready for me.

"As you ordered, my lady, your horse and men ready to do your bidding. The only thing lacking now is direction," Aiden said with derision, still sore at me for outsmarting him so early in the morning.

"If you gentlemen would be so kind as to point me in the direction of the east road that heads out of town, we will be on our way," I responded, climbing up into my saddle, without assistance from Aiden's outstretched hand.

"This way, my lady," Caleb gestured with his hand, as Aiden handed me the reigns.

The sky was beginning to lighten, turning a brilliant pink hue, making traveling the tricky Irish roads much easier than in the dark. I kicked the horse I was riding in the sides, leading the way by instinct.

Thirty minutes later, trees and landmarks began to look familiar and I recognized the area from my dream. Stopping my horse by the side of the road, Caleb and Aiden came up alongside of me.

"What seems to be the matter, Lady Isabella?" Aiden inquired.

"Nothing is wrong, but the house will be just around the corner." I indicated with my head. "The men left behind will most likely be asleep, but in case they are not, we need to have some plan of attack. And by plan of attack, I mean we need to take them alive, so we can find out where Shames has taken my brother."

"Caleb, you stay here with Isabella, and I will take the men and secure the area. When I give you the signal, you bring her in," Aiden ordered as a knowing look, passed between the two of them. "Is there anything in particular I should know before I go?" Aiden asked, directing his question at me.

"Yes, watch out for the man hanging out around the back side of the barn. He's an unscrupulous sort," I cautioned.

"I will keep that in mind," he winked before handing Caleb his reins.

Caleb hitched the other five horses together so they would follow in a line when we received the signal from Aiden. Every second felt like an eternity as Caleb and I waited there in the predawn light. Ten minutes had passed, before we finally heard the signal.

Aiden let loose with a loud whistle, I swore could have wakened the dead. Kicking our horses into motion, Caleb and I rounded the corner that led into the farmhouse yard. Not waiting for Caleb to come around and help me down, I leaped from my horse, and ran straight for the barn.

Throwing open the door, I stood there a minute until my eyes adjusted to the dim lighting, glowing from the far stall. Aiden stood victoriously over one of Shames's henchmen. Propping himself up against one of the stall walls was a slightly beaten, but still living, friend of my brother's.

"Lady Isabella, may I introduce you to Lord —" Aiden began to say.

"Tommy!" I shouted, cutting Aiden off, as I threw my arms around Tommy's neck. "I am so happy to meet you," I cried and laughed at the same time. Holding him out from me now at arm's length, I gave him the once over, scrutinizing him with a critical eye. "Are you hurt?" I inquired.

"Charlie said you would come for us," Tommy's voice cracked with emotion. Relief and gratitude laced his words as he reached up and touched my face. "I can't believe you are real and that you found me."

"I would walk through fire for Charlie," I proclaimed, with an emotional chuckle.

"He said the same thing about you," Tommy whispered, staring up at me, still not sure if I was real or imagined. Tears filled his eyes and he almost laughed to himself. "At first I thought they had come to take me away," Tommy said, jerking his head toward Aiden.

"The only place we will be taking you is back to our hotel room, where you can eat and sleep without fear of further harm," Aiden assured Tommy.

Tommy's eyes wandered around the darkened barn taking everything in. I touched his face, gently directing him to look at me. "Do you know where Shames and his men took Charlie and Ashton?" I asked, unable to keep the hope from my voice.

"The only thing I heard was something about continuing northward, but they would know the plan better," Tommy said, lifting his chin in the direction of the two men, face down on the ground, held in place by Aiden's men.

"Tommy, do you know anything about a symbol of a large oak tree inside of a heart?" I caught movement out of the corner of my eye.

"No, they kept us locked up most of the time. The only way we would hear anything was if they thought we were asleep," Tommy replied.

Caleb bolted through the door. "They only left a few horses. What do you want to do, Aiden?"

"It's not safe to hang around here too long. We don't know who or how many men are due to come and relieve these men. Tie those two to a horse," Aiden instructed, helping Tommy to his feet.

Pulling Aiden aside, I quietly spoke in his ear. "Aiden, I think the young man you were standing over, might talk, if he were given the right kind of incentive. Why don't you separate them, and tell the younger man what the future holds for him, if he doesn't cooperate," I whispered, and then glanced down at the boy, giving me with a wary look. "I swear I felt something from him when I mentioned the symbol of the oak tree inside a heart. The other man is too far gone, his heart has hardened beyond repair. You will never get anything out of him."

Aiden looked over his shoulder at the kid who couldn't have been more than fourteen years old. Casually walking over to the older man, who was still sitting against the wall, holding his head between his hands. Aiden had clocked him in the skull so he couldn't alert anyone else. Squatting down to examine his handy work, Aiden narrowed his eyes at the man, and then whistled through his teeth. "Man, I really did a number on you. Caleb, why don't you and James take this gentleman out of here and bandage his head before we get on the road?" Standing up, Aiden gave Caleb a few hand signals over the man's head that only Caleb could interpret. Aiden then continued to talk, "Boy, I would lay odds that your head is pounding right now."

"All right old chap, up we go," Caleb said, roughly helping the man to his feet.

The older man glared at Aiden, and then narrowed his eyes at the younger man still on the ground near my feet. Jerking his arm away from Caleb, he nearly fell again, determined to walk out on his own. Evidence of a serious injury was displayed down the back of his shirt where blood had already begun to dry.

The moment Caleb shut the door I began grilling the younger man. "Let's start with your name, shall we?"

The boy glared at me with his big hazel eyes, his left eye already show-ing signs that it was going to turn purple. "I'm not talking," he said sullenly.

"Let me tell you something, young man, I'm certain that I saw some-thing in you when I mentioned the oak tree and heart symbol, so you might as well spill it," I fired back, determined to get something out of him.

"I ain't no snitch," he yelled at me, his cockney accent coming out loud and clear as he cast his eyes downward and folded his arms over his chest like a petulant child.

I lifted his chin with one hand, and slapped him hard across the face with the other.

"Didn't hurt," he growled between clenched teeth, while his defiant eyes dared me to do it again.

"I didn't mean for it to hurt, you silly child. That slap was meant to wake you up," I replied frankly. "If you are so hell bent on throwing your life away for those gutter snipes, I figure you will want to be completely awake, just before you swing from the tree limb next to them."

The boy's eyes opened wide. "What are you talking about, lady?" he asked, confusion registering in his eyes. He no longer looked like the grown man he was pretending to be. Instead he instantly transformed back into a fourteen year old child in need of comforting from his mother.

"Well," I said, keeping him in suspense a moment longer, as I got in his face, "this man here, standing over my shoulder, is going to make you an offer. If you choose not to take him up on the offer, he will have no other choice but to make the very same offer to your friend outside. Whoever cooperates first will get the deal, and the other person will not be so lucky," I said, pulling a very sad face and shaking my head side to side, trying my best to induce an atmosphere of panic.

The young man's face fell like a sack of wheat to the ground. "Just how unlucky are we talking about?" he asked in a shaky voice.

Aiden crouched down beside me. "I've got a long rope, and not a lot of time to check with the local magistrates regarding their protocol for kidnapping and murder. There were two other men here today, that we need locating. Someone hauled them away by cart earlier today, and if they turn up dead…" Aiden concluded, purposely leaving the rest of that sentence up to the young man's vivid imagination, "well then, I will have no other choice but to…" Aiden continued, making the universal sign of a slit throat, drawing his finger across his neck, from ear to ear.

The young man's eyes opened even wider now in disbelief. "Honestly?" he asked.

"Honestly!" Aiden confirmed, sounding absolutely serious.

Fifteen minutes later, we walked out of that worn down barn, with all the information we needed. The young man's name was Timothy Connor, and he had been personally recruited by Shames O'Malley six months earlier. It was Timothy's job to find locals willing to leave their homes and hard work behind, in exchange for a goodly amount of money.

People had been told that The Hearts of Oak gang were planning on starting a revolution and intended to take over the government. It was a secret organization, started by a group of Irish thugs dissatisfied with the current state of affairs in Ireland. More to the point they were dissatisfied with their particular political standing. They had started out protesting the high rent and taxes exacted on them by their government, but things soon turned violent when further tithes were sanctioned on the Irish to establish the Church of Ireland.

The Church of Ireland was a Protestant based religion, while the majority of peasants paying tithes were Catholics. They were a hard-working group of people trying to feed their families, while the king's Government of Ireland, and the Irish Parliament, continued to take cuts of the offerings and taxes for themselves. In essence, the rich got richer while the majority of people went hungry, unable to feed their families.

The straw that broke the proverbial camel's back came when the government confiscated common lands and started evicting people on the flimsiest of charges. Essentially stripping away family lands, livestock, and lively hoods, the government was hacking away at the very foundation of the Irish people, splitting the country down the middle, at its very seams, simply because they wanted the choicest properties for their own heirs.

Shames O'Malley, and men like him, began a rebellion, by implementing intimidation tactics. They committed violence against the landlords, killing or maiming livestock, tearing down fences and enclosures, to basically create chaos throughout the different counties.

I had two questions for Shames O'Malley and men like him. *'When exactly did the bullies of Ireland decide that it was a good idea to travel across the water to inflict their brand of terror upon the commonwealth of England? And when did kidnapping our young men and dragging them down to the depths of their depravity become an acceptable form of protest?* None of it made any sense.

We also discovered from the young man, that Shames was headed northward, toward the township of Bainbridge. And that Shames O'Malley was not the actual leader of the Hearts of Oak gang, but merely a lieutenant who took his orders from someone much higher up. Just exactly who the true leader was, still remained a mystery. According to Timothy, most of the men had never met their fearless leader face to face. This not only protected the allusive leader's identity, giving him anonymity from the Hearts of Oak masses, but it also gave him the ability to move about the countryside, eluding government agents wishing to prosecute him for his crimes.

Timothy further divulged that the leader of the unscrupulous group of thugs was rumored to be a highborn, dissatisfied and unhappy with his prospects. Rumor had it that the he was a second born son of a prestigious family, who was not content to wait for his meager scraps to fall from the table. Timothy confessed to us, that no one had actually told him who that disgruntled "highborn" was, because he, himself was too low down in the ranks for that kind of information.

Shames O'Malley had been one of the first members to eagerly join the outlaw band of thieves. He had been angry at the loss of his family's lands, combined with the implemented laws that prevented him from being educated at any of the universities in Ireland or abroad, because of his religious affiliations. Shames had left Tommy behind because he had sold him to a pirate he knew. The pirate was to pick Tommy up in two nights and move him by wagon across Ireland to his ship, illegally docked off the coast of Galway. Tommy would never actually be a shipmate, but someone they called an involuntary ship hand; a person who is waylaid and forced into a life of servitude. A prisoner of sorts, until the day he was no longer needed, at which point he would be resold to another passing ship, or dumped overboard as fish bait.

Young Timothy and his older, larger, more jaded companion were told to wait for the pirates to arrive and deliver Tommy into their hands. Then they were to travel northward, to the safe house in the Bainbridge area. There they were to wait for further instructions from Shames.

Aiden made a show of leaving five men behind with a long rope, instructing them to clean up the mess and take care of the prisoners. Aiden figured he would let young Timothy Connors draw his own conclusion and possibly scare him away from ever joining another gang of thugs in the future. It would be a long time before the lad forgot the day he nearly lost his life to a gang of ruthless mercenaries out for blood.

Aiden left orders that Timothy would be afforded the opportunity to escape, but not before he was witness to the preparations for the hangings. But after Timothy's escape, Aiden's men would be transported the prisoners to the local magistrate, where they would be tried for kidnapping, then hung for crimes against their countrymen. Timothy would be allowed to return home and remain in a state of paranoia, forced to look over his shoulder for the rest of his life. Aiden felt it was punishment enough.

The other men Aiden left behind would stay put, and lay in wait for the pirates. When they showed up, they were to be captured and turned over to the local magistrate as well. When our men had completed their mission, they would meet back up with us at Castle Blayney.

20

Time to Pay the Piper

Y THE TIME WE REACHED the hotel, Maria was ready to go. The carriages were packed, and she had whipped the men into shape. Making a quick switch for fresh horses, we were back on the road, having left Tommy behind at the hotel to recover from his ordeal.

I chose to ride astride a horse, instead of being trapped inside the confines of the slower moving carriage. I wished to spare myself the constant banging and bouncing on the badly rutted roads. In the end, I was thankful that I chose to make the journey to Castle Blayney on horseback, because of the freedom it afforded me. Caleb, Aiden, and I were able to cover ground more quickly.

Aiden's ominous words, *'If they should turn up dead,'* kept ringing in my ears. It urged me to keep going, even though I was in pain from sitting in the saddle so long.

The sun had begun to sit low in the sky, when we finally made the outskirts of the Bainbridge Township. Caleb estimated that we had only another hour of daylight left, so we kicked our horses into a gallop. Gritting my teeth through the pain, I kept telling myself, *'I can do anything for a small while, if it gets us there faster.'*

Aiden decided that it best for everyone concerned if we continue our original ruse of being a couple, taking in the sites of the Irish countryside.

Our journey brought us to the castle of Lord Andrew Thomas Blayney, the eleventh Earl of Castle Blayney, who, as luck would have it, was a good friend and ally to the Townsend family and long time trader of goods with the Deverauxs. The Blayney's and Townsend's long friendship extended back several generations, so Aiden was confident that we would be taken in with open arms, and no questions asked.

Sore, exhausted, and starving, we managed to arrive just before dark, where we were met by a handful of stable hands, waiting our arrival.

Two of Aiden's men had ridden ahead, perpetuating the ruse, and alerting Lord Blayney of our impending arrival. Upon arriving, I sat perfectly still on my horse for a few moments longer than I first thought necessary. I was attempting to gather up my courage for a dismount, because I was all together unsure that my legs would work or even support me after so many hours in the saddle. I felt as if I had blisters on top of blisters. My right leg was cramping up and my left leg was completely numb.

Aiden saw my distress and gallantly came to my rescue. "May I be of some service, my lady?" he offered with a mocking chuckle, trying to hide his amusement.

"I am perfectly capable of dismounting from a horse on my own," I assured him, snubbing his gallant efforts, out of some misplaced pride.

"As you wish, my dear, but perhaps you will allow me to hold your horse still while you try. That many hours in a saddle can make standing on solid ground difficult, especially if the horse is moving," Aiden taunted, not even trying to hide his amusement this time.

I noticed Caleb looking at me strangely, while making his way over to us. "Why are you holding her horse?" Caleb asked, coming to stand on the left side of me. "You should be helping her down," he added, giving Aiden a most unflattering look as he reached up to me.

"I did offer to help her," Aiden said in a subtle tone of exasperation. "But she insisted on getting down on her own."

"Well, that is ridiculous," Caleb replied, looking first to Aiden then back up at me, "Give me your hand, Lady Deveraux," he insisted.

"I am perfectly capable, Mr. Daughtery," I stated politely.

"See, I told you. She wants to do it herself," Aiden added smugly.

"Well now, she is just being stubborn," Caleb protested, taking several steps back to stand next to his friend.

"A polite man would have just said that she was determined, instead of calling the lady stubborn," Aiden chided Caleb.

"Well, if you aren't the pot calling the kettle black," Caleb exclaimed, folding his arms over his chest.

"I swear the two of you sound like an old married couple," I teased. "Would you like me to give the two of you a moment alone?" I inquired with drollness etching my words as I swung my leg over the saddle slowly, and then hesitated a moment before lowering my leg all the way to the ground. The mere act of moving my legs was excruciating. I couldn't figure out for the life of me how I was going to remove my foot gracefully from the stirrup, then remain standing on both feet.

Removing my foot from the stirrup brought involuntary tears to my eyes. I gasped, sucking in air that I then blew out again between my clenched teeth. I stood beside my horse, leaning my head against the saddle, unable to move, and far too embarrassed to ask either one of them for help.

"Is anything wrong, Isabella?" Aiden asked, shifting his tone to reflect surprise.

"Aiden, don't tease her. Can't you see she is in some amount of pain?" Caleb said, squatting down, and then looking up at my face.

"Well, I tried to tell her," Aiden said, sounding superior.

"Ah… oh… um!… It's true he did try to warn me," I moaned, moving away from the horse.

I managed to take two steps on my own, before my legs gave out and I dropped like a sack of stones. Lucky for me, Aiden and Caleb had anticipated my fall from grace, and each of them grabbed hold of an arm to keep me from hitting the ground.

"You might need some assistance with that cramp in your, well, posterior… ah," Aiden stammered, giving me a sheepish look and a wolfish grin at the same time while choosing his words carefully and stifling a laugh.

"Aiden, let's not forget that we are in the presence of a lady," Caleb reminded.

"In that case, I am happy to be of service to you, my Ladyship," Aiden graciously volunteered with a smile and a wink.

"I will be properly scandalized and mortified when I am no longer in pain and I can feel my legs again," I said facetiously, contorting my face into a grimace of pain.

"Oh, this is ridiculous," Aiden admonished, lifting me into his arms. Carrying me through the stables, Aiden headed for the castle's courtyard, with Caleb close on his heels.

"This is most inappropriate, Lord Townsend," I gasped, wrapping my arms around his neck.

"The ruse isn't very affective if you refuse to call me by my Christian name, Isabella," Aiden shot back.

"I can't possibly meet the Earl of Blayney this way," I indicated. "It would be unseemly," I protested, as color spread up my neck and leeched through my cheeks.

I caught myself staring up at his profile, admiring the pleasant way the creased corners of his eyes and his lips turned up when he found something amusing.

"That is absolute nonsense, my dear," Aiden laughed heartily. "I am a knight in shining armor who has come to rescue my damsel in distress," he added with bravado. Aiden caught me studying him out of the corner of his eye and turned to gaze directly at me, with a confident grin.

Suddenly blushing, feeling self-conscious, I pushed against his chest, to free myself from his intimate embrace. "I thank you for your assistance, sir, but I think I can walk from here."

Tightening his grip, Aiden continued to grin down at me, humored by my feeble attempts to dislodge myself. "Stop being so obstinate, Isabella," his tone suddenly changing.

"I thought you said it would be impolite to call a woman stubborn?" I chided, continuing to look up into his face. I was unsure what had changed, but suddenly something about Aiden felt different.

Lord Blayney called out to us, and without missing a step, the Earl of Castle Blayney made us all feel instantly at home and welcomed as he greeted us. "Welcome, welcome. It is so good to see you again, my dear boy. It has been far too long since your last visit," he laughed good-heartedly, slapping Aiden on the back and grasping Caleb's hand.

"I do apologize for not giving you any advanced notice of our arrival, but it was a spur of the moment decision," Aiden assured him sincerity.

"Think nothing of it, my boy, think nothing of it. My home is your home, and the doors are always opened to you and yours," the Earl said, with flourish, as he suddenly shifted his attention to me. "Now, who do you have here? A little something you picked up on the road?" Earl Blayney asked with a wicked chuckle.

The Earl was a jolly, flamboyant individual, who stood about five feet eight inches tall. He was slender and fit and showed signs of having a rascally personality. I could tell that his hair had once been blond, but was mostly white now. My eyes were drawn to his manicured mustache, which only added to the charming characteristics of his features. His blue eyes sparkled with much mischief, as he greeted me with a wink.

"Where are my manners? Lady Isabella Deveraux of Bayonne, I would like to introduce you to Andrew Thomas Blayney, the Eleventh Earl of Castle Blayney." Aiden said, making the introductions with a great deal of enthusiasm.

"Please excuse me for not standing, Lord Blayney. It would appear that I have over done it today, and I am a bit saddle sore and unable to walk. Lord... I mean Aiden here has gallantly come to my rescue," I quickly corrected myself.

"Nothing serious, I hope," Earl Blayney said with concern.

"Nothing that a hot bath and a massage won't cure," Aiden said with a rakish grin and a wink to the Earl.

"Oh, I am so delighted to hear that," the Earl replied with a nervous laugh. "Oh, I almost forgot. I received some other unexpected guests last night. I believe you might know them, my dear," the Earl said with flare, stepping aside. "Lord Townsend may I introduce you to —"

"Father!" I cried, unable to hide the surprise and sudden distress in my tone.

"Did you just say Father?" Aiden inquired under his breath. I could feel his muscles flexing, as he squeezed me just a little closer to him.

My father walked up to us both, looking Aiden directly in the eyes. Sapphire shards flew back and forth between them, as they sized each other up. It was at that precise moment that I noticed that they both shared a common trait. A muscle flexed in their jaw when perturbed.

Never breaking his eye contact with Aiden, my father's voice took on a low, but calm tone. "So you are the man I have heard so much about. The way I hear it told, you have swept my little girl off her feet," he paused for affect.

Aiden had never met my father before, so he had no reason to be alarmed, but suddenly every nerve in my body went taut, and alarm bells were going off in my head.

"It appears that I can take that statement literally, as well as figuratively," my father concluded, raising his left eyebrow to indicate my current position in Aiden's arms.

Meanwhile, I felt like the sacrificial lamb, staked out in the middle of a field, with adversarial beasts on either side of me, ready to tear me apart. My heart was pounding so hard I was certain everyone could hear it.

"And who exactly did you hear this from? If it isn't too bold an inquiry, Lord Deveraux," Aiden bristled, his tone, frosty to my ears, causing me to cringe inwardly.

"Why, from me, dear brother," Ian Townsend confessed, while stepping out of the shadows. "He heard it from me," Ian almost sounded giddy. "I was filling Lord Deveraux in on all the sordid details," Ian indicated using his index finger to point at Aiden and then me. "Oh no, was your affair supposed to be a secret?" Ian feigned embarrassment, immediately followed by regret.

I felt Aiden's muscles flex again and I thought for sure he was about to throw me into my father's arms so he could strangle his brother right there on the spot. Instead, Aiden shifted, smiled graciously to my father, and then to his brother, Ian, begore squeezing me possessively against his chest. "No, dear brother, no secrets here," he announced with a dangerous smile that turned up on one side of his mouth. The air cracked with electricity between the three men. I was about to feign a case of the vapors but was afraid my father would see right through that ruse.

"I am very glad to hear it," my father said so calm and low that I nearly missed it. Now turning his attention to me, his eyes were like daggers to my heart. That silent deadly calm of his was my undoing.

"How did you know where to find me?" I asked looking into those great big sapphire eyes of Father's. I knew from years of dealing with the man that it was always best to not show fear or weakness.

"Your mother," he answered, tilting his head slightly to the side, as if to say, who else?

"Of course," I replied, the words dropped from my lips like a flat note from an opera singer. "And how is mother?" I inquired, attempting to make polite conversation while my heart lay on the ground before me.

"She is well. Why don't you talk to her yourself? She is just up stairs changing for dinner," he informed casually, indicating the path to my redemption, with his hand.

I could feel my nerve begin to crack and I wanted to scream out, *"It's not true Father. It is all a lie we concocted to get Charlie back."* But something was holding me back from confessing everything to him.

Maybe it was everyone who stood around witnessing my humiliation, or maybe it was the tone of his voice and my stubborn streak that made me keep my secret. Regardless, I was not yet ready to turn loose of my ruse. Aiden gave me a reassuring squeeze as I turned my head to look at him. My uncertainty must have been written on my face, because when our eyes locked, he gave me a smile and a wink that helped.

Lord Blayney stepped in. "Your father was just telling me earlier that you are like a rare jewel, my dear. And now I see how he would feel that way. Just look at you," he said stepping in between Aiden and my father. The Earl's momentary distraction from my father's looming presence was greatly appreciated. "Oh, I do hope I am not embarrassing you?" he said, graciously. "Shall I have a hot bath sent up to your room?"

Too late for mere embarrassment, I thought to myself. *I was now praying for a large hole big enough to fling myself into and be swallowed whole, preferably sooner than later.*

"Maybe you should put me down," I said, leaning close to Aiden's ear so only he could hear me.

"What?" Aiden asked, as his look suddenly changed from his usual confident self to complete confusion. "But what about —" he started to say when I caught sight of Caleb, who gave me a slight shake of his head, as he narrowed his eyes at me. I suddenly imagined Caleb to be an excellent cards player, because his face immediately turned passive, giving nothing away.

"On second thought," I announced boldly. "Please take me up stairs, so that I might get out of these dusty clothes before dinner?" I looked adoringly into Aiden's eyes. His confusion turned to surprise, and then quickly masked over with an expression of assuredness once again.

All I kept thinking was, *I must keep up the charade for Charlie's sake.* After all, we still didn't know who was behind this divisive rebel group, terrorizing the countryside.

"Please tell Mother that I will catch up with her at dinner," I exclaimed, looking my father in the eye, as I gave him a well practiced poker face of my own, just as he had taught me when I was child. I smiled, lovingly up at him. "Please excuse us, Father, but I really must get out of these clothes and into a hot bath."

Turning to Lord Blayney, I blessed him with a magnificent smile, as I turned on the charm. "Lord Blayney, I would adore a hot soak to ease my saddle weary muscles. If it wouldn't be too much trouble or cause everyone to wait dinner for me."

"I can have it sent up to your suite immediately, my dear, and please don't worry yourself over dinner. We like to eat late," Lord Blayney replied with a solicitous tone. "Don't hesitate to let me know if you are in need of anything further. Will you need a maid to assist you?"

"No, thank you. You have been so kind and done so much already. Maria should be along any minute. She was riding in one of the carriages," I said, gracing Lord Blayney with a sincere smile.

Looking around I locked eyes with Caleb. "Would you mind terribly checking to see if the carriages have arrived yet, and send Maria up to me as soon as she does?" I said with bravado, giving Caleb a look that screamed, *'Help me please.'*

"It would be my pleasure, Lady Isabella," Caleb gallantly bowed, then turned on his heels and headed for the stables.

Lord Blayney snapped his fingers, and immediately two servants appeared at his side. "Sam, if you would, see that the fire is properly stoked in the west wing suites." The Earl's tone seemed to have changed in an instant from ostentatious and showy to one of authority as he gave instructions to his servants.

"Very good, my Lord," Sam muttered, as he turned to do Lord Blayney's bidding.

"Jane, show Lord Townsend and Lady Deveraux to their rooms, and see to the Lady's bath until her maid arrives," Lord Blayney continued.

"Father," I coolly quipped, dipping my head in his general direction as Aiden carried me past him. Tightening my grip around Aiden's neck, I focused my eyes lovingly on him, refusing to look in my father's direction.

Just by chance I happened to catch the astonished look on my father's face out of the corner of my eye. A string of expletives could be heard as

Aiden carried me through the front door. Every word of his tirade was in French; of course, and one thing was for certain — my father was not happy. In fact, judging by the look in his eyes, and the tone of his voice, he was furious, but so was I.

I was not yet ready to forgive, nor forget what he had done to Charlie and me three years prior. And more to the point, I was still bitterly angry over the loss of my other half. That proverbial, better half of myself, that made me whole and complete.

I suddenly wished to feel anything except the empty shell of a human I had become. It was as if I had been living a lie these past three years. Showing the part of myself to the world that was acceptable, and for all intent and purposes I was the picture of perfection. I walked and talked as if nothing was amiss, but it was all a lie, and I for one, was tired of the phony pretense I was forced to endure, day in and day out.

When it came to my father or Shames O'Malley, I was not looking for some kind of polite justice to satisfy some judicial obligation. Oh no, that would be too civil a word for what I had in mind. I was looking for someone's bloody head, served up on a silver platter. Preferably while it was still bloody well warm!

I was now properly motivated to see this charade through to the end. I was willing to take this as far as I had to, if it meant getting Charlie back alive.

21

Let The Charades Begin,
With Earnest and Conviction This Time,
If You Please

"BUT SHE IS MY MOTHER, Aiden. I should tell her the truth. Maybe I can keep this matter from getting out of hand," I argued. Aiden and I were sitting in the ante-chamber that connected the two rooms together, when I broached the subject of telling my mother the truth about our relationship.

Aiden was dressed in a handsome black jacket with charcoal gray trousers, black boots, and a dark green silk cravat. His white linen shirt, crisply pressed by one of Lord Blayney's maids, stood out against his tan features.

"And I am telling you, if you tell her the truth, word will get out and then all the work we have done thus far will be for not," Aiden said pointedly.

"How in the world am I supposed to pull this off?" I countered, glaring at Aiden sitting so calm and collected in a chair. I could not understand how he could be so nonchalant, while my parents were in another room thinking the worst of me.

"Come here," he said in a tone that sounded more like an order than a request.

"Why?" I asked suspiciously.

"Don't look at me that way. I only wish to show you something," Aiden replied, smiling provocatively as he bid me to come to him with a mere flip of the hand. Taking several steps in his direction, I stood directly in front of him, still not convinced that honesty was not the best route to take with my mother.

"Now stand behind me and rest your hand on my shoulder," he suggested.

"I still don't see how this is going to convince everyone that we are entangled," I said reluctantly, while doing as he bid.

"Do you always have to be so capricious?" Aiden scolded, with an exasperated tone. "Let's just say that we have finished dinner, and we are all gathered together in a room enjoying a nice talk. How convincing do you think it will be if you come up behind me and rest your hand on my shoulder?" Aiden asked casually, as if he were directing a play. "Come on, this could be fun."

"Would you like me to pretend to laugh as well? You know, just to make the scene complete?" I said sarcastically while giving a fake laugh.

"Only if you think it would help," Aiden fired back, taking a hold of my hand, in his large, work roughened grasp. I felt disconcerted by the warmth of his touch and the way that it affected me each time he touched me now. I wouldn't show him weakness by pulling my hand away.

"And say I was to reach up and grasp your hand like so, then bring it to my lips," Aiden continued, lightly touching my fingers with his as he rolled my hand over placing the slightest of kisses upon my wrist. I could feel the nerves up my arm begin to tingle as I gazed into his deep blue eyes. Aiden's intense gaze sucked me in like a muddy bog after a three-day rain.

"Then say, I was to pull you around me like so and you should sit upon the arm of my chair, thusly," Aiden continued, demonstrating everything as he spoke. "And perhaps I would place my arm possessively around your waist," he stated, continuing to demonstrate.

Slowly Aiden stood up, as his soothing words drew me in to his ruse even deeper as he reached out to pull me up against him. Bending his head down to touch his lips gently to mine, gradually deepened the kiss, his tongue felt like velvet as it darted between my lips. The sensation caught me by surprise and I felt helpless to struggle or push him away.

I sighed with my eyes still closed as he pulled away, and I felt like I was in a dream state when I opened my eyelids slowly. "Yes, now that is how you sell a charade," Aiden said pensively. His own voice sounded rich and smooth like warmed ocean breeze, as he tried to hide his own emotions. "If you should look at me in that manner this evening, not even the most skeptical of cynics will see beyond our ruse," Aiden assured, then cleared his throat, trying to convince himself that what he was feeling at the moment was all part of the elaborate charade.

Still under his spell, my gaze was locked with his when Maria entered the room. "Perhaps you would like to practice that move once again?" Maria retorted, after clearing her throat.

Taking a step backwards, I suddenly felt caught off guard and foolish. "We were just practicing… because I was… concerned that I didn't —" I stammered and fumbled for words.

"I know what you were just practicing," Maria grumbled, cutting me off, with a suspicious undertone. "And I would caution the two of you to be careful around your father. I heard one of the maids talking. Seems he was none too happy with the way things ended in the courtyard earlier. I heard he wanted to bust down the door and murder someone. At least that is what Mary in the kitchen told me," Maria cautioned. "Mary said he was rambling like a madman in French, and your mother, had to step in to calm him down."

"Perhaps I'd better go and talk with my mother after all. You have no idea what my father is capable of," I shuddered. "Mother would tell us stories when Charlie and I were children," I warned, concerned for Aiden's safety.

"I strongly suggest we stick to the plan," Aiden replied, taking my hand in his, and leading me to the door and out into the hallway. "Are you sure that you are able to walk?" he asked with a wicked grin.

"Yes, I'm feeling much better, thank you for your unwarranted concern. The soak worked, and the salve you gave Maria did the trick."

"I still think you should have let me apply it for you. Who knows if Maria applied it correctly?" Aiden teased, placing my hand over his arm, as he gave me a mischievous grin and a playful bump of his elbow. The sound of his hearty laugh thrilled me for some reason, as we began to descend the staircase together.

"Oh, you are a wicked tease, Aiden Townsend," I laughed with real pleasure, forgetting for just a moment the reason I had come to Ireland.

We teased back and forth down the stairs until we came face to face with the very disapproving glare of my father. Standing next to him was my calm, but subdued mother, The Duchess of Bayonne, Lady Angelina Deveraux. She was elegantly dressed in a royal blue gown and looking as stunning as ever.

I leaned over, placing a kiss on both her cheeks, as was customary in our family. "You look well, Mother. Sorry I didn't have the opportunity to greet you earlier," I said stiffly.

"All is forgiven, Bella, my love," she warmly replied. I knew Mother was smiling, even though I was no longer looking at her, because I was too busy watching my father glaring dangerously at Aiden.

"Father, you remember The Viscount of Buckinghamshire, Lord Aiden Townsend," I said boldly, taking a step forward, placing myself between Aiden and my father in hopes of defusing the tense situation.

"Yes, Bella, I recall meeting your companion earlier," Father replied with great restraint. I could tell it took great effort on his part to control his anger and I must admit, it gave me reason to pause. Out of respect, I leaned forward to greet my father, kissing him properly on both cheeks.

"So, Father, you didn't really get the chance to tell me what has brought you to Castle Blayney?" I questioned, keeping my tone polite and solicitous.

"I came on a mission to retrieve my eldest son, but now it would appear that both of my first born children are in need of saving," he replied, redirecting his attention back to Aiden.

Still holding onto Aiden's hand, my fingers involuntarily dug into his flesh as my heart jumped into my throat for a second time that day. I truly feared for Aiden's life, and at that moment would do just about anything to prevent the loss of it, even if it meant coming clean to my father, despite Aiden's warnings.

"Father, you don't understand —" I began to say, while feeling as if my lungs were about to burst. My corset suddenly felt like it was squeezing the very life from my body.

"Oh, but I do understand, Bella, better than you know," he replied with a menacing tone.

I bit my tongue and took a deep breath. Self righteous indignation began to rise up, and I snapped back, "I am a grown woman, Father, and I have the situation well in hand."

"I can see that. A fact you have made abundantly clear to all who have eyes in their heads," he said, chastising me, while his eyes frosted over. They reminded me of an ice storm at sea, bitterly cold and ultimately dangerous to all whom had the misfortune of getting in its path. I shivered. I had never seen my father truly angry before, but suddenly all the stories my mother had told Charlie and me about Father's ferocious nature came flooding back to me, in vivid detail.

In an instant, I was transported back to that vulnerable little girl, powerless to change my circumstance. My hands began to shake and my knees knocked together when my mother took hold of my arm. "Come, my dear, the men need to talk," I heard her say as my hand slipped from the only solid thing, keeping me grounded.

"Wait!" I protested, but it was useless. Mother continued to drag me toward the dining room. Glancing over my shoulder I saw Father and Aiden walking away, toward an empty room at the end of the hall.

I pulled Mother to a stop and watched Father. Opening the doors to Lord Blayney's study, he locked eyes with me and all I could do was stare at him. I had never before seen that particular look which was now upon his face. His jaw line looked chiseled, as if it was made of stone, and the coldness reflecting back at me would have frozen the heart of any good man.

Attempting to pull away from my mother's grasp was useless, because she knew what was going on and I just had to wait to learn the outcome.

"Come Bella, they will be fine. Your father only wishes to have a word with Lord Townsend," Mother coaxed, patting my hand to assuage my fears, and redirect my attention toward the dining room.

Upon entering the salon, Earl Blayney and his wife greeted us warmly. Several of the guests also came up to introduce themselves to me. I was surprised by the number of people invited to the Earl's dinner. It appeared to me that we had arrived in the nick of time for a party of some kind.

Where had all these people come from, and why were they here?' Yet, I did not give it a lot of thought or ask any questions. Instead my mind was on a different matter taking place in the other room. An inkling of concern kept nagging at me, but I continued to push it aside.

I grew more anxious with the passing minutes, and had nearly gathered enough courage to walk out of the room and down the hall to the Earl's office, when Lord Blayney distracted me. "Lady Isabella, please don't worry. I am sure everything will work itself out for the best.

Now what was that supposed to mean? I thought.

Lady Harriett Blayney leaned over close to my ear and whispered, "His Lordship never keeps anything sharp in his office."

I bobbed my head absently, surprised and a bit shocked by Lady Harriett's strange comment. My mind began to wonder after that exchange and I didn't listen to what she was saying after that. My nerves were raw and I felt sick to my stomach.

Feeling the need to be polite, I tried to make conversation. "Thank you for taking us into your beautiful home on such short notice. It is very generous of you," I said, glancing nervously at the door.

"Please, Lady Isabella, don't concern yourself. I am happy for the opportunity to help your family out. Not to mention how grateful I am to you for the distraction. It can become so tedious around here, as one ordinary day blends into the next." Lady Harriett confessed, with a laugh.

"We have saved you seats over here," Lord Blayney said, directing Mother and me to the table. "Where are Lord Deveraux and Lord Townsend?" he asked, then suddenly catching himself, "Oh, oh, yes. Forgive me, Lady Deveraux. A thousand pardons."

"My husband and Lord Townsend will be along shortly, Lord Blayney. Please, I insist we not wait for them," Mother suggested with a forced smile.

"Oh…OH!" Lord Blayney declared as if he just understood my mother's meaning. "Of course, anything for your family, my dear," he said, clearing his throat before seating me, and then my mother.

That nagging voice inside my head, telling me something was amiss, was no longer quietly talking to me. It had turned into a loud scream that was trying to warn me that all was no longer well with my world.

Leaning over to my mother, I whispered in her ear. "How do you know Lord Blayney?"

"Your grandfather has been trading with Lord Blayney's family for many years. They are well known for their beautiful linens in this region," Mother calmly stated, before turning her attention back to the couple across the table that she knew.

Caleb, who had been visiting with someone in the corner of the hall, came over when he noticed that Aiden wasn't with me. "Where is Aiden?" he asked, taking the chair next to mine.

"My father was waiting at the bottom of the stairs, when we came down tonight," I whispered. "They have been in Lord Blayney's study, ever since. Just between you and me, I'm beginning to get concerned."

"Well this should be interesting," Caleb nervously laughed.

"Why would you say such a thing?" I scolded, startled by Caleb's lack of concern for his best friend. "Clearly you and Aiden underestimate my father's reputation as a dangerous man."

"I told him he was making a mistake," Caleb chided, shaking his head like a know it all. "But no, let's not listen to the voice of caution," he lamented.

"What are you talking about?" I asked, unsure I understood his meaning.

"When he decided to tell the doctor that you and he were involved, I told him it would come back to bite him in the butt, and it has," Caleb said smugly.

"I'm confused," I blurted out, trying to understand what he was implying.

"So was I, but I figured he knew what he was doing," he replied, keeping an eye on the door, "since Aiden always has a contingency plan for everything."

"I thought he didn't have a choice in the matter. In fact, Aiden explained that his hands were tied and he had to come up with that ridiculous story about us being involved, so that we could move about the countryside unencumbered," I argued, suddenly feeling duped. Then with a small derisive snort, "Well, all I can say is I hope Aiden has a contingency plan for my father, because he is going to need it," I continued, as anger began to seep up from someplace deep inside of me.

Caleb made a derisive sound then chuckled. "Oh, I highly doubt that anyone could have a contingency plan for your father," Caleb announced, jerking his head in the direction of the door. "But judging by the look on Aiden's face, we are about to find out what happened," he finished then stood to wait for Aiden to make his way over to us.

Turning slightly in my chair, I watched as Aiden and my father entered the room. Aiden made a beeline directly to Caleb and me with a somber look upon his face.

While my father displayed a smile from ear to ear as if he had just closed a lucrative trade agreement, Aiden walked up to the chair Caleb now stood in front of and gave him a strange look. Caleb simply moved over one chair and sat down silently. Then pulling out his chair, Aiden took his seat, and stared straight ahead.

I was about to ask him what had happened, when Mother leaned over close to me and whispered in my ear. "Bella, whatever happens tonight, just know your father loves you very much, and that everything will work out for the best in the end. Oh, and don't be angry with him," she finished. Immediately, I knew that I was not going to like what was about to happen.

"Why does that phrase sound so familiar to me, Mother? That's right, I've heard this one before, just before I was packed up and sent away to boarding school," I stated drolly.

Leaning over to my other side now, I pulled on Aiden's sleeve. "What in the world happened in there?" I questioned, trying to get his attention. But it was like talking to a brick wall.

Father took the chair on the other side of Mother, but instead of sitting down, he stood and cleared his throat, to get everyone's attention. The room fell silent as my father began to speak. The clear, crisp, pitch of his tone rang out in that enormous dining hall.

"Ladies and gentlemen, I would like to thank our hosts, Lord and Lady Blayney, The Eleventh Earl of Castle Blayney, for putting together this lovely dinner party this evening. Most of you have no idea why you were called here tonight, so I would like to enlighten you. You have been called together this evening for a very special surprise. We will be celebrating the wedding nuptials of my daughter, Lady Isabella Deveraux, to Lord Townsend the Viscount of Buckinghamshire."

I heard my father talking just as everything in my head went silent. Just to be clear, I could see mouths moving, to congratulate Aiden and me, but there was a strange ringing in my ears, that prevented me from understanding what everyone was saying. Aiden covered my hand with his and gave it a squeeze as I sat in my seat, dazed and confused. Disbelief clouded my thoughts, as everything seemed to slow down. And when the ringing ended, I could not believe the words I was hearing. How could this be? The entire matter was absurd.

Before I knew what was happening, Aiden had placed a glass in my hand and everyone was clinking their glasses together over our happy news. Aiden knocked his glass of wine to mine and downed the entire contents of it in one swallow. I was speechless and merely stared at him when he reached over and tipped my glass up to my lips and glared at me until I sipped the contents.

The next thing I remember, Aiden was pulling me from my chair and guiding me down the hallway, out the door, and toward a new room — the castle's chapel.

How convenient, the castle has its own chapel. And then it hit me, as we began to walk down the aisle to the priest who just happened to be waiting for us at the altar. Halfway down the aisle I tried to pull away from Aiden, but he held tightly to my arm and didn't stop his forward march.

I looked at his stoic profile and noticed that his normally good humored smile was gone. His eyes did not crinkle at the corners and his lips did not turn up at the ends. This was no joke. We were really doing this. We were getting married, right now.

"Aiden turn loose of my arm, this is a mistake," I whispered quietly, under my breath.

"No, my dear, it's either this or your father and I will have a proper duel, out on the front lawn, in front of all these witnesses. The choice is completely yours of course," Aiden said flatly. "I just thought this would make for better dinner conversation than grown men shooting at one another," he finished saying, just as we reached the altar.

I stared at him in disbelief. *Someone pinch me, because I think I am having a very bad dream*, I thought to myself.

"You might want to answer yes or I do, to the following question, if you wish for us both to get a good night's sleep tonight," Aiden suggested.

Clearly understanding the inference, I obediently did as I was told. I told myself that we would sort this all out later, and of course, everyone would have a good laugh over the circumstances.

But deep down inside, I couldn't fight the sinking feeling that continued to grow. It was like stepping into quicksand and then squirming about to free yourself, only to discover that you had just made everything worse.

22

More Than Misdirection

HE ENTIRE CEREMONY ONLY TOOK a few minutes before I heard the priest pronounce us husband and wife. Aiden stared into my eyes for what felt like an eternity before leaning down to kiss my lips. When we turned to face family, friends, and people wishing us well, I felt sick. Forcing a smile to my lips, the entire situation felt surreal.

How did Lord Blayney entice a group of people out to his castle on such short notice? More specifically, how did he dupe everyone into witnessing the spectacle, orchestrated entirely by my father, in a matter of just a few hours?

My head was still spinning and it felt light and airy, like it had been stuffed with pillow batting. Oh, not the kind of lightness one feels when they are giddy with delight over such an event, but in the sense that everything was moving far too fast for me. Lord Blayney had arranged for the evening to be topped off with a champagne dinner, followed by entertainment and dancing. When the evening was finished, Aiden and I stood before all the guests, as he graciously thanked everyone for coming on such short notice to share in our happy nuptials.

I felt like such a fraud, smiling like a baboon in a cage, when all I really wanted to do, was explain to everyone that there had been a terrible mistake, we didn't truly love one another, and the entire matter was a mistake.

When the guests had all left, there remained Lord and Lady Blayney, Aiden's brother Ian, Caleb, and my parents. I could feel the tears building at the back of my eyes, so I kept breathing in and out, to keep them at bay. Aiden noticed my sudden distress and placed his arm around me possessively as he gave me a reassuring squeeze.

Aiden politely thanked the Blayney's for their generosity, kissed my mother on the cheek, and gave a curt incline of his head to my father. Saying a polite goodnight to his brother and Caleb and headed toward the door and waited for me to join him.

I followed Aiden's example like a puppet and graciously thanked the Blayney's for the use of their home, or rather their castle. I said my goodnights to Caleb and Ian, kissed my mother on both cheeks, and then stood in front of my father for a full minute before deciding exactly what I wanted to say to him. "I am fairly certain, that you are expecting me to thank you, for intervening on my behalf."

"Well, it would be the proper response." Father conceded, in a teasing tone.

I scoffed slightly and blessed my father with a half smile that didn't quite reach my eyes. "If you would allow me to finish, and not interrupt me again, I was about to say that none shall be forthcoming. And furthermore, someday I intend to repay you in kind, for all that you have done here this day." Our eyes clashed, and I saw confusion and then the pain I had just inflicted. Pain inflicted by my words, as they hit their mark. Then finally recognition, as my words true meaning sank in.

I felt neither sorrow nor regret for my hurtful words at that moment, but instead satisfaction, and vindication for the years of being on the outside of my family. The walking wounded, as some might call me. Apparently, I was still a little bitter over the pain I felt he'd caused Charlie and me. Taking Aiden's arm, we walked from the room, a united front, as we ascended the staircase together.

"Now what do we do?" I asked the moment the door was closed behind us.

"What do you mean? We are married in the eyes of God, and everyone who was gracious enough to attend," Aiden said sardonically.

"So how do we undo this? We should have just gone to my father in the first place and avoided all of this," I reasoned, watching him pace back and forth in front of me, deep in thought.

"I believe that bridge has been burned all to hell, my dear," Aiden off handedly, pointed out. I could see the wheels turning in his head, as he continued to pace back and forth. He didn't even bother to look up when he answered me, but instead, seemed to be talking to himself.

Maria heard us come in and entered the room, as if on cue. "Would you like me to turn down your bed, Miss?" she asked, not yet sure how to react to all that had transpired over the last few hours.

"Not just yet, Maria, we need a minute to talk," Aiden absently answered, still pacing the floor in front of the window, with a faraway look in his eyes. Maria stood in the middle of the room gawking at him, as if he'd suddenly sprouted two heads and a tail.

"I will be fine, Maria. Please, go on to bed. The hour is late, and I can turn down my own bed, just this once," I said, reassuring her with a half smile.

Maria hesitated at first, then covered a yawn, and did as I asked.

"Well?" I said impatiently.

"Well what?" Aiden replied, sounding irritated that I had interrupted his chain of thought.

"Why didn't you just tell my father to sod off?" I asked, stepping in front of Aiden's path, causing him to stop short.

"Because your father is not the sort of man one tells to sod off," Aiden replied, as if this was common knowledge to everyone who breathed air.

"I tried to tell you that, but you are the man with the plan, so now what?" I asked impatiently, plucking pins from my hair. My head was splitting, and the weight of all that hair piled on top was making it worse.

"We have a mission to complete," Aiden stated stoically, sidestepping me to take a seat on the settee, as if our getting married was just part of the master plan all along. "We will liberate your brother and his friend and figure out the true identity of this mysterious man who leads the Hearts of Oak gang," Aiden said, looking at me intently. "The rest will have to sort itself out later."

"I still don't know what that means. You and I will still be married for better or worse," I pointed out. "So how is this going to work itself out?" I questioned, as I placed the pins on the table in front of me and shook my head to free my hair, letting it cascade down my back.

Aiden gave an appreciative stare then cleared his throat, "You don't believe in tip toeing around anything, do you?" Aiden patted the seat next to him.

I rolled my eyes, and then conceded the matter. Not wishing to argue any further, I took the seat next to him.

"Your father was looking for a fight. I just chose not to give him one. A duel would have meant that one of us would have ended up being maimed or killed and that would have put a real damper on the evening, don't you think? Especially for me, if I had been the unfortunate bloke to be injured or killed. Your father is a formidable man and prone to speaking his mind, as well," Aiden responded, making a noise that sounded like admiration for the man. Aiden smiled, remembering their meeting. "So I made a judgment call," he said, sounding so matter-of-fact.

I was flabbergasted. "My father challenged you to a duel?"

"Your father didn't do anything that I wouldn't have done, if the shoe were on the other foot and you were my daughter," Aiden added, putting his hand over mine.

"But I'm not your daughter, and you could have told him the truth. He would have listened. I know he would have," I said, feeling more than mildly frustrated. "Now we are married, and that is that."

"Married less than a day, and already you are complaining," Aiden teased, attempting to lighten the mood.

"How can you joke about this?" I scolded, "The entire situation is unacceptable."

"I'm not really such a bad husband, am I?" Aiden's easy going ways were beginning to wear on my last nerve. "Look at me, Isabella. I give you my word, when this mission is over, I will happily give you an annulment, no questions asked. I swear it," Aiden promised, placing his hand over his heart.

"How can you be so undaunted by the entire matter? Wait, is this a trick?" I asked, suspiciously.

"Cross my heart," he assured me, looking sincere.

"Fine, I will give you the benefit of the doubt, and take you at your word," I said, somewhat comforted, but still feeling ill at ease about the entire ruse. "Well, I don't know about you, but I am exhausted and need some sleep," I yawned.

Standing up, I headed for my room when I realized, I would have to sleep in my gown, unless I asked Aiden for his help. The buttons were in the back, too high for me to reach. Turning around, I must have had a strange look on my face, as I stood there trying to decide whether to ask him for help.

"What is it?" Aiden finally asked, lifting an eyebrow.

"Never mind, I will be fine," I replied, rather unconvincingly.

"Honestly, what do you need?" He asked again.

"Well, it's just that I… I sent Maria to bed and… well, never mind, it would be inappropriate," I stammered. Turning back around, I took another step to leave, intending to put space between us.

"I would be happy to assist you with your problem." A devilish grin slowly spread across Aiden's face, followed by a lecherous laugh as he jumped up, rubbing his hands together. "After all, I've already seen you in a state of undress."

"A real gentleman would never have brought that up," I retorted.

"Then it is a good thing that I am no gentleman," Aiden shot back.

"I can just sleep in my gown. I truly will be fine," I suggested, suddenly feeling shy as I backed away from him.

"Don't be ridiculous. I was just kidding. I have plenty of experience undressing a lady. Where I lack skill is getting them back into those complicated contraptions you call a corset," Aiden informed me, as he stood before me now with his hands on his hips. "You do realize that you will need to turn around if you wish for me to unfasten things." I stood staring up at him a moment longer, trying to determine how badly I wanted out of my corset.

Aiden gave me a half smile as if he could read my every thought. He lifted just one eyebrow again, while moving his hand in a circular motion in the air, over my head. The way he looked at me, with that slow but distinctive smile letting me know he knew what I was thinking, was maddening. As if he truly could read my mind. What a ridiculous thought. Oh how he liked to play the rogue with me. I was beginning to think the man was too good looking for his own good.

Not relishing the idea of sleeping in a tight gown and corset, I turned around and presented my back to him, against my better judgment. Slowly I moved my hair to one side, and held my breath, while Aiden's large hands began to work at the delicate buttons of my gown, excruciatingly slow and methodical, they maneuvered their way along my spine, one vertebra at a time, almost like a caress. I could feel the heat of them through the delicate layers of fabric. Goose bumps formed down one side of my body and up the other, with each button that he unfastened. Tiny hairs on the back of my neck stood on end and I could tell Aiden's eyes were staring at me, trying to gauge my reaction. I chanced a peak at him over my shoulder and our eyes locked. I found myself once again holding my breath. A flush of heat spread through me like a wildfire, starting from my core and spreading outward. How I wished I could escape those eyes, scrutinizing and analyzing my every reaction. I wanted to turn around, throw myself into his arms and kiss his pliant lips again. Abandoning all decency, and let myself go, just long enough to experience what it would be like to lay in his arms for one night.

After he unbuttoned the gown to my hips, he pushed the fabric from my shoulders. "What do you think you are doing?" I scolded, shocked by his boldness.

Scarcely able to breath, for fear he had reached into my soul and read every wonton thought I'd ever had, I turned around to face him. Frantically, I grasped for fabric to cover myself, only to discover that he had trapped me between himself and the wall.

"Calm down, Isabella, I only wish to reach the ends of your corset ties. The fabric of your gown was impeding me," he explained rationally.

"Perhaps sleeping in my corset won't be so bad," I suggested in a disapproving tone that was barely more than a whisper. Pushing away from him, I turned to leave again, when he grabbed my arm.

"Now that's just crazy, let me finish undoing you," he reasoned.

Stopping in the doorway of my room, I turned to face him, blocking the entrance. "I have been quite undone enough by you for one evening, Lord Townsend. Thank you and goodnight," I said, putting my hand on his chest to keep him from advancing any further.

"Forgive me, Lady Townsend, I feel terrible for the misunderstanding," Aiden responded in a tone that sounded slightly repentant. After staring into my eyes for a full minute, Aiden let out a sound of frustration as he raked his fingers through his hair. Deciding to approach the problem in a different way, his voice took on a more soothing tone, "We can't have you bound up all night by such a restrictive contraption. Why, I have heard of corsets referred to by some as medieval torture devices," Aiden maneuvered around me, to step through the doorway, looking for a second chance. "I assure you, that I would lose sleep if I had that on my conscious all night. Please, turn around so I may finish."

"Maria did truss me up rather tightly this evening, and the truth is, I can barely feel my ribs any longer," I confessed, looking for any sign of insincerity on his part. Yet, when I looked into his face, all I saw was plaintive eyes and a charming smile.

Cautiously, I turned back around and presented my back to him once again. Moving my hair to the side, I slipped the gown from my shoulders, giving him just enough room to reach the ties.

"Do you need me to stand in the light so you can find the ends?" I asked, cognizant of the fact I was now standing in an area of the doorway void of any real light.

"No, I can feel for the ends, if you promise not to get hysterical and run off again," Aiden teased.

"I did not get hysterical. In fact, I have never been hysterical in my life," I assured him, turning slightly to argue the point further, only to be pushed back into position. Glancing over my shoulder, I could see his eyes studying me instead of looking for the ends of the corset ties.

"That's good to know," he said, smiling seductively once again as his hands seemed to be searching everywhere except the place they should have been searching if he wanted to find the end of my corset ties.

"I am not entirely certain that you have ever truly helped a woman out of her corset before." Then giving a slight gasp of surprise, "And I can assure you, that your left hand is nowhere near the vicinity it should be," suspicion lacing my tone, as I tried to turn back around.

"Now I will admit, it has been a while, but I am sure that I will eventually find the ends of your ties."

"Is that before or after you have felt your way around my entire body?" I said drolly.

"Are you giving me a choice here?" he asked in a tone that was both teasing and playful.

Oh, he is a sly Devil, to be sure. If he only knew what that smile of his does to me. He is ruggedly handsome and seductive, with those blue eyes that sparkle like jewels when he is pleased. He also has a dark side that could make one run for cover. I am certain I would truly be in deep water if he ever figured me out.

"Voila!" Aiden announced proudly, pulling at the ties, and loosening the laces.

Taking a deep breath for the first time that night, I sighed out of gratitude, to finally be free of the confining restraint of my medieval contraption.

Turning to face him, I pulled the fabric up onto my shoulders again and cautiously smiled, not wishing to encourage Aiden further. His nearness affected me in a disturbing way that confused me, but I could never let him know that. "My hero," I pronounced.

"And my reward would be...?" he asked, with a grin, leaving the question wide opened.

"My undying gratitude," I fired back, tilting my head to one side, blessing him with an innocent smile, as I continued to pull the material of my gown about me like a protective shield.

"Well then, in that case, you wouldn't deny me a goodnight kiss, would you?" Aiden crossed his arms and leaned his back against the door jamb. Slowly he brought his right leg over his left, crossing them at the ankle. For all intent and purposes, Aiden appeared to be completely relaxed, but there was an underlying tension just below the surface.

"And a harmless kiss will be reward enough?" I questioned, with a speculative lift of my eyebrow. Aiden chuckled, reaching out and drawing me towards him so quickly I didn't have time to react. Our bodies were so close, that not even a hair's breadth stood between us.

"I never said anything about a harmless kiss, my Lady."

The phrase '*Too late, said the spider to the fly,*' popped into my head, as Aiden's soul seducing smile disappeared, replaced instead by a certain enticing allure that drew me even deeper into his web.

My half hearted attempts to back away were useless, and every time I struggled, his muscular arms tightened about my waist like a metal vise.

His sensuous lips captured mine as his fingers wrapped around the back of my neck, drawing me even closer. Unable to fight back, for fear of dropping my loosened gown and corset, I gave up struggling against his hold, and found myself melting into him instead. A satisfied sigh echoed in my ears, as it escaped from my throat. I could hardly believe that I had made that noise.

His mouth left mine, only to travel downward reigning passionate kisses along my sensitive collarbone and neck. His fingers entangled through my hair, lifting it away from my neck, and I could hear myself moan from the pleasurable sensations he was stirring in me. Making his way to my ear, he nibbled on my earlobe, sending tiny shivers of delight up and down my spine, as another sigh of satisfaction and desire bubbled up from deep in my throat.

My sighs seemingly sent Aiden into a frenzy as his hands pushed the gown from my shoulders, to pool in a soft puddle of material at my feet, along with my corset. Shirking out of his coat, Aiden dropped it to the floor next to my gown.

I reached up, frantically unknotting his cravat, and pulled the silky fabric from his neck. My nervous fingers shook as I worked to unfasten the buttons of his vest, while Aiden's nimble fingers untied several of my petticoats and watched them fall down my arms one by one until he came to the last one.

"Aha!" Aiden laughed, with the joy of a child, who finally had the gift from under the Christmas tree that he had been eyeing for weeks and now has in his hands.

Shoving the vest off his shoulders and down his arms, I gave a small triumphant cry of victory myself. "Voila."

His hand gently cupped my chin, lifting it up as he stared into my eyes, for what felt like an eternity, before his lips captured mine again. I could feel his desire and need as he pulled me close to him. Aiden's lips were so soft and supple it was as if our lips were made specifically to fit the other's. My mind ceased to function, and all I could think about was the passion and emotion he elicited in me.

Aiden's heart pounded hard beneath my hands that rested upon his hardened chest. I feared it might pound through his ribs, and fall into my waiting hands. He groaned deep in his throat, pulling away slightly, still resting his forehead against mine. Our noses were so close they nearly touched. "Before we go any further, I must ask you a question," Aiden whispered.

Pulling back from him, so that I could see his face, the air from my lungs caught in my throat. "What is wrong?" I whispereds, concerned by the serious look I saw on his face.

"I need you to tell me if you wish me to continue." The pain of restraining himself was evident in his tone. "Because I must warn you, that there is a point when no man can stop, and I am quickly approaching that line. I just need to know that you want me as I want you."

Suddenly fear and reality gripped me by the throat. I realized that I didn't know what came next, or even if I wanted him to continue.

If I were to say yes, to him, then what? Did an affirmation mean that I was giving up my right to choose what happened next? Did he even love me? He had never said anything of the sort. My mind was suddenly bogged down with questions flying at me so fast I couldn't think.

Taking two steps back, I pushed against Aiden's chest and out of his warm, seductive embrace. Crossing my arms over my chest, I attempted to cover my near nakedness, as my mind just kept repeating the same words over and over again.

What have I nearly done? This was a mistake, I thought, as I took another step away from him and shook my head, no.

I could never forget the look on his face as he just stood there, watching me retreat. He didn't move or try to stop me, and he never said a word, as I slowly closed the door.

23

I Think I Have Buyer's Remorse

I TOSSED AND TURNED ALL NIGHT, as images of a handsome rogue flitted in and out of my concisions mind. Aiden haunted my dreams.

And then, sometime in the predawn hours, my dreams morphed and changed, into something entirely different. The tone and feeling seemed to shift in an instant, taking me someplace darker and forbidden. Suddenly barns, with stalls and the smell of dairy cows permeated the air. I tried to make sense of the sudden change, and noticed the vividness had changed as well. My mind was grasping the changes and I was beginning to make mental notes when Maria opened the door and barged in, chastising me as she entered.

"What in the world happened here last night? There are petticoats and pieces of clothing strewn from here to there." Her voice sounded loud, and broke into my dream state, pulling me back to the present.

Poking at the blankets with her hand, I realized Maria was checking for the presence of an unwanted male interloper. Not able to see well, she turned and walked in the direction of the windows.

Groggy from lack of sleep, and in a foul mood to boot, I lifted my head slightly, in hopes of discovering the cause of my present discomfort. Shoving stray strands of hair out of my face, I glared at Maria through fingers hastily thrown up to shield my eyes from the sudden harsh light filtering in through the open curtains. "Are you completely void of consideration and grace, or is it just for my benefit that you act like a fish monger's wife?" I growled. Sitting straight up in bed, I blindly threw my pillow at Maria. Of course, I missed her completely, as the hapless pillow fell harmlessly at her feet.

She stopped long enough to retrieve the pillow, and then cautiously approached the bed with her arms full of various articles of garments, fastidiously picked up, in hopes of erasing all signs of what she could only imagine, went on in her absence.

"Nothing happened last night, Maria," I stated dryly. "So shut those bloody drapes and leave me be," I groused at her through my clenched teeth. "I'm warning you right now, Maria, I am in no mood for your attitude today.

"That isn't exactly true, Maria," Aiden called out, from across the room.

Suddenly I felt wide awake, and both Maria and I swung our heads around to see Aiden standing across the room, propped against the doorjamb, as if he never left last night. He looked refreshed, and well rested. A part of me was disappointed that there was no evidence of distress from a night of tossing and turning after our encounter. Aiden's face was freshly shaven and his hair was neatly combed, as he stood, casual as could be, smiling at me. It was infuriating! He stood in his crisp white linen shirt and black trousers that hugged his hips so tightly that even the Holy Mother herself would have blushed. His black leather boots that came just to his knees were freshly polished, that I marveled at their shine, nearly went blind from the glare.

That scoundrel! I thought to myself.

"Lady Townsend needed assistance with her gown last night, and I was only too happy to help her with her buttons and sundries," Aiden said, strolling into my room with a shameless grin on his face. He was grinning from ear to ear, as if he were the cat that had just devoured the canary, and I was to be his next victim.

"What in the world are you about, Lord Townsend?" I cautiously asked, still feeling on edge.

"Maria, I think, Lady Townsend is in need of a pot of your strongest tea and perhaps some toast with eggs," he suggested with a serious smile. "If it wouldn't be too much trouble," Aiden added, while looking directly into Maria's eyes. It was a thinly veiled attempted to get rid of her for a few minutes, but I didn't yet understand why. "I'm sure after last night your mistress is in need of some nourishment," he added with a wicked grin and a wink. "That could account for the foul temperament you are currently witness to."

Walking over to the other side of the bed, Aiden shamelessly plopped himself down and propped his booted feet up. Then placing his hands behind his head, he casually crossed his legs, giving Maria a questioning glare. "Run along, Maria, you don't want to keep Lady Townsend waiting." Maria gave a disgusted harrumph, then turned and rushed from the room, with her arms still full of unmentionables.

"Alright, what is this big show of ownership about, Lord Townsend?" I asked dryly.

Rolling over to face me, Aiden propped his head up on his hand. "If we are to appear to everyone, including Maria, to be husband and wife, might I suggest that you get into character." He added with an heir of frustration, "And perhaps you could try and remember to use my Christian name, even in private. That way you will be less likely to slip up in public," he scolded. "Oh and before I forget, you need to be ready in an hour," Aiden added, just before he leaned over, placing a kiss on my cheek. I gave him a questioning look, before he rolled off the edge of the bed.

"What am I doing in an hour?" I quietly asked, still startled by the kiss.

"Lord Blayney's personal jeweler will be here with a selection of rings, so that you, Lady Townsend, can be properly adorned with a ring befitting your lofty status," Aiden informed me with the same flamboyance and flare, that mimicked Lord Blayney's perfectly.

"Oh," I said looking down at my empty finger. We had borrowed rings for the ceremony and then returned them once the ceremony was over. It had not occurred to me that we would be taking the charade to the next level.

"Oh. Oh! That is all you have to say?" Aiden said very animated. "Most women would be jumping out of bed and running to get dressed, if they knew they would be picking out a ring."

"I am not most women, Aiden. I thought we had already established that," I stated flatly, feeling slightly put out that he would pile me in with the general population of women.

"No, apparently, you are not," he responded. Then softening his tone, he came around the bed, and sat down on the edge next to me. Taking my hands in his, he finally asked, after studying me for a moment. "What is wrong, Isabella?"

"It's just that a ring is such an expense, and in the end, the extra expense is for not. I just find it frivolous and silly, that's all," I admitted, pragmatically, forcing myself to feel nothing as Aiden sat so close to me.

"You can't think of it that way. Besides we don't know who is watching us or if there are spies among the staff here," Aiden stood up abruptly and took several steps toward the window. He continued to talk with his back to me, "I can only pray that we still have the element of surprise on our side," he said, turning to face me now. "Tell me that you still have the stomach for all of this, Isabella."

Lifting my chin an inch, I took a deep breath. "We have come this far," I answered, stiffening my spine with resolution. "I am willing to do whatever it takes, no matter what."

"That's the spirit," he added with enthusiasm. "And whatever you do, it is imperative that even Marie believes that this is real. You know how maids and servants like to talk. We don't need the wrong thing said at the wrong time," Aiden warned. "Loose lips sink ships."

Looking up at him, I responded with a tone of exasperation, "I understand."

Maria announced herself before entering the room, as she carried in the tray of food, "I have a nice hot pot of freshly brewed tea, and eggs just the way you like them, Lady Isabella."

"Lady Townsend," Aiden corrected, still looking directly into my eyes for a few seconds longer. Then Aiden turned his head to look at Maria. "I guess that would be my cue to leave you ladies," he announced, giving me a wink as he leaned down to kiss me passionately on the lips, in front of Maria. I must confess, I could not be sure just how much of that passionate kiss was for show and how much of it was for his own pleasure.

Maria watched him leave the room before she spoke. "That one is very cheeky. So, what's he about, my Lady?" she asked suspiciously.

"What do you mean, Maria?" I questioned, climbing out of bed to look over the tray of food she brought me. But mostly, I needed a distraction from my own, clouded emotions.

"Well, one moment you're supposed to be involved, but you're really not and the next minute he's acting like the king of the castle. That's what I mean," Maria said pointedly, giving me the eye.

"It seems that I find myself entangled and married, Maria. Lord Townsend is my husband, for better or worse," I declared, while dipping my toast into the soft center of my egg yolk. "Now help me figure out the proper outfit to wear for picking out my new wedding band," I said adamantly, refusing to make direct eye contact with her, as I popped the crust into my mouth and moved toward the wardrobe cabinet.

It took longer than an hour to make myself presentable, so I was rushing out of my bedroom when I ran smack dab into Aiden. He caught me by both arms, preventing me from falling backwards, as I bounced off his solid chest and cried out in surprise.

"No need to rush. The jeweler has only just arrived," Aiden said, holding me out at arm's length, making sure I wasn't hurt.

"I was running late and thought everyone would be waiting on me," I explained breathlessly.

Aiden rubbed his thumb over the red spot forming on my cheek where I had just run headlong into his chest. "Let them wait. You've hurt your cheek."

"I've done worse," I said softly, suddenly feeling awkward, as I looked up at him through my lashes.

"Still, I am sorry. I was just coming to see if you would be much longer," Aiden explained, tipping my chin up to meet his eyes. "But we really must do something about that look."

"Is this not a proper dress?" I cried, suddenly looking down at my gown. I had chosen a moss green, wool dress, and Maria had fashioned my hair on top of my head, in a sophisticated up do, befitting my new status.

"It's not the dress, my dear, it's the look in your eyes that is all wrong," he muttered, bringing his mouth down upon mine. Our lips softly touched, gradually becoming more demanding as Aiden's arms tightened about my waist and back as he pulled me against his solid form. Half heartedly pushing against his chest at first, I soon realized that my attempts to protest were futile.

Aiden smelled of lavender soap and leather saddle polish. The combination assaulted my senses and drove me to distraction. I entwined one hand through his glorious silken hair and the other hand rested on his chest. I couldn't help but give a slight groan of disappointment when he slowly pulled away. Looking up at him, I sighed and reached up to touch my swollen lips.

"Now that is the look you should always wear upon your face," Aiden smugly said, with a satisfied smile. "Let's go pick out our rings. No one will notice the red splotch on one cheek because they both match now," he teased.

"Oh, you!" I exclaimed, as Aiden pulled me toward the stairs. "You are a terrible rascal, but I am sure I would not be the first person to tell you that," I proclaimed as we descended the staircase arm in arm.

"I believe my mother has mentioned it once or twice," Aiden quipped, as he threw his head back and laughed.

And that was the moment it happened. My heart swelled and skipped a beat all at the same time, and I knew in that instant that I was in love with Aiden Larkin Townsend, the Viscount of Buckinghamshire. I swallowed hard to keep the emotions down, as they threatened to overwhelm me.

What am I to do now? To Aiden this was merely a job, a mission that had to be completed before he moved on to the next job. Oh, what had I done?

"What happened to that look?" he asked, as a perplexed look furrowed his brows.

"What?" I said, snapping out of my morbid thoughts. "It's still here, see," I declared, looking up at him, and forcing a smile to my lips. "No one will ever know." Aiden eyed me suspiciously and then continued down the stairs.

"Here they are, the happy couple," Lord Blayney proclaimed, walking out of the sunroom.

"Yes, here we are," I said. "I am terribly sorry to keep you waiting."

"Think nothing of it, my dear. It was no inconvenience at all. May I say, you are looking radiant today, don't you agree Lord Townsend?"

"Without a doubt, my good friend, without a doubt."

Oh, he's good, I thought to myself. *He truly knows how to play the game well.*

Lord Blayney continued to play the consummate host. "Please come along, you two lovebirds, and let us get you fitted with a set of lovely rings."

His enthusiasm made me feel even more uncomfortable about the situation, and I looked up at Aiden when he squeezed my hand. Pulling me along behind him, Aiden guided me into the room.

The jeweler was a small man, with pointy, sharp features that reminded me of a bird. His hair was combed back with an oily substance that held it in place. His spectacles were worn half way down the bridge of his nose. This allowed him to look at people over the rim of his glasses, without removing them while examining the stones at the same time. His clothes were of high quality, and every piece had been hand tailored to fit him to a tee.

"Lady Townsend, I have already met your husband, so allow me to introduce myself; I am Thackeray Hamilton, of The Hamilton Jewelers. It's a pleasure to make your acquaintance," Mr. Hamilton said with a curt bow.

"I assure you, Mr. Hamilton, the pleasure is all mine," I smiled warmly, trying hard not to laugh at his overly professional and sterile gestures.

"If you will allow me, Lady Townsend, I just want to look at your hands before we begin," Mr. Hamilton requested, putting his hand out, as he waited patiently for me to comply.

"But of course, Sir," I chuckled, placing my left hand in his outstretched one.

"No, my dear, I need both hands. An artist wouldn't paint someone's portrait if he could only see half the person."

"But of course, Mr. Hamilton, a thousand pardons."

"Long tapered fingers, slender wrists, your hands are very lovely, my lady," he mused almost to himself, before curtly nodding and patting the back of my hands. Walking over to the large satchel he had brought with him, he began to methodically rummage through the drawers. The jewelry case stood approximately two feet high and one foot wide, and was guarded by two very large men, at least two and a half times the size of Mr. Hamilton.

The diminutive jeweler opened a drawer and flipped back the satin cover as he studied the jewels lying before him. Then shaking his head, he closed the drawer again and opened the next drawer down. He repeated flipping back each satin cover. Finally satisfied that he had the right drawer this time, Mr. Hamilton, pulled the entire shelf from the box, and presented it to us.

"Shall we?" Aiden suggested, with a gesturing of his hand, pointing at the couch.

"Of course," I said, forcing another smile to my lips.

I examined the contents of the velvet lined drawer, picked up a piece, and then tried it on. I held my hand out in front of me, and then handed the piece back again. Nothing seemed quite right.

"What else do you have, Mr. Hamilton?" Aiden asked, while looking over the contents before him on the tray. "All of your pieces are quite lovely, of course, but nothing seems to be…well, spectacular."

"Aiden, these are fine," I assured, looking up at him, and then over at Mr. Hamilton, hoping he was not offended by Aiden's comment.

"But darling," Aiden began with a solicitous smile and a wink, before turning to Mr. Hamilton. "I am certain that Mr. Hamilton has been chomping at the bit to parade his most spectacular pieces before us. Perhaps he is unsure of my commitment to the matter. Wouldn't you at least like to see them?" Aiden asked, as he presented Mr. Hamilton with a most gracious smile.

Thackeray Hamilton suddenly lit up, as if someone had set off firecrackers under his seat. He was instantly animated, and very excited to finally be able show off his best pieces, the ones he kept in reserve for only the best clientele. He raised both eyebrows in excitement, and plucked the ring from my hand, which he immediately placed back on the tray. Quickly walking back to the case, he slid the entire tray back into place without even covering the jewels with the satin cloth. Almost simultaneously, he reached for the drawer at the very bottom of the case and, with an expectant look in our direction Mr. Hamilton pulled the tray out and ceremoniously carried it to where we sat.

"This tray contains the rarest jewels that I keep for only the most discerning clientele, Lord Townsend," Mr. Hamilton reverently said, barely able to contain his enthusiasm. Gently, but with flourish, he pulled back the satin cover as if he were revealing the baby Jesus himself. "As you can see, each piece was hand crafted by only our best jewelers and meticulously set in the finest gold," he added, holding up a beautiful, large emerald cut green stone. It was set upon a quarter inch wide, gold band with six tiny pave' set diamonds, encrusting each side of the stone. Handing the piece to Aiden first for his inspection, Mr. Hamilton barely took a breath as he waited anxiously for Aiden's reaction over the top of his glasses.

"It is beautiful, dare I even say exquisite, Mr. Hamilton. Perhaps you should have led with this piece, and saved us all a lot of time," Aiden declared holding the piece up to the light. "It's perfect," he stated with a half smile before reaching out, capturing my left hand, and slipping the ring upon my finger.

"Aiden, this is far too extravagant for my needs," I said, attempting to remove the ring from my finger.

"It reminds me of your eyes, darling, and I will hear nothing more on the matter, except how much you love it," Aiden insisted, as he placed a hand over mine to prevent any further protests.

I looked up into his face and found only sincerity there. "Please wear the ring for me," Aiden pleaded.

"I was told that the jeweler had arrived," Mother announced, as she entered the room.

"Perhaps once my business is concluded with the lovely couple, you and your husband would like to take a look at the pieces I have brought today. Say for an anniversary or special occasion," Mr. Hamilton inquired, solicitously.

I could see him mentally calculating the money in his head, from the sale he had just made, as well as the sale he foresaw with my parents.

"What do you think, darling?" Mother said turning to my father who had walked in behind her.

Mother crossed the room to sit beside me, as Father took the chair across from us, looking as if his pride was still stinging from the night before. A part of me wanted to forgive him for forcing Aiden and me to marry, and another, more childish part, wanted to make him work for absolution.

"Oh Bella, this is exquisite. Did you pick it out yourself?" Mother asked, examining the ring on my finger. "The way the stones sparkle, and the setting, why, I have never seen anything like it."

"Aiden picked it out. I think it is too extravagant," I stated, pragmatically.

"Nonsense, it's perfect," Aiden declared. "Now, Mr. Hamilton, perhaps you could find me a simple gold band and we can conclude our business," he proclaimed, kissing the palm of my right hand.

"My pleasure, Lord Townsend," Mr. Hamilton, said covering the tray and placing it back in his case. Then counting four trays up from the bottom, he pulled out the drawer and carried it over, placing it in front of Aiden.

"Were you looking for a simple but elegant band, Lord Townsend, or would you prefer something a little more ornate?" Mr. Hamilton inquired.

"I prefer simple, but elegant if you please, Mr. Hamilton," Aiden answered, still looking at me. Then focusing his attention back to the tray, Mr. Hamilton picked up several bands and handed them to Aiden to try on.

Finally, deciding on two different rings he turned to me. "I need your advice, my dear. Which one do you prefer?" Aiden asked, presenting the two gold bands to me.

Taking the rings from him, I examined them both, slipping them on my thumbs, and then holding them up to examine them again. Finally, I held up my right thumb, "This one," I declared removing it from my appendage. I had chosen the quarter inch band with beveled edges and rounded on the inside for comfort when worn. "I think this one looks more like you," I proclaimed. "It won't rub your finger raw when you twist it around, playing with it."

"How do you know I will twist it around?" he asked, taking the ring from me.

"Because most men do when they are not use to wearing one," I said, with a knowing smile.

"Would you do me the honors then?" Aiden requested, placing the other one back on the tray and presenting his hand to me.

"It would be my pleasure," I replied, slipping the ring on the ring finger of his left hand.

I sat there smiling up at him, knowing all the while he was merely playing a roll. As he leaned down to give me a gentle kiss on the lips, he said, "Why don't you run along now, while I finish up with Mr. Hamilton, and I will come find you in a while."

"That is a splendid idea. I have a matter to discuss with Mother anyway," I said, reaching over taking Mother by the hand before turning back to Aiden. "And thank you, darling, the ring is lovely," I said with a bit of sadness, because I knew the truth of our little charade, and just for a moment I wanted to forget that I knew.

"Mr. Hamilton, it was a pleasure, and I wish to thank you for taking time out of your busy day to assist us," I said, flashing him a radiant smile.

"Please, Lady Townsend, it is I who should be thanking you and your generous husband. I hope that Hamilton Jewelers can be of service to you and your husband again in the future," he added with zeal, as he not only shook my hand, but also caressed my fingers with his other hand before turning me loose. "You truly have lovely hands, Lady Townsend. I hope you wear your ring in good health."

Taking hold of Mother's hand again, I beat a hasty path out of the sunroom and down the hall, looking for a quiet room that would provide us privacy.

"You wouldn't happen to know where Lord Blayney's library is?" I asked, opening yet another door in the enormous hallway.

"Across the hall, um, I think it is this room over here," Mother said, opening the door, "Yes, this is it," as a triumphant cry sprang from her lips. "What is it you wish to discuss?" Mother asked, taking my hand and drawing me into the room.

"I don't feel connected to Charlie any longer. I think he is blocking me, or something. And then I had this crazy idea last night when I couldn't sleep," I began.

"You had trouble sleeping last night?" Mother asserted, while giving me that all knowing look that said 'I know what you were doing last night.'

"Mother!" I exclaimed with shock.

"Oh, Bella, your father and I were young once. Sometimes I still feel like we are," she continued, with a dreamy look in her eye.

"Yes, I know all about your youthful enthusiasm, Mother," I exclaimed, with a perturbed look when my childhood suddenly flashed through my mind.

"And what is that supposed to mean?" she asked

"I did the math," I informed her flatly, "And I assure you that Aiden and I are nothing like you and Father."

"Bella, you are far too restrained and serious. It can't be healthy for you," Mother smiled. "Your husband, Lord Townsend, is very handsome. Did you want some advice regarding a man and a woman... and say —?"

"No! No, no, no!" I waved my hands in front of me, "I really don't think I need to hear the rest of that sentence, Mother," I cried suddenly raising my eyebrows. "My love life isn't up for discussion, and I really don't want to discuss yours, for that matter," I hastily said, pacing back and forth in front of the window. "I'm having difficulty connecting with Charlie, that is all," I began. "The only thing I do feel is despair and hopelessness when I close my eyes and think of him. I can't get a clear read on him any longer. I'm scared Mother, I can feel him slipping away from me," I lamented, as a single tear ran down my cheek.

"How can I help?" Mother asked, reaching out to comfort me like she would when I was a little girl and had scraped me knees trying to keep up with Charlie.

"I thought maybe we could try to find Charlie together. Maybe my connection to him would be stronger that way," I said reasonably, looking up at her. "Does that sound crazy?"

"I don't think it's crazy at all, Bella," Mother lovingly said, looking into my eyes as she cradled my face in her hands. "In fact, I was going to suggest the very same thing."

"When I was younger and wanted to find Charlie, I would sit quietly and clear my mind and think of nothing but Charlie. I thought if we could do that together, just maybe..." I began, then let my words trail off.

"Well, it couldn't hurt, and we have to do something. I don't know about you but the waiting is getting to me," Mother cried in frustration.

"I will pull the curtains if you lock the door," I told her, as I made my way towards the window.

"Good idea," Mother agreed, sounding like a coconspirator in a devious plot.

We sat as close together on the couch as we could and held hands. Mother gave a prayer asking for the safe return of Charlie and Ashton, and then we both fell silent. It felt like an eternity as we sat silently together in that library.

Tipping our heads together, I tried to match her breathing. Mother had slowed her breathing down, and I would have sworn she was asleep, but then she squeezed my right hand.

Another ten minutes passed and nothing happened until a sharp splash of color entered my inner-sight so intense I felt blinded by it at first.

Mother squeezed my hand gently and then more color began to come into focus. I could hear voices talking about the governor who was coming for a visit. One of the men put two bowls down in front of Charlie and Ashton. It was as if I were seeing everything from Charlie's point of view. My head began to hurt and I felt hunger pains so intense that even the bowl of porridge sitting before my eyes seemed to me like a feast.

The man, who had set the bowls down in front of Charlie and Ashton, was himself shabbily dressed. He wore an old dirty, dingy, stained shirt and a pair of well worn trousers held up by suspenders and a piece of string to keep the pants from gaping open. His work boots were cracked from abuse and appeared caked with layers of mud and muck.

I suddenly thought to myself, '*What is that awful smell?*'

It smelled as if someone had been walking through animal dung or rolling in it, I couldn't tell which. Either way the smell was making me sick, so I began to breathe through my mouth to keep from heaving my guts up.

Charlie and Ashton appeared to be shackled by their legs to a stall in a barn. Their beds a thin layer of hay, piled on the ground. They had each been given a thin, moth eaten, blanket for protection against the cold.

As Charlie looked around I could see more of the barn's structure. It was a large building with a ladder that led up to a loft for hay storage. I could see an orange tabby cat, hanging around one of the haystacks on the ground, with five kittens pestering her. Three of the kittens were orange like the mother, one was black, and the other was gray, and somehow I knew that the kittens had the most amazing green eyes.

It was also becoming clear to me that the farm was a dairy that produced cheese and butter for the surrounding area and had been owned by an elderly couple who had suddenly retired. The couple's two sons, had become entangled with the Hearts of Oak gang in hopes of bettering their circumstances, now ran the farm. But instead of being happy with their current arrangement, the two brothers had become disillusioned with their new bosses. In fact, the two brothers still worked just as hard as they had been in the past, but now, instead of receiving a large influx of cash that they were promised, they took orders from a total stranger. Someone they'd never met, who always dipped into their pockets for a bigger cut of the money they worked so hard for, day in and day out.

A commotion in the yard, outside the barn caught Charlie's attention, but he couldn't see what it was. Just then, a man dressed completely in black from head to toe, walked into the barn and into Charlie's line of sight. The man was clever and kept his face turned away from the prisoners. He stood in the shadows with a scarf covering his face. A large black hat sat upon his head, casting an even darker shadow to hide his identity. To say the man made my skin crawl would be an understatement. He had this evil, omnipotent vibe about him that also smacked of depraved indifference. I felt an involuntary shiver go through me. *That must be the man they call the Governor. The infamous leader of the Hearts of Oak crew,* I thought to myself.

The man walked up to Charlie and Ashton, stopping a mere fifteen feet from them. He appeared to be examining them for some reason, but never spoke a word or removed the scarf from around his face. He would be impossible to identify, because he didn't have any distinctive marks or missing limbs, and the shadow over his face made it impossible to see his eyes. There was nothing about him that stood out. So how would I ever be able to point him out in a crowd? Perhaps that was the point. Anonymity gave him all the power and freedom to move about without fear of retribution.

After what felt like a long examination of Charlie and Ashton, the man in black walked back to the two men guarding the door. Then, he made his first mistake; he laughed. His laugh was his distinguishing mark. It was filled with mockery and scorn, punctuated with disdain for anything descent. He didn't realize it yet, but I was coming for him.

I was determined to find him and when I did, he would pay for the pain he had caused my family. Revenge is a dish best served cold the saying goes, but I didn't buy it. As far as I was concerned, revenge was a dish best served up anyway I could get it!

24

I'll Have Mine On A Silver Platter, Please

RABBING MOTHER'S HAND, I PROCEEDED to lead her from the library and down the hall in search of Aiden.

"Slow down, Bella, I'm not as young as I use to be," Mother complained, as I dragged her behind me.

"We don't have much time, Mother. Something bad is going to happen. I can feel it and I will never forgive myself if we are too late," I insisted, tracing my steps back to the sunroom, only to find my father and Mr. Hamilton still talking.

"Where did Aiden go, Father?" I cried, coming off sounding rather short with him in my haste.

"Oh, now you deem me worthy to speak to?" I could hear the hurt in his tone, and I supposed he was still stinging from our exchange the day before; but I didn't have time for soothing sore tempers.

"Don't be verbose, Father, this is serious. Do you know where he went or not?" I demanded impatiently.

"He headed up the stairs to find you. What is it? Did something happen?" he called after us when I immediately turned and headed out of the room.

"Mother and I have to find him immediately," I called out while pulling Mother behind me as I ran from the room.

I could hear my father telling Mr. Hamilton that they would conclude their business later, and then he too was following quickly up the stairs after us.

Entering the suite, I called out to Aiden. He rushed from his room, and I began talking the second I saw him, "Aiden you will never believe what has happened. Mother and I were able to connect our abilities somehow. But that isn't the best part. We know where Charlie and Ashton are. Well, let me clarify we can describe where they are," I said excitedly, blathering on without bothering to breath between sentences.

"Why, that is incredible! Where are they?" Aiden asked, as he took three long strides across the room to me.

"You know where Charlie is?" Father exclaimed upon entering the room behind us.

"We can describe it, right, Mother?" I said, turning to her and realizing I had been squeezing her hand tightly. "Oh sorry, I didn't mean to hurt you. I just got so excited."

"That's quite alright, dear," Mother replied, rubbing her hand, attempting to get the circulation flowing again. "They are being held on a farm northeast from here. The place is run by two brothers," she absently stated while wiggling her fingers.

"It's a dairy that makes cheese. They sell their products locally," I interjected.

"Could you be a little more specific?" Aiden asked with some trepidation.

"Should I tell him, or would you like to do the honors, darling?" Mother exclaimed, turning to me with that all knowing smile of hers.

"I think I will give it a go, if you don't mind? But by all means, please feel free to jump in if I leave anything out," I said, nearly singing the words, as my smile mirrored Mother's.

"Of course," she replied.

Closing my eyes to bring everything back into focus, I began. "There is a tree at the entrance of the property that has been struck by lightning. But the tree lives and continues to grow despite the gaping, black hole left in the trunk. You will know the tree instantly because it's just so shocking that a tree that badly damaged continues to grow. The farm is run by two brothers who are rather large men. They feel quite disillusioned by their affiliation with the Hearts of Oak group. In fact, they are regretting their decision to involve themselves with the group altogether. One brother in particular, grumbles a lot about how they do all the work and get none of the rewards of their labors. Oh, and the older brother has a nasty looking scar over his left eye, from a kick he sustained to his face from a cow, when he was ten," I added without taking a breath. Then opening my eyes to look directly at Aiden, I continued, "It seems that something is about to happen. People were a bit shaken up by the sudden and unexpected visit from their mysterious leader."

"Is there anything else?" Aiden asked, astonished with all the details we were able to provide.

"Yes, there is," I replied, looking up at him. "The man we are looking for calls himself the 'Governor'. He likes to cover himself completely in black, from head to toe. I didn't get a look at his face because he was so covered, but he has a distinctive laugh wouldn't you say Mother?"

"It was eerie and decidedly sadistic, but I am fairly certain the man had blue eyes," Mother answered, giving a shiver as she remembered the entire scene in her mind. Father put his hand on Mother's shoulder as she looked lovingly up at him.

"I didn't get a look at his eyes, because the brim of his hat cast such a shadow on his entire face. Just standing next to him in my mind gave me a case of the willies, and I couldn't stand to look any closer. But the sound of his laugh will forever be seared into my brain," I replied, with a shiver of my own.

"Mine too," Mother said, touching my shoulder as I felt another shiver crawl up my spine.

"I will get the men ready to ride," Aiden interjected, heading toward the door.

"My men will come too," Father insisted, calling after him.

"Of course, and I will be grateful for the assistance," Aiden added.

"And I will be coming with you both just as soon as I get changed," I called out while heading toward my bedroom door.

Both men turned on their heels and said simultaneously, "Oh no you are not!

Stopping mid step, I swiftly turned on them both. "Oh yes I am," I countered in a tone that left no room for negotiations. "And neither one of you is going to stop me."

Maria, hearing all the commotion stepped into the room. "Maria, I need a change of clothes. I'm going for a ride today," I called out to her without turning around. Then to make a point, I added, "Incognito! And would you be a dear and get my boots out of the trunk. I will be in momentarily to change," I stated while glaring at Aiden and my father.

"If you value your employment, you will disregard that last order," Father ordered, threatened Maria with a menacing glare.

"Maria does not work for you and let me assure you that I will not be terminating her employment today," I stated emphatically, gesturing to Maria with my head. Then turning my head and making eye contact with her, I silently sent her a message that I would meet her in the other room. I watched Maria beat a hasty path out of the room and far from the immediate line of fire.

The moment Maria left us I was bombarded by Father, Mother and Aiden.

"Isabella, it isn't safe," Aiden argued, trying to reason with me. "I will —"

"Bella, do you really think it is wise to go?" Mother said, cutting him off as she shoved herself in front of him. "I would be heartbroken if something were to happen to you."

"Bella, this is insanity. You could get hurt or worse," Father added, now all three of them vied for my attention.

"The three of you are acting as if I were a little child. Do you truly think I am unaware of the dangers? I have dreamt them. I have felt such terror through my brother's eyes and it has chilled me to the bone,"

I cried out, petitioning my case as tears formed in my eyes, clouding my vision. "I just don't think any of you get it. I have felt my brother's desperation, fears, and pain. It haunts me even when I am awake," I swiped at the tears as they rolled down my face. "So yes, I realize it is dangerous, Lord Townsend," I yelled directly to Aiden's face, before turning to my mother. "And yes, Mother, I do realize the heartbreak I would cause you if something should happen to me. But I cannot be concerned for my own life when it is Charlie's life I truly fear for."

Turning to my father, I gazed into his eyes a full minute before I could get past the lump in my throat to speak. He stood with his arms folded across his chest, looking stoic and unmovable, like a statue. "You have allowed me certain freedoms growing up that you now wish to curb," I boldly proclaimed. "And yes, Father, I do understand the implications involved with me dressing like a man to go along with you. I realize your men and others may deem me unfit or perhaps insane. But don't you think that some people would consider what Mother and I do the very definition of insanity?"

Backing away from the three of them, I continued to speak while wiping away the tears that now rolled freely down my cheeks. "But to be perfectly frank with the lot of you, I don't really care!" I glared defiantly at them now while taking a deep breath that only strengthened my resolve. "My mind is made up and the three of you don't get a say in this, so you can all hang yourselves. I am going, and that is final."

Turning on my heels, I walked toward the bedroom chamber door when I heard my father say, "She gets her stubborn streak from her mother," just before I shut the door to my chamber. "Don't look at me that way, woman, you know it's true," Father boldly stated, when Mother eyed him.

Emotions, raw and volatile boiled up, from somewhere deep inside of me as I mentally prepared myself for the journey. Anger, disgust, as well as fear and apprehension, culminating in my stomach all at once, causing me to double over in pain. I wrapped my arms around my mid section and sat on the edge of the bed for a moment.

My mind was racing. *What will we find when we reached the gang's present hideout? Will they still be there? Will we find Charlie and Ashton still alive?* Worry tugged at my mind. I couldn't breathe, feeling as though I had been punched in the gut.

After a few minutes, I gathered my courage and dressed in black trousers, a white shirt, and a grey vest with black, leather, knee length boots. The black wool jacket was slightly too large for me, but Maria made it work by rolling the sleeves up.

Pulling my hair back, Maria quickly braided it and secured it with a brown leather strap, in hopes of containing my unruly hair.

A black satin scarf was tied about my head, to hide my hair, and was topped off by a wide brimmed hat, meant to further disguise my gender. After handing Maria my new wedding ring, I grabbed the pair of leather gloves sitting on the table and headed for the stables.

Mother was waiting at the bottom of the stairs for me when I came down. "I understand why you must go and I respect that, but are you sure you won't change your mind?" Mother pleaded, taking hold of me by my shoulders to keep me in place long enough to look directly into my eyes.

"No, I won't," I gently said, hoping to soften the blow of my leaving. Then kissing her on both cheeks, I continued, "I'm going to bring Charlie back to you, Mother. I will be fine, I promise."

"I'm sure you will, Bella," Mother said, "But I will be coming as well, to see that you keep that promise."

"What are you talking about, Mother? That is absurd. What if you get hurt?"

"You heard me, I said I will be coming too, and there will be no further discussion to the contrary!" Mother answered, dragging me by the arm toward the stables, with my mouth still hanging open.

"But what did Father have to say about this?" I questioned, giving her a sidelong look.

"He was not happy. You leave your Father to me," Mother advised, giving me a big smile. "I know how to handle him," she confident chuckle.

Finding my horse, I climbed into the saddle without assistance, barely noticing the stiffness in my legs and posterior, as thoughts of Charlie ran through my head. I was determined not to be a hindrance or bother to anyone. Chancing a glance in Aiden's direction, I noticed he was still preparing his horse, as he intently watched every move I made. Lifting my chin a smidge higher, I looked around for my father who was with his own men, giving last minute orders.

Mother led her horse over to him and waited till he noticed her standing there. He finished with his men and hurried to give her a hand up onto her horse.

Mother was very capable of mounting her own horse, but I found her ploy interesting and watched her closely. I was struck by how effortlessly she maneuvered my father. It was as if he were under her spell. His entire countenance changed when he was around her. The scowl was gone and his shoulders seemed to relax as he gazed into Mother's eyes. She smiled at him then leaned over, giving him a kiss to thank him for his help. Perhaps I could learn a thing or two under Mother's tutelage after all.

Caleb rode up beside me. "Aiden is in a foul mood. You wouldn't happen to know the reason for it, would you?" he quipped while raising a questioning eyebrow at the same time.

I forced a pleasant smile. "I can't imagine."

Making a sound deep in his throat to let me know he wasn't buying what I was selling, Caleb tried again. "It wouldn't have anything to do with the fact that you are going with us, would it?"

"Don't be ridiculous, Mr. Daughtery. I have come to believe that Aiden's foul mood is possibly his natural disposition. So how can I be blamed for that?" I reasoned, nodding in Aiden's direction, placing a placid smile on my lips. Caleb made that sound again deep in his throat, before handing me a set of throwing knives and holster. "Aiden said you might know what to do with these."

"Thank you, Mr. Daughtery, these truly might come in handy," I replied, while testing their weight in my hand, before strapping them to my chest and hiding them beneath my vest and jacket.

"I know exactly what to do with these," I said under my breath, as soon as Caleb rode away.

25

An Army is Strengthened, When They Fight as One

ITH FATHER'S TWELVE MEN AND Aiden's fifteen, we had a small army that wouldn't move quietly. In fact, with two such strong leaders heading our expedition, I was concerned that we wouldn't move at all.

My father and Aiden both stepped forward at the same time to address the men gathered together in front of the stables. They eyed one another intently for a moment, before Father raised his eyebrows, and with a grand gesture, nodded his head and swept a hand in front of himself with a bow to Aiden. Aiden did not hesitate to take the lead.

"Since we know the general direction we are heading but not the exact location of this farmhouse we seek, we will be splitting up," Aiden said as he addressed both companies. "There are two roads out of town that head in the northeastern direction. My company will take the road to the left when it forks, and Lord Deveraux and his company will take the road to the right. We will meet up where the two roads converge again," he continued, as he placed his foot into the stirrup and hoisted himself into his saddle.

"If one company comes out on the other side and reaches the second fork in the road without finding the damaged tree, you need to assume that the other group has stumbled upon the hideout, and needs your assistance." Aiden finished by looking directly at my father, before turning his gaze to me. "Are there any questions?" while his blue eyes sliced through me like a knife. "Good. Let's fall out."

Aiden turned his horse toward the road and rode out a bit before stopping to wait. He never turned his head or indicated why he had stopped, but somehow I knew he was waiting for me. Caleb turned around impatiently and nudged his horse over to the side to make room for me. Taking a deep breath, I kicked my horse forward, taking my place beside Aiden. He then waved his hand in the air, motioning for the men to move out. Father and his men were already on the road ahead of us.

We rode for twenty minutes before coming to the fork in the road Aiden had mentioned. Father, saluting his farewell, took his men and went right, as we cut off to the left.

We rode without speaking for nearly the entire journey until Aiden broke the awkward silence between us. "Are you sure you will recognize the place when you see it?" he asked more formally than usual.

"How would your wife know where we are headed, Aiden, and more to the point, what exactly are we looking for?" Caleb asked, narrowing his eyes suspiciously at me.

"Yes, of course I will," I answered looking directly at Aiden, while trying to ignore Caleb and his awkward question.

Not one to be put off so easily, Caleb attempted to interrupt us again by asking his question one more time, "Aiden, how does she know where we are going?"

"She just does, so let's leave it at that for now," Aiden answered, sounding testy, as he gave Caleb a look that spoke more than mere words.

Four men had been sent ahead of the group to scout out the road before us and two of them were now heading our way, quickly.

"Smith, report," Aiden called out before the men fully reached us.

"There is a possible match to your description, about a mile up the road," Smith replied.

"Were there any men on the road or standing guard near the entrance to the property?" Aiden asked.

"No, Sir, none that we saw. The farmhouse sits back on the property about a quarter of a mile from the road," Smith continued. "Roberts and I disengaged from the others and came back to report. I gave them orders to stay out of sight," Smith concluded.

"Very good, Smith," Aiden replied. Then waving the rest of the men in close, Aiden quietly called out his orders. "Smith and Roberts, I want you to take four men and make your way through the woods on the south side of the property, taking positions behind the house and barn. Keep out of sight until you hear the signal. Dismissed," Aiden commanded.

"Caleb, you take the rest of the men and break up into two teams. Stay off the main road, but make your way due east until you come to the farmhouse and then wait. Leave the horses tied up just off the road so they don't give us away before we are ready. Lady Townsend and I will make our way down the main road posing as Lord and his… male apprentice," Aiden added looking at my attire strangely, which caused some of the men to chuckle. "We will try to stay out of sight ourselves until I have had time to assess the situation. If you are discovered, you all know what to do. We will be going in on my signal. That is all," Aiden concluded then waited for his men to disperse.

My horse could sense my anxiety and began to dance around under me while Aiden addressed his men. Every instinct told me to charge, headlong down the road, in search of the landmark and my brother. I would barge my way in and demand they release Charlie and Ashton, immediately.

My heart was pounding and I wanted to scream at Aiden to hurry up, but he acted as if we were on a Sunday ride out in the country, merely to observe the flora and the fauna. It was simply maddening.

"Aiden, why are we traveling so slowly? I am about to lose my mind," I quietly demanded, under my breath.

"You never know who may be watching or who exactly is listening, so we play the game," he replied, looking sideways at me. "Why are you so irritated?" Aiden asked.

"I don't know. I feel…I feel," I stammered, then fell silent for a second. "I feel Charlie, Aiden, I can feel Charlie," I cried out in surprise.

"What do you mean you can feel Charlie?" Aiden inquired quietly, lowering his voice, so that we wouldn't be overheard.

"When we were children we could each feel the other's presence. Especially, when we were near one another," I said, turning to Aiden. "I can feel him again," I cried as tears glistened in my eyes.

Barely able to contain my excitement, I stopped my horse in the road before leading him off to the side. Closing my eyes, I concentrated all my thoughts on Charlie. Tears flowed down my cheeks and my stomach began to hurt, causing me to groan in pain and double over.

"Isabella, are you alright?" Aiden frantically grabbed for me as I slipped to the side of my saddle.

I could hear the concern in his voice as he immediately jumped from his horse and hauled me the rest of the way off my horse when I didn't immediately answer him.

He kneeled on the ground and cradled me in his arms. "Isabella, answer me," he growled under his breath while giving me a good shake.

"Something is wrong with him," I groaned.

"With whom, Isabella?" Aiden asked, suddenly confused. "Something is wrong with whom?" he gave me another sharp shake.

"I'm talking about Charlie, of course! I think he is sick," I cried when I was able to answer. I shoved away from Aiden. "We must hurry. Please!" I insisted, as I attempted to climb back onto my horse.

"Isabella, stop." Aiden demanded, pulling me backward and off my horse. "I thought something had happened to you. What was that all about?" he snapped, tipping my chin up and forcing me to look at him. I could see the concern in his eyes and it touched me to know how much he cared, but I needed to get to Charlie; he was my first priority.

"I told you. I can sense Charlie and everything he is feeling. Charlie and I have been able to do this since we were very young. Maybe even since birth, I don't know," I continued impatiently. "I'm sure he knows that I am near," I insisted, grabbing his face in my hands. "And he needs us to hurry, so help me get back on my horse. We need to go now," I ordered. Our eyes clashed for what felt like an eternity, as Aiden stared down at me with that discerning gaze of his, trying to decide if he believed me. "Please, Aiden, hurry," I pleaded with some degree of desperation. Finally breaking the spell, Aiden relented. He helped me up, giving me a boost, back into my saddle.

"If we are going to do this, we need to be smart about it and you need to listen to me," Aiden said, after taking another deep breath, sounding more like my over-protective father than my mercenary husband.

"Fine, fine, anything you say; just be quick about it. Charlie has been sick for a while now and he is getting weaker," I interrupted. And let's face it, at that point I was willing to agree to anything, as long as it got me to Charlie quicker.

We rode in silence for ten more minutes before I saw the tree. "Aiden, that's it. That's the tree," I called out, louder than I meant to, forgetting for a moment that I needed to be quiet.

"Great. Just keep going. Don't stop here," Aiden cautioned, motioning with his head for me to follow him.

I opened my mouth to say something, and then immediately shut it again. In the end, I put my head down like the good servant I was pretending to be.

Silently, I followed Aiden down the road, even though every fiber of my being urged me to run my horse headlong down the other road, towards the farmhouse.

We rode till we came to a bend in the road and Aiden was confident that no one was following us. Leading our horses into the trees, we tied them up out of sight of anyone passing by. Doubling back, we silently made our way to the property and as close to the barn as possible.

"What are we doing sitting here? The barn is right there," I whispered in frustration, gesturing to the barn with my hand.

"We are observing," Aiden informed me, grabbing my shirttail and yanking me backward, while never taking his eyes off the barn.

Moments later a very large man stepped out of the barn and shut the door. Standing in front of the door he stretched his back and casually looked around as if he didn't have a care in the world.

Recognition hit me. He had been one of the men who had surrounded Charlie and his two friends the night they were taken from the London Wharf. My body stiffened with the relization, and Aiden clamped his hand over my mouth, pulling me to the ground on top of him when he ducked behind the log.

Our eyes locked and I nearly screamed at him, until I saw the look on his face. He silently gestured with a finger to his lips, then shoved me behind him, as I crawled over his legs and took my new position.

After the man walked away, Aiden whispered to me over his shoulder. "That is why we wait and watch. So you keep your britches fastened and wait till I give the signal," he ordered with authority.

"Good to know," said an unfamiliar deep male voice, directly behind us.

26

I'm All In

SIMULTANEOUSLY, AIDEN AND I TURNED, and I again landed squarely in Aiden's lap as I took a step backwards.

I recognized the man holding the riffle that was aimed directly at my head. He was the older disgruntled brother from my vision, the one with the nasty scar over his left eye.

"So, why are the two of you sneaking around my dairy?" he asked in a menacing tone that was rather unnerving, especially considering the riffle he held in his hands.

"I had a horse come up lame a ways up the road. I was wondering if I could borrow one of yours to get us the rest of the way home," Aiden explained.

"That still don't explain why you would be sneaking around my farm. I think you both best get up and head for the barn," he insisted, jerking the riffle in a manner that indicated his impatience.

I stood up, and Aiden followed, pushing me in front of him so that he would be between me and the gun.

"And keep your hands in the air. I don't want no funny business," he ordered.

"We just moved to this region from Langford. Do you know the place?" Aiden asked in an amiable tone, as if we had just stumbled upon the place. "Certainly, if I had known that people were so inhospitable in this part of the country, we never would have settled here," Aiden said, sounding rather put off.

"Open the door," the man ordered when we reached the barn. Silently I obeyed his order, anxious to get inside and find Charlie. It took a few seconds for my eyes to adjust to the darkened interior. I could see that there were other men lurking about the barn. I counted three, but I couldn't be sure if there were more.

"Move!" he said, shoving Aiden in the back with the butt end of his rifle. "And keep your hands up high, where I can see them."

"So what have you brought me today, Boyd?" another man said, coming out of the shadows to my left. Suddenly, my heart froze in mid beat and all the fury I had been carrying around with me these past few weeks came bubbling up to the surface. It was Shames O'Malley in the flesh, the shiftless, blackheart, savage, beast himself.

Pointing at Aiden with his gun, Boyd explained, "This bloke here says he's just moved here from Langford and that his horse pulled up lame down the road. Personally, I'm not buying it, or the load of manure he's selling. I found them ducked down behind a log, spying on us."

"And the smaller guy here, what's his story?" Shames asked, nodding his head toward me.

"That's just my servant boy. He holds my horse and shines my boots when I need him to," Aiden interjected, stepping between Shames and me.

Shames growled, then balled up his fist, and landed a blow to Aiden's jaw that crumpled him to the ground like a rag doll. "I was not speaking to you, and I would thank you to hold your tongue unless I ask you a question," Shames hissed, while taking another step towards me.

Normally, I would have felt fear and trepidation standing so close to a lumbering giant of a man towering over me. I couldn't say why I didn't shrink from Shames. Perhaps, I was merely channeling my brother's unbridled rage and righteous indignation. I could feel Charlie stronger than ever now and knew he was furious. His mind was shouting his anger and hatred for this man in my head. I could hear him clearly, as if he were standing beside me, shouting wrathful words at this man himself. He raved on incessantly over the cruel, inhuman treatment he and his companions had endured at the hands of the ogre-like being who stood before me now.

I felt sickened by the mere smell of the black hearted beast as his fettered breath wafted past my nose. The fact that Shames O'Malley was continuing to breathe the same air as decent human beings infuriated me.

I heard Aiden as he slowly stood. I heard him trying to laugh the entire matter off, while shaking his head from side to side. "Duly noted, Sir, and I will try my best to remember that for the future," Aiden said, getting to his feet, and at the same time reaching out to pull me behind him. I took the opportunity to slip one of the blades I was carrying, into Aiden's trouser waist band as he shielded me from view. Again Shames belted Aiden in the stomach, this time doubling him over.

"I thought I made myself perfectly clear. I want you to shut your pie hole," Shames yelled with a harsh tone. My eyes locked with Shames, who wore a large sadistic grin across his mouth. Revulsion gnawed at my insides.

Just then, I heard Charlie groan from a darkened corner of the barn behind Shames's stocky form, and I was unable to hide my expression of surprise. Turning my head in the direction of the noise, I bit down hard on my tongue, to keep from crying out to him.

Shames took the opportunity to reach around Aiden and grab hold of my wrist, viciously yanking me from behind Aiden, and causing me to cry out in pain. This was followed by a string of unladylike curses in French and a vicious act of my own, as I stomped on the instep of his foot, catching Shames O'Malley by surprise.

Aiden growled under his breath and I turned to look at him. Then quickly shaking my head, I gave him a stern look. Shames turned loose of my arm, then gleefully crowed like a proud rooster as he strutted around me, giving me the once over. "Looky, what we have here, boys. A woman dressed like a wee lad," he announced sarcastically while taking a hold of my arm again and parading me in a circle as he removed my hat and scarf. My hair spilled out over my shoulder and he laughed, as if he had told a funny joke. I could see the look in Aiden's eyes as I came back around. I gave him another quick shake of my head, and used my free hand to wave him off. Yanking my arm away from Shames's grasp, I turned to face the huge hulk of a man. Those eyes of his burned like fire into the deepest part of my soul and I felt a moment of hesitation.

"Look here, *Monsieur* O'Malley I have come to reclaim my brother and his friend," I stated very matter-of-factly, while glaring up into his repugnant face. My French accent always seemed to be more pronounced when I became angry, and it had become quite thick at that moment.

"Is that so? Then you won't mind telling me how you and your help-less body guard here," Shames sneered and pointed in Aiden's direction, "plan on accomplishing such a feat of brilliance and liberate my two pitiful captives?" He laughed and crossed his arms over his barrel of a chest. Shames scoffed, clearly showing us that he was confident as his men joined in the amusement, at our expense. The darkened interior seemed to erupt into scornful laughter.

"That my dear, Monsieur O'Malley, is a surprise," I remarked with a wicked smile.

"Watch him, boys," Shames said pointing at Aiden. "The lady and I are going to have some fun," he informed everyone with a wicked smile of his own.

The two men grabbed Aiden's arms while he fought with all his might to free himself. By the look on his face, he knew exactly what Shames had in mind for me.

Shames's men continued to subdue Aiden, bringing him to a kneel-ing position, as Shames let out another hearty laugh as he led me away, squeezing my sore arm again, causing me to cry out in pain. We were headed in the direction of Charlie's groan and I could barely contain myself when we drew nearer.

"Look alive, you sorry excuses for human life. You have company," Shames announced, kicking Charlie's foot to roust him.

Charlie and Ashton lay before me, each with a leg shackled to the stall wall. They had been given just enough chain to reach a filthy bucket, sitting just feet away from them, filled with excrement. They lay on a pile of filthy straw, with one wholly, moth eaten piece of cloth for a blanket. It was the only thing to protect them against the winter cold. But I knew all of that because I'd already seen it all in my vission

"Charlie," I softly cried, attempting to pull my arm free of Shames's grip. Hatred, pure and hot formed in my heart, and burning deep in my soul. Looking up into Shames's face, something inside of me broke as an animalistic growl gurgled up from deep in my throat. I swear that in that moment I could have murdered Shames O'Malley where he stood with my bare hands. Shames looked shocked and immediately turned loose of my arm.

I fell to my knees and cradled Charlie in my arms like a child. I remember thinking to myself, '*He is so thin*' while running my hand gently over his bruised cheek. I wanted to cry, and then scream out in a fit of angry frustration, but I didn't. The fact that I had finally found Charlie and he was still alive was enough for the moment. Now all I had to do was clear my mind and think. I rocked Charlie back and forth in my arms as tears of gratitude filled my eyes. Impatiently, I swiped at them with the back of my hand, because there was no time for useless tears.

"You told me she would come for you, Charlie, but I didn't believe you," Ashton said, sounding as if he disbelieved his own eyes even as he stared at me.

"Charlie, Father and Mother are here too," I whispered in my brother's ear. While I examined him closer, I bent down to kiss his hallowed cheeks. Relief flooded my mind and I just kept repeating over and over again, '*I found him and he is still alive. God be praised.*'

He was weak and barely able to hug me back as my tears of joy turned to tears of outrage. "Why?" I cried out loud, not really looking at Shames.

"Why what?" Shames asked in a derogative tone.

"Why did you take them?" I screamed, turning to look at him now.

"Why not?" he replied with a wicked smile, completely unashamed of his despicable actions.

"That's not an answer, Sir," I stated, slowly standing now to face him.

"I've got to hand it to you," Shames exclaimed, eyeing me as if I was a juicy piece of pork chop and he was a starving man, "You have some pluck. I think you and me will get on just fine."

"And how is that?" I snapped, eyeing him with fire in my eyes for the harm he had caused my family.

"I think that when I am through with you, I will sell you to this foreign bloke I know. He likes his gals with lots of back bone," Shames crudely replied, yanking me away from Charlie. "Although, when I am through with you, I can't guarantee just how much backbone you will have left, if you know what I mean," his vulgar meaning registering loud and clear. Complete revulsion caused me to shiver at the mere thought of his touch. Shames, gripping me by both arms now, pulled me so close, that I could smell his feted breath as he leered in my face.

"Selling people into slavery seems to be a running theme with you, *Monsieur* O'Malley." I snapped back at him, while trying to remain calm.

"Look at you standing there so calm and saucy. I bet you have ice water in your veins," Shames said derisively.

"And what were you hoping for?" I asked curiously.

"I was hoping for a little screaming or crying, maybe some begging. It always makes the whole thing much more enjoyable for me," Shames jeered at me with excitement in his eyes.

"What, and waste all this desire for revenge on a little tantrum?" I said coolly, answering his lecherous smile with a glare of my own. "Just so you know, I'm going to tap down this fury and rage that has been building up inside of me. No, *Monsieur* O'Malley, I am going to stew in it until it is well cooked. Then I am going to cultivate my one and only desire," I informed him with a vicious sneer. "Can you guess what that one desire might be?"

"No. But I am guessing that you are going to tell me," Shames answered with a cool but cocky attitude.

Giving Shames an evil smirk I continued. "It is to kill you with my own hands," I said with a sadistic smirk as I widened my eyes for emphasis. "And here is the best part, so listen up, you dim-witted goat."

"Dim-witted goat, is it?" Shames repeated, giving me a harsh shake.

"I'm going to visualize the most masochistic, gruesome ways that any one person can be killed," I taunted, "and then I am going to figure out the most painful way possible, just for you, of course."

"Of course," Shames added smugly as he humored me.

"But I won't stop there, because I don't believe in giving up easily or only giving it half an effort. No, I give any endeavor my all, and this will be no exception. So I am making you this promise. I will survive just so I can watch the spark drain from your eyes, *Monsieur* O'Malley," I stated between clenched teeth.

"Damn woman, if you aren't blood thirsty and a little bit twisted. I have half a mind of keeping you all to myself," Shames said smirking back as he drew my face to his, cruelly pinching my cheeks between his fingers.

"Well, you have half that statement right," I taunted. "What makes you think I will let you live long enough to take me?" I sneered at him confidently.

"Just what makes you think you won't enjoy it?" Shames replied, his lecherous meaning further implied, as he wagged his bushy eyebrows at me.

"You are a little on the brutish side for my taste, you '*gros con*'," I stated in French, glaring at him.

"What did you just say?" Shames snarled out the words in my face.

"She said that you are a big fat idiot," Charlie spoke up as he chuckled through the pain while holding his sides.

"Oh ya?" Shames exclaimed, giving me a rough shake.

"*Fait chier*," I said with a sigh, as if he were a mere imposition. Charlie and Ashton looked at one another then began to laugh.

"What did she just say, Deveraux?" Shames growled.

"She is simply annoyed by you," Charlie answered. That old familiar spark lit in my brother's eyes as he laughed even harder this time. I turned my head to smile at Charlie and Ashton, snubbing Shames which infuriated him. He retaliated by slapping me across the face so hard that I was knocked backwards onto the ground.

Charlie tried to catch me as I fell on top of him. I turned quickly, dropping the other knife I had tucked against my chest, between his legs, before Shames could snatch me up again. Even though I had only a few seconds, I looked Charlie in the eyes. And in those few seconds we communicated everything that needed to be said.

Shames grabbed me by the hair and lifted me up. "Perhaps we should have a little fun right now, since my life, according to you, is going to be cut short," he said with another wicked grin. "And look, we have an audience. I hope you don't get stage fright," Shames snarled through his rotting teeth, while ripping the coat from my back, as I kicked at him viciously.

"Get your hands off my wife, you bloody bastard!" Aiden yelled, struggling frantically with his two captors.

"It seems I am already spoken for, you filthy pig," I sneered, while frantically struggling to block his attempts to disrobe me further.

"Not to worry, my good man. Leftovers don't bother me none. I will even let you watch. Bring him over here closer, boys, so he can see how it is done," Shames laughed as he ripped at my vest buttons. "Now what do we have here?" Shames asked eyeing the nearly empty leather strap across my chest with suspicion.

"Aiden, if you are going to send out the signal, I think now would be a most splendid time," I called out over my shoulder.

Aiden let out an ear splitting whistle that echoed so loudly through the entire barn, I was sure people from the next county heard it. Within seconds, we heard gunfire and men yelling outside the barn. Aiden caught both men by surprise, reaching into his waistband, to retrieve the hidden knife, and stabbed the first man in the stomach, and then slit the throat of the other one, all in one fluid motion.

The barn doors in the front and back of the barn, opened almost simultaneously, as men flooded in with the light from outside.

Shames grabbed me by the waist and lifted me off the ground, using me as a human shield. "What do we have here?" he growled, while reaching for the last knife I had strapped to my chest. "It's a shame that we didn't get to have our fun. I was looking forward to showing your husband how a real man does it," his lascivious tone reverberating in my ear. "You really are a crazy woman."

I scoffed, and then turned my head so that I could see his eyes. "If you like crazy, just wait a minute and I will introduce you to my father. He should be coming through that door any second now," I announced, with a flick of my head. "You can't possibly judge crazy until you have met him. Wouldn't you agree, Charlie?"

"That's far enough," Shames warned Aiden, turning quickly and presenting his back to Charlie and Ashton, while pulling me up even tighter to his chest. I could feel Shames's hand shaking, while his heart pounded against my back.

"Oh, did I forget to mention that my father was a ruthless pirate in his former life?" I added innocently, while Shames pulled the blade even tighter against my throat, nicking me slightly. I could feel several drops of blood trickling down my neck.

Bringing my hand up to steady Shames's shaking hand. I hoped to prevent the blade from cutting me further. "I know you don't really want to hurt me, *Monsieur* O'Malley, so why don't you just take a deep breath and put down the knife. Perhaps my father will let you live," I suggested.

"Bella!" Father yelled from the doorway, as he came through and saw the situation.

I heard Mother gasp, as she attempted to push her way past Father. "Jude, do something," she demanded.

"Let's just all stay calm now," Aiden suggested. "See, I am going to put down the knife," he added, throwing the blade toward the open doorway, sticking it into the door jam. "Let's just talk a minute before things get out of hand."

"Stay where you are. Don't come any closer, or I will slit her throat," Shames threatened.

"Where are my manners?" I stammered. "Father, allow me to introduce you to Shames O'Malley. Shames, you don't mind me using your Christian name, do you?" I asked, trying to sound calm, even though my heart was trying to beat its way out of my chest while I waited for Shames to nod his head yes. "Good. Shames, this is my father, Jude Deveraux and that would be my mother behind him, Angelina Deveraux. But you may address her as Her Grace. They also happen to be the parents of Charlie over there," I said slowly, turning my head slightly, now only able to look at him out of the corner of my eye because of the knife. I was trying to gauge whether my words had the desired effect of calming him down. Shames looked puzzled. "Oh, did I fail to mention that Charlie and I are twins? My apologies," I quipped. "As you can well imagine our parents have grown rather fond of us, after nineteen years, so might I suggest you not slip my throat with that very sharp knife, you have clutched to my throat.".

"Stop talking, woman," Shames demanded. "This is how it is going to work," he said, while backing up a couple more steps. "I am going to ride out of here with your daughter as my escort," Shames continued, looking around nervously as he adjusted his arm, crushing my ribs. I chanced a look over my shoulder and saw the desperation in Shames's eyes. Suddenly, in that moment, I realized that he was a man with nothing to lose. "And if I make it down the road and no one follows us, I will simply let her go. I give you my word, that she will still be breathing when I leave her," he said coolly, leaving little doubt in my mind that I would not continue breathing the rest of the day if Shames O'Malley was allowed to leave with me.

"But if anyone attempts to follow us, I will slit her pretty little throat as easily as I carved the Christmas goose, and that will be that. I've lived a full life," Shames continued, with a controlled chuckle, his eyes on Aiden and my father. "But this delicate little thing," he announced with a degree of cynicism in his tone, giving me a shake, and then a sloppy wet kiss on my cheek, "well she has just begun to live her life. And wouldn't it be a shame to see it end so soon?" Shames said, purposely posing the question to cause the most distress. He smelled my hair as he nuzzled my neck. "And ain't she a fine specimen of a woman, so sweet and feisty all at the same time," he smiled sadistically at Aiden. "So what says you, gents? Is she going to live to see the sunrise tomorrow or do we end this right here and now?" Shames stated with a menacing smile, as he readjusted the knife at my throat.

"If you hurt her, O'Malley, death will be a blessing when I get my hands on you. You mark my words," my father growled as he took another step towards us.

Then I heard a slight rattling of chains behind us, but didn't dare turn my head as Shames took another step backwards. I knew it was Charlie and that he had a plan.

"Then I suggest that you stay where you are, and not come any closer," Shames stressed by purposely nicking my neck, causing me to yelp in surprise. "I just thought I would make a point, gents. This thing could end one of two ways," Shames chuckled nervously, "What's it going to be?" The murderous look in my father's piercing blue eyes would have reduced most men to a puddle of liquid on the floor in a matter of seconds. But Shames O'Malley was living on borrowed time as it was, so he didn't care.

"Poppa, it's alright," I cried. "I will be fine. Just take care of Charlie," I said, trying to reassure him.

"Bella," Mother cried.

I could see the concern written on her tear streaked face. "It's alright, Momma. Everything will work out," I called to her.

"You!" Shames yelled, looking directly at Aiden, "Get me a horse," he ordered. "And be quick about it. My arm is starting to twitch, and you know what that means," Shames said before laughing directly in my face. His retched breath made me gag and I had to turn away.

Aiden ran outside, then brought a horse through the doors and lead it over to us quickly, almost too quickly.

"Wait!" Shames shouted. "Not that fast," he cautioned Aiden.

"A thousand pardons, Mr. O'Malley. I was under the impression that you were in a hurry to be gone," Aiden said smoothly, leading the horse closer to Shames than he was comfortable with, causing him to back up two more steps.

"Put the reins in your wife's hands, and then back up," Shames ordered, as he began to get jumpy and nervous all of a sudden. "And if you make a grab for the knife I will slit her little neck before you can blink an eye," Shames warned.

Aiden placed the reins in my hand and squeezed it closed. Then, patting the saddle with his hand, Aiden backed away, never taking his eyes off me. When he had stepped back about eight feet, Aiden nodded his head to me and I knew by the look in his eyes what he had done.

Suddenly, I felt Shames jerk, attempting to look behind him. Just then he let out an animalistic growl from deep in his throat, and dropped the knife he had been holding to my throat, his right arm suddenly rendered useless.

I didn't hesitate to make my escape. Freeing myself from Shames, I reached over the top of the saddle, while Shames was still trying to figure out what had just happened. I frantically ran my hand along the edge of the saddle, searching desperately for the knife I knew Aiden had hidden there. I chanced a quick look over my shoulder to make sure Shames wasn't coming after me. When I saw him turn on my brother and Ashton with a murderous gleam in his eyes, I panicked.

Ashton came around and hit Shames with a large wooden stick he had been hiding under his pile of straw. Scrambling, I jumped up and pulled myself over the saddle so I could see the knife. Grabbing it, I jumped down and turned to see Shames on his knees with his hands wrapped around Charlie's neck, while Ashton lay on the ground next to him, out cold. Jumping onto Shames's back, I was surprised by his agility when he threw me to the ground and I landed next to Ashton.

Charlie reached his hand up, to hit Shames directly in the face, which only served to enrage him further. Shames reached around, pulling the knife out of his left shoulder where Charlie had stuck it. The noise he made as he removed the knife was awful, somewhere between a scream and a guttural growl of a wounded beast. Charlie was too weak to move or defend himself and Shames knew this. He sat on the lower half of Charlie's legs, keeping him pinned in place and immobilized.

I frantically searched through the hay for the blade I had dropped. With horror, I saw the intent in Shames's eyes as he drew his arm back and I screamed, "No!" as I laid myself across Charlie's body to shield him from any more harm. Closing my eyes tightly, while throwing an arm across my face, I braced myself for the impact of the knife, I knew would be coming.

At the same time, I heard a strange gurgling noise. My hand and face were sprayed with something warm, wet and sticky. I didn't instantly comprehend what it was, and then slowly recognition sank in. Realization hit me when the searing pain I had expected never came. Slowly, I opened my eyes and saw my father with one hand wrapped around Shames's head and the other holding the knife he had just used to slit Shames's throat. Aiden held tightly to Shames's arm, preventing him from stabbing me with the knife that still sat clutched in his cold dead fist.

I breathed a sigh of relief and rolled off Charlie, praying that I didn't cause any more damage to him. "Charlie, Charlie!" I screamed, cradling his face in my hands. "Talk to me Charlie," I desperately cried.

"Can't you see I am in pain here? Stop shaking me as if I were made of rags," Charlie said with a weak smile, as he slowly opened his eyes.

"Oh Charlie, you're alive!" I clutched him tightly to my chest, rocking back and forth while I cried. "Look, Poppa, he's alive," I half laughed and cried all at the same time.

Mother fell to the ground next to us and wrapped her arms around Charlie and me and sobbed grateful tears. Father joined in, wrapping his large arms around everyone that would fit. "I haven't heard you call me that since you were a little girl," Father said, hugging us even tighter.

"Are you crying, Poppa?" Charlie asked with astonishment.

Ashton came to, opening his eyes and coughing to get our attention. Father and Mother both turned toward Ashton, but when I looked over at him, he opened them even wider, "Charlie, why is your sister covered in blood?" he asked in horror. "She looks utterly blood thirsty and warrior like, just as you described her. But I never took you literally, old man," Ashton stated while looking between Charlie and me.

I laughed and then cried when I noticed that a bruise had already starting to form on Ashton's beard stubble cheek, where Shames had punched him hard.

"Yes, but isn't she the most beautiful sight you have ever seen, blood and all?" Aiden insisted, dangling a set of keys in the air. "Let's see if we can get you out of these shackles, gents. I just happened to come across a set of keys no longer being used by their previous owner," he said, slipping the key into Ashton's lock and then Charlie's.

"Sir," Roberts said coming to attention in front of Aiden.

"What is it, Roberts?" Aiden asked as he turned the key releasing Charlie from his shackles.

"We've located your horses and detained the two brothers who run the dairy. The older one seems to have plenty to say," Roberts continued, while standing at attention.

"At ease, Roberts," Aiden chuckled. "We'll take them back with us. I want this place cleared and everyone ready to head out in thirty." Aiden stood up. "Gather any horses left behind and get them saddled."

"Yes, Sir, right away," Roberts saluted, before turning to bark out orders.

27

Properly Propositioned

HE JOURNEY BACK TO CASTLE Blayney was a long and arduous ride, and we were all exhausted when we got there.

Yet, I felt exhilarated as well. We had found Charlie and Ashton, and we would soon be going home. Home, it was a strange thing to think of. Where would I call home now?

Father had sent two men ahead to advise the Blayney's of him condition, giving them time to send for a physician. Charlie was unable to support himself so Father held Charlie in front of him the entire journey back, just as he had when we were children. He was so malnourished and weak from his ordeal that my heart ached for him. Ashton was a trooper and managed to ride alone with a few stops along the way to rest.

I caught myself crying, as I watched Charlie's face contort in pain. It made me want to retrace my steps and kill Shames O'Malley all over again. The fact that I already wore Shames's blood on me, gave me little solace. I couldn't wait to wash the filth of him from my skin.

I had plenty of time to think, and found my thoughts wondering as we traveled. I couldn't make sense of this unknown man who referred to himself as the Governor. All we knew about him was that he had come from a good family, possibly even a wealthy one. A man who had become disenchanted with the inheritance law that prevented him from sharing in the family fortune. Because of this law many of the privileged class's second born sons were out of luck and on their own.

What I couldn't reconcile was why someone like that would take up with thugs and thieves, to back a group of men who went about steeling and causing mayhem among the very people he came from.

Aiden had ridden ahead of us and was dismounting his horse when I came into the courtyard. He walked up to my horse and offered to assist me down from my mount.

"This is most unexpected," I said, surprised by his gallant gesture.

"It shouldn't be. I am your husband," Aiden replied, cocking his head to one side as he lifted an eyebrow at me.

"It's just that the mission is over and my brother has been restored to us," I stated, while dismounting my horse with his help. As I turned around, I expected Aiden to back up and give me room. But instead, he came in even closer, pinning me against the horse.

I inhaled deeply. Aiden smelled of dust mixed with leather and musk and none of these scents were unpleasant to my senses. He reached up to brush a stray hair from my cheek and our eyes locked. He leaned in, stopping a hairs breath from my cheek with a seductive smile on his lips. My breath caught in my lungs, and I felt my pulse begin to race.

"I will be up in a little while, when I am done with the prisoners. There is something I wish to discuss with you," Aiden informed me, caressing my cheek with the back of his hand. As he walked away leading the two horses behind him, I stood there a moment longer. I felt puzzled by the enigma before me.

I looked up to see Caleb staring at me and wondered just how long he had been standing there. My face turned a bright shade of red this time as I turned on my heels and headed to the castle and straight up the stairs.

Lady Blayney stopped me on the landing. "Oh my dear child, how good it is to see you have returned in one piece. I look forward to hearing all about your ordeal at dinner. You will be coming down for dinner, won't you?" she inquired, as uncertainty showed in her eyes. "Oh my, please forgive me. You are covered in blood. It must have been horrible.

And listen to me rambling on so about dinner. I will order you a bath, straight away, you poor dear," Lady Harriett said, taking my hand and patting it as she led me to my room. "I will also order you some warmed wine, as well. I insist." I let her prattle on because I had nothing to add. She seemed perfectly happy to carry on a one-sided conversation.

The moment Maria saw me she rushed to my rescue. "Lady Isabella—I beg your pardon, I mean, Lady Townsend, let me help you," Maria said, taking my arm from my companion.

"The poor dear has been through so much. Why, she hasn't even said a single word to me the entire time. It must have been just awful out there," Lady Blayney continued. "I don't know what her husband was thinking, letting her go out there with those bloodthirsty men," she continued. "I promised her a hot bath and some warmed wine, to steady her nerves. I will make the arrangements immediately," she said, as she softly closed the door behind her.

"Isabella, are you alright? Was it just the worst thing ever?" Maria asked, concerned by Lady Blayney's words and my continued silence.

"Yes, Maria, I'm fine. It's just that Lady Blayney wouldn't stop talking long enough for me to get a word in, so I just played mute. It seemed the easiest thing to do," I admitted, taking a seat in the bedroom.

"A hot bath and some warm wine in you and you will be right as rain," Maria insisted, trying to sound light and cheery as she bustled around the room, getting things ready for my bath. Putting my head in my hands, I began to weep, giving myself permission to cry uncontrollably, until I heard the maids coming with the hot water for my bath.

Minutes later I heard Maria as she brought in the tray of warmed wine and fresh baked rolls, still dripping with melted butter. Maria poured me a glass, placing it in my hand, and then she placed my emerald wedding ring in the other. "Drink," she ordered then closed the door behind the young ladies when they had finished filling the bath. Slipping the ring on my finger, I stood and walked to the window, looking out at the dimming sky line as the sun was setting over the hill.

"This will fix you right up," Maria said. "Janice has lit the fire for you, so you can sit in the bath as long as you like, my lady," Maria babbled on, leading me to the tub and helped me out of my dirty, blood splattered clothes.

Testing the water with my hand before stepping into the tub, I noticed that the water was very hot, but it was exactly what I needed. Dunking my head under the water to wet my hair and wash the blood off my face, the heat was like a balm to my tattered nerves. Maria began to scrub the blood from my hair with a special soap she concocted from boiled soap and herbs that made a wonderful lather. It always left my hair shiny and clean, after which, she would add some oils to the ends of my hair, leaving it till the end of my bath before rinsing it out. It was like heaven itself as the scent of lavender and mints permeated the air. It had the added benefit of calming and soothing my raw nerves.

After handing me another glass of warmed wine, Maria excused herself from the room, giving me a few moments to myself, to reflect on all that had taken place that day. I was beginning to relax with my second glass of warmed wine when I heard a knock at the door, which I ignored. Setting the cup on the table next to my bath I sunk under the water again to rinse my hair. Holding my breath as long as I could, was a game Charlie and I use to play when we were children. I laughed inwardly to myself, because I could always beat him. Coming up I blew out my breath and wiped my eyes only to find Aiden sitting on the stool beside my tub.

"Attempting to drown yourself just to avoid talking with your husband is what I call commitment," Aiden teased with a smirk.

I jumped, then tried to cover myself with my arms. "What are you doing here?" I cried out, as I turned three shades of red.

"I told you I would stop in when I was finished with the Banning brothers," he retorted, lifting an amused eyebrow.

"No. I mean, what are you doing here, in this room, while I am taking a bath?" I asked again, more than a little annoyed. "Where is Maria?" I questioned.

"I don't know. I didn't get a response when I knocked," lifting his shoulders as a way of explaining.

"So you figured you would come into my chambers anyway," I said with a slight tone of outrage.

"For a split second I thought you had drowned yourself. But just before I reached in to pull you out, I noticed little bubbles floating to the top," Aiden explained, leaning back on two legs of the four legged stool, as he crossed his arms over his chest with an amused smirk on his lips.

"I bet that's not all you observed," I fired back, the words coming out as an accusation, while I turned yet another shade of red. "Well, now that you have eased yourself of any trepidations of a dead wife due to an accidental drowning, you may go," I said dismissively. Lately, just the thought of Aiden sent heat crawling up the back of my neck. But I couldn't decide if the intense hammering in my chest was from anger or something else. Either way I found it impossible to breathe with his nearness.

I studied his face, wishing to understand what he was about in the same moment Maria entered the room.

"What is this?" Maria questioned, visibly flustered as she rushed into the room.

"Just a husband visiting his wife, Maria, it's not a crime where I come from," Aiden stated flatly, bristling slightly at her tone. "I believe we were having a conversation." That's when I decided to sink a little deeper into the tub, attempting to avoid weighing in on the matter.

"Perhaps you would like to step out of the room a moment, until Lady Isabella is done with her bath and I have helped her dress," Maria suggested coolly.

"No," is all Aiden said, as he fixed Maria with one of his cool, stony stares, the one he used to let people know that they were on thin ice with him and should choose their next step carefully.

"Please give our regrets to Lord and Lady Blayney this evening, Maria. I believe Lady Townsend and I will be dinning in tonight. It has been a very trying day. Oh, and have a tray sent up for us, if you please. I am starving," Aiden ordered while looking intently at me, and in a tone that suggested to Maria that his wishes were to be carried out without further debate or delay.

Maria looked at me first, then dropped a slow but deliberate curtsy in Aiden's direction, "Very good, my Lord," was all she said, before slowly walking out of the room, closing the door as she left.

Aiden continued stared at my face. Patiently, he sat down again on the stool next to the bath, tipping back on two legs. "So tell me what has changed. You barely said two words the entire trip home."

"I find I no longer have the stomach for our charade," I said, boldly studying the angles of his face.

"What part of this charade exactly do you object to?" Aiden asked, narrowing his eyes at me.

"I fear I have ignored my fractured heart until it has become indifferent to my desires. I seem to have shriveled and hardened beyond recognition," I mused, looking away, feeling embarrassed by the intimacy. "I feel myself slipping away, piece by piece until I hardly recognize myself," I continued, "trying to untangle the emotions of the last three years that had been exasperated by the events of the last few days." I swallowed hard trying not to cry, even though tears already glistened in my eyes. "I'm afraid I have become someone unworthy of love," I concluded, looking down at my hands.

"Then stop," Aiden said, setting the stool down on all four legs with a thud. He leaned forward to study my face. "Just stop, and share your burdens with me."

"But how?" I asked, looking back at him. "How do I suddenly become this soft and loving person, after guarding against such gentleness for so long?" I felt my lower lip quiver.

"You share everything with me. That way we don't end up two people who are married, but separately. I don't wish to doom myself or you to a life of endless nights locked away and alone in our secret chambers, with nothing but covers and fireplace embers to keep us warm," Aiden pleaded passionately. "I refuse to become two people traveling separately down the same road, feeling vindicated by our many sins. I will never be satisfied to merely survive until the day comes that I draw my last pathetic breath, and you shouldn't either."

"But this is a marriage on paper only, your words!" I said accusingly, reminding him of the stupid deal we'd made. "And now the mission is over and…" The rest of my words stuck in my throat, making it impossible to finish the sentence.

"All I am proposing is that we give it a go," he began, floundering for the right words. "We are married, but I will leave it up to you if you wish to make it real or not," Aiden said, raking his fingers through his hair as he stood up and began pacing in front of my bath. "I have desired you ever since that moment you threw that bloody sword at my feet. You stole my breath away, along with my heart, without even trying. Oh, you were so fierce and fiery, standing up to me the way you did," Aiden laughed, stopping to look at me. "And all I've thought about every day since that day is what a bloody shame it would be if I were to die before I had the chance to tell you how I really feel," Aiden squatted down beside the tub now, with his arms resting on the side. "So what do you say, darling, shall we give it a go?"

Confused and taken aback by his heart felt words, I was left speechless. I opened then closed my mouth a couple of times, unable to formulate coherent words or come up with anything witty to dispel his powerful words.

Aiden stood up and stared down at me for a moment longest before retrieving the soap and rag, dunking them both into the water. Then kneeling down behind me he began to scrub my shoulder.

"What are you doing?" I questioned, sitting up just an inch taller in the water before realizing what I was exposing his eyes to. My cheeks burned red with embarrassment, which caused me to bend forward, hugging my knees to my chest again.

"I was going to scrub your back for you," he answered as if it were an everyday occurrence.

"But, but..." I stammered, searching for words to rebuke him, but found nothing immediately came to mind. I didn't dare move a muscle for the fierce pounding of my heart.

Aiden lifted the hair from my back and laid it slowly over my left shoulder. Then, very gently, he began to soap my back. But instead of merely scrubbing my skin like Maria normally did, his touch felt more like a caress, stirring feelings in me never before awakened.

"Are you cold?" Aiden asked.

"No," I softly answered back, turning my head to look at him over my shoulder.

Aiden reached up to wash my neck and I turned back around and closed my eyes, suddenly enjoying the indulgent feeling of his caressing touch. Perhaps it was the two glasses of warmed wine before he had arrived that allowed me to justify my complacency with his presence, or perhaps it was his words that began to mingle with my curiosity. I could almost hear the smile in his tone as Aiden continued to wash behind my ears, moving my hair from one side to the other.

"Do you even have any idea what I have truly come to love about you?" Aiden asked quietly, and then continued without waiting for my reply, "Your sense of adventure," he replied, clearing his throat, then he grew serious again. Soaping the rag once more, he began to soap the front of my neck while he explained his proposal in earnest. "To annul our marriage would be a true crime. So, I propose we move forward with this marriage, if you are amenable with going forward with what we have started?" he argued, rather boldly, nodding his head to one side. Aiden paused a moment, mid scrub, to raise his eyebrows at me.

I took this slight gesture as a silent question, while he rested his hand just between my neck and chest, waiting for any sign from me, that I was in agreement.

I had my knees pulled up to my chest, like one of those pill bugs that would tuck themselves into a tight little ball the moment you touched them.

Aiden waited patiently for the slightest sign of consent, while looking intently into my eyes. How could I feel such stirrings, such secret, insidious, sensuous stirrings that Aiden seemed to arouse in me, by simply staring into my eyes? A shiver ran down my spine along with a burning desire to have questions answered. I had so many questions of the carnal nature that only he could answer for me.

Staring up at him, I lowered my knees and tried to relax against the back of the tub. I could barely breathe as my mind and body waited in anticipation for what would come next. My heart felt like it was in my throat as I stared into his eyes, while they reflected the firelight jumping about in his glistening orbs. Aiden continued caressing my skin with the rag, as he ran it over my chest, while another wave of goose bumps formed.

The very air in the room was enough to send sensations through my entire body, while Aiden's hand now skimmed below the water and along my stomach. The forgotten rag now floated in the bath, as my head fell against the rim of the tub. Aiden's lips softly came down upon my partially opened mouth and his free hand cupped the back of my head, pulling me closer. His embrace becoming more urgent as his desires became my desires. I felt emboldened by his touch, wrapping my arms around his neck, our kiss deepened. His hand slid down even further, causing a sudden intake of air while my heart raced and his fingers explored the juncture between my legs. A groan of desire and pleasure deep in my throat escaped and I clung even tighter to his neck.

Aiden slowly pulled away and sat back on his haunches staring at me a good long moment, running his wet hand through his hair. I took this as a gesture of indecision, before he stood up. Pulling his wet shirt over his head, Aiden dropped it where he stood. His muscular physique was magnificent and his desire and need was quite evident.

Looking about, Aiden retrieved the bath sheet and held it up in front of himself. I stood and stepped out of the tub, walking into his embrace as he wrapped the towel about me and gently led me to the thick plush rug before the fire.

"What have you in mind?" I questioned curiously.

"You will see, now just be patient and sit down," he said with a sly smile.

Stepping into the sitting chamber between the rooms, Aiden returned moments later with a tray. Closing the door with his foot, he gingerly balanced the tray in one hand, as he reached around to flip the lock on the door. Aiden grinded with a satisfied smile, and gave me a wink. Setting the tray of food on the ground next to me, he walked over to the nearest chair and sat down to remove his boots and stockings.

"Now let us see what Maria has managed to scrounge up for us to eat, shall we?" Aiden said with the childish delight of one opening presents on his birthday. He sat down across from me and began to carefully lift covers and peer under them before immediately placing the covers back again, making sure that I didn't see anything. I truly was famished and needed something in my stomach.

Pouring the wine, Aiden handed me a glass, "A toast to my lovely bride," he announced, turning to me. "May our skies be fair, our seas be calm, and our life together an adventure. And may my wife be as bonny and bold as she was today, until the day I die," he finished with a rakish smirk, as he clinked our glasses together.

Then, tilting his glass back, he downed the entire contents in two swallows, giving a satisfied sigh when he was done.

"You enjoy playing the rake when you are around me, don't you," I pointed out, as I studied his profile.

"Why do you say that?" Aiden asked while rearranging the two plates sitting on the tray. He even slapped my hand away when I reached for one of the covers.

"Ouch," I yelped in surprise.

"New rules," Aiden insisted. "You cannot feed yourself the entire night and must eat whatever I put in your mouth. And when I feed you the delectable delights under these covers, you must respond, by telling me that it is your favorite. You may even add an Aiden my love, or a darling in there, if you really must," he added with a wicked grin.

"Now you are just teasing me, aren't you?" I replied.

"No. No, I'm not. Those are the rules and you must follow them or suffer the consequences," Aiden added with another wicked smile.

"But what if I don't like what you put in my mouth?" I suggested.

"Doesn't matter, the answer is always the same," he replied. "Come on, where is that sense of adventure that I have come to love so much," Aiden said, goading me on.

"All right, fine. I will play your silly little game," I finally said, giving in and conceding to the rules.

Picking up the napkin from the tray, Aiden began to fold it over a couple of times. "Did I mention that you will be blind folded the entire time?" he added with a laugh, as he came around behind me to tie the makeshift blindfold over my eyes.

"No, no, no," I vehemently objected, reaching out my hand for the blindfold.

Aiden again slapped my hand away. "Don't make me tie your hands behind your back as well," he threatened, with a serious tone, and then paused a second, "Come to think of it, that might make things more interesting."

"I do believe the blindfold will be adequate," I replied flatly, placing my hands obediently in my lap. Shifting to the side, I tried to maintain some modesty as I reached up to make sure the end of my towel was tightly tucked in.

I heard him remove the cover from one of the dishes after he had finished tying the blindfold around my eyes. "Oh, you are going to love this," Aiden assured me, as his fork clanked against one of the covers.

Scooping the fork into the plate, he brought it to my mouth, "Open wide for your first mystery bite."

"What is first?" I questioned.

"You know the rules," he scolded.

"Fine," I relented, then opened my mouth reluctantly. "What in the world is that?" I asked, screwing my face up, trying to politely spit it out. "Ew...that is simply hideous —"

"Come, come now, how many times must I tell you the rules?" Aiden chided good humoredly.

I found it difficult, but I swallowed the vile bite. "Alright, fine," I stated rather sarcastically. "That is my favorite thing ever," I continued unconvincingly.

"I want you to say it like you mean it," Aiden protested, with a muffled chuckle.

"Alright, give me something else, and I will do better this time," I exclaimed, trying to get into the spirit of Aiden's game.

"As long as you behave yourself, I will give you something tasty. But if you are naughty, I just might give you something not so tasty," Aiden announced.

"And why do you get to keep changing the rules as we go along?" I asked, feigning outrage.

"Is that dissention and sarcasm I hear in your tone? Either way, you're not behaving," he playfully scolded.

"Absolutely not," I countered, with a good-humored chuckle. "What would make you say such a thing?"

"Good, because there is an entirely different penalty associated with discontented participants," Aiden cautioned.

I laughed. "Of course, I might have known. Please, may I have another delectable bite of my favorite things, darling?" I said sweetly as I played along. "I realize you are unable to see my eyes at this very moment, but I am fluttering my eyelashes at you."

"I might have known you were a woman used to getting her way, by use of her womanly wiles," he joked while trying to feign disappointment. "And since you have asked me so sweetly, it would be my pleasure to serve you something else."

Aiden brought another fork full to my mouth, and I obediently opened wide. "Oh, yum. Now that was good. Thank you, darling, I believe that was the best thing you have put in my mouth thus far," I complied, giving a satisfied moan.

"But wait my dear, the night is still young and your next bite is only a forkful away," Aiden cheerfully quipped.

I swallowed and then opened my mouth again as he placed a spoonful of chocolate mousse in my mouth. "Oh...yum," I gushed, savoring the rich chocolate flavor as it melted in my mouth, then licking my lips. "That, by far, is definitely the best thing you have put in my mouth!" I gushed on with delight.

"That just goes to show how little you truly know darling. Because..." he paused long enough to remove my blindfold as he pulled me into his arms, "The best is yet to come," Aiden said, while licking the remaining chocolate from my lips. "I fear I have denied every single impulse and desire I've had for you, out of some misguided sense of duty and chivalry."

The intensity of his words and the heat of his stare sent a thrilling shiver through me, while tiny butterflies danced in my belly.

"I have never been a patient man, willing to wait for someone or anything for that matter to come to me. If I wanted something, I took it," Aiden said. "And the heavens above know that I have been a very patient man where you are concerned. It feels like I have wanted you for an eternity. You've haunted my dreams and my waking hours. I've tried to deny it, but I have come to realize that you are impossible to deny, my love," he concluded as his piercing blue eyes traveled up and down my entire form, assessing me with such intensity that it set my blood to boil.

The emotion of his words and the passion in his eyes, choked out any words I could have spoke. *'How can this man feel so fiercely about me?'* But there it was, reflected back at me through the windows that were his eyes.

I could not deny it any longer. "I need you," I sobbed, taking a second to catch my breath as my eyes wondered over the corded muscles of his shoulder. I traced my fingers over his tan bare chest. "May heaven forgive me, but I find that with all that I am, I need you," I whispered.

His free hand wrapped around the back of my neck pulling my lips to his. Any thoughts of modesty went out the window in that moment. His lips melted into mine and his velvety soft tongue pushed its way past my lips, exploring the recesses of my mouth. He gently laid me down, placing passionate kisses on my cheeks, eyes, and forehead. I heard the tray of food scatter along the floor, and the dishes clanking together, when Aiden pushed everything tray out of the way.

In his eyes, I caught a glimpse of seduction, so raw and powerful, it made me catch my breath with anticipation. My lungs felt tight and I couldn't breathe. Every nerve in my body was heightened, as if a single touch or a well-placed kiss would send me over the edge. He gently pressed the weight of his body over mine and I could feel his warmth and need through the thin layer of sheet. His fingers frantically searched for the end, as he tried to remove it. His lips moved magically down the column of my throat and across my chest, leaving searing hot, passionate kisses along my skin.

Swept away by the moment, I closed my eyes and arched my back towards him, desiring to be even closer to him. I didn't even care or feel ashamed as I felt his hands removing the towel from around me. I gasped with surprise when the cool air hit my skin, opening my eyes as he stood up. Our eyes locked as he stood over mee me with the firelight glowing against his bare skin.

I studied him, running my eyes boldly over his chest, then down to his taut washboard stomach with the thatch of blond hair below his navel that disappeared beneath the waistband of his trousers.

Aiden reached to unfasten those same trousers and I could clearly see the urgency of his need. Chewing on my lower lip, I gasped when he slid the material from his hips, fully exposing his form to me.

He stood there staring at me for a moment, trying to gage my reaction, until I sat up and reached for him. Taking my hand, I pulled him toward me, never looking away. Something in his gaze emboldened me, making me desperate for his touch. It was entrancing the way he looked at me, as if I was the only person in the world.

I finally understood my parents and the strength of their bond. They would joke when Charlie and I acted as if we were dying every time they showed affection for one another. But suddenly, I understood. This is what they felt, every time they stared longingly into each other's eyes.

"I want you," I sighed. A red hot ember began to burn deep inside of me. "Show me everything," I pleaded.

His lips turned up at the corners as he captured my mouth with his and his breath came out in harsh rasps of desire. His free hand ran the length of my body, cupping my bottom as he pulled me up against him. I moaned in pleasure when his lips left mine and began their downward decent, trailing burning, passionate kisses as he went, until I nearly lost my mind.

"Please," I pleaded, as my breath came out in short gasps, as an longing ache began to burn deep in my belly.

"Please what?" he asked between kisses he generously dispersed along my stomach now as he looked up into my face. My thigh flexed involuntarily and I moaned with emotions and feelings I had never felt before. I inherently knew that I was about to embark upon something that I had never dreamed of, or even imagined. The only thing I did know with any amount of certainty was that I couldn't stand the suspense of waiting any longer.

"Aiden, please, I want you," I cried desperately, arching my back towards him as his teeth nicked my flesh while he inched his way up my body, ever so slowly.

With my heart pounding in my chest, I felt a pooling inside my belly. A desperate hunger that tore at my core, and I was unsure of how to quench it.

Knotting fingers through his hair, I pulled his mouth to mine and feasted hungrily. Surprising myself, I gently bit his lower lip, as my fingers dug into the flesh of his back. My lips felt swollen and I moaned again in pleasure as my breath came out in a combination of sighs, mingled with my desperate cries to be fulfilled.

Aiden growled, as he used the last bit of restraint he had, not to rush the moment. Running my hands over his bare chest, I marveled at the texture of corded muscles beneath my fingers, and gazed into his smoldering eyes. I heard him suck in his breath as I innocently explored every inch of him with my hands.

"You truly are the most astonishingly, beautiful woman I've ever laid my eyes upon, Isabella Townsend." His eyes involuntarily closed, as he enjoyed the feeling of my touch, when his eyes opened wide and he captured my hand in his, pinning it to the floor by my head. He rolled me over and balanced himself above me.

"I will beg your forgiveness ahead of time, my love," he said, placing a hand on my cheek, when I looked confused. Then bringing his lips to mine, all thoughts and confusion were banished in an instant, replaced instead with raw animalistic desire.

Aiden's warm, masculine bouquet of musk, mingled with freshly shaven skin, assailed my nostrils, creating illicit thoughts and desires as they stirred my wild imaginations once again. I felt oblivious to anything else around us. The world could have been falling apart at that moment and I would have never noticed.

Pressing his manhood against the stubborn barrier of maidenhood, Aiden broke through as I cried out in surprise. I was not expecting to experience pain, mixed with pleasure, but I quickly forgot everything else except my own carnal desires and hunger that needed to be satiated. Aiden covered my mouth with his and waited for the tension to pass before he began to move his hips. His kisses became more insistent as his body began to move in a rhythmic motion, causing a ravenous need to build up inside of me, that became a tidal wave that wouldn't be stopped. All coherent thoughts was gone, replaced with raw passionate desire. Arching my back, I called out to him and dug my nails into his back, until I could do nothing else but cry out in ecstasy. I called his name over and over again between harsh ragged breaths as he stroked my face and then I felt him stiffen and cry out as well.

We clung to one another as the incredible sensations began to dissipate, and our limbs intertwined, as we both gasped for air. A few minutes passed before Aiden rolled to his side, pulling me with him.

Cradled in the crook of Aiden's arm I closed my eyes as he ran his fingers through my damp hair. I could feel his eyes studying me.

"Why are you staring at me?" I asked without opening my eyes.

"How do you know I am looking at you?" Aiden asked with a smile on his face.

"Because I can feel your eyes staring through my eyelids, and why are you smiling?" I chuckled.

"And what makes you think I am smiling? Maybe I am scowling at you or maybe I'm not looking at you at all," he countered.

Slowly opening my eyes, I looked up at him. "You know that you made a huge mess for Maria to clean up, when you kicked that tray over and scattered dishes and food everywhere. She is going to figure out what we did here," I pointed out, suddenly having an attach of guilt.

"Something tells me Maria is going to know exactly what went on here, and as far as the mess is concerned, she should be thanking me," Aiden interjected with a lift of his eyebrows. "It will give her something to do all day, besides gossip with the other maids. And technically we are married, so stop acting like a school girl who was caught behind the school house with a boy."

"Fair enough," I blushed, realizing how silly I sounded. "You never answered me. Why were you staring at me?" I asked, turning onto my side and propping my head up in my hand. I began tracing my fingers over his chest, averting my eyes, because the look he was giving me was too intense.

Tipping my chin up with his hand, Aiden forced me to look at him. "You looked so peaceful laying there. I wish you could see your face right now. You've already changed."

Cupping his face with my hands I kissed his lips, "Thank you for changing my heart, Aiden Townsend."

28

A Snake Has Slithered Into My Happily Ever After

 HAT BEGAN AS A VERY pleasurable evening rolled into a fitful night, filled with strange emotions and a prickling sensation at the back of my neck followed by a disconcerting sense of dread that completely encompassed me.

"Shh... shh..." Aiden soothed as he gently held me close, shaking me awake. "It's just a bad dream."

I awoke with a start, to Aiden stroking my face, as he brushed tears from my cheeks. "Something is wrong," I cried sitting up in bed, pulling the covers up higher to ward off the chill that had invaded my whole body.

"What are you talking about?" He asked, pulling me closer to him. "You just had a bad dream," he reassured me.

"No, Aiden, I am telling you, something is wrong," I insisted, pulling away from him, and climbed out of bed. Finding my robe, I slid it on, tying it at the waist while I walked over to the window.

"Isabella, come back to bed, it's early," Aiden pleaded.

I could feel his eyes following me as I yanked the curtain back and stared down into the courtyard. I was looking for anything that was different or out of place. But I saw nothing. I should have been reassured by this fact, but I wasn't. The nagging feeling persisted. I tried telling myself that I was being silly...that as Aiden had said, it was nothing. But the feeling wouldn't leave me, and I involuntarily shivered.

Climbing out of bed, Aiden put his robe on and stood behind me to see what I was looking at. "You see, there is nothing unusual going on down there," he said, pointing at the courtyard below. "Now, won't you come back to bed with me," he begged, turning me around in his arms. "I think I have a few more things to show you yet," he smiled alluringly.

I smiled up at him, unable to shake the feeling that the other shoe was ready to drop, when suddenly someone began urgently knocking at our door.

"Who the devil?" Aiden cursed under his breath when he felt me jump. He turned and headed toward the bedroom door with me following closely behind him.

"The other shoe," I said dryly when he looked at me with a strange look on his face.

"What are you talking about?" Aiden asked, turning to look at the door when someone urgently knocked again.

"Answer the door, Aiden," I insisted, trying to open the door when he didn't immediately do so, "And that question of yours should be answered." I said, as he gave me the queerest look. Taking a hold of my hand, Aiden pulled me behind him, and then opened the door. It was Caleb on the other side.

Caleb blurted out, "We have a problem," the moment the door was opened. His normal air of good humor and light tones were gone, as he continued. "The Banning brothers are both dead, as are the two guards on detail."

I audibly gasped before covering my mouth with my hand. Aiden swung the door open wider and pulled me from behind him.

"Whose men were they?" Aiden asked, visibly shaken.

"They were our men," Caleb said with a mix of sorrow and anger in his voice.

"What were their names?" I asked holding my breath.

"Roberts and Smitty," Caleb answered, and then quickly looked down when he noticed tears in my eyes. Turning away I walked back into the room, taking the closest seat I could find as Aiden and Caleb continued talking quietly at the door. Aiden walked up behind me he stood there for a moment without speaking.

"Do you believe me now?" I questioned, without turning around.

"I will never doubt you again," he answered. "Never!" hitting the top of the chair with his hand before heading to the window and staring out at the courtyard below. Emotion reverberated in his voice as he spoke and I could tell he was badly shaken by the senseless loss.

Getting up from my seat, I joined him. "Who could have done such a thing?" I asked, looking up at his profile, as he stared blankly out the window.

"I wish I knew," anger slicing through Aiden's words now as he turned to look at me, "By all that is holy in this world I wish I knew. When you awoke, you were crying. Did you see anything in your dream that would be useful to us now?" Aiden asked.

I searched my mind closing my eyes desperately trying to remember my dream and why I had been crying. "Nothing is clear or in focus. It's all these flashes in my mind. Everything was happening so fast," I growled in frustration, because I couldn't see any one thing clearly. "It was a blur, as if my mind was trying to see everything at once. I know there was more than one person present, of that I am certain. Maybe even three people."

Tears ran down my cheeks as I thought of Roberts. "I think I knew that Roberts was dead, but I didn't want to believe it," I cried, burying my face in Aiden's shoulder. "Oh Aiden, it was so awful," I sobbed. "They slit his throat and left him there gasping for air. There was so much blood." I felt Aiden's arms tighten around me, trying to comfort me. He didn't say a word. He just held me until I stopped crying.

Maria softly knocked on the door as she entered my chambers and I felt Aiden nod his head.

Pulling back some, Aiden looked down at me, "I have to dress and see to the men. Will you be alright for a little while?" he asked gently.

"Yes, Maria will be with me," I sniffed and blew my nose in the handkerchief Aiden handed me from his robe pocket. My eyes felt swollen and I looked away, embarrassed by my tears.

"Don't leave the castle without me, Isabella. I know how you like to take your rides when you are upset, but I need you to promise me today you won't go out without me," he cautioned, as his fingers dug into my shoulders.

"I promise," I replied softly. "I was planning to look in on Charlie. I swear I won't leave the castle," I winced slightly, and he let go suddenly, realizing that he had been digging his fingers in to my flesh.

"Maria, watch after her until I return," Aiden said, his request sounding more like an order than a polite petition. Then spying the mess he had made the night before, Aiden turned. "Maria, I wish to apologize now for the mess I made last night with the food tray. The entire thing is my fault and I am sorry," he said with all seriousness.

"Don't mention it, my Lord. It's quite alright," she replied, eyeing the mess even before he said anything to her. "I will clean that right up good as new," Maria said under her breath almost sarcastically when he was out of earshot.

"I heard that," I said to her. "You realize the mess wasn't entirely his fault," I chided.

"Yes, I think I am beginning to get the picture quite clearly in my mind," Maria answered, bending over to scoop some of the food onto a plate, and placing the entire mess on the over turned tray.

"Get that later or better yet, get one of the maids to do it for you," I sniffed again then blew my nose. "Help me get dressed, please," I insisted. "I have to check on Charlie."

"I thought maybe the blue dress would be nice today," Maria said, standing up and making her way to the changing room to retrieve the gown.

"I will leave it up to you and your expert opinion," I replied passively. "Just don't forget my dagger," I added as an afterthought.

"I would never forget that," Maria reassured me. "It would be like forgetting your undergarments."

An hour later I was headed down the hallway toward Charlie's room when I came across Ian coming out of his room. He was closing the door when he noticed me. "Good morning, Lord Townsend," I called out my greeting as I passed by him.

"Wait up, dear sister," Ian called back to me, as he rushed to catch up. "I fear I didn't truly have the opportunity to congratulate you properly, when you and Aiden wed," Ian added as he took a hold of my arm. "Where are you off to in such a rush?"

"I wanted to check on my brother Charlie this morning," I replied, taking a deep breath to stem my frustration at being delayed. But mostly I was in a rush to speak with my mother.

"Why don't I walk with you and you can tell me how my brother is doing. It is such a shame that Aiden and I are not as close as you and your brother... Charlie, is it?" Ian said, feigning sadness. "There was a time when Aiden and I were thicker than a couple of theives. It seems like an eternity ago. I really don't know what happened; something changed at some point. Oh, how I miss those days," Ian sighed, looking down at me. I could tell he was lying about his sadness and missed opportunities with Aiden. But I didn't know why, nor did I truly care to delve into the matter at that moment. My mind was working overtime to solve the mystery of my dream, or lack of any real clear visions, and why I couldn't remember more.

"Well, this is Charlie's room. I would invite you in, but I don't think he is ready for visitors just yet," I offered, as an explanation, while disentangling myself from Ian's grasp.

"Oh, do not concern yourself, Lady Townsend," Ian paused a moment before continuing. "Say, would you mind terribly if we were less formal, dear sister?" Ian asked, adding a pleasant smile, almost as an afterthought.

"Please, call me Isabella, we are family after all," I replied.

"And I insist that you call me Ian," he demanded, bending over to take my hand and place a chaste kiss upon it. "Well, I am off to meet with Lord Blayney's second son, Lance. You haven't met him yet, have you?" Ian asked, with a hint of mystery in his tone. "Lance and I grew up together. It seems that he and I have a lot in common."

"Oh and how is that?" I asked, wondering to myself at the same time what his true agenda was.

"He too is a spare son, as they say in the succession and family ranking," Ian snorted his derision.

"Is that how you truly see yourself, Ian, simply as a spare?" I asked curiously, placing my right hand into my dress pocket, resting it upon the cool hilt of my jeweled dagger. Wrapping my fingers around it, I was comforted by the knowledge of its presence. There was just something off about Ian. But I couldn't put my finger on it yet.

"Well, what would you consider me, since I am not eligible to inherit my father's wealth?" he said, narrowing his eyes.

"I believe you to be a man worthy of joy and happiness. You may do as you wish with your life. Please don't tell me that you feel held back in life by a mere matter of birth order," I argued coolly.

"Sweet, naive Isabella, that just goes to show what you truly know of family, society, and politics," Ian answered, patting the back of my hand almost patronizingly. "Well, this is where we part ways, dear sister," Ian kissed my cheek before turning on his heels to make his way down the hall in the opposite direction.

Just as he had taken about five steps, Ian turned back around and said the most bizarre thing. "Oh Isabella, do be careful when you are wondering about this old dusty castle. I have found that it can be full of secrets and hidden dangers," his ominous tone and thinly-veiled threat made me shiver as I watched him turn and continue on his way, whistling a happy tune.

Squeezing the handle of my dagger one more time before removing my hand, I watched Ian turn the corner. Placing my hand on the doorknob, I took a deep breath before knocking, then entering Charlie's room.

Mother was standing at the window staring out into the courtyard. She never turned around when I came in. She didn't need to, she knew instinctively who had entered the room. I joined her at the window, putting my arm about her waist, and leaning my head against her shoulder.

"It's just awful what happened last night," she said without looking directly at me.

"I dreamt about it last night, Momma." I quietly replied, lifting my head up to look at her. She pulled her eyes away from the activity in the courtyard to look at me. "I remember having a bad dream and I must have cried out, because Aiden woke me up. But I can't remember the details, except for the blur of blood, death and emotions. There are no real details that stand out clearly to me. Nothing seems to be in complete focus. It's as if my dream was made up of everything that occurred, but it's garbled and mixed up," I whined, looking to her for answers and clarity.

"The experience was too much for your mind to comprehend all at once. When your mind is ready to except what transpired in that room, it will become clearer," Mother assured me softly, touching my face gently with her hands.

"I don't think you understand," I cried. "I can't do this any longer. I fear I am not strong enough to endure these visions," I blurted out in a harsh whisper, trying not to disturb Charlie. Tears blurred my vision and I wiped at my eyes, turning back to the window.

"You are the strongest, toughest person I know," Charlie uttered in a hoarse voice, as he tried to sit up in bed.

"Charlie," I cried out in surprise, wiping at my eyes again before turning around and crossing the room to help him sit up, "I didn't mean to disturb you."

"Don't be ridiculous," Charlie grasped my hand with more strength than he had the day before. "I can feel myself getting stronger already, just being near you."

I buried my face in Charlie's shoulder and hid my tears.

"I knew you would come for me. I could feel your strength and tenacity even when everything was so bleak. It's what kept me alive," Charlie admitted, patting my back, before squeezing me tightly. "You can't let me down now by turning into a sissy girl."

"But I am a girl, you idiot." I exclaimed, while delivering a half hearted punch to his arm and pretending to be offended. "Oh Charlie, how I have missed you." I wiped at my nose with my hand as Charlie held me at arm's length. "Isabella, you have this untapped wealth of courage and strength that you haven't even yet realized. I know this because I can feel it in you. Even if you cannot feel it for yourself, it's in there," Charlie grasped my shoulders. "Together the three of us will figure this out."

Mother stood behind me looking down at Charlie while resting her hand on my shoulder. "It will all become clearer with time," she said reassuringly. "But first things first. Charlie needs his rest if he is going to get stronger. I believe he too has a wealth of untapped abilities not yet realized," Mother stated proudly.

"I just hope we can wait," I said dubiously, pondering the future, as another chill of foreboding chilled my bones.

29

To Breathe a Sigh of Relief, or Not To? That is The Question

VENTUALLY MANY BEGAN TO BREATHE easier in the three days since the murdered men were discovered in the guesthouse. Everyone that is, except me.

Aiden assigned a man by the name of Donovan as my bodyguard. He followed me everywhere when Aiden wasn't by my side. Donovan had been given Aiden's old room across from what was now the master bedroom. I found him sitting in the common area, between the two rooms, waiting for me to emerge each morning. He was a very large man with bulging muscles and large hands. But the thing that impressed me about him was the arsenal he carried. I never saw any one man pull more implements of death from so many places on his body. The man truly was impressive. I asked him to demonstrate this marvelous magical act the first day we were introduced and he was more than happy to do so.

He began by pulling out the two pistols from his waistband and placing them on the table before me. He then reached into his vest and produced three throwing knives, assuring me he could accurately hit a fly on the wall from twenty paces. Donovan then removed a dagger from one pocket, and a set of connected metal rings, that he wore on the fingers of his right hand, from the other. He said he could stop any man with one punch. Putting his left leg up on a stool, he reached under the pant leg and pulled out another knife, placing it on the table as well. Then he informed me, with a wide grin, that he had two other weapons hidden somewhere on his body, that he never revealed to anyone, not even me. The only question that continued to plague me was, where in the world did he hide the other two weapons?

Donovan and I got along great and I even implemented some of his tricks by carrying a pair of throwing knives, strapped to my thigh, everywhere I went. I may not have been as accurate as Mr. Donovan, but I was good enough to do some real damage, if a situation should arise.

Charlie and Ashton continued to heal and would be heading home in another week, on the *Tempest* with Mother and Father.

Father and I mended our broken relationship, while Aiden and I continued to work on improving ours, although we had not yet discussed what came next or where we would be living.

All in all it had been a very productive three day, yet something kept nagging at my mind. I never felt completely at ease and was constantly on edge, waiting.

I sat at my dressing table, quietly pondering things, while Maria worked her magic. She had piled my hair high upon my head, threading ribbons throughout the curls as they cascaded down the back of my head.

"Perfect Maria," I gasped. "It is simply perfect."

"I love this color of red on you. The tone brings out your coloring beautifully, my lady," Maria exclaimed, handing me a white laced fan as I stood up.

"Oh Maria, you have done it again," I gasped, eyeing myself one last time before heading from the room.

Aiden was in the outer chamber talking with Donovan when I walked into the room. All talking ceased, and I noticed that Aiden stood a little straighter, as a devilish grin played across his lips.

"I think I will be escorting my beautiful wife to dinner now, Donovan, so your services are no longer require this evening," he announced, while maintaining eye contact with me. "In fact, why don't you take the night off, and I will see you first thing in the morning."

"If I were you, I would keep that one all to myself, as well," Donovan confessed, elbowing Aiden in the side before inclining his head in my direction as he excused himself and left.

"You are truly a vision this evening, my dear." Aiden crossed the room taking my hand in his and placing a kiss upon the back of it. Holding my breath as Aiden gently ran the back of his hand across my cheek, I felt my heart pounding in my chest. "Are you happy?" he asked.

"Yes," I replied, reaching up to pull his glorious mouth to mine. Aiden pulled back from me a moment and I could still feel his breath next to my cheek as he began to recite a verse of poetry to me:

"What does love have in store for me?
One happy minute, or hour, or perhaps years to come
Will her love end my pain the moment it begins anew?
I pray that no day be void of this bliss and pleasure,
And if we are blessed to escape our time of death
May cupid guard the door forever more to keep us,
From such a time, when death comes to seize us no more.
Causing time to stand still and no one would know
For I would contend myself with you, every hour
Basking in your light, where I would find delight.
If time and death would depart, leaving us
Unharmed or marred by its passing
For love, has found a way to live, by dying."

"Aiden, that is absolutely beautiful. But I don't recognize it," I said, with a sigh.

"It is by an unknown, if not obscure, author of little consequence," he replied,
hovering over my lips with a devilish grin.

"Oh, pardon me," Maria said, clearing her throat and surprising us as she entered the room. "I thought you had left for dinner already."

"Oh no! What time is it?" I gasped, suddenly shocked that I had lost track of the time. I began looking around for a clock in a panic. "We are late, everyone will be waiting on us."

"Let them wait," Aiden calmly said, still looking down at me so intently that I was certain he meant to kiss me right there in front of Maria.

"But Aiden —" I began to say when he interrupted me.

"Shh... now, everything will be fine. If we leave now we will only be fashionably late," he teased, giving Maria a wink, as he passed her, pulling me out the door behind him. Rushing down the stairs, we laughed like children sharing a joke which came to an abrupt halt when we ran into Ian and another man.

"It would seem the two of them are getting on rather well. Wouldn't you say, Lance, old friend?" Ian laughed in a mocking tone that sent a tingle of apprehension straight through me. I glanced up at Aiden only to see him clenching his jaws together.

"Indeed, old friend, they are getting on very well indeed," Lance echoed Ian with a small chuckle.

"Well, if it isn't my brother Ian, and his pet parrot," Aiden scornfully fired back, stepping in front of me as if to shield me from the unpleasantness of the two men.

"Brother dearest, I mean you no harm. But you go for the jugular, every time," Ian replied, pulling a sad face as he feigned sadness, while Lance Blayney looked as if he was going to take Aiden's head off.

"What's the matter, Lancelot, didn't you get your proper rations of crackers and seeds this evening? You always did like following Ian around, picking up his crumbs," Aiden taunted as he advanced on Lance, blocking his view of me.

"Now, now boys, do I have to split you two up? Or will you agree to play nicely?" Ian asserted, stepping between them both to prevent the exchange of blows, and inevitable bloodshed that would occur.

"Lance, this is Lady Isabella Townsend, my new sister in law," Ian explained, reaching around Aiden to grab me by the hand, and pull me forward, as if nothing was amiss. "Isabella, meet Lord Lance Blayney, the second son of Lord and Lady Blayney," Ian offered, as if he were merely trying to defuse the situation he had deliberately provoked. "His real name is Lancelot, but he hates to be called that, so we use his preferred name, to keep the peace."

"It's a pleasure to meet you, Lord Blayney," I blurted out, trying to sound gracious as I offered him my hand.

Lance gave my hand a contemptuous look, and then glanced up at my face. "The pleasure is mine, madam," he stated, unconvincingly, with a curt nod.

Dropping my hand back down to my side, I attempted to be polite and smooth over the awkward moment. "Well, if the host's son can be late to dinner, then all is not lost," I said with a nervous laugh and a quick glance back at Aiden.

"We aren't having dinner with you tonight," Ian stepped in to explain. "I am afraid that Lance and I have some… um… urgent business to attend to," Ian quickly said, then giving Lance a strange look, he gestured with his head that it was time to go.

"Perhaps we will catch up to you both later," I added as an afterthought, when they had turned to leave.

"Perhaps you will," Lance answered cryptically, with a sadistic smile over his shoulder as they headed for the door.

"I'm not entirely sure I understand everything that just transpired," Aiden said, taking my hand in his as we stood and watched Ian and Lance walk away. My body involuntarily shivered, and my head felt suddenly fuzzy and numb, so I grabbed ahold of Aiden's arm for support. "Are you alright?" Aiden asked with concern.

"Just give me a moment." I said cautiously, closing my eyes and taking several deep breaths until the strange feeling left me.

"What just happened?" Aiden asked.

"I am not sure," I answered. "It was a very strange feeling, but I think I'm better now."

"Perhaps you over-exerted yourself today," he added, smoothing his thumb over my pale cheek.

I tried to smile. "Maybe that's it, and I need some food," I replied, as I allowed myself to be led toward the dining hall. Chancing a glance back down the hallway, where Ian and Lance had disappeared, I felt another involuntary spasm spread through my body. "I hope they are serving soup," I absently commented.

"If not, I will go to the kitchen and make you some myself," Aiden sweetly replied, glancing at me out of the corner of his eye.

30

Beasts and Monsters Are Real And
They Lurk in Dark and Scary Places

INNER WAS AN EVENT ROLLED into a night of entertainment. The Blayney's never failed to invite fascinating people, and that evening was no exception.

Lord Blayney had solicited one Mister Ronald Whickem to dinner that night, who was the local proprietor of the theatrical play house in town.

Mr. Whickem was a flamboyant, dapper gentleman in his mid-forties, who brought along two actors headlining at his theater.

Miss Lara McBride was stunning, with blond hair. The color reminded me of wheat fields ready to be harvested. Delicate little ringlets piled high atop her head, spilled down her back, with wispy curls framing her heart- shaped face. She was blessed with long dark lashes that fringed her gentle brown eyes that crinkled in the corners when she laughed. She also had brilliantly white teeth that sparkled like pearls when she smiled and laughed. She was very captivating and I could feel myself being sucked into the vortex that was Lara McBride.

Mister John Hayes, on the other hand, was a very handsome man, with chestnut brown hair, hazel eyes, and a thin but attractive frame. He was a charismatic yet funny man, with full pouty lips that were meant for kissing. He often turned his attentive hazel eyes toward Miss McBride, who seemed not to notice his longing looks or solicitous gestures.

Miss McBride opted instead to turn her full attention to the dinner companion to her left, my unwitting brother Charlie. This treasonous act of betrayal by Miss McBride seemed to cause Mr. Hayes great distress. They both were members of a ten person traveling troop that sang, danced, and acted its way across Ireland. The group would end their tour in Galway, the home base for this troop, which would bring to an end their seven month tour.

Lara explained to us that the traveling troop of performers would take two months off when they were through with their tour. Afterwards they would spend two and a half months preparing another production, adding and subtracting players as necessary. I found it profoundly telling when she mentioned subtracting members, Miss McBride looked directly at John Hayes for the first time that evening. In turn, Mr. Hayes looked truly crushed.

She then turned her attention back to us and went on to say that the troop would again be on the road, for seven consecutive months, making the rounds of popular playhouses.

As a special treat after dinner, Mr. Hayes and Miss McBride, being accompanied on the piano by Mr. Whickem, performed several scenes from their show that included a love ballad, which lacked conviction on Lara's part, but was very convincing when Mr. Hayes sang his part. After their riveting performance, we were encouraged to sing along. I had developed a headache during dinner, which was made worse by all the noise and excitement in the room. Slipping quietly from the room, I headed upstairs to find Maria, and see if she would make me a tonic. Upon entering my chamber, I noticed a dim light in the dressing room, just off the bedroom, and figured Maria must be tidying up in there. I called out to her, and turned to rummage through my trunk for a shawl. "Maria, I just came back for a wrap and to see if you could make me a tonic for my headache," I absently said, over my shoulder. "Found it," I continued, as I pulled the white shawl, with the tiny rose buds stitched along the edge, from my trunk. "Maria?" I called out again to her, as I wrapped the shawl about me. Turning around, shock immediately registered when I found two men dressed completely in black standing in the shadows of my room.

"I would advise you not to scream or call out for help," suggested the man, holding the knife to Maria's throat. "I understand that you are fond of your hand servant," he said with a derisive snort.

"Please don't hurt her," I said in a panic. "What do you want, money, jewels? I asked in desperation. Then turning back to the trunk, I began to dig into the corner to retrieve a bag of coins I kept tucked away. "Here, take it," I cried with a degree of recklessness, throwing the bag at his feet. "Just let her go. She hasn't done anything. Please!"

"Oh, but she has done something. She served her part very well indeed," the other man said callously. "She has managed to keep you in check, and as I hear tell, that is quite an accomplishment indeed," he continued, not even trying to hide his identity.

Recognition suddenly hit me, "Ian?"

Dramatically removing his hat and scarf Ian had a sardonic smirk on his lips. "Isabella," He calmly replied.

"And that would make your accomplice Lord Blayney. I can only assume that this is the business the two of you needed to take care of tonight," I remarked, with distain dripping from my lips.

"Look at her, Lancelot, isn't my sister in law just the cleverest girl?" Ian's sarcastic tone and self assured stance told me he didn't fear being discovered.

"Why, Ian?" I cried, my voice sounded strange to my ears, "Why would you do this?" I continued in disbelief, as the cloud of confusion lifted.

"I find the best way to hurt the ones I love is to hurt the ones they love," Ian snorted his derision, as if he were the cleverest person in the room.

"So what happens now?" I asked, as reality began to sink in and panic threatened to take over. "Do you intend to butcher us like you did those men the other night?" I asserted, trying to stall for time. Involuntarily shivering with revulsion as the memory of my dream came flooding back, playing out in my mind again. Only this time everything was crystal clear, including the sheer pleasure on Ian and companion's face when they slit the throats of Roberts and Smitty, and watched them bleed to death, gasping for their last breath of air. I felt sick to my stomach and had to swallow hard when I tasted bile in my mouth.

"No, that would be too swift," Ian confessed, taking several steps toward me, causing me to shrink back from him involuntarily. The darkness that surrounded him turned my stomach again, and I knew that I wouldn't be able to stop it this time. I grabbed the basin off the dresser and proceeded to empty the contents of my stomach into it. I pushed Ian's hand away when he tried to give me his handkerchief to wipe my mouth, opting instead to use my own.

"I don't just want to hurt my dear brother this time. I want to crush his spirit and rip out his heart. So that means you, sweet sister, must disappear," Ian gloated, as he clenched his fist in my face, making me jump back with a start.

"Do you mean that you killed Aiden's first wife and son?" I managed to whisper, shocked by his thinly veiled admission.

Ian walked around me boldly assessing me. "Are you accusing me of duplicity in Aiden's family's death?" Ian cynically asked. Stopping directly in front of me, he leaned in close to my face. Momentarily unable to speak, I simply stared back at his dead eyes. "Well, unfortunately I didn't," he declared finally, glaring at me. "But their deaths nearly drove Aiden to the madhouse. It was quite a scene to behold," Ian said with a sadistic laugh. I gasped when I heard the coldness in his voice. It turned my blood to ice and I could feel all the color draining from my face, because suddenly I realized who the Governor was. "You suddenly look pale, dear sister," Ian's patronizing tone was grating, as he feigned concern.

Taking several deep breaths, I closed my eyes to gain control again. My head felt like it was spinning and I felt I might be sick again. "You are the infamous Governor that everyone has been whispering about, aren't you?" I quietly asked, as I slowly opened my eyes to look into Ian's, cold, grey orbs.

"Do you hear that, Lancelot? I'm infamous!" Ian cooed.

Finding my composure once again, I clasped my hands to keep them from shaking and betraying me. "Why have you done this, Ian? Are you truly so callous and heartless that you did all of this because you are displeased with your birth order? Choosing to tear your family and country apart just to destroy your own brother over money. fear you have truly lost your moral compass, and I will pray for your soul."

"If you meant that to be cutting, I am afraid you have missed your mark," Ian scoffed then snorted, as if I had just told a dandy joke. "Come, come, I know you can do better than that."

"Ian, we have to go," Lance insisted, as his eyes darted around the room nervously only to land on the door once again.

"As always, you are my voice of reason, Lancelot," Ian turned to look lovingly at his companion and partner in crime.

"I told you before that I don't like it when you call me that," Lance scolded, under his breath as if the open familiarity embarrassed him.

"You heard the man, we must be off at once," Ian cackled, turning to me, unruffled by Lance's rebuke.

"What makes you think I would go anywhere with you?" I argued, sounding bolder than I felt.

"It's simple, really. If you don't come along like a good girl, I will slit Maria's throat, and make you watch as she struggles to take her last breath. And let me assure you that it really is quite gruesome," Ian replied without emotion.

"You're insane!" I spat at him.

"Yes, that fact is well known, but to what degree has always been a matter of some debate," Ian smirked, giving me a push, forcing me to move forward, toward the dressing closet. "May I suggest you both grab a heavy cloak on your way out. It has begun to rain, and I wouldn't want you to catch your death, just yet." Maria grabbed my two heaviest cloaks, handing one to me.

Lance led the way to a panel, hidden in the dressing room. Moving clothes to one side, he felt around on the wall for the hidden lever that released the panel, causing it to open. Two torches burned brightly in the blackened interior of the secret passageway, no doubt placed there in the ancient rusty hooks on the damp walls by Lance and Ian before coming in through the panel.

"I gave you fair warning when I told you that this old castle was full of secrets and hidden dangers," Ian insisted so matter-of-factly as he shoved me toward the opening when I hesitated.

"Wait," Ian called out when we had walked down a few of the dimly lit steps, "place your hands together," he exclaimed, pulling a thin strand of leather tie from his pocket.

"Is that really necessary, Ian? What if I slip on the damp steps? I won't be able to stop myself from falling," I reasoned.

"What can I say, Isabella? Your reputation precedes you," Ian said with a grimace. "I would caution you to be careful, but when all is said and done, who really cares."

His callousness caught me by surprise and I gasped. "Are you truly afraid of a woman?" I taunted, holding my hands together in front of me. Ian's hand shot out, slapping me across the face so hard that my head snapped back and I momentarily saw stars. Then, grabbing my hands, he roughly wrapped the leather strap around my wrists several times, insuring that it was tight.

Maria's cry was cut short, as Lance clamped his hand over her mouth in warning. Then Ian reached into my right front pocket, and pulled out the jeweled handle dagger I always carry. "There now, we can be sure that there will be no funny business on our journey." With a self satisfied smile on his lips, Ian continued. "Lancelot, would you and Maria be so kind as to lead the way out of this ancient, decaying, rat infested corridor, so that we might be on our way to our desired destination," he gestured with his hand for everyone to get moving. I glared at Ian, as he took hold of my arm and propelled me forward down the dark, slippery steps.

We walked for about fifteen minutes, turning and traversing the darkened corridors of the castle's secret labyrinth. Finally, we came out on the other side of the ancient stonewall that once protected the castle's interior from being breached by invading forces. Waiting just beyond the tree line were five men on horseback with three horses in tow. I recognized one of the men as being part of Aiden's group of mercenaries. So, what was he doing here? I looked directly at him as he gave me a cold stare. I kept searching my brain to remember his name, but it wouldn't come to me.

"You ladies will have to share a horse. We had only anticipated retrieving one of you from the castle tonight," Lance explained as he tied my hands to the saddle, after helping me onto the horse.

"You won't get away with this," I argued.

"So you have said three times already," Lance stated blandly, appearing to be less than interested in what I had to say. In fact, he looked angry that I was still breathing.

"Well, will you at least tell me where we are going?" I demanded.

"And spoil the surprise?" Ian scoffed, "Lance wouldn't dare," he cried, coming around the horse with Maria. The two of them managed to lift Maria up, placing her behind me on the horse. I bit back the string of expletives I wanted to throw at them, but opted instead to present them both with a gracious smile that didn't quite reach all the way to my eyes. "Well, I suppose the best part of any journey is the adventure of getting there," I declared with sarcasm.

"Now that's the spirit, old girl." Ian's words dripped with sarcasm. "I keep telling Lancelot that he should develop a more positive attitude," he laughed close to Lance's face, while still looking at me. Then turning his full attentions back to his companion in an intimate way, before laughing once again and slapping his back.

Lance took the horses lead, pulling us roughly behind him as he muttered a few profane words and something about Ian's questionable parentage, under his breath, before climbing onto his own horse.

Maria was softly sniffing behind me. "I'm sorry, Isabella. I never even saw them until they were on top of me in the room."

"Maria, none of this is your fault, so put it out of your head," I assured her, as she encircled my waist. "Right now, I am concerned with surviving until someone comes to rescue us. And you can rest assured that they will come for us," I whispered, with confidence. *Just play it smart old girl and we will get out of this alive*, I said to myself, as I silently sent up a prayer, and a call for help to my twin, Charlie. Maria hugged me tightly and buried her head in my back trying to stem her sobs.

My eyes kept going back to the man from Aiden's team that I recognized. I was racking my brain for his name. "Gershwin? No, Grainger, Garretty? Yes, that's it, Garretty," I repeated the name under my breath.

"Did you say something, Isabella?" Maria whispered close to my ear.

"Yes, that man over there," I gestured with my head, as I tried not to draw too much attention to myself, "I recognize him. He's one of Aiden's men. So what is he doing here?" I pondered out loud. "His name is Garretty. The only thing I don't know is which side he is truly on. Ours or theirs?" I mused out loud again, while hanging onto the saddle as Lance continued to work out his issues with Ian, by jostling our horse roughly behind him. "Keep your eyes and ears open, Maria, but don't be too obvious about it," I said, twisting around to look at her. "And if you are a religious person, now would be a good time to pray."

31

The Search for Isabella Begins

NGELINA DEVERAUX FOUND AIDEN TALKING to Mr. Whickem. She touched his arm gently to get his attention, "Aiden, where is Isabella?" Angelina asked with a touch of concern in her voice.

"She said that she was going to get a tonic from Maria for her headache and that she would be right back. Maybe she decided to go to bed," Aiden concluded, pulling his watch from his breast pocket to check the time. Surprised when he realized that an hour had passed, since he last saw his wife. "I will go check on her," Aiden said, excusing himself.

Angelina grabbed Aiden's arm before he could turn to leave. "I just sent one of the maids upstairs to check on her and she said that there was no one in the room. She also advised me that she hasn't seen Maria all evening. I'm concerned, Aiden, Charlie told me ten minutes ago that something was wrong with Isabella."

"We can't jump to conclusions, Lady Deveraux," Aiden said, trying to reassure her, as a feeling of dread began to creep into his conscious mind.

"I'm telling you that something is wrong. I will find my husband. Charlie stepped outside to see if he can locate her," Angelina said, sounding distressed, with her hand still resting on Aiden's arm.

"I will go look for her as well," Aiden insisted. "I'm sure she is fine. She either stopped to visit with Maria in the kitchen or she is talking to someone in another room."

"Aiden, you are not listening to me. Isabella is gone. She has told you of our family secret," Angelina questioned, with a degree of discomfort.

"What family secret?" Aiden asked, feeling disjointed and confused.

"The gift we were born with," Angelina asserted, pausing to look around, making sure that no one had overheard her before going on. "The gift that Isabella and Charlie share… their ability to sense things," Angelina explained, still waiting for the light of understanding to dawn in his eyes as she pulled him off to a quiet corner. "How do you think Isabella knew exactly where Charlie was?" she whispered.

Understanding suddenly dawned in Aiden's eyes, as he tried to focus on the conversation with his mother in law. "Yes, she has told me all about it and I find her astute observations, remarkable, but I must admit, I still don't understand it," Aiden confessed, giving her a perplexing look.

"Mother," Charlie called out, his father following close behind him.

Angelina took Aiden's hand in hers still trying to make him understand. "Isabella and Charlie have had a heightened sense of one another ever since they were born. They get it from my side of the family. It's inherited through the blood line. My mother and I both have the gift, as well. When I tell you that something is wrong, you just need to take my word for it," she persisted as her penetrating green eyes stared into Aiden's crystal blue ones.

"Isabella," was all Charlie said before he wrapped his arms around himself and shivered.

"We should search the castle again, just to make sure," Aiden insisted.

"She isn't here, Aiden," Charlie scolded in a loud whisper of frustration, looking around to see if anyone was staring at him.

"Don't waste your time. If my son says that she isn't here, then you can be assured that Isabella isn't here and something has happened to her. I've never known Charlie to be wrong when it came to his sister. You're going to have to learn to take these things on faith, son," Jude concluded, slightly exasperated, having to explain it to his new son in law.

"How could she just disappear?" Aiden mused.

"I don't know, but Charlie and I will confer, and get back to you. Just be ready to go," Angelina said, fixing Aiden with a serious look.

"I can't just stand here and do nothing," Aiden swore under his breath, as he took a hold of Angelina's arm when she turned to leave with Charlie.

"You can't go in search of her if you don't know which way to go or what you are looking for," she growled, sternly looking at Aiden's offending hand preventing her from moving forward.

Aiden followed her eyes and released his vise-like grip on her arm immediately. "I'm sorry."

"We will come to find you as soon as we have anything. But right now, we need a quiet place to concentrate," Charlie insisted, placing a comforting hand on Aiden's arm.

"Father, you better ready the men and get the horses saddled," Charlie directed, as he pulled his mother from the room.

Lord Blayney noticed the disturbance. "Is everything alright?" he asked with concern.

Aiden combed his fingers through his hair, taking a few cleansing breaths to steady his shattered nerves. "Isabella and her handmaid are missing," he announced, looking about as he tried to decide what he would do next.

"But I just saw her go up the stairs a few minutes ago." the Earl insisted.

"It has been over an hour," Aiden replied, as he rushed from the room, Lord Blayney followed him.

"Where are you going, my boy?" Lord Blayney rushed to catch up to Aiden as he took the stairs two at a time.

Aiden entered the room he shared with Isabella, thrashing about like a bull in a china factory, he was searching the room high and low for clues. Retrieving the white shawl carelessly tossed on the floor, Aiden buried his face in it, inhaling deeply of Isabella's scent. An anguished growl from deep in his throat escaped Aiden's lips as he exhaled through clenched teeth. He continued to scan the room with the eyes of a hawk, searching for anything else that might be out of place. Lord Blayney placed a sympathetic hand on his shoulder.

"I can't lose her!" Aiden's anguished voice cracked slightly.

Suddenly spotting the bag of coins in the middle of the room, Aiden rushed to where the bag sat on the floor, the coins scattered about. He noticed a few more coins near the dressing room door and the lantern still lit in the room. Picking up a black scarf carelessly tossed on the floor just inside the dressing room, he stared at it.

"What is it, my boy?" Lord Blayney inquired as he followed Aiden into the small room.

A petticoat had been dropped on the floor and a few hangers were scattered about, as if someone had been in a hurry. Aiden began sliding clothes to one side and knocking on the panels as he listened. When he came to the portion of the panel where the clothes had been in disarray, he knocked and a hollow sound reverberated back.

"Does this wall move?" Aiden asked, tossing clothes out of his way. Lord Andrew Blayney stammered a moment, trying to think back to his youth. Aiden looked intently at Lord Blayney and directed his attention to the spot he spoke of by pounding on the wall. "It's a simple question, Lord Blayney. Are you aware of secret passages in this castle?"

"When my brother and I were younger, we discovered a few of them, but I never had the stomach for adventure like Timothy. I found it too dark and musty down there."

"But there are secret passages, and you know how to open the panel?" Aiden questioned desperately. "Show me!" He insisted, grabbing at Blayney's arm.

"There is a latch somewhere…" Lord Blayney mused, reaching around to the side and inching his fingers around the edge of the panel.

"Here!" he cried, thrilled that he'd remembered how to open the panel after so many years. They both jumped back as the panel popped open.

"Where does this tunnel lead?" Aiden asked, licking his lips as his mouth went dry.

"It all depends on which way you turn. Turn one way and it leads to a room in the castle, turn another way and it leads you out of the castle and beyond the wall. But if you don't know which way you are going, you could get lost down there," Blayney cautioned, stepping back from the opening.

"Aiden!" Caleb yelled as he rushed into the small dressing room. "I just heard," Caleb blurted out, falling silent when his eyes fell upon the opened panel.

"Round up the boys, Caleb, we have another mission. We are going after my wife," Aiden ordered, like the mercenary captain he was.

His mind raced three steps ahead, trying to make sense of the sudden turn of events.

"Where does this lead?" Caleb asked, still trying to digest the existence of a secret tunnel.

Aiden turned to Blayney. "Do you know which way to go, when we get down there? I am going to assume that whoever took my wife planned on leaving the castle," he stated. "So, do you know exactly where this tunnel comes out at?" he asked again, pulling Lord Blayney closer to him and looking more like a desperate man than a mercenary.

"I think so. It has been a very long time, but I think I still remember," Lord Blayney replied, disentangling his coat collar from Aiden's grasp.

"Get me our best tracker and as many lanterns as you can find," Aiden ordered Caleb, pulling Lord Blayney behind him, as he left the room.

"Slow down, my boy. I'm not so young anymore," Blayney cried.

"There's no time to waste, Lord Blayney. We have no idea who took Isabella and her handmaiden, or why they were taken," Aiden shot back over his shoulder.

"We do now," Charlie said, as he stood in the doorway of the bedroom.

"Who is it?" Aiden asked almost desperately. "Spit it out, Charlie, we don't have time to waste."

"The Governor," Charlie replied. "Mother will meet us in the stables."

"We just discovered how they left the house without anyone noticing them. There is a secret passageway in the dressing room," Caleb blurted out.

Taking a few more steps before stopping short, Aiden turned around, with a stricken look on his face, and addressed the three men following him. "So it had to be someone who knows this castle well," Aiden declared as if everything had just fallen into place for him. "And if I find out that this 'Governor' is my brother or Lancelot, they are dead men. Do you hear me? I will strangle them with my bare hands," Aiden growled between clenched teeth as he looked directly into Lord Blayney eyes, with an icy glare. "I swear it!" He declared emphatically, with a second growl to no one in particular.

32

Going, Going, Gone, Sold to the Highest Bidder

IDING THROUGH THE NIGHT AT a fast pace, as if the Devil himself was trailing after us, we stopped just before dawn at a farm that was sympathetic to the cause.

I could tell that we had been headed south for the better part of the night. But I was unsure of exactly where we were, because I was unfamiliar with the countryside. I had studied Ireland in school, but it was very different seeing it in person.

I found it rather odd that Ian and Lance made sure they stood between me, and the farm's owners.

"Lance, make sure they are out of our way for the entire day," Ian ordered, in a tone that said he was the one in charge. "Pay them off if you must, but I don't want them around when the others show up. I will have no interferences today."

Ian then turned to Maria and me. "I am sure the two of you would like to stretch your legs and use the privy," his tone suddenly changing to one of a solicitous nature.

Smooth and approachable, he advanced on our mount. Pulling Maria off the horse none too gently, Ian held her up while she found her legs again. Then turning to me, he reached up to pull me down, when I surprised him, kicking him squarely in the chest, knocking him backwards a few steps, before he regained his footing.

"Oh, you are going to pay for that mistake," Ian growled at me through clenched teeth.

"Please pardon me, dear brother in law. It appears we have been riding too long and I have experienced a leg spasm. I'm truly sorry," I replied without any true remorse, followed by an insincere smile. "If you don't mind, I would prefer to dismount myself and prevent any further misunderstandings with spasmodic muscles and all," I sweetly cooed.

"By all means," Ian snarled, backing away from the horse with a stiff courtly gesture. Climbing from the horse, I tested my sore muscles by bending my legs a couple of times, while keeping an eye on Ian. Advancing on me the moment I turned around, Ian grabbed me by the throat. "Might I suggest for your own preservation, that in the future you learn to control your spasmodic muscles." Then coming in even closer, Ian whispered into my ear, "The next man that owns you, may not be as understanding as me."

Turning loose of my throat, Ian gave my cheek a quick slap, then grabbed me by the arm and motioned for Maria to follow us. "I'm so glad that we could have this little chat, and that we have now come to an understanding," he proclaimed in a rush, leading us to the privy at the back of the house. The crudely built structure measured five feet across by three feet in depth. The entire shack was riddled with worm-holes, that didn't allow much privacy for the occupant.

Ian's mood suddenly changed again as he appeared to gain control of his temper. "I have to hand it to you, Isabella, your persistence and fortitude will serve you well, wherever you end up," Ian said with a wicked smiled on his lips. Then opening the door to the small rundown outhouse with flourish. "Well, look at what we have here, a side-by-side privy. And I bet you were thinking that they were terribly uncivilized in this part of the country," he mocked, while untying my hands. Shoving us both headlong into the filthy shed, Ian slammed the door shut behind us. The sound of his sadistic laughter rang in my ears, as he continued his reign of terror on us. "I would suggest that you both hurry and don't dilly dally too long, because I will be opening these doors in exactly five minutes. And oh, how I do hope you are decent by then," Ian added with another sadistic shriek of laughter.

"And I am hoping for your humanity to return in the next five minutes. But I truly feel that would be too much to hope for, since it is highly doubtful that you ever had any humanity in the first place," I yelled back at him through the flimsy door.

"Dear sister in law, your barbs are like daggers to the heart. How you wound me to the quick," he gasped dramatically, feigning distress.

"It is a requirement to have a heart before you can take a dagger to it. Unseemly conduct is still unseemly conduct, no matter how you choose to dress it up, Ian," I volleyed back.

Exactly five minutes after shutting the door, Ian suddenly opened it, without warning, just as Maria and I were putting our skirts down. "You are a sadist!" I hissed, glarimg at him.

"Oh, how you do like to carry on," Ian laughed, rolling his eyes as if I had just paid him a compliment.

"So what do you plan to do with us now?" I asked, with a sinking feeling in the pit of my stomach. Ian marched us toward the run down farmhouse, shoving me from behind, and knocking me into Maria when we had reached the door. Maria would have toppled to the ground if I had not grabbed her by the arm, bringing her upright again. In a show of defiance, I gave a good natured chuckle under my breath and pretended that everything was normal, even though I was seething. "I couldn't help over hearing you instruct Lancelot to get rid of the homeowners for the day. I believe you said something about others showing up. Would you care to elaborate further?" I asked.

"I would not. And don't let Lance overhear you referring to him as Lancelot. He doesn't like it much. Come to think of it, he doesn't like you very much, either," Ian stated, while pursing his lips together in a disapproving way. "As for what I have in store for you, well let's just say that I am entertaining offers. You will be sold to the highest bidder," he added.

"That's it?" I felt like I had just been punched in the stomach. "That's your great plan?" I sputtered indignantly. Maria placed a gentle hand on my shoulder and I quickly glanced at her.

"Oh dear Isabella, is my plan too simplistic for your sensibilities?" Ian chuckled slyly, shocked at my less than enthusiastic response. "I, on the other hand, happen to think my plan is brilliant!" he bantered, grabbing my hands to secure the leather tie around my wrists again. "You have to see the bigger picture here," Ian continued with enthusiasm. "I sell you to the highest bidder, who then sails away with you to a faraway land, never to be heard from again. My brother Aiden is left brokenhearted, wondering what could of happened to you as he searches in vain for the rest of his miserable life." He exclaimed, dramatically clutching his hands to his heart, while jutting out his lower lip, feigning sadness, then pausing for affect, he looked directly at me. "Either way I win," he added, dropping the dramatic stance and smiling sadistically.

"You are a monster!" I screamed. "I would have thought that you, of all people, could be a little more original than that," I ranted.

"You apparently do not understand the brilliance of my plan. The money I raise from selling the two of you will go toward the cause," Ian countered.

"And what cause is that?" Maria chimed in.

"Why, The Hearts of Oak, my dear. I'm doing this for the good of the common folk," Ian stated innocently.

"Save it, you sadistic miscreant. You do what you do, for no other reason than your own misguided sense of revenge," I spat out. "You wish to line your pockets and gain the upper hand! And for what, to come out ahead in this twisted game of yours that began on the day you realized that you would not inherit your father's fortune because you were born second instead of first?" I scoffed. "You cloak yourself behind this disguise and call yourself the 'Governor' to give importance to the cause. But really you just want revenge against a brother who has never done you any harm," I cried, glaring at him as I looked him in the eyes and searched for the chink in his armor. "What's the matter, Ian? Did daddy's favorite little bootlicker turn out to be a major disappointment?" I hissed.

Ian's agile reflexes were brutal as he rewarded me with a vicious slap to my right cheek, knocking me to the ground. I could taste blood in my mouth and feel my lip begin to swell. Kicking me in the ribs when I tried to get up, Ian stood menacingly over me. He clasped and unclasped his fists, rapidly breathing in and out. Finally, he narrowed his eyes and took a step back.

"You're not a very good business man now are you, dear brother?" I said with a derisive laugh.

"What are you babbling on about, you foolish woman?" Ian snapped back.

"A good business man would never bruise the fruit before putting it out on display if he hoped to get a good price for it," I stated sarcastically as I slowly got to my feet, smearing the blood on my lip across my face, with the back of my hand.

"I wouldn't expect a simple woman to understand the complexities of my cause and what drives me," Ian began to say.

"Stop it! Just stop spouting your platitudes about the cause. You care nothing about the cause. You are nothing more than a common thug and a thief. Unfortunately for me, I am the collateral damage you choose to leave in your wake," I said, cutting him off. I stood before him now with pure defiance in my eyes and a heaving chest, as I spat blood from my mouth.

"Oh my dear, nothing about this situation is that simple —" Ian coolly retorted in a patronizing tone.

"And a dog doesn't bark because he has anything in particular to say. He barks because it is what he does. It is simply in his nature to bark at the moon," I continued, cutting him off again. "I truly think you gain some morbid satisfaction, running around, all cloak and dagger, through the countryside. I'm sure you relish the accolades you receive from the simple folks as you masquerade in your disguise, pretending to be this so called Governor."

"Touché," Ian said with a smirk. "If only the rest of us could take such a moral high ground or share your capacity for reasoning. But alas, it is not to be," he lamented. "And although you seem less than thrilled over the prospect of being sold to the highest bidder, I want to assure you that this is going to happen as scheduled, regardless of your objections," he continued, gently stroking my cheek with the back of his hand, almost solicitous. "But I want you to know that there is a part of me that truly regrets destroying something as bold, defiant, and beautiful as you."

Momentarily stunned by his words, I did not notice him pulling a blind fold from his pocket until he turned me around, pulling me up against him, so that my back rested against his chest. Roughly tying the material over my eyes, Ian continued to speak, "Don't get me wrong, you really aren't my type at all. But I can still appreciate a beautiful piece of art." Turning me back around, I could feel his eyes on me as I stood blindfolded and stunned by his actions. Reaching out his hands, Ian tore the bodice of my gown at the neck, exposing my corset, slip, and ample breasts that nearly spilled out. I screamed in surprise, and my knees began to shake.

"You cad!"

"There, that's better," he snickered. "The least we can do is give the paying clientele a good show and a little peek." I could hear the smirk in Ian's voice as I tried to cover myself. "That should drive the price way up," he asserted, roughly pinching my cheeks with his fingers, to bring the color back to my face. "That's better. You looked a little pale for a minute, my dear."

I was teetering between shock and rage when I heard Ian turn to leave, whistling a tune as he went. "Maria, be a dear and clean that blood off her before she comes out. Wouldn't want the gentlemen thinking I bruised the fruit," Ian quipped, without missing a step. "Oh, and one more thing," he said, turning back around as he called from the door, "could you give us a little seductive pout when you are put on view for all the rich patrons?"

"You are an atrocity!" I screamed, indignation and anger causing me to shake all over. I felt Maria put her arms around me.

"You do say the most outrageous things, my dear," Ian taunted.

"I hope Aiden kills you," I hissed.

"He can try," Ian responded, "but he will have to catch me first."

Opening the door, Ian motioned to his men standing just outside, giving them instructions. The next thing I knew, I heard heavy foot-steps coming at us. One of the men grabbed Maria and roughly dragged her away from me.

"Maria!" I screamed, grabbing for her arm again, as she was being torn from me. I tried to follow her loud protests, but fell to the ground, when my toe caught the edge of a chair.

"Isabella!" Maria cried out, as she was dragged through the doorway.

I was then roughly pushed back down when I tried to stand. "No need to hurry. They won't be needing you for at least ten minutes," a man stated with a chuckle. "I was told to clean you up a bit."

I could hear him rustling around in the kitchen area of the two room shack. Then coming back to where I sat, he squatted down and wiped my face with a wet rag.

"That should take care of it," he said, as his hand and rag strayed below my neck headed towards the ripped bodice.

"Get your filthy hands off me, you coward," I spat.

"Now is that any way to talk to your caretaker?" he cajoled.

"You're going to be a dead caretaker, if you keep it up, you son of a putain."

Grabbing my face between his thumb and fingers, he squeezed tightly, until I cried out. "And here I was thinking you were a lady," he said, delivering a rough kiss to my already tender lips.

Pushing back with all my might, I clamped down on his bottom lip with my teeth and kicked him at the same time.

Crawling away from his grasp the moment he jumped back from me, I grabbed the chair that I had nearly tripped over and brandished it in front of me. "Stay back or I will *really* hurt you next time."

He spat on the ground what I hoped was his blood, and then began to chuckle again. "Some people have to take all the fun out of the simplest of pleasures. Well, come on then, we have to go now," he said taking a hold of my arm and lifting me off the dirt floor. He proceeded to dust the dirt from my tattered gown. Then taking hold of my arm he steered me through the room and out the door.

"Don't do this," I pleaded, while trying to pull my arm from his grasp, when I recognized his voice. "I know you. You're one of Aiden's men."

Desperation had taken a hold of me and I dug my heels into the ground, pulling my arm back at the same time, stalling the inevitable. "I recognize your voice. Your name is Garretty, right?" I cried, trying to make a connection with him.

"So, What of it?" Garretty replied, his tone sounding defensive.

"Aiden and my father will be coming for me. I can tell them that you helped me."

"That won't help me none. My family already lost their home and property to the highbrows. I ain't got nothing left to lose," Garretty answered.

"Things aren't going to end well for your fearless leader," I assured him.

"What would you know of it? Now get moving, or I will be forced to pick you up and carry you," Garretty replied, and I could tell he was grinning when he said it, as if he was daring me to challenge him further.

"That won't be necessary," I said, lifting my chin a bit higher. I allowed myself to be led from the dwelling, refusing to lower myself any further by begging him for help. I figured he would get his in the end, when Aiden and my father arrived. I just hoped they would show up in time.

I heard talking just before Garretty and I entered the barn. Pulling on his arm, I stopped him before he could push me through the entrance. "Perhaps you can allow me a small amount of dignity and see that I don't step in anything," my voice sounded scared, even to my ears. Clearing my throat, to stave off the hysteria that I could feel building up inside, I took two more deep breaths to stop the tears that were forming. Then I nodded, giving Garretty the signal that I was ready to continue.

When we entered the barn, all talking ceased, and a low muttering noise began. It was very eerie and disconcerting. My senses were assaulted at once and I nearly choked on the pungent odor of thick cigar smoke. I felt sick to my stomach and off kilter, and in that moment of weakness I grabbed for Garretty's arm with my free hand when my knees buckled.

"I see the main attraction has arrived," Ian's voice echoed through the small barn. "Didn't I tell you she was worth the trip? I must give you fair warning though, she is a handful." The room erupted into laughter and I could hear men all around me as if they stood in every free corner of the barn. The room had a circus like atmosphere and I was standing smack dab in center ring. Garretty passed me off to Ian, who grabbed me by the arm and paraded me about like a prized show horse.

"Maria!" I called out, while reaching up to remove the blind fold at the same time, only to have my hands slapped away. "Maria, where are you?" I screamed out again.

"Didn't I tell you she was feisty?" Ian laughed as he led me back to the center of the room. Coming around behind me now, Ian took hold of my shoulders as he leaned in close to my ear. "Maria is already gone. Now behave yourself or I will be sure to humiliate you even further," he hissed between his teeth.

"You mean more than selling me to the highest bidder, you pompous giddy?"

"I think we will start the bidding just a bit higher this time, gentlemen. Who will give me two hundred pounds?" Ian began calling out amounts and taking the next bid, as they jumped in increments of twenty five to fifty pounds at a time. He maintained his grip on my shoulders, while lifting his hand and pointing to the person who had just made a bid. I could hear men calling out, making distinctive noises from different areas of the barn, as if they were merely affirming a bid at a Saturday morning cattle auction.

I struggled to break free of Ian's vice like grip. His fingers dug into my flesh every time the bid climbed higher. "Get your filthy paws off me, you bloody bastard," I screamed, pulling free of his grip and yanking the blind fold from my eyes, before throwing it on the ground at Ian's feet. Then I turned to face my brother in law.

The only light in the interior of the dingy, dank barn came from two lanterns that hung just above Ian's head in the center of the room. The rest of the barn's interior was nearly in complete darkness. Visibility was made worse by the cigar smoke. I tried to make out faces, but they were merely outlines, as they all seemed to slither even further back into the shadows, when I removed the blind fold, assuring them complete anonymity.

The look of shock on Ian's face was worth the vicious slap he delivered to my left cheek, knocking me to the ground. The animalistic growl from deep in my throat gave Ian warning as I launched myself at him. Unfortunately for me, my hands were tied and my range of motion limited. I did, however, manage to startle him when I viciously scratched his face. Ian then balled up his fist, hitting me hard in the stomach. I doubled over and fell to the ground with a very unladylike thud. After what felt like an eternity of rolling around on the ground, gasping for air, like a fish out of water, I felt the rush of life-saving breath, as it finally entered my lungs.

Managing a partially kneeling position, my eyes once again landed on Ian. I glared at him standing only two feet away from me, as I plotted my next move. Then he motioned with his head to someone behind me, and before I knew what was happening, Garretty clamped his arms around my waist, lifting me off the ground as if I were a rag doll he could move about at will.

Biding my time, I went limp in Garretty's arms, pretending to be out of it still. As Garretty stepped closer to Ian, I startled everyone by lashing out, kicking Ian in the upper thigh, just shy of his family jewels. This caused Ian to fall to the ground on one knee, and place his hands over his groin. Momentarily stunned, he took several deep breaths to calm the rage that was building inside of him. He stood up slowly, and for the first time, I have to admit, I was truly afraid of the murderous glint I saw reflected in his pale, steely-gray eyes. There was no doubt in my mind that he would have slit my throat, without hesitation, if there hadn't been so many witnesses. Ian slowly dusted the dirt from his trousers, and then looked at me, as Garretty grasped me even tighter about the waist. Ian narrowed his eyes for a moment longer, then suddenly smiled back at me.

Slipping effortlessly back into his role as the consummate ring leader, he turned to the crowd once again. "Did I mention that she was spirited?" Ian exclaimed, raising his hands in the air while turning about in a circle like a ring master at a circus show. "Now where were we, gentlemen? I believe we ended the bidding at eight hundred pounds to the gentleman on my right, here," he continued in a jovial tone, as he smiled and pointed toward a darkened corner of the room.

The men chuckled, but I wasn't fooled by his act. I knew he was furious and had no doubt he wanted to kill me.

"A thousand pounds!" Someone yelled, from the center of the room, directly in front of me.

"Now that is more like it, gents. I have one thousand pounds over here. Do I hear one thousand one hundred?"

"Aye."

"Thank you," Ian said, pointing to another area of the darkened interior.

"One thousand five hundred," the gentleman called out from the far left corner.

"It seems we have someone with discriminating taste," Ian chuckled, good-naturedly.

"Two thousand pounds," the voice rang out clear and strong from the gentleman directly in front of me again. The only visible evidence that he existed was the red glow of his lit cigar as he gave two strong drags on it. Squinting my eyes, I peered into the darkness, trying to see the man's face, but the light from directly above me, prevented it.

"I have a bid here of two thousand pounds. Going once, going twice…" Ian gave a dramatic paused, hoping for an even higher bid, "Sold!" He called out, "to the gentleman with impeccable taste," he finished, sounding almost giddy with delight, like someone who had consumed too much champagne. "If you will come along with me, good sir, we will complete our financial transaction before you leave," Ian concluded with a sadistic chuckle as he stared into my eyes. "As for the rest of you gents, better luck next time."

"Garretty, prepare her for the journey," Ian called over his shoulder, while following the man with the winning bid from the barn. I strained to get a glimpse of this wealthy stranger, but my feeble attempts were blocked by Garretty's rather large personage, as he stepped in front of me, blocking my view.

Now struggling in earnest, I kicked wildly at Garretty, when he lifted me from the ground and tossed me over his shoulder like a sack of grain. "You need to settle down before you get hurt," he warned, slapping my backside with his enormous hand.

"You are the one who should be worried," I growled at him, through clenched teeth. "When I dispense with my captor, I will be coming back to finish you off, right after I slit Ian's scrawny, little throat. You are both bloody well going to pay with your lives!" I screamed at him, kicking and thrashing with all my might.

"You are wasting your breath, my lady, and your strength. Now settle down," Garretty laughed, slapping my backside again, for good measure.

"Give me back my dagger, you sadist, and we will see who is wasting their breath, you bloody turncoat," I screeched. "See if you are still laughing when Aiden gets a hold of you. You... you piece of filth."

"Ouch!" Garretty cried out in surprise, as I landed a direct kick to his stomach. "Don't make me hurt you, Lady Deveraux."

"That is Lady Townsend, you retched scum," I corrected, with an undertone of disdain.

"Pardon me," Garretty said mockingly, "my mistake."

Garretty shifted me from one shoulder to the other, with little effort. Taking long strides, he reached the door of a fancy carriage in five strides. Opening the door, he thrust me onto the seat, momentarily knocking me silly when I hit my head against the paneling. This gave him time to climb in after me.

"What do you think you are doing, you bloody ogre?" I berated.

"I am preparing you for travel, as I was instructed," he replied. Pulling a length of rope from his back pocket, Garretty grasped my already tied hands, which he secured to the interior lantern ring.

"Is that really necessary?" I asked with derision.

"I was told it would be and you know how I tend to follow orders," Garretty said, finding pleasure in my pain, as he tightened the rope. When he'd finished tying my hands to a metal ring, he reached up and tweaked my cheek, then tauntingly patted my cheeks.

Turning his back to me was Garretty's first mistake. As he placed his right foot on the first step, I placed my right foot in the middle of his backside, and sent him flying out of the carriage door. He landed face first in the muck and filth two feet beyond the carriage. I heard a beast like growl, as he lifted himself from the mud and animal dung, spitting and spurting gunk from his mouth, along with a string of expletives that would have made even a hardened sailor blush. He stood up and shook himself like a dog, flinging brown goo from his person. Another guttural growl escaped his mouth, as he reached up, wiping the muck from his eyes and face with both hands. I couldn't actually see his eyes through the dripping muck from his brow as he reached for the carriage door, but I knew full well his intent. He was going to strangle me if he got his hands on me.

Garretty was well on his way through the carriage door, when he was yanked backwards, by the scruff of his collar, by another man with an even stronger grip. His face registered surprise as he fell backwards, smack dab into the mud once again, landing on his butt this time with a loud thud.

I held my breath, momentarily hoping that it would be Aiden or my father who had come to my rescue. But my hopes were quickly dashed by the sound of a foreign man's voice.

"Hold up there, good sir. I cannot have you laying your filthy hands upon my shiny new acquisition, because of your misfortune or poor judgment," the man said. Garretty sat there in the mud, covered in muck, dripping from his chin and hair.

"I thank you for your diligent service, good sir, but I will take it from here," the man concluded with authority, while removing a handkerchief from his coat pocket, to wipe the mud from his hand.

Garretty slowly stood and reluctantly backed away from the carriage. An evil smile formed on his lips before he bowed to me, as if he were gentry. "Adieu, my lady, until we meet again," his words were said to taunt me, and yet I was grateful to be on my way.

"Adieu, good sir," I replied, taunting Garretty in return. *At least I would have a chance of outwitting a total stranger who did not know me.*

I could smell the pungent odor of the gentleman's cigar before I saw his face. It was the same smell as the dingy, dank barn I was just in, only minutes before. Disappointment caused me to turn my face toward the window to hide my dashed hopes.

The carriage shifted as he climbed in, closing the door with a resounding thud. I felt him take the seat across from me, as he sat himself down and stared at me. I swallowed hard and took a deep breath, before placing a disinterested glower on my face. Turning slowly, more from curiosity than anything else, I wished to study my new proprietor.

He was a tall, well dressed, proportioned man, with shoulder length, jet black hair. His hazel eyes studied me intently, while seeming to take everything in at once. He wore knee length, black leather boots that cuffed at the top. He had on a pair of tight black pants that conformed to his muscular legs, and his jacket was a bold red brocade with gold threading that ran throughout, with large brass buttons. He had a mustache and a patch of hair on his chin that had been trimmed in the traditional Musketeer style. I nearly laughed but held my disinterested gaze as I slowly assessed him from head to toe with my eyes.

"If I had to guess, I would say that, by your accent, you are either from Spain or Portugal," I said engaging him in conversation. "But you long to be a Musketeer of the Guard by your dress." I couldn't help throwing in a small dig at the end of my statement.

"You have a very good eye, as well as ear, my dear. I am Romero Alonso Garcia la Toya of Barcelona, at your service," he added with a courtly incline of his head.

"Since my soon to be dead brother in law didn't see fit to introduce us, please allow me. My name is Isabella Monique Deveraux Townsend. My father is Lord Deveraux the Duke of Bayonne and my mother is Lady Angelina Marguerite Amelia Deveraux. And just in case Lord Townsend neglected to inform you, my husband is his brother, Lord Aiden Townsend," I informed him, in hopes that my words would carry some weight and persuade Romero Alonso Garcia la Toya of Barcelona to set me free.

"He did not mention a husband. It must have slipped his mind," Romero countered with a sigh of regret. "But no worries," he continued, as he rapped on the roof of the carriage with his cane.

"What do you mean no worries? Will you not return me to my family?" I cried, as a disquieting feeling began to creep into my thoughts.

"Yes." He nodded his head affirmative. "I am not going to return you to your family. That is the correct usage for that word is it not? Your English is so confusing at times," he added with an engaging smile.

"But I don't understand? Clearly there has been a mistake made. I am not a common trollop to be bought and sold to the highest bidder."

"I agree, and that is why I paid so much for you," la Toya announced with a solicitous tone, as he lifted an eyebrow.

"But you are an attractive man. Why would you feel the need to buy a woman?" I asked, feeling slightly hysterical.

"I was on my way back to my ship, when I received an invitation to attend an unusual auction. I was promised that it would be well worth my while. I believe that was the way it was presented to me," Romero said remembering back. "Anyway I thought, maybe I would attend this unusual action and stand in the background to observe. But then you were brought in, and there was something so intriguing about the fire that burned in your eyes, once you removed that ridiculous blindfold. I am afraid I was captivated by you."

"Let me guess, you are in love. You men are all so predictable," I said sarcasticly, rolling my eyes in exasperation.

"But that was the moment I knew that I had to win the bid, so I could possess you. *Si.*"

"And then what? You thought I would be so impressed with the amount of money you spent to *possess me* that I would fall into your arms and beg you to take me," I jeered, jerking on the bindings at my wrists. "Why are you even here in Ireland?" I asked, frustrated by the lack of give to the ropes binding my wrists.

"I was here on business," he answered ambiguously, refusing to go into details.

"So which are you, a thief, or a smuggler?" I quipped.

"Let's just say I was down here doing some trading of goods," Romero answered cryptically.

"So you are a smuggler."

"No, my dear, I am no smuggler," he said with a good natured laugh.

"Then you are an honest business man. You buy and sell products, to ship here and there," I said, with a derisive scoff.

"Something like that," he answered again, trying to evade the question.

"So, I ask you again. Which one are you, a thief or a smuggler?" I bantered, making direct eye contact with Romero.

"If you are well known for your smuggling abilities, you are doing it all wrong," he answered, feigning modesty.

"So you wish to go down on record as a cunning thief," I pointed out accusingly, trying to make him squirm. "Your mother must be so very proud, indeed."

"In my opinion, there is a problem with your narrow mindedness, my dear. You lack the ability to admire the finer points of bad behavior," he added without remorse, placing a hand upon my knee.

"I can assure you, Mr. la Toya, that I neither lack the appreciation or imagination for bad behavior," I said with dead calm, as I glared at his hand, resting on my knee. "In fact, if you lay a hand upon me again without my permission, I will show you the very definition and meaning of the words bad behavior," then added under my breath, between clenched teeth, "assuring that you will never wake up again," while delivering a sharp kick to his shin.

"Ouch!" Romero cried out in surprised. "You little vixen," he chuckled good naturedly, as his mood suddenly changed back to solicitous. "Why would such a lovely woman talk like this? I believe we could have a mutually, beneficial relationship. If you make me happy, I will make you happy," he said in a soothing tone.

"Well, you just might wish to batten down the proverbial hatches, because I am predicting a particularly bad storm headed your way," I advised, moving as far away from him as I could manage. Then, to add insult to injury, I ignored him all together.

"Why must you be so difficult? I already have a surprise for you that I am sure will make you very happy," Romero coaxed, trying to draw me into conversation. When I refused to answer him, Romero tried again.

"Come on, I bet you can't guess what it is."

"Your head served up to me on a silver platter," I added dryly.

"No, no, no," he laughed again. "I know you can do better than that, you're not even trying," Romero coaxed, trying to sound lighthearted.

I snorted in derision. "And you need to understand, the only two things that will make me happy is to witness your lifeless body lying at my feet, or to be reunited with my husband and family. Anything short of that, and I can assure you that I am not going to be happy," I argued, glaring at him.

I felt the carriage come to a stop, and felt a sinking, sick feeling in my stomach. I could smell the salt of the ocean breeze blowing through the window and knew that we had reached our destination.

Romero reached over to untie my hands from the window. Dragging me from the carriage, I was unceremoniously draped over his shoulder when I refused to come along willingly. I discovered he was stronger than I had anticipated as I tried to squirm free of his hold. Then he had the nerve to pat my rump and chuckle as he approached a large merchant ship.

Tipping his hat to someone at the top of the gang plank, Romero paused a moment to shift my weight when I suddenly kneed him in the chest. I felt vindicated, though, when I heard a small cry of pain escape his lips.

"What have you acquired now, la Toya?" a man called out, as Romero maneuvered the gangplank with me in tow.

"I would hold still if I were you," Romero said coolly. Reaching up, he gave me a pat on the buttocks once again, in a macho show of superiority for the crew and captain's benefit. "It truly would be a shame to drop you into the water below when I have invested so much," he added with a hearty laugh, as he unceremoniously deposited me on the deck.

My eyes were like daggers, as I shot green shards directly at his cold heart. "Untie me and we will see who ends up in the water," I threatened.

"Stop looking at me like this, or I may begin to think that you truly do dislike me. I have such a wonderful surprise waiting for you in my cabin," Romero said slyly.

"Is it a knife so that I might cut out your blackened heart," I taunted with cold distain.

"No, it's better," Romero chuckled, reaching down to help me up. Slapping his hand away, I stood up without his assistance and dusted off my soiled, ripped gown.

"Then I'm not interested," I replied, snubbing his attempts to be friendly.

"This one, she is quite a handful," the captain said, leaning into Romero with a sly grin.

"I am counting on it," he winked, and gave the captain a devilish grin that said more than words alone as he grabbed hold of my arm.

"Unhand me, you barbarian," I screamed, attempting to shake free of his vice like grip.

"We will come to an understanding before the night is through," Romero said under his breath as his mood seemed to change, to one of a more serious nature. "Of this I am sure."

"Oh, we will have an understanding of some kind. That you can count on, sir," I said with bravado, "Mark my words, Romero Alonso Garcia la Toya," I stated in a mocking tone, parodying his accent.

"Now look at you," he said jovially, stopping in his progression to his cabin, to place his right hand over his heart. "You have remembered my full name, and here I was starting to think that you did not care for me at all," he retorted, flashing me his most charming smile.

"It is important to pay attention to first impressions, *Monsieur* la Toya," I sweetly smiled, narrowing my eyes. "And I suppose it is only time, that will bear me out." I said with a derisive snort. "The slow marching of time indeed will be the deciding factor," I added, arching my eyebrows for emphasis.

"Oh, how I love to watch your lips move when you speak," Romero blurted out, maintaining eye contact as he moved in closer, stopping mere inches from my lips. Placing my hands against his chest, I prevented him from moving in any closer for the kiss he intended to place on my lips. Turning my face to the side, I could feel his breath against my cheek as he continued to speak while unbinding my wrists. When Romero signaled to the man standing guard at his cabin door, the man stepped aside.

"I will yet win you over, *Mademoiselle*," he assured me, flashing a confident smile as he slowly reached for the door to his cabin. "You will see." Throwing the door opened, Romero pushed me forward, through the doorway and waited for a reaction.

A woman was standing at the window, looking out to sea. I did not recognize her at first and then she turned around to face me.

"Maria!" I screamed and ran to her. Tears sprang to my eyes as I embraced her. "I thought I would never see you again," I cried, wrapping my arms tightly around her. "How is this possible? Ian told me you were already gone before I was led into the auction room," I wept, looking into her eyes.

"I could tell that she meant a great deal to you, when you called out for her," Romero said, coming to stand beside me, "So I made arrangements with the man who had purchase her, offering him double the price. Who can say no to me? So you are pleased?"

I looked up at him with a conciliatory smile. "You did this for me?" I asked in disbelief.

"Yes," he simply said, with a self assured smile on his face.

Then turning around, Romero walked to a cabinet along the far wall of the cabin and opened the doors. "You will find something a little more suitable to wear and fresh water for your needs," he added with a grand gesture. "I will leave you, ladies, to attend to business. I need to take care of things on deck," Romero informed me, before bowing at the waist. "I will take my leave, unless you wish to throw yourself into my arms now," he added with his hand on the door's latch and a hopeful smile playing on his lips.

"I think not. But I will give you one last chance to do the right thing. You will be handsomely compensated for your losses," I vowed with genuine gratitude.

Romero's smile slipped from his face, "I assure you that no amount of compensation would be enough."

"As you wish," I bowed my head, as my disappointment rang out loud and clear in those three simple words.

Romero turned and walked out of the room.

33

One Last Battle to Fight Before I Can Rest

ARIA AND I MARVELED AT our good fortune, but only for a few minutes, before we got down to business.

"What are we to do now, Isabella?" Maria asked, wringing her hands together.

Pacing the floor, I felt the need to think, to gather my courage and come up with a plan. "Shush, Maria," I scolded, "you worry too much." I walked to the cabinet and began rummaging through the gowns, and picked the lightest one I could find. Then examining the petticoats, I found the perfect one. "We will clean up and make ourselves presentable, that is step one." Pulling another gown from the cabinet I held it up to Maria, "This one will look lovely on you."

"Oh no, miss, I couldn't," Maria protested.

"But of course you could, and you will," I insisted. "You are just as much a lady as I am. Now let's make ourselves presentable, shall we?" Grabbing a cloth and wetting it, I began to wash my face and arms as Maria assisted me out of my soiled, ripped gown.

"My brother and mother will find us soon, don't you fear. They are coming," I reassured her with confidence.

"But how can you know that?" Maria cried, turning me to face her.

"How else do I know anything, Maria?" I blinked, then took her by the shoulders and shook her gently. "I feel them, and I can feel Charlie getting stronger," I smiled, "Now stop wasting time, Romero could walk in on us." I stepped out of my soiled slip, and Maria gasped with surprise. Strapped to my leg were two throwing knives.

"Why didn't you use the knives earlier if you had them strapped to your leg the entire time?" Maria inquired.

"Because Maria, they are only affective if you have the element of surprise on your side. It also helps if you aren't outnumbered," I said with a giddy laugh. "Now help me get dressed before we are discovered," I insisted, slipping into a clean petticoat and dress.

I Looked at Maria with a critical eye, when she had changed into the gown I picked for her. "You look lovely! Now we just need to fix your hair. And Maria, no matter what happens, I need you to stay calm and play along with whatever I say," I looked directly into her eyes. "Can you do that for me?" Maria stammered, looking a way for a minute, not quite sure how to answer my request.

"Maria! I need you to snap out of it. I can't do this alone," I admitted, shaking her by the shoulders again.

"Yes! Yes, I am fine, Isabella. I just can't seem to catch my breath," Maria said, clasping her chest.

"I'm scared too, Maria. But that just means we will have to work harder to cover our tracks. Romero can't know that we have anything planned," I whispered, in case the man at the door was listening.

"What do you want me to do?" Maria asked, coming out her daze.

"We need to make our way up on deck. I don't wish to be trapped here like sitting ducks when all hell breaks loose."

Maria combed out my hair, and I gave hers a good brushing as well. Finally, when we were presentable, I opened the door and gave my most dazzling smile, using every ounce of English charm I could muster.

"Excuse me, kind sir, would it be possible for us to make our way to the deck? It is terribly stuffy in the small cabin and I am feeling like the walls are closing in on me," I sweetly pleaded with the stern faced young man standing guard.

"I don't think —" he began to say.

Placing my hand on his arm, I played the sweet, innocent, debutante to the hilt. "My apologies, good sir, but I don't think that we have been properly introduced. My name is Lady Isabella Townsend, and you are…" I asked, trying to catch him off guard, and make him feel unbalanced at the same time.

"Marcos," he stammered, taking my hand in his, he gave me a gentlemanly bow, "Marcos Torres, my lady."

"It is a pleasure to meet you, Monsieur Torres."

"I have my orders," he insisted, with less severity than before.

Pouting slightly, like I had seen other young socialites do to get their way, I continued to push my advantage. "Of course, I understand and wouldn't want to do anything that would get you into trouble. It's just that small spaces make me feel anxious and then I find it difficult to breathe," I added, heaving my slightly exposed chest, up and down dramatically, while fanning myself, for emphasis. "I was beginning to feel quite faint and thought that the ocean air would help with the vapors," I said, as I turned all of my charms and attention to Torres, while leaning on his arm for support. "Oh please, I beg you. If there is any way that you could see your way clear to allow me and my handmaiden out of this room, I would be ever so grateful," I implored, while batting my eyelashes at him, with a wide-eyed glance that promised everything.

The young man turned three shades of red and took a look around him to see if anyone had been watching. When he had assured himself that no one had witnessed the exchange and therefore could not accuse him of dereliction of duty, he laughed a little to himself. That is when I knew that I had him hooked.

"If you promise to behave yourself, I will sneak you up on deck, but only for a few minutes," he added as an afterthought. I was warned that you could be trouble. I truly hope you don't make me regret my decision," Torres said, with a weary look on his face.

"I promise to behave myself, and thank you for your kindness. I really am very grateful to you, good sir," I innocently gushed, giving Maria a wink.

34

Allow Me To Introduce Myself

RYING NOT TO SEEM TOO anxious, we followed Marcos Torres to the deck as I babbled on innocently about the weather and what a mild winter it had been. Marcos, who was not immune to my charms, took a cautious look around the deck, before stepping out of the passageway with us directly behind him.

I immediately spied Romero la Toya on the upper deck, talking with the captain and I was grateful that he didn't notice us as Mr. Torres skirted us just out of Romero's view.

While Marcos kept a diligent eye out, I took the opportunity to pull Maria aside, just out of ear shot of our guard. "Maria, whatever we do, we must stall them from setting sail," I whispered in her ear.

"But how do we do that, my lady?"

"I don't know, but we have to figure it out," I exclaimed, while casually looking toward the shore for any sign of my father or Aiden.

"What will happen when they get here?" Maria asked, making a show of taking in deep breaths of air.

"I don't know. But I'm betting Romero isn't going to turn us over, without a fight, so we need to be prepared for anything," I whispered and turned to smile reassuringly at Mr. Torres.

"Prepared for what, my dear?" Romero questioned, with an heir of suspicion in his tone.

Maria and I nearly jumped out of our skin as we turned around to find Romero la Toya standing directly behind us. The color drained from Maria's face, and I was momentarily left mute, unable to come up with anything remotely plausible to say.

"How lovely that color is on you, Isabella. I am so glad you were able to find something to wear," Romero added solicitously. I was trying to figure out if he was fishing for something or just trying to give me time to collect my wits.

Looking down at the gown I was wearing, I decided I would go with it, "Thank you, *Monsieur* la Toya," I purred. "How thoughtful of you to provide us with clean dresses. Just one thing I was curious about — how did you happen to come by so many gowns in your closet, when you didn't know that you would be returning with us? I asked, scrutinizing Romero, while trying to turn the tables.

"I pride myself on being prepared for anything," he smoothly replied, with feigned humility. "Now stop dancing around my question. What is it you feel you need to be prepared for?" Romero asked, taking another step towards me, and tipping my chin up with two fingers to gaze down at me.

Clasping my hands together in front of me, I dug my nails into the palm of my left hand to stop from shaking. Taking a deep breath I smiled sweetly feigning gentility. "Why, we were just discussing what might become of us when we reached your home land. Maria had some concerns about what you intended to do with us," I lied, but continued batting my eyes at him. "Once we do reach your home in Barcelona, I mean." I took another deep breath and turned my head to the side as he leaned down to kiss my lips.

"Oh my dear, you wound me with your rebuffs." Romero said playfully, placing his hand over his heart as if I had mortally wounded him. "Am I truly that repugnant to you?" he asked as his Spanish accent grew thicker.

"No, not at all. In fact, I find you to be a very pleasing man to look upon. It's just that I don't know you at all. We have only just met, and well..." I stammered, searching for just the right words.

"Well, what my dear?" Romero prodded, his vanity getting the better of him.

"I am afraid that it takes time for me to become comfortable with someone," I exclaimed, putting my head down slightly, as I stared at the ground, pretending to be shy.

"Well then, perhaps we should go below and I will introduce myself to you properly," he added with a sly smile, as he took hold of my arm, attempting to drag me with him.

"No!" I yelled a little more forcefully than I intended to. Digging my heels in, and yanking my arm free. "I mean, that would be delightful, of course. But the room is just too stuffy and closed in and I am enjoying the fresh air." My voice began to shake as I backed up a step or two. "Couldn't we stay up here just a little while longer?" I pleaded, with a shy smile.

"Captain, riders approaching and they seem to be in a hurry," a crewman yelled from his lofty perch high up in the rigging, while pointing in the direction of the incoming riders.

"I am afraid, my dear, that I am going to have to insist that you and your maid accompany me to my cabin," Romero insisted, grabbing at my arm, frustrated by my maneuvers to dodge his grasp. "Right now!" he growled, between clenched teeth in frustration as I continued to move just out of his reach. Evading Romero's grasp, while trying to get a good look at how close my rescuers were, all the while keeping Maria behind me was a trick.

"I find your behavior a bit deceitful," Romero scowled, narrowing his eyes at me.

"I refute such an allegation, whole-heartedly..." I retorted, while still making my way toward the other side of the ship so I could get a better look at the approaching riders.

"But your actions speak otherwise, my dear," he countered and cut me off.

"That is an impertinent allegation, good sir, as well as preposterous," I stated with bravado, praying desperately that my knees would stop shaking.

"And yet, I do not believe you." Romero's brown eyes suddenly turned hard, as he viciously grabbed my arm when I turned to leave.

"Ouch!" I yelped, in surprise. "Unhand me, you cad." Twisting my arm viciously behind my back, Romero tried to force me in a different direction. "You act as if I somehow knew that they were coming," I grumbled, still trying to break free from his grasp, while Maria broke free and ran for safety on the other side of the ship, just as the rescue party arrived.

Leaping from their horses, before they had even come to a complete halt, Father, Aiden, and Charlie, were the first to run up the gangplank, while the captain and his crew, worked frantically to weigh anchor and drop the ropes tethering the ship to the dock.

"Wait!" I screamed, stomping on the instep of Romero's foot and sinking my elbow into his stomach.

"Oufff…" was the only noise that escaped from Romero's mouth as I knocked the air from his lungs.

Running towards the gangplank, I was immediately cut off by three large men. Subsequently, Aiden, Charlie, Maria, and my father were stopped, and therefore hindered in their efforts to assist me by five very large men with pistols and swords drawn and at the ready. My mother and a few of Aiden's men came up the gangplank next, only to be forced to stand helplessly by and watch what transpired next.

"I am sorry to be so inhospitable, but I do not give leave to board my ship," Captain Anton called out.

"Isabella!" Aiden called to me.

"Yes," I replied loudly.

"Are you hurt?" he inquired.

"No, I am unharmed. And you, how do you fare?" I called back, giving the men blocking my way the evil eye.

"I have had better days, my love," Aiden called back, clenching his jaws, in frustration.

Romero came up behind me, placing a possessive arm about my waist, fully prepared to square off. "Why do you trespass upon my ship, gentlemen?" Romero mockingly challenged.

"Allow me to introduce myself properly. My name is Lord Aiden Larkin Townsend, Viscount of Buckinghamshire. You are detaining my wife," he accentuated the last words with gritted teeth and a throaty growl. Taking a couple of deep breaths to calm himself, Aiden continued, "I have reason to believe that she was abducted from the Blayney Castle last night, by my brother, Ian Townsend and his accomplice, Sir Lance Blayney. She was subsequently sold to you, and I am willing to double the price you paid so that we may resolve this matter peacefully, and you can be on your way."

"This delectable morsel I hold here in my arms now belongs to me," Romero crowed proudly, moving my hair to the side, as he took a long, deep breath, inhaling my scent, in a show of possessiveness. Looking up slowly, with a devil-may-care smile on his lips, Romero eyed Aiden and my father. Placing his free hand across my throat, Romero continued with an air of complete calm. "Terribly sorry that you have lost such a valuable prize, but I happen to be the one in possession of her and I intend to sail from here with all that I own," he declared, calling out even louder his orders. "Drop your weapons on the deck, and kick them away from you, or I will break my new toy."

"Don't do it —" I yelled to my father, only to have my words cut off by Romero's fingers, as they tightened around my throat. He gave me a good shake, before loosening his grasp, when I started to pass out, from lack of air.

"Why do you push me to do such things, my dear?" Romero cooed in my ear. "I wish to give you the world," he continued, as if we were already lovers. "Just the thought of losing you makes me crazy," he said, then stroked my cheek with the back of his hand. "I didn't mean to hurt you."

"Excuse me, good sir, but I don't believe I caught your name," my father called out, attempting to distract Romero.

"I don't believe I gave you my name, good man. But I can guess who you are," Romero said benevolently, as he pulled his eyes away from mine to converse with my father. "You must be this lovely woman's father. And could that striking young lad behind you possibly be the twin brother, Charlie, whom I've heard so much about? I must admit I have the advantage. Your daughter could not stop talking about you on our long ride here. Although I do believe that the family resemblance is uncanny. Don't you agree?" He remarked, momentarily diverting his attention from me.

"I do," my father simply replied.

"And that enchanting vision with you must be your wife, Isabella's mother," he smirked, as if he already had everything worked out in his mind. I was getting the feeling that Romero Alonso Garcia la Toya was a bit unhinged.

"Please allow me to make the introductions," I said, with a forced smile, trying to sound pleasant.

"By all means, my dear, please introduce me to your lovely family," he replied with an imperious tone.

"This is, Romero Alonso Garcia la Toya, of Barcelona, Spain. He is a Smuggler of the highest quality," I blurted out before Romero tightened his fingers around my neck again, severely cutting off my air supply. "Was I not supposed to say what you did for a living? Or did I not accurately depict your chosen vocation?" I whispered with distain while trying to pry his fingers from my throat.

"I am a business man. I deal in many different commodities," he insisted. "Let's just say that I move high demand merchandise, from here to there, for which I am well compensated for my services." Romero said loud enough for my family to hear.

"So you consider yourself a good smuggler, then?" I taunted, under my breath. Romero was scowling at me when my brother called to him.

"Why not cut your losses now, and make a clean escape. My sister will only slow you down. Why take the gamble with the authorities hot on your heals? And I guarantee, they will be coming after you," Charlie cautioned, playing it off as if it all boiled down to a matter choice. "You don't really want her. Why, she will most likely cut your heart out one night, while you sleep."

"I have no delusions of your spirited sister's short comings. I know she has claws. I was warned. I like it when they put up a bit of a fight," Romero scoffed, giving me a sadistic smirk. "That is what makes her so valuable to me," he laughed, giving my cheek a tweak. Adding under his breath, in a low tone so that only I could hear. "How am I to get caught, if all the eye witnesses are dead?" He murmured, while smiling cordially at Charlie. "No eye witnesses, no charges, problem solved. "Kill them!" Romero shouted with authority, "Kill them all!"

"Wait!" I screamed, desperately grabbing for his raised hand, while pulling his face around to look at me. "Please," I groveled as fear gripped my chest.

"Wait!" Romero called out, staring into my eyes. "Why, my dear, you are a complicated creature after all. I was beginning to think that you were made of ice."

"What if we strike a bargain, just the two of us?" I said in desperation.

"What kind of a bargain?" Romero answered with a sly, sadistic smile.

"Isabella, please no!" Aiden yelled.

I never even looked away, but continued to stare into Romero's eyes. I could feel tears forming at the back of my eyes, but I refused to let them spill. My heart was beating so fast that I feared it would pop out of my chest.

"I do not believe you truly wish to make a bargain with me. You only wish to stall the inevitable," Romero interrupted, lifting his hand in the air once again, to give some kind of signal to his men.

"No, I mean it!" I pleaded, while a cold sweat broke out across my brow. "Look at me, please," I cried, liking my dry lips as I grabbed for his hand again, preventing him from giving the signal. "I swear it, an agreement between you and me. I beg you. Just let them live."

"What sort of agreement?" he asked, curiosity getting the better of him.

"A gentleman's agreement, struck between two honorable people, and hopefully something we can both live with," I replied.

"Oh no, no, no!" Romero said, clicking his tongue at me, disapprovingly with a sour look upon his face. "A gentleman's deal will never do. I think you will have to sweeten the pot, as you English like to say."

"And what exactly is it that you would suggest?" I questioned, taking a deep breath, along with a step back.

"If you should win, I will set your family free, unharmed, with the understanding that they will not follow us," he stated, gesturing toward my family, "and you will agree to come away with me. But if I should win, I will dispense with your entire family as I see fit, and you will still come away with me, willingly or not, it matters not to me." My heart was beating so hard I could barely hear the words coming out of his mouth over the sound of rushing blood between my ears.

I looked at my family and Aiden as they stood helplessly surrounded by Romero's men. I could see the anxious looks in their eyes. I deliberated in my mind as my heart was breaking, chewing on my lower lip, frantically trying to think my way out of this mess.

I weighed the pros and the cons in my head, and it felt more like I was striking a deal with the Devil, himself, than a mere mortal man.

"If I win, they go free, with no fear of retaliation from you or your men. And if you win, I will go willingly, and serve in whatever capacity..."

"Isabella, no!" my father and Charlie yelled at the same time.

I looked towards them both, and saw the shock and horror, on their faces. Taking a deep breath, I slowly brought my eyes about to meet with Aiden's gaze. I feared in my heart that I would see the same in his eyes. But instead of anger, accusation, or disappointment, I saw understanding and pride when our eyes locked.

"… in whatever capacity you deem fit," I repeated, completing the rest of my sentence as I reluctantly brought my eyes back around to Romero's.

"You wouldn't be playing me for a fool, now would you, my dear?" He asked accusingly as he raised his chin just a touch higher to study me.

"No," I replied, coolly. "I am, if nothing else, an honorable person. I swear that much to you. But, how can I be certain that you will keep your word to me? You are after all, a dishonest man by trade," I countered.

Laughing it off, Romero acted hurt, by dramatically bringing his hands to his chest, as if I had just stabbed him in the heart. "My dear woman, you are just going to have to trust me."

"I trust you about as far as I can throw you, *Monsieur* la Toya."

"So tell me, Isabella, which game of chance shall we take up? Which one of your proper, English dueling implements will you choose?" Romero asked, walking around me, with his hand on his chin, speculating as he walked. "We certainly couldn't have a duel with pistols. I have too much invested in you at this point to put a silver bullet in you. After all, a bullet to the head can be so final," he pondered the matter as he scrutinized me with his dark piercing eyes. "No, a duel with pistols just won't due at all," he concluded.

"Perhaps we could use rapiers?" I suggested, while looking at him from the corner of my eye, while he came around me again.

A wide satisfied smile broke out on his lips, as he fingered his mustache, "My dear, you are full of surprises. Rapiers, then."

"Shall we use buttons or no buttons? Since you have so much invested in me and all." I questioned, taking a deep breath, while anxiously waiting for his reply. Unpleasant memories flashed in my mind, jumping to the front of my thoughts, as I remembered what had happened the last time I offered up a friendly game of dueling with blades. A feeling of déjà vu washed over me, and I involuntarily reached for my left arm and shivered.

"I think we will make this interesting by fighting without the buttons," he replied, as his smile reached clear to his eyes this time. "That should make things quite interesting indeed," Romero mused to himself.

"Sanchez, fetch my rapiers," Romero ordered, pointing to a man standing guard near the gangplank. Sanchez lit out like a shot, running to do as he was ordered.

Moments later he returned with the two weapons, gently clutched in his hands, as if they were the Holy Grail. "As you requested, Sir," Sanchez said, standing before us in a very formal stance, presenting the blades to Romero.

Again Romero fingered his mustache with a satisfied grin dancing on his lips. Looking over the two blades resting in Sanchez's hands, Romero bowed, and gestured toward the blades. "I believe in being a gentleman, so I must insist that the lady chooses first."

"Isabella, you don't have to do this," my mother cried out. "Please *Monsieur* Romero, I beg of you."

"Madam, your silence is appreciated," Romero said, turning to address my mother. "Your daughter is a very brave girl and we wouldn't want her distracted by your dramatic outbursts, now would we?"

"Sir, you claim to be a gentleman, and yet you keep my daughter against her will," Father called back in disgust.

"I could simply kill you all now, and be done with it, if you wish," Romero replied in a menacing tone. "Otherwise we can settle this matter in a gentleman's fashion as Isabella has requested. I would like her to feel as if in some small way, she is in charge of her own destiny," Romero shouted with an air of superiority, before regaining his composure.

Turning to me, Romero grinned and winked. "Please choose a weapon, my dear."

Feeling my anger building, like a fire that had just been doused with accelerant, I narrowed my eyes at Romero, and grasped the rapier closest to me. I felt the weight of it, and then placed it back, and retrieved the other blade resting in Sanchez's hand.

Again testing that weight of the weapon in my hand, I grinned back at Romero with renewed confidence. "I think I will use this one," I announced, swiping the blade in the air several times, getting use to the unfamiliar blade in my hand.

"We can start when you are ready," Romero gallantly bowed.

"May I have a drink first? My throat is terribly dry," I pleaded, coyly.

"Whisky or sherry?" he asked, signaling to one of his men.

"Whisky. Irish, if you have it," I said, swinging my blade and thrusting back and forth to work out the jitters.

"Bring the lady a glass of Irish whisky, and Desmond, see that you pour it from my personal stock."

"Right away, Sir," Desmond replied, as he quickly moved to do Romero's bidding.

Brandishing my blade in the air, I positioned myself so that I could see Aiden. He stood tall and straight like a statue, barely moving. But his eyes said everything to me that his lips could not. He nodded his head, sending me a silent message. The movement was very slight, but in that instant, it was as if we were connected and I could read his mind. I gave a slight, but distinct nod in reply, before turning back around to face Romero. My face was now an unreadable mask, as I put my nerves and fears in check.

Desmond arrived with two glasses, containing a rich, caramel colored liquid, which he presented to us on a silver tray. Romero and I each took a glass. I lifted my glass to him in a silent solute, and drained the cup. Relishing the burn, as the liquid slid down the back of my throat, like a shot of liquid courage, it awakened me from the inside out.

"Smooth," I choked out hoarsely, placing the glass back on the tray. Bowing my head, I said a silent prayer and took a deep breath.

"Just to clarify, are we using house rules or regulation rules?" Romero questioned.

"Since I have no way of knowing what your house rules are, I am going to have to insist on regulation," I replied.

"Excellent, shall we begin?" he stated calmly, as if we were about to take a leisurely ride around the park.

"*En Garde*," I called out, crouching in the classic fencing stance, as I prepared for him to charge me.

Making the first move, Romero came in making a direct assault, as he playfully batted my blade around, then retreated back to his original position. I thought, *he is either a terrible fencer or he is simply playing with me.* Either way, I was determined to win my family's freedom.

I lunged with a direct attack trying to get a feel for Romero's style, as we parried back and forth for a few strokes. The playful banter, back and forth with our weapons, went on for another ten minutes. I believe it was a courtesy warm up before the real action began.

"You, Sir, are a real gentleman, giving me time to work out the kinks in my legs, after our arduous ride earlier," I stated casually.

"Yes, well, I would be happy to call the whole thing off, before things get serious and you lose," Romero countered.

"And who said that I intend to lose to you, *Monsieur* la Toya?"

"I am afraid I haven't been exactly transparent with you, my dear," he said, making an advanced forward cross step and sweeping my blade in a full circle before crossing our blades up, and trapping my blade between us. Taking his free hand, Romero held my bladed hand next to his, as he came in close. With a sinister smile plastered on his lips, Romero leaned in next to my ear. "I neglected to inform you that I trained at the *Canne de Combat Ecole* for a time, in hopes of becoming a Musketeer of the Guard."

"So what you are telling me, Sir, is that you couldn't cut it as a Musketeer of the Guard, so you decided to take up your current dream life as a career criminal," I smugly stated, pushing off from him to reset. "*En Garde*," I called.

"Did you not hear what I just told you?" he asked indignantly, confusion marring his features.

"Oh, I heard you. Were your words meant to frighten me?" I countered. "So did you train with Lecour or Charlemont?" I questioned, lunging at him, with a perfectly executed corps a corps, making body contact as I pushed off from his left side, causing Romero to lose his balance and trip.

"That was an illegal move, my dear," Romero stated, with a most perplexed look upon his face.

"You did not answer my question, la Toya. Perhaps you never really studied at the *Canne de Combat Ecole* after all, and wished to merely frighten me with your tall tales," I continued, hoping that my taunt would throw him off. The ploy worked and my blade nicked his wrist slightly, as I countered his advance.

"Ouch! Why you little vixen," Romero hissed.

"Charles Lecour or Joseph Charlemont?" I asked, again.

"Charlemont," Romero barked out, with a most ungentlemanly grunt.

"Charlemont is a very good instructor, but Michel Casseux was always deemed to be the better fighter. He taught strategic fighting, rather than basic tactics. In fact, he was deemed to be the best there was," I stated, with a smug glare.

"Casseux no longer instructs students at the school. He is a legend among swordsmen," Romero said, in awe and reverence as he countered my thrust, coming in close to command my blade again with his off hand.

"You realize you have done that illegal move twice now," I scolded, while wagging a finger at him. I knew that I was playing with fire by taunting him, but I no longer cared. "Charlemont would have booted you from the match, for such a move," I advised, disengaging from Romero with a stomp to the top of his booted foot and a quick rebound attack.

When I came to a full reset, Romero looked down in surprise to notice that I had cut off the corner of his finely tailored coat. Making eye contact with me, he narrowed his eyelids. "How would you know what Monsieur Claremont would have done?" he asked suspiciously.

Taking a step back I smiled confidently, "Because Monsieur Charlemont forced me to abstain from practice one entire day when I pulled that stunt. He was most displeased with me."

I witnessed several emotions simultaneously cross Romero la Toya's face, "Why you duplicitous little —"

"Oh, did I neglect to inform you that I was trained by both Monsieur Charlemont, *and* the legendary Michel Casseux himself?" I asked with a drollness that was meant to get under his skin. "He insisted that Charlie and I refer to him as Uncle Michel. We were practically family."

Gritting his teeth and then giving a low growl, Romero lunged at me with his blade raised, as he began slashing wildly. I decided that I had poked the bear one too many times and maybe my luck had possibly run out. Stepping back, to get out of the way of Romero's frantic slashing, I countered his attack with a slick move called the envelopment. It is accomplished by sweeping the opponents blade around in a full circle and then up, trapping the two blades between you.

I suddenly felt a breeze of cool air between my legs and looked down to see that the front of my gown was slit open from mid skirt to hem.

"One moment, if you please, Monsieur la Toya, while I rectify a small problem you seem to have created for me," I stated with an air of distain. I refused to show Romero that I was shaken by his unorthodox fencing method.

Romero gestured his agreement to my request, by sweeping his blade to the side and then down. He took several deep cleansing breaths to gain control of his anger. Blowing air out through his mouth and in through his nose seemed to have calmed the beast for the moment. "But of course, my dear, take your time," he finally replied.

I looked up and noticed that Romero was now staring down at me with curiosity. Ripping at the skirt where it was cut, I removed the dangling material. Then cutting and ripping at my petticoats, I removed the extra cloth, to give myself room to move about more freely, without getting tangled in material.

Grabbing my arm the moment I stood back up, Romero leaned in close to my face. "If you fail to hold up to your end of the deal, the consequences to you and your family will be utterly apocalyptic," he warned.

"And if you fail to hold up to your end of the bargain, you will learn the true meaning of the term, 'hell hath no fury like a woman scorned,' I retorted, ripping my arm from his grasp.

"Fair enough," Romero replied, with a smile.

"*En Garde,*" I called out at the same time I charged, displaying a few signature moves I had been saving as a surprise for la Toya. He countered by reverting to a cutting like action to block my blade from hitting its mark.

"You are quite clever, Isabella," Romero admitted with great admiration. "There are only a handful of men who would have made such a move."

"And yet you continue to speak, instead of fight," I taunted while resetting into a proper starting position.

"*En Garde,*" he called out, with a salute of his blade. He began by initiating a charge, then crossing over and nicking my hand in retaliation. I backed up several steps, easily dodging his advances, and then I countered, forcing him to retreat.

"You ultimately will lose, you know," Romero offered with a smug smile, trying to keep things light by bantering as we dueled.

"I wouldn't throw dirt over my grave just yet."

"You English have such strange sayings," Romero countered.

"Tyranny like hell will never be easily conquered," I countered, while charging at him. "And nothing too simply achieved can ever be held in high regard." I accentuated my word by cutting his coat button off, then thrusting and swinging my blade as I countered. "The more difficult the fight, the more glorious the triumph in the end," I said, emphasizing the word *triumph* by cutting the sleeve of his coat, and his arm at the same time.

"Are you quite finished?" Romero growled in frustration just as his eyes traveled downward to his cut arm.

"No, I don't believe I have completed the stance." I grinned and advanced before he was ready. "For it is the dearness of the prize," I replied with a forward hop and then a lunge, grabbing his blade with my off hand, binding him up and catching him off guard. "That gives life its greatest value!" I finished by tweaking his nose with my free hand, before pushing off from him.

I suddenly laughed, hopping backwards two steps and pointing my blade downwards. "Care to surrender now, Monsieur la Toya? Because I fear you are the one who will be on the losing end of this match today," I taunted, with a jubilant tone, heckling him on purpose, attempting to throw off his rhythm again. In hindsight, perhaps it was not the best move to make. But I was tired of his superior attitude. It was grating.

Charging me with a wild look in his eyes, I could see his renewed determination, as I countered his forward attack. Romero forced me to retreat a step or two, and I nearly tripped over my own feet from the viciousness of his attack.

I could hear Maria and my mother gasp, when Romero began to advance with earnest, forcing me backwards. Binding me up so I could no longer wield the blade, Romero stripped the rapier from my hand, and threw me against the wooden mast, pinning me by my throat. He then stepped in close, between my legs to keep me from striking out, or kicking him.

I screamed in surprise, and gave a low growl as I struggled to breathe. I pummeled his chest with my fists, striking out in the only way I knew how.

Then Romero dropped his rapier to the ground and the metal handle made a clanking sound as it hit the wooden planks and rolled away from us. Clasping my chin between his finger and thumb he brought his face in close to whisper in my ear. "Let us dispense with the charade," Romero said, dropping a gentle kiss upon my cheek when I turned my face at the last minute. He gloated with a smug smile that floated before my eyes, while he loomed over me. "I have won and you have forfeited. Simply say the words and be done with it."

I heard a commotion coming from the gangplank, but felt helpless to do anything about it in my current situation. My full attention was mainly focused on Romero and his ever looming presence, just inches away from my face.

Lifting my chin a touch higher, I took a moment to look to my left. Charlie had to restrain our father as he attempted to charge the man standing in his way. Mother just stood there stoically, while Maria bowed her head, no doubt praying for a miracle. And then my eyes met Aiden's crisp blue orbs that seemed to spark with so much emotion as he nodded nearly in perceivably. I could almost hear the words his eyes were shouting at me. They were the very same words that were running through my own head. *You have the element of surprise, so use it.*

"Were you looking for me to concede, Monsieur la Toya?" I managed to whisper as my voice choked with emotion. Slowly, I brought my jade green eyes back around to stare into his dark brown, scrutinizing glare, only to find him intently studying my expression. I realized that Romero's demeanor was not that of an angry man determined to destroy me and my entire family. Every emotion the man was feeling at that moment was written all over his face. Romero Alonso Garcia la Toya of Barcelona, Spain, was a man completely captivated by a woman.

And that woman was me. I had to stop myself from laughing out loud, deciding instead to change tactics and quickly.

"It would be the honorable thing to do," he added, impatiently waiting for me to speak the words he longed to hear.

Coyly I smiled, looking at him through my lashes. I chewed at my lower lip as if taking a moment to think about my options. This definitely felt like *déjà vu*, all over again, only this time it was with a man I despised with every fiber of my being.

Surprising even myself, I lifted my right leg up, resting it against the side of his leg, in a provocative way. I prayed the entire time that Romero wouldn't try to run his hand up my leg and discover the pair of surprises I had waiting for him. Turning the charm up a notch, I gave Romero a coquettish smile, as I lifted my chin to give Romero a seductive full pout.

He smiled widely and chuckled to himself. "I knew you would come around. You and I are going to get along very well, my dear," Romero concluded, turning loose of my wrist, anxious to run his hand along the leg that was now propped against his hip.

Grabbing his hand before he could run it up to my thigh too high, I distracted him, by bringing his hands together between us. Then running my left hand over his chest, I slipped my finger into his shirt, where his strings had come untied.

Romero grinned even broader, giving me the perfect opportunity to slip my free hand beneath the hem of my skirt, to retrieve my blades, before he knew what was happening.

"Perhaps we should take this matter back to my cabin, where we will have a little privacy," he added looking over his shoulder, toward my family, then back at me, almost feverish with desire.

"But I have not conceded yet, *Monsieur* la Toya, and rules are rules," I added with a slight pout, which would have tipped off anyone who truly knew me well.

"It is really just a formality, my dear, and truly not necessary, since you have dropped your blade and lost the bet," Romero said quickly.

Suddenly chaos and noise erupted on the docks. Thirty men came to a rushing halt on horseback in front of the ship, hastily dismounting, before rushing the ship.

"After all, a deal is a deal, is it not?" Romero muttered under his breath, momentarily distracted by the commotion just beyond the railing of his ship. With a queer look in his eyes, Romero turned back to study my face, gauging my reaction, to the new comers.

"Yes, Romero, my dear, it certainly is," I hissed, with a renewed confidence, just before I viciously jabbed him in the groin with one of my knives.

Romero began swearing in Spanish, as he jumped back.

I could only understand every third word, since I had not paid attention during my Spanish lessons, but I understood the gist of his disappointment.

The new comers rushed Romero's ship and crew with pistols and swords drawn, and I heard someone order the crew to stand down, or be killed. Romero's men dropped their weapons, without a shot being fired, and surrendered with even less fuss.

"You are not only a crafty opponent, Isabella, but you are a very conniving woman," Romero ground out the words between clenched jaws. As he backed away from me, I heard Charlie's voice shouting in my head.

"Watch out Bella!"

Romero glanced down at his rapier, lying on the deck.

"I would not attempt it, if I were you," I warned, as I brandished my weapons. "I'm not opposed to removing a few fingers or your hand, la Toya." I knew I had the upper hand, and I intended to use it to my full advantage.

Romero smiled placidly, while continuing to inch the toe of his boot closer to the hilt of his rapier, still lying on the deck.

I threw my blade, sticking it into the wooden plank, just between Romero's boot and his rapier, causing him to jump back in surprise. "Or a toe," I added, giving him a cold, hard stare.

As if from out of nowhere, Romero produced a blade, and hurled it in my direction. I had been so distracted by his foot inching its way toward the discarded weapon, I failed to see his hand, reaching for the hidden blade, until it was too late. I noticed movement out of the corner of my left eye, but didn't have time to think twice about it, I only reacted. Instinctively arching backwards, to avoid Romero's blade, I threw the remaining blade in my hand.

Suddenly, I was knocked to the deck by a force I never saw coming. Propelled backwards, I hit the deck hard with a loud thud, knocking the air from my lungs. I fought and struggled, frantically against the weighty burden that covered me and kept me pinned to the deck. Desperately I thrashed, trying to breathe again. Seconds ticking by like an eternity.

Finally, air flooded my lungs and I gulped for more, while blindly pummeling at the chest of my unknown assailant, fearing for my life, unsure exactly who had knocked me down. My shoulder and head felt like they were on fire, as recognition slowly penetrated my jarred brain. Aiden's voice whispered in my ear.

"Isabella, it's me," he quietly said, lifting the majority of his weight off of me slowly.

"Romero? Aiden, where is Romero?" I asked in desperation.

"He's dead, Isabella!" Aiden's voice cracked with emotion, as he cupped my face in his hands. "Shh, shh, shh, my love, I have you now and you are safe. He will never hurt you again."

I was comforted by the sound of Aiden's voice, but at the same time I knew that something was wrong. I could hear it in his tone. I could not imagine what possibly happened and tried to peer around Aiden, but could only see that the crew and captain had been subdued.

"Is my family alright, Aiden? Did anything happen to my parents or Charlie?" I frantically asked.

"Do not trouble yourself, everyone is safe," Aiden soothed me, with his words, while placing a gentle kiss on my lips, cheeks, and eyes.

"Is she all right?" Charlie yelled over Father's shoulder, as they both fell to the deck next to us, trying to get a better look.

Looking up I squinted and shielded my eyes against the bright sunlight. Then peaking around Aiden, while I gave him a hard push, I was puzzled when he groaned slightly.

I could see Romero's lifeless form, lying on the deck only feet away from us. He had a blade sticking out of his chest, where his cold, black heart should have been.

"Are you certain he is dead? I questioned, still unable to believe that I had hit my mark.

"You did it, Bella. Your blade hit true," Charlie cried out gleefully, as happy tears welled up in his eyes.

"Charlie, what is the matter with you?" I asked.

I suddenly turned my head to look at my mother, when I heard her gasp in horror.

Blissfully naïve to what the problem could be, I felt perplexed once again at such a reaction. I felt fine, except for the splitting pain in my head and shoulder where I hit the deck. "What is the matter? You're acting as if somebody just died or is about to," I said flippantly.

Narrowing my eyes at Father and Charlie, I began to push at Aiden's chest in earnest, attempting to free myself. "Aiden, what is wrong with you?" I demanded. "Let me up."

"Darling, I seem to be having a little difficulty moving at the moment," Aiden confessed, his voice sounding strange to my ears.

"Well, don't just sit there with your teeth in your mouth, help him up," I demanded, while still trying to move out from under Aiden's large form. Caleb, Charlie, and Father all took a hold of him, so I could slip out from under him. Then they gently laid him back down on the deck as Caleb pulled his friends head into his lap, gently cradling him.

My eyes instantly fell upon the blade, protruding from Aiden's left shoulder. I thought I would be sick. Gulping air for a few seconds, I turned my back to him. I needed a second to gather my wits about me, so Aiden didn't see the fear in my eyes. Panic momentarily gripped my heart, as my mind raced for answers.

"Darling, everything is going to be fine," I assured him as I turned back around and plastered a pleasant expression on my face. Calling out orders, like I had seen my mother do a thousand times before, I sounded more like a general. "Maria, fetch the surgeon. Take two of Father's men with you. We wouldn't want any more mishaps today. Mother, find the captain's quarters, and prepare the room for Aiden. Charlie, I need you to find the galley and prepare two large pots of boiling water. Then bring them to the captain's quarters," I said without even taking a breath. In reality, I was afraid that if I stopped for even a second, I would fall apart.

"Isabella, I have a knife protruding from my shoulder. How are you so calm?" Aiden asked.

"As long as you are still breathing, I will have faith," I answered, getting down on my knees, next to him and Caleb. I gazed up at Caleb and our eyes locked. In that instant, I read everything in his eyes. Caleb was scared for his best friend's life.

"Well, gentlemen don't just stand there twiddling your thumbs. Let us move my husband to more comfortable accommodations, shall we?" I suggested, trying to sound unconcerned and confident.

Then turning quickly, I led the way, before Aiden or anyone else could see the tears that formed in my eyes. Gently picking Aiden up, Caleb, Father, and two other men followed me to the captain's quarters, to wait for the surgeon.

While we waited for Maria to return, Caleb related how they had surprised Ian and Lance on the road that day. Ian refused to give up any information when interrogated by my father. He even seemed to revel in the pain and rough treatment being administered. But Lance had been a different story.

Caleb delighted in telling me how Lord Blayney, had nearly fainted at the sight of his own blood when Aiden started in on him. Lance had caved, pinning everything on Ian, in an effort to save his own skin. It was from Lance that they learned that Maria and I had been sold to a rich Spaniard, who intended to leave the country that day.

Caleb splintered off from the others to gather reinforcements from the local authorities. And it had been Caleb who arrived in the nick of time, saving Maria and me from a life of who knows what.

Aiden weaved in and out of lucidness as he continued to lose blood. I tried to keep him awake with cold water and lively conversation, but I felt I was losing the battle.

"Aiden, darling, just hold on, I'm sure Maria will be back any minute now," I cried, trying to assure him, while stroking his face, as fear started to creep into my thoughts.

"You sound worried, my love. Don't you know how this is all going to turn out?" Aiden teased, with a feeble smile. "And here I thought you had some special powers, or connections."

"Of course I do, darling. Everything is going to be just fine. I have it on good authority that you will make a full recovery," I said, trying to sound confident. All the while my insides were melting like hot wax down a candle stick.

"Could someone check to see where the bloody hell Maria is with the surgeon?" I yelled over all the idle chatter. I took several deep breaths, to calm my raw nerves, trying to quiet the fears that kept going through my head.

Caleb, and Father called out in unison, "I'll do it," as the two of them turned on their heels, leaving the room in a hurry.

"I will give you two a moment to talk. I have to go to the galley and check on the water," Mother responded, giving me her all knowing look, before shutting the door behind her.

"Why did you do it, Aiden? Why did you throw yourself in front of me? I would have been fine."

Reaching for my right hand that was cooling his brow with a damp cloth. Aiden pulled my fingers to his lips, then placed a loving kiss in my palm. "That was a chance I could not take. Your continued life means far too much to me to leave it up to chance."

With tears in my eyes now, that I could no longer hide, my true emotions and fears came flooding to the surface. "Aiden, if something should happen to you…" I choked back, unable to continue.

"Nothing is going to happen to me. You've assured me of that," Aiden gently prodded, as his piercing gaze locked with mine. "And I have not known you to be wrong yet."

"If you were lost to me, Aiden, surely my reason for breathing would soon follow," I cried, laying my head on his chest.

Aiden stroked my hair with his hand, and I felt his breath catch in his chest. "When you disappeared, I was like a madman. I thought I would lose my mind. The mere thought of never seeing or touching you again made me crazy." Lifting my head up, I gazed into his eyes as he tenderly wiped tears from my cheeks with his thumb.

"I would not have stopped searching for you, until you were found, or I took my last breath." His steady tone and loving words touched my heart, as fresh tears silently rolled down my cheeks.

"But, I … I…" I started to say, when Aiden placed a finger over my lips, silencing my words.

"Shush, my love, I would gladly pay any price required of me, to assure your continued breath, for just one more day," Aiden defiantly said. Looking to his left shoulder, he half smiled and then chuckled, through the pain. "Besides, this is merely a scratch. You will see."

I could see that he was lying. His skin had turned pale, almost ashen and his eyes looked dull. I was beginning to think that the surgeon would be too late, if he did not arrive in the next few minutes.

"Promise me you won't leave me, Aiden. I wouldn't survive it," I cried, trying to stem the flow of more tears by biting my lower lip.

"You would survive it," Aiden insisted, with the knowledge of a man who had lived through his own loss.

Charlie burst through the door with Maria on his heels. She had managed to locate a qualified surgeon from the nearby town. Doctor Harrison was a serious individual with sharp angular features and a no-nonsense bedside manner. He entered the room, assessed the problem, and immediately opened his black bag to remove a device that would allow him to listen to Aiden's heart.

Next, he ordered water to be boiled and brought to the room just as Mother walked through the door with two large men carrying the pots.

Then he examined the area that had the knife protruding from it, pursed his lips together as if he were thinking. "It seems, my good man, that you have a bit of a problem," Doctor Harrison pronounced.

"It would seem to me, Doctor Harrison, that you have a way of stating the obvious," Aiden retorted, without humor.

"No cause for rudeness, good Sir."

"I'm sorry Sir, but I tend to get a little cranky when I have a knife sticking out of my shoulder!" Aiden replied, in a derisive tone.

Then I looked at Maria over the Doctor's shoulder, and silently mouth the words, "Where did you get this guy?"

"Who is this woman, and why are you still here?" the doctor asked, while staring at me.

"I am his wife, and I will not be going anywhere," I informed him, in no uncertain terms.

"Very well then, you will follow my instructions, and stay out of my way. And if anyone gets woozy over the slightest bit of blood, leave now," Doctor Harrison ordered, without compunction.

"I think I speak for everyone in this room when I say we are well past that," I retorted.

"Then you may stay, but you will follow my every instruction to the letter," he reiterated, turning his back to us, as he began preparing his instruments.

"As you wish," I replied, reaching up to push a stray hair out of my eyes with the back of my hand.

Aiden reached out and grabbed my hand to get my attention, "If something should happen to me —" he began.

"Nothing is going to happen to you," I assured, cutting him off as I gazed into his eyes.

"But if something should happen, promise me..." Aiden said with a catch in his throat, "promise me that you will not stop living," he said quickly before I could cut him off again.

"Darling, nothing is going to happen," I admonished, before leaning down to kiss his forehead.

"Isabella, swear to me. Swear you will go on living," he pleaded.

Gently touching his face, and then running my thumb over his lips, I studied his face a moment, before leaning down again to kiss his lips lightly. Tears ran down my cheeks, bathing his face with salted drops. "I'm afraid I can't do that, my love," I replied, letting out the breath I didn't even realize I'd been holding. Placing my head next to his, I spoke quietly into his ear as emotions causing my voice to crack and catch slightly in my throat. "You are the air that I breathe and the blood that runs through my veins, each minute, each second, of every day."

Lifting my head up, so that I could look into Aiden's eyes, I desperately searched his face, memorizing every line and curve of his sun-kissed features. I took a deep breath, breathing in his scent with a smile. Slowly bringing his hand to rest on my chest, so that he could feel the beating of my heart, I continued, "Aiden, you are as much a part of me now, as this heart, beating in my chest, giving me life. You give me a reason to continue fighting when I want to give up. My heart has been changed, because of you," I desperately cried, gulping back emotion, as I held back more tears. "You have to fight! Please darling, I beg you, don't give up. We have only just found each another. I can't even fathom saying good bye so soon."

Then swallowing hard as tears ran freely down my cheeks, I slowly leaning down, and kissed his lips gently once again. "My heart swells with pride, because I am your wife and I swear it skips a beat every time you are near. Aiden Larkin Townsend, I forbid you from dying on me."

Aiden gave me a half hearted smile, just as his hand went slack in mine. His eyes closed, and I desperately called his name over and over again. "Aiden... Aiden, open your eyes, darling!" I screamed, as hysteria began to build in the pit of my stomach. "Aiden, please... please, I beg you, open your eyes darling... Aiden, look at me!" I softly called. Clinging to him, I refused to let go, until my mother and Charlie pulled me from him.

The doctor moved in, blocking my view as Charlie and Caleb physically drug me from the room, while I continued to scream out Aiden's name.

Taking a hold of my hand, Charlie squeezed it tightly. "Isabella, stop it!" he ordered. "You can't help him this way."

My mind screamed out, *I'm scared Charlie. I don't think I can do this. I will go mad, if he dies.*

"I'm here, Isabella, I'm here now. Don't be scared, everything is going to be alright," Charlie answered out loud, as our minds continued to connect. He removed his coat and rolled up his shirt sleeves.

"I need more time, Charlie, I need more time. I have to tell him how I feel," I babbled out loud, through my uncontrollable tears. "I didn't get to tell him how much I —" I began, trailing off.

"He knows, Isabella." Charlie said, empathetically patting my hand. "And I'm here for you. The doctor will fix him, you'll see. Aiden is going to be just fine. He's is a fighter,"

I heard someone open the door and then heard the doctor, call out over his shoulder. "I need volunteers to give blood. Now!"

"Certainly, Doctor I will be right there," Caleb called back through the door, as he squeezed my shoulder and hurried back into the room. Placing my back to the wall, I slid to the floor, when my legs gave out. Charlie silently sat down next to me, placing his coat over me and taking my hand into his. I placed my free hand over my eyes and took a moment to reflect on the last month of my life. How differently I felt about everything since Aiden had come into it.

I felt Charlie let go of my hand and step away, disappearing into the room to assist with Aiden. My mind continued to ponder thoughts, as a question kept turning over in my mind. *At what point did we cease to be in control of our destiny, choosing instead to allow life to simply unfold?*

Part of me wanted to rejoice in the fact that I had been loved and transformed by the simple act of that pure love. I felt such great sorrow, in my failings and short sightedness, learning too late that being loved and loving in return meant everything to me.

Why did I always feel the need to be so strong, so independent? Like an island, unto myself. Did I wait too long to give my heart over to someone, only to lose that love upon discovering it?

I found, that in that moment, I suddenly gained great clarity, because I was willing to turn lose of the things in my past that had held so much power over me. Things that kept me imprisoned and trapped in their web of lies.

I had been dangling in the same place for far too long, trapped in a single paralyzing moment of time by pain, anger, and regret.

At some point I had made a choice to go right instead of left, and my life was forever changed. And so my lot was cast by nothing more than a handful of choices. Choices that not only stood to determine my fate at this moment, but Aiden's as well.

35

Four Years Later... A Gathering to Celebrate Life Anew

 BREATHED IN AND OUT SLOWLY, enjoying the sensations and smells that caressed my nose. Everything was blooming again after the harsh Dublin winter, and I found myself in a reflective mood, as my family and extended family gathered to celebrate the end of the long cold winter.

For some reason my mind kept drifting back to that terrible day, four years ago, when I found such clarity, just as life threatened to rob me of everything I held so dear. In that defining moment, I feared that my grief would consume me.

I believe that death knocks at our door from time to time, to remind us that we are all merely mortals, subject to the same frailties and short comings that befall all human kind. Perhaps, prompting each of us to remember that life is precious, yet limited, and meant to be lived to the fullest, each and every day. I realized that day, that I had been hurt by things in my past, which caused me to build walls around my future. Walls that were intended to surround and insulate me from further hurt and pain, only to discover that they could never accomplish the very purpose for which I had built them in the first place. Instead, they further isolated me from my life and the world around me, giving me a false sense of security.

When my past fears collided with my future hurts, everything became hopelessly entangled. I was like a child who cried out in the middle of the night, from nightmares of imaginary creatures hiding beneath the bed. I fought against everything that was harsh or hurtful in my eyes. Then later, I found that none of it was true. And the fears I clung to, like a life raft for survival, were nothing more than childish rants. It wasn't until I let go of my perceived hurts and childish fears that I was free to live or even see things clearly.

It was as if the gray clouds had parted and the sun's rays beat upon my face for the first time in my life that day. There is nothing like true forgiveness to resurrect a soul, and make one finally free to be whole again. My choice was made simple, and it came down to this; give up on life or live it fully and with true purpose of heart every day from then on.

So here I sit, overlooking the beautiful Dublin countryside, with my family surrounding me.

I count my blessings every day, and among those, my greatest blessing is my daughter Olivia, sitting in my lap, gazing up at me with an angelic smile upon her three year old face. A face I have come to cherish, speckled with tiny freckles across her perfectly formed nose.

I love telling her that the angels kissed her nose, and left their mark behind so that she would always know where she came from. It never failed to make her laugh. Her delicate blue eyes sparkle and dance with mischief just like her father's and it took my breath away.

"Mommy, please let me down," Olivia, politely orders, as her cherub hands push against me.

Ginger colored curls bounce about her rosy cheeks as she runs head-long into her grandfather's opened arms, making me laugh and cry all at the same time.

I believe each of us is put here on this earth to learn, love, share, and appreciate what we have been given. I found that I had to be willing to give myself over fully and completely to loving someone else, before the true joys of life could be revealed to me.

No one person is given the clarity or insight that tells us when our time here on earth is done. So instead of focusing on the negative,

I chose to focus on the positive. Life is fragile, unpredictable and too easily snatched away in a single moment.

I believe this to be God's way of reminding us to make the most of every day, because our lives are limited at best. Time is doled out in different amounts that are neither fair, nor equal. Time is a precious commodity. It is to be used wisely and not squandered, nor thrown away like last week's spoiled produce. But it is to be viewed as a gift and meant to be cherished and spent judiciously every day.

I look to my right and see Evelyn Townsend sitting on a swing under the shade of the large oak tree. She is gently rocking back and forth, playing a sly game with my brother, Charlie. She coyly smiles to herself, while pretending not to notice Charlie, who is attempting to peak her interest in higher learning.

He is reading to her from Immanuel Kant's, *Groundwork of the Metaphysics of Morals,* a recently acquired book Charlie has been combing through, with the critical eye of a scientist. He is looking for those rare little nuggets of truth that he can incorporate into his own philosophies of life.

Directly in front of me, my mother and Judith Townsend are playing a game of Paille-Maille, or as some have nicknamed it Pall-Mall, which is Latin for ball and mallet.

Paille-Maille is a game played with a round, wooden ball, which you strike with a mallet. The players attempt to move this ball through a maze of arches placed in the ground. The arches are made of a thin iron that is shaped into a u shape. The one who can hit the ball through the arches with the fewest blows, or at the number agreed upon, wins.

There have been several heated discussions this last week alone, in regards to the game's origins. It seems there is some dispute over who can claim the official proprietorship to this silly game. Aiden's father, John, claims the Irish invented the game and that he knows for a fact that the game was introduced in Galway at the Bishop's Palace Garden, but they called it "Croquet." My grandfather, on the other hand, is sure that the English invented the game and that he has proof, because Samuel Johnson wrote about the game in his dictionary in 1755. My father objected vehemently and claimed that the game of Paille-Maille or Croquet was invented by the French. He even went so far as to say that he remembered the game being played on the palace lawns many years ago, when he was just a young lad. To tell the truth, I don't care who invented the game, I only know that it is fun to watch.

"Mommy, Mommy!" Olivia cries as she runs toward me.

"What is it, Olivia?" I answered, looking into her precocious, blue eyes.

"Daddy is coming!" she exclaimed, rather boisterously.

"Darling, we had this discussion already. I told you why Daddy couldn't be here with us," I stated as gently as possible, reaching out my hand, tucking an unruly stray curl behind her ear.

"But Mommy, Coco told me Daddy was coming," Olivia insisted, "And he has a surprise for me."

"Olivia, who is this Coco you have been referring to all day? I don't know anyone by that name."

"Coco is my sister, Mommy," Olivia innocently said, with a giggle.

"Olivia, my darling, you are my only child," I replied, giving her a stern look. "I think I would know if there was more than one of you running around here."

"Oh Mommy, Coco isn't born yet." Olivia laughed with the innocence of a three year old. "She told me she is coming for my birthday and that you and Daddy will name her something silly like Catherine," Olivia said with a serious tone. Then leaning in close to my face, as if she was about to share a big secret with me, Olivia placed her hand to my ear and whispered, "But she told me she wants to be called Coco, because she likes that better." Then placing both of her hands on either side of my face, Olivia forced me to look into her eyes. "Oh thank you, Mommy, for my wonderful gift," she said, kissing my lips before running off again. Caught off guard, I faltered and sat perfectly silent for a moment, stunned by her unexpected news, delivered so matter-of-factly. Finally finding my voice, I called out.

"Wait, I don't think I understand," I said dumbfounded.

Stopping in her tracks Olivia turned around and motioned for me to follow. "We have to go now, Mommy," she insisted, before turning back around and running ahead.

Olivia, who realized I hadn't moved to follow her, stopped again to find me still sitting in the same spot staring after her. Trotting back to me, Olivia took me by the hand and coaxed me up, "Come on, Mommy," Olivia demanded.

"But where are we going, darling?" I asked, still perplexed by the unexpected news she had just delivered.

"To the garden house, Mommy, Coco says it is going to rain," she stated as if everyone should already know this fact.

The garden house as Olivia called it was really an atrium that was built five years earlier. It housed beautiful flowering plants that would not normally survive the harsh Dublin weather.

"Alright darling, but I don't think…" I said as I looked up toward the sky, to see fluffy rain clouds blowing in quickly. My words died on my tongue, mid sentence as I fell silent again and just stared at Olivia.

Finding my voice again I called out to my brother and his companion, "Charlie, Evelyn, we are headed for the atrium, apparently it is about to rain."

"We were just coming in anyway," Charlie called back to me.

"Tell Uncle Charlie not to forget his book, Mommy," Olivia insisted, giving me a serious look.

"What darling? Did you just say something?" I questioned, still lost in thought as I stared up at the clouds again.

"Coco said Uncle Charlie will forget his book. Tell him not to forget his book," Olivia reiterated, with a look of real concern on her little three year old face.

Turning around I called out to Charlie who was headed my way with Evelyn in tow, "Charlie, Olivia says don't forget your book."

"What?" Charlie asked confused as he looked down at his hands. Then with a queer look on his face, Charlie stared at Olivia in disbelief. He smiled awkwardly and pursed his eyebrows together. "How did she know that I had forgotten my book?"

"Coco told her," I stated with an awkward laugh then I smiled at him.

"Who the bloody hell is, Coco?" Charlie asked, giving me an even queerer look.

"Charlie!" I gasped.

"Ooh, Uncle Charlie just swore." Olivia laughed, covering her mouth with her hand.

"I will tell you later," I said to Charlie, "But for now, I would suggest you retrieve your book before it gets ruined by the rain."

"But there isn't a cloud in the sky...." Charlie said looking up as I had done moments before. "Bullocks, where did those come from?" he grumbled.

"Ooh! Uncle Charlie said another bad word, Mommy!" Olivia informed us with another volley of titters of laughter.

"Uncle Charlie!" I scolded half heartedly. "Don't you think you have educated your niece enough for one day? Just get the book and meet us in the atrium. We will be having lunch there instead of out on the lawn."

"Oh yes, of course. Where are my manners?" Charlie stammered before he turned around and trotted off to retrieve his book.

"Come on, Mommy. Daddy is waiting for us," Olivia called to me. Her excitement could not be contained any longer and she ran ahead of me, while looking to her right as if she were having a conversation with someone.

"I thought you told me Aiden couldn't join us," Charlie interjected with an air of surprise when he caught up to me, his new book in hand.

"Apparently, there are things of this world that you and I are not privy to, but my three year old daughter is. I swear sometimes I think she is really a thirty-year-old woman stuck in a tiny person," I stated in a half joking tone.

"Don't be ridiculous Bella. She's only three," Charlie chastised.

"She talks to spirits, Charlie. Look at her. Presently she is holding a conversation with her sister, Coco, whom she insists will be born on her birthday," I stated in a high pitched voice that sounded somewhat hysterical.

"What?" Charlie asked in disbelief.

"Honestly, I wouldn't lie to you. How do you think I knew to remind you not to forget your book?" I asked.

"That was Olivia?" Charlie questioned.

"No, Coco, your niece to be, haven't you been listening to a thing I've been saying," I corrected.

"So let me get this straight. Olivia told you that you are with child, but she learned of it from my niece to be, who isn't even born yet, but will be arriving on the very same day Olivia turns four?" Charlie questioned with a measure of shock. "And to top it all off, you didn't realize that you were with child, did you?"

"Yes! I mean no. I didn't realize I was with child," I answered, with a measure of my own disbelief. "Don't look at me like that Charlie. I'm not making this up."

"You're not, are you?" He said, tilting his head to the side as the news began to sink in.

"Is that rain I'm feeling?" I questioned, putting my hand out in front of me, as the first drops of rain pelted my face.

"Yes, so we had better run for it," Charlie urged, taking off his coat and placing it over both our heads to keep the rain from completely soaking us.

Tucking my arm around Charlie's waist, we ran toward the covered atrium. And just for a brief instant, the years melted away as we laughed like we did when we were carefree children running through the rain. We would put on our thick boots, so we could slosh about in the puddles, making a royal mess of our starched white clothes. Oh, how our nanny would scold us when we finally came back inside, all caked in mud and drenched to the bone.

I felt such pure bliss in that moment as we entered the atrium.

"Mommy, Mommy, I told you Daddy would be here," Olivia's shrill voice could be heard across the entire room.

Aiden was crouched down next to her as he placed something in Olivia's little arms. She carefully cradled the object and headed towards me after one last glance back at her father.

"What do we have here?" I asked, glancing at her arms suspiciously.

"It's a puppy, Mommy. Daddy brought me a puppy," Olivia's excitement was unmistakable.

"Oh is it now? And who is going to take care of this little ball of fur?" I inquired, bending down to get a better look.

"This sounds like a private discussion, I would rather not be involved in," Charlie assured me, as he headed off to find Evelyn.

"Me, Mommy," Olivia cried, peering up at me through her lashes. "Can I keep him, please, Mommy? Daddy said you have the final say. Oh, please, oh please, Mommy? You have to say yes." Large innocent blue eyes stared up at me pleadingly.

"Olivia, a puppy is a lot of responsibility," I added, looking up to see my husband standing behind her now, with an equally pleading pout on his face.

Aiden was tilting his head to one side at the same time he protruded his lower lip. Then he pressed his palms together, like a child begging for forgiveness, after doing something he was told not to do.

"Oh, let me see it," I said in a resigned tone, knowing that I didn't stand a chance against the two of them.

Taking the small, black ball of fur Olivia gladly relinquished to me, I held it up to examine.

The puppy was only about nine inches in length and so round, it truly reminded me of a ball. Its face was well proportioned and its eyes were large and black, but nearly lost in all that hair. I was instantly lost, as I fell in love with the puppy.

"She looks like a miniature bear," I laughed when she began to lick my hand. "Where in the world did you find her, Aiden?"

"She came in on one of the merchant ships two days ago. Apparently, the ship's mascot tangled with a male counterpart just before the ship left port and then gave birth at sea. She had seven puppies and the captain was looking to lessen the number of mouths to feed. She is a Black Norwegian Elk Hound. I was told they are very smart and excellent companions for children," Aiden assured me, bending down beside us.

"What shall we call her?" I asked, nuzzling the puppy's cold, wet nose to Olivia's, just so I could hear her squeal with laughter. "And make it a good name because she will have to live with it the rest of her life," I added.

"We could call her Dalia," Aiden suggested, "It means raven haired, I think."

"Well, I can see someone has given this matter a lot of thought already," I laughed.

Pausing a moment as if someone was whispering in her ear, Olivia tilted her head thoughtfully for a moment. "Oh Daddy, that's silly. Besides, Coco says she doesn't like it. We like Winnie instead," Olivia announced, proudly.

"Darling, that is a wonderful name. Winnie it is," I said, placing the little ball of fur in Olivia's outstretched arms.

Aiden's head suddenly snapped up and a puzzled looked crossed his face. "Who is this Coco, and why does she have a say in the puppy's name?"

"Olivia, run along and show everyone your new puppy," I said, giving her a kiss on the cheek. I waited until Olivia was out of ear shot before replying to Aiden's question.

Clearing my throat first, I was trying to come up with a way to break the news to him gently. "Coco is our daughter," I stated.

"Our what?" Aiden retorted, with an incredulous tone.

"Let me try this again. Coco is our unborn daughter, to be exact," I added, stepping closer to him, I picked up his arm and placed it around me, as I nuzzled my face against his chest. I took a deep breath, smelling of his masculine scent. "I really missed you this time. You were gone so terribly long," I added with a slight pout for emphasis. "I was beginning to doubt that you would ever come home to us," I laid my head against his chest, and wrapped my arms around his waist.

"Wait. I'm still confused. Could you please explain who Coco is again?" Aiden insisted, tilting my chin up to look at him.

"You know how I told you that our daughter was precocious?" I began.

"Yes," Aiden answered with a suspicion tone as he pursed his eyebrows together, giving me that look of his. I could tell he was wondering where exactly this conversation was leading.

"Well, it seems our daughter is more than precocious. She also has some abilities," I stated, while looking directly into his piercing blue eyes, trying to gage whether or not he fully understood what I was saying.

"What do you mean, she has abilities?" Aiden cautiously questioned, placing me at arm's length. Then giving me the once over, from head to toe, Aiden placed the back of his hand against my forehead.

"What are you doing?" I suddenly asked.

"I was checking you for a fever. You look flushed to me," Aiden answered.

"I'm fine, darling. Thank you for your concern, but the flush is most likely a reaction to the news that was just delivered to me by our three year old," I admonished, brushing his hand from my brow. "Olivia can speak to spirits," I added, then paused to wait for his reaction.

"She can what?" Aiden gasped.

"There!" I said pointing at the expression on his face. "That is the same exact reaction I had when I first learned the news myself, and I was born with abilities. It's all very perplexing," I admitted with a shake of my head. "You might want to prepare yourself for the possibility that Coco may have…uhm… well…abilities as well."

"This is all very disconcerting, my love," Aiden confessed as he walked in a circle with his arms over his head, trying to make sense of the news. "And can you tell me why we are naming our unborn child Coco?" he asked, coming to a dead stop in his circular path, to stare at me.

"That's just it, we didn't name her Coco. She has named herself that. Apparently, we decide on the name Catherine for her," I added, becoming flustered. "But it seems the child would prefer to be called Coco," I stated flatly, with a stiff smile.

"This child, who isn't even born yet, is already dictating her demands?" Aiden interjected.

"Yes, Aiden, the child that isn't even born yet," I added flatly. "But I think you are missing the point."

"And when were you going to tell me that we were having another child?"

"Now that is a funny story," I awkwardly laughed, then cleared my throat again, when I noticed the stern look on his face.

"How can this be, Bella?" Aiden asked with a look of concern which quickly turned to confusion as he began to pace back and forth in front of me again. "Oh Bella, I'm not sure I fully understand all of this yet. We have a precocious three year old, who talks to spirits. And now you lead me to understand that there is definitely another one on the way. And this one has even picked out her own name, from the great beyond!"

"Little Olivia will soon be four my love, and keep your voice down," I scolded.

"Do you think she heard me?" Aiden shouted, not really concerned who might hear his discontent. "This unborn child of ours," he clarified.

"I wouldn't be surprised," I said blandly. "But then I think everyone two miles away heard you as well," I added. "I remember telling you this sort of thing runs in my family."

"But I didn't think I would have to deal with this … this … particular thing until our children were much older," Aiden stammered, flailing his arms before taking a deep breath and blowing it out through his mouth.

His face took on an exasperated, defeatist look that I had come to recognize these days as his way of giving into what life choose to throw at him.

Slowly he reached out, drawing me into his embrace, and placing one hand over my stomach. "It's a girl?" he asked, as his entire continence slowly changed, "We are having another daughter."

"Are you disappointed?"

Tilting my chin up to meet his gaze, Aiden genuinely smiled now. "I could never be disappointed in you. my love," he replied, lowering his lips to mine, passionately kissing me in the middle of the atrium, with the sound of rain hitting the roof.

"Daddy, Daddy!" Olivia's boisterous voice called out to us, before she entered the room. Olivia burst through the doorway, running as fast as she could, with her tiny new playmate, following close on her heels.

"Winnie is so wonderful," Olivia cried with such exuberance. "Oh, Mommy, I love you and Daddy and Coco and my new puppy, Winnie so very much. I can't wait for Coco to get here, so we can all play together." She giggled as her puppy crashed into the back of her dress, when she stopped suddenly.

"Darling, when Coco arrives, she won't be able to play with you for some time," I pointed out.

"I know, Mommy. But I still can't wait for her to come."

"Did my ears hear correctly?" my father interrupted. "Olivia has informed us that she has a baby sister on the way."

"Yes, Poppa, I wish to make it official, and inform everyone that there will be a new arrival this fall. Olivia has informed us that it will be a girl, and she wishes to be called ..."

"Coco!" Olivia shouted, interrupting me, "Her name is Coco," she proclaimed stubbornly. "She doesn't like the other name Mommy and Daddy give her," she added, bending down to pick up her puppy.

"Apparently, our precocious daughters have picked a name, and I am just the hatchery," I added facetiously, which caused the room to erupt into laughter.

Bending down to whisper in my ear, Aiden added, "The name is growing on me."

"Seriously?" I blurted, looking at him as if he had just lost his mind.

"Seriously!" Aiden assured me with a devilish smile and a wink, "I have given up fighting against the things I do not understand. I find it is better to go with the tide, rather than against it."

Suddenly, I felt movement in my belly, like butterflies fluttering around in a circle. "I must say, I believe our little Coco, heartily approves of your new philosophy."

"Splendid then, everyone is happy, and I will rest easier at night," Aiden proclaimed, triumphantly.

"I dare say, you are about to have another beautiful, yet extraordinary daughter. You, Sir, will never rest peacefully again," father informed him, with a half smile and a rye look.

"Honestly, you couldn't have kept that piece of information under your hat, Father?" I scolded, when I saw the look of concern on my husband's face.

"Now what would have been the fun in that, my beautiful, extraordinary daughter?" Father exclaimed, as he tweaked my cheek. Just then Mother came through the doorway.

"Look who has just arrived."

"Honore, Nicolette, I have missed you both!" I squealed, running to them and throwing my arms around them both at once. "Could this day get any better?" I proclaimed through my tears of joy.

"Well, I'm not sure, but we picked up a couple of stowaways on our journey here." Honore grandly proclaimed, redirecting my attention towards the door.

"Grandmother, Poppy, I am speechless," I cried out, practically throwing myself at them, and wrapping my arms around my grandparents, Jonathan and Clarisse Stewart.

"The doctor gave me the thumbs up to travel, so we were on the next ship, which just happened to be the same one these two were on," Grandfather explained.

"I still can't believe it," I squealed, beaming from ear to ear.

"Jonathan, let's be honest, you bullied that poor doctor, until he relinquished," Grandmother protested.

"Darling Clarisse, you worry too much," Poppy chided, trying to smooth Grandmother's ruffled feathers, "I feel just fine. Never better." I had no doubt that Grandfather's health was a bone of contention for the majority of their journey from England.

"Darling, Nanny would like to know if you want her to take Olivia yet?" Aiden asked, interrupting the blissful reunion.

"Nanny has a name, my love, and no, I don't want her to take Olivia yet. I think this is a special occasion and everyone has only just arrived. Perhaps Olivia would like the opportunity to get to know her great-grandparents. Who knows how many more opportunities she will have?" I said, while resting a hand on his arm to stall him a moment longer. "Could you tell the footman to set four more places at the table? It would seem that our modest little gathering just grew exponentially."

"Of course, my love, I would do anything for the most beautiful woman in the world," Aiden exclaimed, bringing my hand to his lips.

I stood there for a moment watching the endless activity of everyone interacting with one another. My family and in laws reacquainting themselves, as the staff readied the table. My heart swelled larger, and I could scarcely take it all in. *This is perfect, I am so happy at this moment.*

"Mommy," Olivia said, tugging at my skirt.

"Yes, darling," I replied, stooping down to her level.

"There is a boy following Grandfather."

"Is that your grandfather Jude or my grandfather?" I asked, not sure that I under stood what she was trying to tell me.

"Your grandfather, Mommy, the boy is following him," Olivia said, pointing at my grandfather, who had just arrived.

"There is a boy following Poppy?" I mused, quite puzzled by her queer statement, "Tell me what he looks like."

"He has red hair and says his name is Charlie. I've never seen him before, Mommy."

"Everything will be alright, my little Angel. I think I know who he is and why he is here," I said with a heavy heart, as I gave her a kiss on her forehead and pushed her towards the gathering, "Now go on and have fun with everyone, I will join you in a minute." I stood slowly, taking a deep breath, as I watched everyone gather around the table to take their seats. My mind scrambled to take it all in at once. I wanted to remember every minute detail before it all disappeared.

Then a thought hit me like a bolt of lightning from above and I realized that no matter what became of our lives in the future, nothing could replace or erase that moment from my mind.

For in that one exquisite moment in time, my life was perfect, and nothing could change that. It would forever be preserved in my memories and in my heart, as the most perfect day.

Authors Note

Thank you so much for reading my book. If you enjoyed it please consider posting an honest review on Amazon (https://www.amazon.com/Diane-Merrill-Wigginton/e/B00MS5NV38) and Goodreads (https://www.goodreads.com/book/show/34318579). Please feel free to visit jeweleddaggerpublishing.com to sign up for new book releases or to contact me. It would really mean a lot to me. Thank you.

Diane Merrill Wigginton

A Preview of Book Three in the Jeweled Dagger Series: Olivia's Promise

JANUARY 9, 1804

DUBLIN CASTLE, IN DUBLIN, IRELAND

12 O'CLOCK MIDNIGHT

"O LIVIA, WAKE UP." THE HOARSE whisper sounded harsh next to my ear.

Slowly I opened my sleep-filled eyes and recognized my best friend, whom I hadn't seen in months, "Lilly. What is it? What's the matter?" I asked, with a degree of shock at seeing her dress disheveled and torn, standing in my bed chambers. Slowly sitting up in bed, I rubbed the sleep from my eyes.

"I need your help," she said, pulling her shawl tightly around her slender shoulders and sounding desperate as she walked to the end of my bed.

Reaching over to the night stand, I struck the flint and lit the candle, while absently answering her, "Anything, Lilly. Name it," I replied, turning back around to get a better look at her.

As my eyes adjusted and fell on Lilly, my heart sank to my stomach, because I just realized that she was no longer among the living. She was now just one of the many spirits paying me a midnight visit before crossing over to the other side.

Quickly bringing my hand to my mouth to keep from crying out, tears filled my eyes and all I could do was stare at her ethereal form. The feeling of loss was so raw it hurt. I swallowed a gasp, at least I thought I had.

Lilly's eyes flew to my face. "What's wrong? Why are you staring at me like that, Olivia?"

"What happened to you, Lilly?" I cried, feeling despair overwhelm me. "I have been inquiring after you for months now, but all your sisters would say is that you were away visiting a relative in England."

"I can't remember off the top of my head where I've been exactly, but I don't believe I went to England," Lilly replied, with a stricken look.

"Then tell me where you did go."

"That's just it, I can't remember. The only thing I do recall is feeling happy and excited that I was going someplace. Ever since Mama died, I've wanted to be happy again, Olivia," Lilly whined. "Truly happy!" she added, with emphasis, poking out her bottom lip slightly. "I grew tired of the mask I wore every day to appear happy to everyone." Lilly clutched her fist to her belly, then wringing her hands in her gown, she began looking around with confusion, unable to remember how she had come to be there.

"We will figure this out. I just need you to stay calm. I have something to tell you and I'm not entirely certain how you are going to take it," I prefaced my next statement, while climbing out of bed and walking over to her.

"Don't be silly, Olivia, you can tell me anything."

"Forgive me for being blunt, Lilly, but I don't know any other way to say this," I stated, through sniffles while trying to soften the blow. "You're dead, Lilly."

"That is ridiculous, Olivia Townsend. You don't know what you are talking about," Lilly retorted, looking down at her bare feet and torn dress, before running over to the full-length mirror. I followed behind her with my candle in hand.

"I'm so sorry, Lilly."

"No, no, no, no, no, no…" she kept repeating, bringing her hands to her face in disbelief, when she couldn't see herself in the mirror. Her celestrial form began to fade before my eyes.

"Lilly. Lilly, come back here. I insist you come back here this minute!" I stomped my bare foot on the hardwood floor. "Oh please, Lilly, I promise everything will be alright." I cried, holding the candle a little higher. "Please come back, Lilly." I sobbed.

The door to my room slowly opened and I turned suddenly in surprise.

"Olivia?" Coco's voice was tentative as she looked back over her shoulder before stepping into my room and shutting the door. "Who were you talking to? I heard you calling out to Lilly and thought maybe you were having a bad dream."

"It wasn't a bad dream, Coco. It's was a nightmare," I sobbed into my hands, slumping into the nearest chair, wondering what I was going to do next.

"I don't understand, Olivia. Tell me about your nightmare." She sweetly coaxed, setting her candle down on the dresser and kneeling beside me.

"Oh, Coco," I gasped, setting the candle next to me on the little table and covering my mouth with the back of my hand.

"What is it, Olivia? What's happened?"

"Why have I been cursed with this ability?" I snapped, suddenly angry that I had been given the ability to see spirits. I'd always considered it a gift and a blessing to help people to cross over to the other side when I was younger, but lately it had become a curse.

"What are you talking about, Olivia?" Coco questioned, "I don't understand. You're not making any sense." "Oh, never mind," she uttered, reaching out to take my hand and easily slipping away to the place she goes when she sought answers. Coco closed her eyes and fell silent.

Quickly turning loose of my hand, Coco jumped to her feet and gasped. Her beautiful eyes registered her shock and horror at what she had just witnessed. "This can't be, Olivia! I don't believe it."

"You don't believe it," I sniffed, "I don't believe it!"

"How did this happen to her?"

"I never got that far in our conversation. When I told Lily she was dead, she disappeared on me and I don't know where she went," I cried again as tears trailed down my cheeks.

"But she is coming back?"

"Where else would she go?" I bluntly stated.

"Olivia?" Lilly whispered, causing me to nearly jump out of my skin as I turned my head toward her voice and re-affirmed body.

"Is she back, Olivia? Olivia, answer me!" Coco demanded, growing impatient with my silence. Coco took a hold of my hand so that she could see what I was seeing.

"Lilly, I was so worried about you. Where did you go?" I asked, sniffing loudly and drying my tears with the back of my hands.

"I was scared and when I couldn't remember what happened to me… well, I just felt myself begin to fade away and I didn't know how to stop it." Lilly's voice cracked with emotion.

"Well, did you remember anything more?" I questioned with a loud sniff. "I want to help you, but I need to know where to start. Did you leave your home with someone? Did you take a carriage or a ship? Do you remember if you stayed in Ireland or sailed to another country? Was it a man or a woman that you went to meet, and did you know them well? What is the very last thing you do remember?" I asked in quick succession without taking a breath in between questions.

"Stop it, Olivia. Just stop! You must give me a minute to catch my breath. I did just find out that I am dead. Give a girl a chance to blink, would you?" Lilly responded, shaking her head and turning her back to me as she looked off someplace far away, falling silent for a few minutes.

Reaching back into, her memories, Lilly quickly turned back around, excitedly by her new revelation. "I remember, there was a man and we were in love. Oh, Olivia, I was in love! He was terribly handsome too, now that, I do recall."

"Can you describe him to me?"

"He is very tall and has the most beauty hair. Oh, and a beard. He has a beard and the sweetest brown eyes. I felt like I was melting inside every time he looked at me," Lilly swooned.

"Yes, yes, that's all very nice, Lilly, but you still haven't told me anything about the man or what he does for a living. Telling me that he is handsome and beautiful brown eyes gets us nowhere," I stated with irritation. "You have to give me more to go on, than he makes your insides melt," I was pointing out, when I got an idea.

I separated Coco's hands and gave her a gentle shake.

"Why did you do that?" she complained.

"Because, Coco, I need you to do something for me. Run and get your sketch pad, and be quick about it," I added, watching my sister snatch up her candle and move quickly toward the door. "I need you to sketch the man as Lilly describes him to us. Then we will at least have a picture of him," I said, sitting down in the chair next to me with a plop, before murmuring under my breath, "I hope!"

Coco quickly returned with sketch pad in hand, drawing the man as, Lilly gave us every detail of him.

Holding Lilly's gaze, I said very solemnly, "Lilly, I am going to make you a promise. I swear that I will find out what happened to you, and with my last breath, I will make the person responsible for hurting you pay dearly."

An hour later we had an accurate drawing of our mystery man, a few more details from Lilly of what she could recall of this man, including where he was from and what he did for a living. Then I formed a plan of attack, one that I was not sharing with anyone else.

I was certain Coco would try and stop me, or at the least talk some sense into me, if she knew what I was planning. I was even more certain our mother would know instantly what I had in mind if I put words to it and return home on the next tide. So, I kept all thoughts of my crazy plan to myself.

Thank goodness my parents were out of the country and not due back for another five to seven days. I seriously doubted that they would go along with my crazy scheme.

Printed in Great Britain
by Amazon

37750689R00199